The Mountain Flowers Have Bloomed Quietly

Lu Xing'er

Panda Books

First Edition 2005

ISBN 7-119-03358-1

© Foreign Languages Press, Beijing, China, 2005

Published by Foreign Languages Press

24 Baiwanzhuang Road, Beijing 100037, China

Website: http://www.flp.com.cn

E-mail Address: info@flp.com.cn

sales@flp.com.cn

Distributed by China International Book Trading Corporation

35 Chegongzhuang Xilu, Beijing 100044, China

P.O. Box 399, Beijing, China

Printed in the People's Republic of China

CONTENTS

CONTENTS

Editors' Note

WHEN the Cultural Revolution came to an end in 1976, especially after 1978 when China adopted the policy of reform and opening to the outside world, one tidal wave of creative writing after another has washed over the face of Chinese literature. Chinese women writers have added their indelible inscriptions to this New Age Literature. Their works present a good cross-section of life in China. Among these writers are Shen Rong, Wang Anyi, Zhang Jie, Cheng Naishan, Tie Ning, Lu Xing'er, Chi Li, Zhang Xin, Fang Fang, Chi Zijian, and Bi Shumin, to name only a few.

The late 1970s and the early 1980s was a period of literary renaissance, thanks to the relaxed political climate and growing democracy in China. Many women writers emerged, dealing with all kinds of subject matters and attracting widespread attention. The school of "wound literature" took shape, which mainly focuses on people's lives during and after the Cultural Revolution. Shen Rong's "At Middle Age" raises the problems of middle-aged professionals, who enter the new age with marks left on them by the Cultural Revolution and who have to divide their time between career and family and more often than not neglect one or the other. Cheng Naishan, perceptive, objective, penetrating, and compassionate, captivates her readers with stories about the lives and loves, the destinies and the emotional entanglements of the industrial and business families of China's metropolis, a class which has weathered political vicissitudes before and during the Cultural Revolution. "The Blue House," her representative work, is one such story describing the turmoil going through the Gu family, the former steel giant in Shanghai who owned the Blue House.

Women writers were truthful spokesmen for the youth who suffered during the Cultural Revolution. Problems of the young people of the time were frankly dealt with, such as their disrupted education; lack of interesting employment; the difficulties met with by boys and girls sent from town to the countryside; the low incomes and overcrowding which threaten to break up young couples' marriages; their mental confusion after the turbulent years in which traditions were thrown overboard and bureaucracy, nepotism and corruption were rampant. Zhang Jie's "Love Must Not Be Forgotten" had aroused considerable interest as well as much controversy. Boldly unconventional, idealistic and intensely romantic, the story sheds interesting light on the changes in the attitude to love in socialist China, still strongly influenced by feudal ideas about marriage at the time.

While reform was still dawning on the Chinese horizon, Zhang Jie captured the historic social changes of this mood of reform in her important novel, "Leaden Wings." First published in 1981 and an instant bestseller, the story has as its central theme the modernization of industry. The publication of this book aroused further controversy. Exposing various abuses and man-made obstacles to modernization, it came under fire for "attacking socialism." But many readers welcomed it as painting a truthful picture of modern Chinese society of the time.

In the mid-1980s, seeking out and examining the roots of Chinese culture became the dominant trend, hence the term "root literature." Leading this trend was Wang Anyi's novella "Xiaobao Village," which dissects the rights and wrongs of traditional moral values by portraying what happens behind closed doors in a tiny village that is generally extolled as a paragon of humanity and justice. The author's rich choice of language and her profound grasp of the cultural life and nature of people in a small village, places "Xiaobao Village" on a par with Ah Cheng's "The Chess Master" and Han Shaogong's "Father."

Wang Anyi, who represents the writers whose formal education was disrupted by the Cultural Revolution knows from first-hand experience the problems of young people who have returned from communes to the cities. In her stories, a sense of humanism appears. She is not one simply to condemn or write off the 10 years of her generation lost because of the Cultural Revolution. In her creative world, authentic human feelings live through the traumatic days of the Cultural Revolution. They are perpetuated along with — perhaps in tandem with — the old class relations, with all their old prejudices, suspicions, and tolerances, too. Wang Anyi analyzes China with an imagination that seems nourished by both pre-revolutionary and post-revolutionary culture. Her stories are alive with such tensions and contrasts. Her stories "Lapse of Time" and "The Destination" have won literary prizes in China.

In the late 1980s, Neo-realism came in vogue in Chinese fiction, of which Chi Li, author of "Trials and Tribulations," and Fang Fang, who wrote "Landscape," are both hailed as founding members.

Chi Li is an active writer on the Chinese literary scene. Her stories, like the above-mentioned "Trials and Tribulations" and "Apart from Love," mostly focus on the female world, their love and marriage, though her attitude has nothing to do with feminism. The detailed and earthy descriptions conjure up a vivid picture of life in the late 1980s.

Fang Fang began by writing humorous stories, which are full of caustic and witty remarks. She then turned to stories about magic in which her characters summon up wind and rain like spirits. But she later changed her style again. She is sort of unpredictable, constantly surprising readers and critics because she does not confine herself to a certain style. One of the most popular female writers in present-day China, she is best known for her stories about urban life, with characters ranging from intellectuals to laborers. Her "Landscape" depicts the relationships between an illiterate docker and his nine children, and the hardships they endure in a raw struggle to survive.

During the transitional 1990s, New Age Literature came to an end. The transformation of social and economic patterns in China has given rise to multiple literary patterns with writers of various pursuits locked in a keenly contested competition. The principle of literature has changed from serving life to serving man's existence, and from presenting people's aspirations for life and the historical destiny of collectives to depicting ordinary people's existence in this world. Works by women writers started to describe the petty vexations of people working to earn and survive in the mundane world. Neo-realism, first appearing in the late 1980s and represented by Chi Li and Fang Fang, has developed to a new height. Chi Li's relatively recent stories, "To and Fro" and "Life Show," have presented a vivid, realistic picture of the life of women in the fast-changing Chinese society. Bi Shumin, a doctor-turned woman writer, focuses on specific social and economic phenomena, revealing the contradictions in modern society and the true nature of man in the face of the social and economic reforms in China. But her works don't just stop there. Her novella "An Appointment with Death" and full-length novel The Red Prescription aim for a broader philosophical meaning beyond the superficial implications of subjects like hospice care, life and death, drug use and rehabilitation.

Today, China's relaxed political climate and growing democracy have resulted in more truthful writing and a wider range of themes. Love, social injustice, the value of the individual, humanism and other subjects formerly taboo are being fearlessly tackled by women writers-often with an unaashed display of emotion.

As editors, we hope that this series of women writers' works,

compiled and published by Foreign Languages Press, will open a
door to the world of Chinese women writers and to the everyday
life of ordinary Chinese, for our readers who are interested in
Chinese literature and China as well.

Oh! Blue Bird

This sounds like a fairy tale. Long, long ago, two innocent children went into the wilds to look for a bird with pure blue feathers, because a fairy maiden had told them that the blue bird would be able to tell them the secret of happiness. And so the children went on their journey, through twists and turns and...

1

SATURDAY.

Yongyong longed for yet dreaded the weekend. She sat quietly at her little desk facing the wall, a desk littered with English text books, dictionaries and scraps of paper covered with miscellaneous words so closely scribbled that they looked like squiggly worms crawling all over the paper. The little desk crammed in between the high double decker bunk and the wall along the door carved out a small area of about one square metre. Behind her, it was a different world.

"Oh, I've got another big bag," muttered Lili as she hurriedly packed up the laundry she meant to take home to be washed. She was her mother's spoiled infant. When she first received the university's notice of acceptance, her mother came with her to help her register just as when she had first gone to nursery school hanging on to her mother's apron strings.

"Don't forget the biscuit tin, kitten," Wang Ping reminded Lili as she sat on the bunk pulling on her new bell-bottom trousers.

"Never fear. Mum got some super cream crackers through a friend this week. Just you all wait." Lili brought down a big biscuit tin from the top shelf and shook it. It was quite empty. Every evening, after study hour, she would open the tin and share her snack with the other girls.

"Hey, girls, how do I look?" Wang Ping turned around slowly showing off her new trousers. She was tall and a prominent figure in the track and field team.

"You've got long legs. Bell-bottoms look good on you. Lovely line!" said Little Ou who was standing on a stool and reaching up to the shelf to rummage through her little suitcase, making a mess of the contents. She kept her hair short with a smooth fringe over her wide forehead like a teenager.

Lines? Yongyong longed to turn round to have a look. She rarely noticed what people looked like and "line" sounded so fancy and sophisticated. While she was working at the Forestry Centre, she felt that plain, rough clothes were the right thing for her. Every time she went back to town for her vacation with her mother, her mum had to go to a second-hand store to look for conservative-style clothes for her.

"Who's got some nylon rope?" asked Ou.

"What do you want it for?" Wang pulled out a rope from under her bedding.

"To camp in the Botanical Gardens. Got to put up a little tent with my blankets."

Lili cast Yongyong's back a significant look. Little Ou caught on at once and jumped down. She put her arms around Yongyong. "Come with me. After a week of hard work, it's time to relax. You should learn how to live."

Yongyong only shook her head apologetically.

"You should go," Wang chipped in. "Otherwise, you'll be the only one left in the dormitory this Sunday..." Before she could say more there was a knock at the door.

As soon as Little Ou pulled open the door, she laughed derisively at Wang. "So that's why you've put on new trousers."

A tall good-looking young man stood there, the collar of a blue sweat-shirt turned out over his jacket. He was a member of the provincial tennis team.

"So long now," Wang smiled as she slung her knapsack over one shoulder, put her hand on the boy's arm quite naturally and walked out without any embarrassment.

"I'm off too," Lili announced, biscuit tin in hand. "Mum will be waiting for me at home."

"Me too!" Little Ou picked up her rolled-up blanket and glanced at Yongyong again. Only then did Yongyong turn round with a forced smile. "Go on," she said.

All the girls left, their chatter and laughter dying away. Yongyong now stood up. It was very peaceful in the dorm all by herself. Living with those jolly, talkative girls, Yongyong looked forward to the peace of the weekend when the least she could do was to memorize the new words on her vocabulary lists. But once the weekend came, the loneliness following the silence would tinge her usually moody nature with more than a touch of melancholy. Lili went home happily. Wang went off with her boyfriend. It wasn't as if Yongyong wasn't envious. But for her?

When she was filling forms at registration, Ou had leaned over to ask, "Do you have a baby?" Yongyong had covered the form with an arm muttering "Uh...um..." She didn't know why she should feel as if she had something disgraceful to hide before this childlike schoolmate whose glance was both curious and friendly. Before coming to university, she had made up her mind that she would not say anything about her baby to the others; she would particularly say nothing about *him*. There was neither joy nor glory for her to brag or mention them.

Perhaps she should have gone with Ou for the nocturnal visit to the Botanical Gardens, squeezed with her into a tiny tent and talking about light-hearted but interesting subjects... No, even if she had gone, she would not have felt at all light-hearted. Last week when they had a class-room quiz she had got a fail mark though she had prepared seriously beforehand, sitting up two whole nights. When she got her paper back, she had stared at it like a fool. The startling red crosses on her mistakes caught in her throat like fishbones, making her unable to swallow her lunch. Suppose in the end she just couldn't manage to get through? She felt like having a good cry, but what was the use of tears? After all, she had brought all this on herself. Why had she come at her age to study in the first place? She was somewhat sorry she had. All the girls in class were much younger. Little Ou was ten years her junior. Now all of them sat in the same classroom. She didn't want people to ask about her age, hating to hear their remarks, full of pity, "You're already so...and still going on..." But the many more years she lived had not given her the things she should have had. It was now too late. She really shouldn't have taken this step.

The ball game on the court outstide her windows finally came to an end. Yongyong was able to push open the window.

There was a splendid sunset. A smudge of lichee-pink spread into a rosy glow and violent shades which merged into the azure of the horizon. Under this canopy of colour the branches of the plane tree appeared bright and dazzling. There was no breeze. Green leaves hung motionless against the canopy as if in deep meditation.

"Why ever did I come to university?" Yongyong's gaze was pinned to the scene outside her window. Twelve years ago, her gang of hot-blooded fun-loving young people with axes stuck into their belts had gone to that fascinating primeval forest and camped under the trees for several nights. Like a huge green tent, the giant trees with their thick foliage covered them snugly, sheltering their excited, exuberant hearts. "We will stay in the forest all our lives!" — was the courageous pledge. But as the years went by, one by one the others had left the forest. Yongyong alone remained. She was leader of the Girls' Logging Team; she was a model worker cited for hard work by the provincial authorities. When was it that she too began to grumble against the forest and eventually leave it?

Shu Zhen was on winter vacation, and Yongyong dashed back from the mountains to visit him, two bulging sacks of pine nuts on her back.

The sawing, the gathering, the squares, the logs... Yongyong talked about everything at the Forestry Centre, but her husband, newly returned to town to study journalism at college, seemed not a bit interested now. Shu Zhen just sat there cracking and gobbling up the crisp hard pine nuts. What else was there to talk about? Yongyong went on doggedly cracking until she had a big handful of delicious kernels for him.

"Let's go to Dinxin Tea Garden for sweet dumplings tomorrow," Shu Zhen finally said.

Yongyong was very pleased. She loved going out with her husband and she loved sweet rice dumplings.

The tea garden was very crowded. They had just found a table when someone called Shu Zhen's name asking him to join them. At a table by the window sat four of his schoolmates, two boys and two girls.

"This is Yongyong," Shu Zhen's introduction was simple.

Yongyong sat down stiffly. She was very disappointed. She rarely came out to eat with her husband; why did they have to bump into this gang, utter strangers to her? He never took her to his college to meet his schoolmates. Perhaps all men were vain and wanted wives to be glamorous and beautiful who aroused the envy of other men so that they could feel proud. Yongyong did not have a youthful look. The winds and storms of the forests were sharp as knives, cutting rough lines into her complexion. Swinging axes or wielding a saw, she worked like her male comrades so she no longer looked as delicate or fragile as fresh young girls from school. As Shu Zhen's wife and a grown woman, she would not pass with flying colours among the college girls. She imagined that he found her looks nothing special. Sitting beside him, she felt she was not in harmony with him. Shu Zhen wore a brown casual jacket which made him look boyish and buoyant. He had a broad forehead under which his long smooth eyebrows made his eyes bright and attractive. His schoolmates liked to call him The Handsome One.

As soon as they sat down the two girls opposite Yongyong glanced at her with a keen and curious look. Yongyong, her hands between her knees, didn't know where to look. Her husband seemed more talkative and animated than when he was with her alone.

"You know that Italian reporter Oriana Fallaci interviewed Nixon, Nguyen Van Thieu and even Khomeini..."

"Have you heard? This is world news!" another boy put in. "There is doubt about the authorship of the Soviet novel *And Quiet Flows the Don*. It's said that Sholokhov was probably not the real author..."

"Have you read the script of those newly-released foreign films?" asked a girl with short windblown hair, hitting the table with her chopsticks in rhythm with her words: "Really fascinating ones, the *Godfather, Fabulous Family, A Courtesy Call*..."

"Oh, yes, yes. *Fabulous Family* is so long it had to be published in two issues of the translation magazine," cried the other girl, gesticulating with her arms as if she was discussing it in a literary salon. "It's very revealing, exposing the whole of society through one single family..." She seemed oblivious that she was merely in a tea garden having dumplings.

Yongyong was unable to put in a single word. She sat there in silence. She knew nothing about those events and the books they were talking about. The remote Forestry Centre where she worked seemed like a natural watertight screen cutting the world into two. Buried in the mountains, she could only live like a primitive being in the primitive forests. Suddenly she felt there was an invisible force pulling her away from the others sitting at the same table, as if there were an impassable gap between them. It was awful to sit like this, quite lonely and apart. How she wished the dumplings could be served at once so that she could swallow them and be gone.

Her husband was still deep in discussion with the others. Just then, a waitress with a pale, cold face passed by their table. Yongyong unwittingly asked, "Why haven't our dumplings come yet?"

The waitress jumped up with a loud cry, as if shot by a pistol. "Don't come here for food it you can't wait!" Her shrill voice rang out over the hubbub of the noisy tea room.

Shu Zhen glared at Yongyong. "What are you in such a hurry about?"

Embarrassed, Yongyong turned away. The others at their table had all stopped their animated conversation to look at Yongyong in surprise. There was a hint of contempt in their eyes. But very quickly, as if covering up, they resumed their conversation. Dejected, Yongyong hung her head.

After saying goodbye to the others as they left the tea garden, Shu Zhen said not another word. Yongyong too walked silently,

her steps getting slower and slower until she gradually fell behind
him. Shu Zhen, on the other hand, quickened his steps. He strode
further and further away in the hurrying tide of people.

"A big forest separated you and me..." Yongyong wanted to
write this down in a letter when she returned to the Forestry
Centre, but eventually she crossed it out after a long hesitation. It
wasn't just a huge forest really. Every Saturday, when Shu Zhen
returned with his bulging canvas knapsacks, Yongyong felt that it
was a magic sack of mystery. Once when he wasn't around she
couldn't resist the temptations to look into it. Books, note books,
even the slips of paper with casual scrawled words on them
seemed to hide tremendous changes and secrets. She realized that
these were not mere secrets but the "world" he was so interested
in. It was this world of his which was pulling them further and
further apart. A scrap of much creased and torn paper floated down
from a textbook.

A ball of fire,
And a poem,
A proud, serene marble sculpture,
An ordinary person who can really work.

This little verse of his was entitled *Wife*. Was this what he
hoped of her? True, she was a ball of fire, but certainly not a
poem. She was indeed an ordinary person who could work but not
a proud sculpture. Obviously, she was a long way off from his
ideal. The few dumplings she had swallowed in the tea garden
were tossing and turning in her stomach as if never digested. They
felt heavier than little lead balls.

Was it because she had wanted to digest those dumplings that
she had gritted her teeth and come to study?

Yongyong turned to pick up a glass of water on her desk. It

was icy cold but she poured it down her throat as if hoping to drown something. The chill of the water sobered her somewhat. She picked up her book again, forcing herself to stuff the printed letters into her head. But her head was reeling again, the small letters darting back and forth in front of her eyes like tadpoles in the water. She had to lean back and close her eyes for a few moments. How tired she felt! She longed to go to bed, bury her head under the quilt and sleep with not a thought in her head for several days and nights. Hadn't she had this sort of feeling before?

Outside the dormitory tent, the loudspeaker hanging overhead was blaring out: "Our Girls' Logging Team was the product of the Gang of Four's ultra-left line..." Yongyong collapsed on her bunk and closed her eyes in a semi-coma. Nearly ten years of hard labour seemed to burst out in accumulated fatigue at this point. She felt utterly exhausted, so tired that there were no thoughts left in her head. Her brains were like a burnt-out forest, all shrouded in whitish smoke. Life too was singed by flames, leaving nothing behind at all. She became very ill. Her heatlth had completely deteriorated. Waves of dizziness kept overcoming her. The doctor said it was anaemia due to over-exhaustion.

Yes, it was time to leave this primitive forest.

As she was making arrangements for departure, she was given a thorough physical. The results she brought back included a positive urine test. Pregnant! Was it a daughter or a son? Her heart thumped as if a tiny being were already breathing there, accelerating her own heartbeat. Surprised, delighted but also a little frightened. She was going to be a mother but she was not prepared. Motherhood? A powerful, new and sacred feeling gushed from her heart like a rivulet in spring surging out of melted mountain snow, a tenderness and tranquility vibrant with new life and hope. For ten years, she seemed to have missed really living properly. Wife, husband,

family all still seemed strange to her. In fact, at the very thought
of him... she still felt bashful. But the fruit of their union, a life
still strange to her, had barged into her consciousness. She should
write to him immediately to tell him the news! No, send him a
telegram. As if dashing out to catch a train, she ran to the post
office. A man passed her a form to fill in her message. Yongyong
flushed red, so stupid of her. How could she write such a message?
"Sorry," she muttered before dashing out of the post office like
someone on the run. Better not to tell him yet. When her departure
was finally settled, she would appear before him and tell him in a
whisper... What would be his reaction? He'd cry out in delight, his
blazing eyes melting into a happy warm smile, bright like the
noonday sun. She sank into sweet imaginings.

The day she finished with formalities at the Forestry Centre,
Yongyong timidly pushed open the door of the local hairdresser's.
Once she was in the big barber's chair, she watched the continuous
changes of herself in the mirror with a fresh and frightened feeling.
Her long plaits were cut off, the shorter hair curled into layers of
waves. When the hairdresser put an oblong mirror behind her head
for her to see the whole result, she felt that her shoulders were
carrying a newly installed head which she was quite unable to turn
round. Was that me? She dared not recognize herself. Still she
liked the change. It was time she said goodbye to her maiden days,
to the past years. The new life within her brought changes into her
heart, she felt that even her voice was now softer and gentler. She
hoped that by the time she got home she would begin everything
anew and bring so much joy to him. Yes, he would be glad.
Hadn't he said long ago that women should be gentle and make
themselves nice looking?

But the moment she pushed open the door, Yonyong felt tense.
Holding tight to her bag, she watched with uneasiness the first
glance of her husband. At first he stared at her in surprise, showing

no joy in her sudden appearance. Then, he shifted his gaze away.

"Isn't it all right?"

"What's that supposed to look like!" Shu Zhen lit a cigarette and took a long puff.

"I...I..." Yongyong was at a loss for words. She was so perplexed that she didn't even remember to put down the heavy traveling bag in her hand.

"Don't try to beautify yourself if you don't understand beauty. Go and get all those flutters cut off tomorrow."

After that, who'd be in a mood to discuss anything? Even the matter of the baby...

"Have you finished reading *What to Do*?" After dinner that evening, he suddenly brought up the question. He had borrowed the book from the library about a month ago to send to her.

"I finished it."

"Like it?"

Yongyong nodded. As a matter of fact, she wasn't quite sure whether she liked or disliked it. The large sections on theory in the book bored her, she wasn't sure what they meant.

"If you like it we should do as the book suggests." Shu Zhen's face no longer looked so stern. He helped Yongyong to smooth the fringe over her forehead. "Leave the forest and return to work in town...since that's what you want. I will not stop your coming back. Once you return here, we will be together all the time. But I cannot imagine just being together and letting ourselves be bound by endless mundane and miscellaneous household matters..." He really felt that way. He was not yet ready to take refuge in the sheltered harbour of home. To him, the vessel of life had to bypass cosy harbours if he intended to sail on towards big seas. "Can we live in the way outlined by Vera in *What to Do*? For the time being, we should not interfere with each other, demand to know all about the other, nor influence or become a drag on the other but keep relatively independent..."

What was this? Yongyong felt unable to understand what he meant. "Chernyshevski's ideas belong to utopian socialism. Is it at all practical?"

"It is indeed a new idea. Marriage should not be just a rope tying two people down together." Then Shu Zhen's words shot out at a tangent. " I hear the announcement for enrolling new university students will be issued very soon..."

Yongyong understood what he was trying to say. He had once advised her to do some studying. "Pretty soon the examination system will be restored. You should make good use of your time and review your middle school lessons..." For her though it was impossible to imagine the moment she would walk into an examination room. How would she answer all those questions? Her hands, so used only to the saw, the axe and other work tools, were rough and unskilled. The pens and pencils would feel heavier than tools in her hands. She did not have the confidence to try. Yongyong kept silent. She did not know how to answer him. The transfer back to town and her joy over the coming baby had filled her heart, she had had no time to think of the kind of life outlined in *What to Do*?

"I wish you would change a bit, Yongyong," Shu Zhen said sincerely. "I don't know whether you've sensed it. Although we have the same background, have much in common regarding thinking and experience, we are vastly different in character, taste, attitude to life, aesthetics... I don't want such gaps to remain there unchanged. Otherwise we will both be unhappy."

Yongyong felt her heart trembling slightly fall like the setting sun. Those wretched sweet dumplings she had consumed the other day in the tea garden were pressing down in her breast, reminding her of the two college girls staring strangely at her and the image of her husband walking faster and faster away from her. "Don't say anymore," she was practically shouting. "Why, why did you marry me...in the first place?" Every word he uttered with such cold precision was like a thorn, its fine sharp point piercing her heart. Unable to control herself any longer, she thrust herself through the door and rushed out.

New Year's Eve.

The 11:30 train to Harbin.

The compartment was practically empty. Who wanted to be rushing around at a time like this? Yongyong leaned weakly against the window gazing outside as if waiting for something. Would he come? If he jumped into the train now, dragged her bags down from the rack, would she go back with him docilely and perhaps, unable to resist the temptation of throwing herself into his arms, say to him, "We are going to have a baby..."

On the lonely platform, only a few uniformed conductors on duty paced up and down. In the icy air, firecrackers burst intermittently. The train slid quietly out without a blast or whistle as if reluctant too to be leaving on such a long journey during this fine festival time. Yongyong hid her eyes in her hands.

It was getting dark. The moon newly risen hid itself again in the folds of the clouds. "The night was dark just like this..." Yongyong felt as if the chair under her seemed to be rocking as if she were still in that night train. No, it was just her dizziness again. She put her hands, icy cold, over her eyes... A year ago, when she had left him without a word of farewell, she had only this to say as she left, "We will not hear from each other for a whole year..." Later, she had felt a shock at her own determination. She had always been considered weak-willed where her emotions were involved.

She had returned to the Forestry Centre without mentioning anything about leaving. Why go back home to him? She had thought things out. Without equality there could be no real love.

She went on working quietly in the forest and just as quietly dug into her books. Then still very quietly she went alone to the hospital.

The operating room of the gynaecology department was behind closed doors. Standing outside, Yongyong eyed the pale-faced wives being helped out by anxious husbands as they moaned a little. A dreadful agony emerging from her very bosom gripped her completely. An elderly nurse came toward her. "Have you come for an abortion?" Experienced eyes swept over her face. "It's a first pregnancy, isn't it? Why don't you want to have the baby?" Why? The baby should be the fruit of love, a symbol of happiness, but where were her love and happiness? Involuntarily, she put her trembling hands over her stomach. She had no answer for the nurse but felt the new life was already stirring. What wrong had the baby done? Why did she not have the courage to shoulder a woman's burden by herself? Yes, why not use her own shoulders to bear the responsibility of life independently. She was not one to complain or falter under hardships. Had she not borne such difficulties in the mountain forests over the past ten long years? Her only fear was that if she kept the baby would she be able to get into college? Would they discriminate against someone who was already a mother? No...no...people would understand that she belonged to that special generation of students who missed their education during those turbulent years.

Yongyong waved her hand apologetically at the elderly nurse and turned away from the operating room. She ran away as fast as she could stopping only when she had left the hospital behind. Then she breathed a sigh of relief.

"The baby should really be fast asleep by this time..." An unbearable, tormenting longing to see her baby came over her again. Several times she had put the photo of the baby at one-month-old into an envelope with the intention of sending it to him without a word of explanation. She had always hesitated and abandoned the attempt. She had thought he might write to her, but he had not. She seemed to be waiting every day but sank into deeper disappointment day by day.

He never did write. It was nearly a year... Her misery, which she had buried deep down, was emerging to envelop her once again. The dozen or so new words she had succeeded in memorizing with sheer doggedness were drowned in her sorrow.

Better go out for a walk, she told herself. All by herself in this forlorn empty dormitory, she was unable to control herself from getting tied up in a tangle of depressing thoughts.

2

There was a knock at the door.

"Who's there?" asked Yongyong.

"Is Yongyong there?" The voice was familiar and yet unexpected.

When she opened the door, Yongyong jumped in surprise. "Zhao Guokai!" She stood stunned in the doorway, her glance hesitant but glad. Was it really him? She couldn't believe it. They'd not seen each other for a whole decade...

"You haven't asked your visitor to sit down!" Guokai's tone was gentle as he smiled as if he were a frequent caller. The twitch of his handsome black eyebrows belied his excitement. "I noticed the name Yongyong on the wall-newspaper in the English Department and I followed the trail here."

"There are lots of people with the name Yongyong."

"If wrong I only had to say 'sorry.' I was prepared to be disappointed."

Yongyong laughed. "You're studying here too? Which department?" As she asked, she guessed that most probably he was in the Department of Political Science. While in middle school he was already a junior "statesman." He had a proud, commanding demeanor and was a natural leader. Their classmates seemed willing to tacitly accept his leadership. During the Cultural Revolution, he was one of the chiefs among the school's Red Guards and also a member of the municipal Alliance of Middle School Red Guards. Yongyong remembered him imbued with the stature of a leader, exuding tremendous confidence and power all of which had once attracted her... But the Zhao Guokai standing before her now seemed similar but not quite the same person. He had changed. In what way? She scrutinized him, comparing him with the young lad in army uniform and a dazzling red arm band. In those days, he would always shake his mop of thick black unruly hair when making a speech or debating with people.

He was now wearing faded old overalls, very ordinarily clothed. His hair was cropped very short and it was getting thin near his forehead. Only his dark eyebrows remained unchanged, though the eyes underneath seemed to have been soothed so that they looked warmer and deeper, without the sharpness and proud command of former days.

"I'm a postgraduate in the Chinese Department," Zhao Guokai told Yongyong. "I didn't expect you to take up foreign languages. How have you been all this time?" He longed to know all about her. His first instinct when he saw her was that she seemed so very different from the person who had stayed in his memory.

"I didn't expect it myself either..." Yongyong sighed. An inbred trust in this friend of old made her unwilling to hide her real mood from him, although it had been a long time since they were in touch. "Better tell me about yourself. I have nothing much to say. The first few years out of school, things went smoothly, and life was boring and uneventful. I didn't learn anything and didn't think much either. Sometimes I felt depressed and just wanted to hide myself away in some cozy niche from life. Then I realized such places don't exist..." She spoke rapidly, her head low, her words flowing easily. She did not need to choose her words carefully with him.

Zhao watched her in amazement. He hadn't expected to see her so listless, like someone newly-defeated in battle or convalescing from an illness. He had heard that she was a model worker at the Forestry Centre, that she had got married and that her husband had been selected for college education. In his imagination, she lived under balmy skies, totally different from him. He had treasured in his heart her happy laughter, as cheerful as the cooing of flying doves under an azure sky. It was this laughter that had given him comfort in his years of utter misery when he had lost his freedom. He had been in jail for a period of time because the Alliance of Middle School Red Guards to which he had belonged made the mistake of joining college students in "bombarding" Zhang Chunqiao. He was glad that before he was jailed he had trekked around the country with so many other students. Yongyong was one of the few who had followed him to the end of the trek —— Jinggangshan Mountain —— a revolutionary base. Now he wanted to tell her that not long after being enrolled in the university, an unexpected opportunity had enabled him to follow the same trail once again. To him it had been a very significant trip. Those strange and yet familiar little villages he went through had aroused so many dreams and memories.

In a little village called Rocky Lagoon, they sang a song of Chairman Mao's quotations as they entered. "Where there are hardships and problems..." A sparkling brook flanked by green rushes ran by the edge of the village. The splashes of frogs jumping into the water could be heard as well as the heavy tread of boatmen pulling their crafts. In the paddy fields, the rice was long and luminous. He remembered the little girl named Lu Aizhen who had shed tears of dismay because the bit of food she'd prepared for her father was not enough to feed those hungry young students. Yongyong had to tell her several stories before she smiled amidst her tears...

Once he and Yongyong were on their own looking for somewhere to stay. They espied a tiny light halfway up the hill. When they knocked, an old woman and two little girls appeared. "You two want a room to sleep in?" asked the old woman eyeing them alertly. "No, no, not one room," Yongyong quickly explained, her cheeks flaming.

At the August 1st Museum commemorating the uprising of the Red Army in Nanchang, a long, long queue waited to get in. Zhao ordered Yongyong to go back to the hostel and rest while he queued. "Come back in three hours," he told her. Yongyong went away. After a while, Zhao sat down by a tree at the roadside for a little rest but fell asleep. He was cold and tired. He woke up suddenly three hours later to find Yongyong's overcoat covering him. He searched for Yongyong the length of the queue, so long that he could see neither the beginning nor the end, shouting her name as he went. Close to the door of the museum, he saw her, a slender small figure, her slim shoulders hunched against the chill wind.

In those days she was a young girl, so delicate and fragile, but she doggedly trekked a thousand miles... When he'd gone by train following the same itinerary, he seemed to see their footprints all along the narrow gravel paths by the side of the rails. A deep feeling like floating wisps of clouds shrouded his heart, a feeling so pure and fine. This sparkling seed in his memory was still strong and vital.

Zhao Guokai did not mention those memories, nor did he tell her about his return to those places they had trekked through together. He locked those sentimental seeds deep down in his heart together with the memory of her merry laughter.

Yongyong's clouded countenance now seemed to have driven the gentle laughter in Guokai's mind further and further away. The vicissitudes of life brought unexpected results. He felt a deep regret over the changes of time. "Yes, there are always ups and downs in life," he said, making his tone light-hearted. "But I knew you'd be able to get yourself into college."

"College?... I'm even thinking of backing out. I failed a test recently." Yongyong bit her lips, unable to stop bitter tears from slipping down her cheeks. She averted her face. "I'm having a very hard time here. I had so little schooling before."

What she lacks is confidence, Guokai thought. In their trek of many miles he had discovered that she was a person with a determination and stamina much stronger than that of most people. Wasn't she aware of that?

"Why do you feel so futile? Whatever you do you must at least have confidence. Otherwise, what can you depend on for support?"

"Confidence comes from a sound basis. I feel that I have never achieved anything of any consequence in the whole of my life. Nothing to show that I have ability or intelligence."

"Not achieving anything of consequence doesn't mean much. We lived in extraordinary times and our failures were due to history. I don't know if anyone amongst our batch of students has achieved anything. But I do know for sure that in the future we will." Zhao Guokai smiled to himself as if remembering something. "Want to hear a story?" He sounded like an adult trying to amuse a little girl.

A smile flickered over Yongyong's tear-stained face. The sight of Zhao Guokai made her feel as if she'd met a long-lost elder brother. He was such a help. "Oh, you, the same old you." She brought out her thermos. "I suppose I have to make you a malted drink." She remembered his old habit. Back in school, he was known for his wonderful stories, but he always had to be given a hot drink, not just plain water before he would tell his stories.

Accepting the hot, sweet drink, Zhao Guokai took a greedy mouthful, choking in his haste. Quite unabashed, he wiped his mouth with the back of his hand and launched into his story. "There was once a little girl who was sure she was ugly. She never tried to make herself pretty nor was she interested in the things around her. She always looked very solemn, which made her unattractive so that people didn't bother to look at her. One day, a ragged old woman came to her. 'Oh lass, I think you have a very pretty face. You're not a bit ugly. Look closely at yourself in the mirror if you don't believe me and then comb your hair properly. Go and pick a fresh flower to put in your hair.' The little girl was unconvinced but she bought a mirror just the same. By the roadside she picked a little red flower. At home she sat long by the mirror watching her own image. Gradually, she discovered that her face in the mirror was, in fact, quite pretty. Thereafter, like other girls she put on pretty, flowery frocks. Soon, young men began to turn their heads as she went by, the way they did with other girls." The story was told like a fairy tale for nursery children. Zhao Guokai spoke with charm and conviction.

"I'm not a child," Yongyong blushed.

"Sometimes we are not aware of the truth that even children understand." He was very sincere. "This story tells of a plain fact. Beauty comes as you continually observe yourself in the mirror of imagination, make yourself attractive and assert yourself. You have to appreciate yourself, look after yourself. Isn't one of the meanings of life to know yourself? How else would humanity have the courage to face the great, infinite world of nature?"

"Self?" Yongyong was aware of a hazy new consciousness. It was true that she never felt she should think of herself. Like that girl in the story she rarely spent time by the mirror looking at herself. She never felt such a desire, nor was she interested in studying herself. At the Forestry Centre when work was at its busiest, she hardly had time even to slip a comb through her hair, to say nothing of looking into the mirror. At any rate she wore a wicker helmet on her head all day long in the forest. So the ugly girl turned out pretty in the end. Perhaps she herself was not really ugly. Yongyong reflected on the story, "What about me? Where is my self?" Self is a word every child knows and feels but Yongyong who rarely thought of herself found it difficult to know herself. Yes, the story told by her friend contained things requiring her contemplation, although she wasn't quite sure what he meant exactly. However, his story brought hope and confidence like the early rays of dawn, making her feel less heavy of heart.

"Tell me about you!" Yongyong said as she poured him more water. "I heard you were under a great deal of pressure at the state farm. Was it because of your participation in the Red Guards' Alliance or was it because of your father's problems?"

"Both. I was constantly under 'proletarian dictatorship' until the Gang of Four was smashed." He said this lightly as if telling her about a pleasure trip. "I learned a vital lesson. Of course when we were fearlessly dashing around making revolution, we really thought that events in China could be shaped by our screams and slogans. I thought a great deal over these past years, bitter thoughts and painful thinking, enough to drive me nearly out of my mind until I finally came to some sort of understanding." He put his thick fingers into his short hair and rubbed his head.

That was why he had lost so much of his thick hair, Yongyong said to herself wanting him to go on. "What have you understood?" Yongyong's eyes searched his face. Someone had once told her that life is full of grief only to those who are pitiable and the world seems to have no meaning only to those who have no purpose. She herself could not find a concise expression to define her own views of life and the world.

"I realized that we ourselves were too inept. Our ardour to reform our country was good but we had no ideas of our own nor much knowledge. We didn't have the ability needed to find practical solutions to solve some of the country's problems. We also knew too little about China and the historical development of the world. How could we know how to reform our country? I was often called an 'arrogant element.' Every time I was criticized, such a cap was put on my head. In those days, whatever nasty names they called me I was always proud of the designation of arrogance. Once I settled down to read, I discovered that my former arrogance was merely an extension of my shallow and ignorant self. For three years I did not go home but dug into books, trying to fill my empty head. Literature, political economy, philosophy... I studied everything and anything."

"And what is your major subject now?"

"Comparative literature. With comparison comes the ability to ascertain. We should try to identify the special features of our national culture from a study of the development of human culture as a whole. It's a question of the source and the flow."

How deep and far-reaching his thoughts are. In the confident, and assured gaze of her friend, Yongyong felt exuberance and vitality.

"Oh, here I go, unable to stop once I start talking. Incurable old habit, blowing my own trumpet." He pushed the glass on the table as if pushing something away from him. "Let's hear about you." He folded his arms. "Nice to have a husband and a home, eh? Where does he work now?"

Yongyong who had just begun to feel relaxed felt a heavy weight again. Was it nice to have a home? She could pretend in front of anyone else, pretend to be very happy and content but she did not want this old and dear friend to get a false impression of her. This trust and willingness to reveal all about herself applied only to a very few in life; it was something she treasured. But, could she tell him in so many words that it was nice or not nice? After a bit of pondering, she just said, "He works for a newspaper."

"A journalist? Not bad."

"True, not bad..." A glimmer of pain flickered over her eyes. He felt it immediately and stopped going on.

"It's a long story, we'll talk about it some other time..." Yongyong sighed, her heart heavy.

Zhao Guokai changed the subject. "You really need to create a proper atmosphere for yourself when learning a foreign language." They discussed other things.

3

When the telephone in his office rang, Shu Zhen had just got back. "Your call, Shu Zhen." Old Zhao, the editor sharing his office handed him the receiver. "It's as if they heard your footsteps."

Shu Zhen thanked him and took the receiver. It was the person he had been expecting, Xiao Diandian, the Youth League secretary at Steel Five.

"You're hard to reach, aren't you? This is the third time I've called you this morning."

"I was out getting a story," Shu Zhen laughed.

"Next week we're arranging a visit to Hangzhou for our Youth League cadres. Would you like to go with us?"

"What's got into you?" Shu Zhen joked. "My going requires permission from your father. He's the chief editor, everyone is in awe of him."

"Nothing to do with him. Are you coming with us or not?"

"Let me think it over."

"Don't give me that. We need a definite answer."

"I'll let you know this evening," Shu Zhen answered stubbornly.

He could have said yes immediately. Steel Five was one of the plants that the paper was intending to write up in its column about Youth League activities, depicting it as a model. Shu Zhen had every reason to join their outing since he was in charge of reporting on the lives of young people in industry. He intended to give her his answer in the evening as he meant to have a talk with her. He was preparing an article about this Youth League secretary. Of course it would not be a real interview or a special personality feature. She was not a heroic model, nor was there any event about her for him to write about. He just wanted to write her up as a practice article, the way artists do sketches for practice. Shu Zhen's enthusiasm for strong and colourful characters and events was like that of an astronomer out to learn all about new "stars" appearing in the firmament. His interest in this particular person named Diandian seemed to have begun the first time he heard her name.

The first time he went to Steel Five to organize a discussion among young workers there, the man in the Party committee office had described her to him.

"The Youth League secretary is named Xiao Diandian. She's very sharp..."

Diandian? A rather quaint name. Interesting. "Is she here?" Shu Zhen asked.

"At the moment she's attending a meeting for the enrollment of new Party members."

"Then I'll wait."

His host decided to let him wait in the Youth League office. When they opened the door, the man said in surprise, "Why are you not at the Party meeting, Diandian?"

A slim, small young woman stood by the newspaper rack reading. She turned to reply, "Meeting adjourned for recess. Will continue in a few minutes." Her eyes were composed, serene like the water in a deep well. There was no sign of the excitement or

exhilaration usual in people being accepted into the Party. So this
was Diandian! A childlike slip of a girl, not at all the image of a
sharp, commanding Youth League secretary. Would those sturdy,
thick muscular young workers by the steel furnaces listen meekly
to her commands? An interesting conjecture.

"I'm a reporter. I'd like to talk to you when you've finished
with the Party meeting." Shu Zhen passed over his reporter's card.

She did not deign to look at it. Turning to replace the newspaper
in her hand to its rack, she asked, "What do you want to talk
about? I'm not going back to the meeting."

"But...if you are one of the candidates being accepted..." Shu
Zhen faltered, rather astonished at her casual tone.

"That's none of your business." The lack of expression on her
face made her look younger.

"This is no joke. A Party meeting for new candidates is not
something to trifle with," the other man also tried to persuade her
to go back to the meeting. Diandian cut in, "It's not just a Party
meeting to accept new candidates but a trading counter. The
members of the Party committee have very divergent views about
the candidates and they are fighting over who should be allowed to
join. It's just a question of bargaining over your accepting my
candidate while I accept yours, simply trading." Diandian said this
quite coolly.

Shu Zhen gazed at her with some uneasiness, not knowing what
to do next. Support her views? He was after all a mere stranger
here, he really did not know the situation. For some reason though,
he thought what she had just said was true. Her frank, upright
spirit which seemed strong enough not to be cowed by power and
authority was something he very much approved of. To risk
personal interests in order to show protest was not something most
people were able to do.

She seemed quite determined not to go back to the Party

meeting.

But when the discussion meeting with the young workers which Shu Zhen came to listen finally started, it was extremely quiet. The theme of the discussion was "Happiness" and "Ideals". Shu Zhen was eager to know what the young workers thought but there was continued silence for quite a while. No one volunteered to speak. Feeling desperate, Shu Zhen cast an imploring look at Diandian, begging her to start the ball rolling.

Only then did Diandian stand up. She was wearing a white shirt which fitted her slim figure and faded khaki trousers with no shape at all. This was the typical outfit of the offspring of cadres who considered themselves grand enough to wear and do anything. Did she think she was that kind of arrogant person? Her face was still expressionless as if it had been the most natural thing for everybody to remain silent. After casting a sweeping glance around her, she finally started, "So why don't you all say something? If you don't we might as well all do something else." Her words were crisp and frank. "You there, Xiao Li, weren't you saying yesterday that the greatest happiness was to be with your girlfriend every day?"

There was a burst of laughter, whispering and exchange of looks before people began to speak. Diandian in the meantime sat down quietly, an unfathomable look of interest in her eyes. Obviously, she wasn't the least interested in such meetings. When the others dispersed after the meeting, Shu Zhen asked her, "Why didn't you contribute to the discussion?"

"What is there to talk about?"

"You are hesitant about saying things?" Shu Zhen asked tentatively.

"No, not at all. I never hesitate to reveal anything I've done or thought about," she said frankly.

"Could we make an appointment some time so I could talk to you?"

"Talk about my approach to happiness?" She smiled slightly, a very wry smile. "I can tell you right now. Happiness is something that doesn't exist. I never think of this word, never!" Her startling calm and candid conclusion announced the end of the interview.

She was frank, like a child who never told lies, but cold like an old woman with a world of experience. Shu Zhen, his curiosity aroused, wanted to know more about the thoughts of this mystifying Youth League secretary. He asked to talk to her the next afternoon. But that afternoon as soon as he sat down at his desk, a phone call came with a summons to the chief editor's office.

Shu Zhen was surprised that the Chief Editor Xiao wanted to see him.

When he went in he found the chief at his desk reading a manuscript. "I've asked you here to discuss the matter of the special column on youth," said Editor Xiao eyeing him carefully, the way he read through manuscripts.

Shu Zhen thought quickly, trying to intuitively sense the man's intentions. He was kindly, gentle and not bad-tempered. Shu Zhen had made inquiries about him in preparation for just such a summons from him. The chief was a veteran reporter from Yan'an days when he worked on the *Liberation Daily*. He was an upright, honest man who took his work seriously.

"We are working on an article about young people's approach to happiness. The first part is extremely important but also rather difficult. Our first step is to do some research. We need to organize a series of meetings..." Shu Zhen went on confidently and in detail about the progress of the article. He spoke like a student at his graduation visa, clearly and logically following a draft he had outlined in his head the night before. He spoke well and with assurance, for he was adept at dealing with such situations. When he was at the Forestry Centre and was one of the office staff there, all the leaders appreciated his brilliance and ability. Whatever material he presented, either the draft of a speech written for someone, a summary of work or a proposal at the Party committee, it was always adopted without demur. When work teams were set up to go down to the different sections of the Forestry Centre, all the leading cadres wanted Shu Zhen to go with them as assistant. In addition to his efficiency and reliability in secretarial work, he was also able to summarize the four pages of *Reference News* from beginning to end while lying on his bunk in the tent so that his superiors, busy all day long, could just listen to him without the need to read anything themselves. These hardworking, exhausted men always enjoyed his interesting retelling of news as they lay in the tent drowsy with sleep.

The chief editor now stood up, evidently highly satisfied, "We are giving you this assignment and it's a decision the whole Party committee has discussed and agreed. We expect you to do some solid research and talk to as many young people as you can."

"I've already been to a few factories like Steel Five and got some young people together to discuss the subject."

The chief editor seemed interested. "Oh? You've been to Steel Five? The Youth League secretary..."

"Has a very strong character. I meant to talk to her again this afternoon."

The chief editor smiled quizzically. "She's got a very sharp tongue."

"You know her?"

"Of course. Father and daughter. She's put me on the spot more than once."

"Your daughter?" Unwittingly, he began to look for resemblances between the two. "No wonder."

"No wonder we both have the name Xiao!" The older man laughed. "There is no inkling of a similarity between us. Everyday she harps on at me with criticisms." Though he complained about her, his smiling face showed love and pride in his daughter.

"Don't blame her. If we can't puncture the mature thoughts of an older generation, what is the use of us younger generation?"

"Looks like you and she are of the same type."

"Hard to say. I haven't had a real chance to talk with her yet."

"You've put it well. Young people's thinking nowadays is extremely confused." He sighed deeply. "There are more and more things which make it difficult for people to understand each other. Hard to bridge the gaps."

The chief was musing about his daughter. They saw each other everyday and everyday they exchanged views on the times, society, life and events but there was no communication between them, as if a strong repellent force kept them from reaching each other. What was the reason? They had different experiences and the times had changed so much. He seemed almost, but not quite, to understand the reason.

"Will you tell me something about your daughter?" This thought crossed Shu Zhen's mind but he throttled it. Mustn't be too rash at this first encounter with the boss.

Back in the office, Old Zhao handed him a *Xinhua News Release* :

"The new students for the '78 class are entering college now. You might go down to the schools to have a look. Get the students to stand up and speak. It'll make our discussions more lively." Zhao followed his words with a personal question, "Did your wife take part in the entrance exam?"

"Uh...uh...probable not..." Shu Zhen's thoughts seemed to have remained behind in the chief editor's office.

"What do you mean by um...uh...and probably...?" Zhao asked with a touch of humour.

"I don't know..." Shu Zhen could only evade the question. Did she take part? He honestly didn't know. She went off in anger leaving him with only the words, "Not write to each other for a year..." All right, if you say don't write, we won't write. At the time, he did not take it seriously. In two weeks she would probable write to him. They had had many quarrels. It was always she who asked for reconciliation. He waited, but in vain. Contrary to his expectation, this time she did not make a move. More than once he took up his pen, though he always curbed his desire to write. "We'll see who can stick it out," that was his masculine pride. He had to admit to himself that he missed her, though not in a sentimental love-sick way. Sometimes he looked back on his own words, wondering whether he hadn't been too radical and impatient. But those words had to be uttered sooner or later. He felt that he was influenced by his own sense of discontent. He was dissatisfied with himself, with her and with their life together. An active volcano will erupt sooner or later. What exactly was he dissatisfied with? To him, life should keep moving on, never stagnate. But she... He liked discussing books and reading periodicals. Every time he got the *Reference News*, the information, trends and items gathered from all over the world, stimulated him so much that he became in turns indignant, shocked, scornful or worried. "Look, the Soviets have increased their intermediate launchers from 200 to 700. They've also stored a lot of nerve gas. The gas can completely disable people within just a few minutes..." He used to tell her, talking in a loud and excited voice but got no response whatsoever. She went on placidly with whatever she was doing. Immediately, he felt his mood plunge very low. After that he no longer wanted to discuss anything with her, though they lived together... Now she had left, sending no news for quite some time, which made him anxious about her. Two months back, when he was writing an article about the first entrance exam for college students after the Cultural Revolution, he wondered whether she was among them. It was reported that there were girls who had fainted from tension, others wept when they found their answers were incorrect. He

realized that the exam was very hard on students like her. For
years she had been a manual worker at the Forestry Centre with no
place or time to do any reading or studying. He felt then that he
understood her a little. Should he write to her and tell her to come
back to him? Was he feeling remorse? No, it was better to let her
go her own way. It was only to be a year of separation... Only 365
days. Someone had told him once, "You're a person who won't
settle down but just likes to make trouble, not only trouble for
yourself but for others." This assessment was true. He was not
willing to let life drag him into a mire of vulgarity or to live out
a plain ordinary existence without getting something done. Although
"trouble" would bring pain, it would always bring vitality, excitement
and change. He could not be satisfied with the present. He was
already thirty years old. He felt that half his life was gone, but
what imprint had he left on this earth?

Would she understand how he felt?

The *News Release* in front of him became a blur as his thoughts
flew away.

4

"On we go, on we go, on we go!"

Several youngsters, canvas knapsacks on their backs, shouted
gaily toward the old man at the door using the words from a
popular new movie.

They had decided to go to Hangzhou by boat.

Xiao Diandian seemed to have made a little effort to look nice.
Instead of her floppy barrel-like trousers, she was wearing silver
grey slacks, quite sleek, topped by a corduroy jacket with a
flowery pattern.

Shu Zhen continued to wear his youthful zipped-up jacket and
black cotton shoes which were neatly cleaned with the edge of the

soles white.

By four o'clock in the afternoon when the boat blew its whistle, they were on deck. All their joy, expectations, and preparations were condensed into the steam emanating from the giant engine as the loud whistle sounded.

Diandian stood by the railing watching the ripples between the wharf and the boat. The water was a pale yellow. "Tell me," she said looking up suddenly to ask Shu Zhen standing by her side. "What colour is this water?"

"The colour of the earth's dreams," answered Shu Zhen without a moment's hesitation. "As for the dream of travelers, shouldn't its colour be the azure of the sky or the blue of the sea?"

"I'm a plain person, can't understand you," Diandian was being sarcastic.

"You're pretending!" Shu Zhen did not let her off. "The ancients composed poems when they were out roaming the hills and waters."

"Haven't you written a poem for this trip, Shu Zhen?" asked two girls. "Read it to us."

"What's the hurry. Wait until the boat's on its way," someone else put in.

The boat gained speed, bucking the headwind. The sun too emerged from the layers of light grey clouds, emitting a gentle, barely perceptible warmth. A copper bell hung near the flagpole. When someone touched it, it gave out a merry, resonant sound.

"Come, let's go to the front," Shu Zhen called and the youngsters rushed forward along the deck, surging along in ripples like the foam of the river.

Diandian followed angrily at the very back.

The boat cut through the smooth water like a sharp knife cutting through pear jelly. The strong breeze over the water tugged at people's hair and clothes as if attempting to ruffle the hearts' wings to bring happiness.

"Read your poem now," urged the two impatient girls. "Poems should be read to cheer up the journey. Come on."

"All right." Shu Zhen brought out a little notebook, glanced at a page and closed the book again.

> *It may be an accidental force which pushed,*
>   *And you started out,*
> *Brushing aside all ties and obstacles,*
> *To test and probe into the darkness of the universe,*
>   *And search the grand panorama of the planets.*
> *Or is it to mold one's tiny breath into*
>   *The giant bosom of the firmament?*
> *To send individual greetings*
>   *From one star to another.*
> *Perhaps it is to see clearly oneself*
>   *From a distance of a thousand leagues*
> *In one backward glimpse at the original position.*
> *Or perhaps there are no thoughts at all,*
>   *Nor any purpose, except*
> *To go out, move away, to fly!*

There were clappings and cries of bravo. Diandian, however, made no move as she continued to stand, one hand on the railing, eyes pensive.

Shu Zhen went to her side. "Well, did you like it?"

"Sorry. I know nothing about poetry." She seemed not in the least interested, just like the time Shu Zhen went to Steel Five for the meeting.

Shu Zhen asked no further, though he felt a little crestfallen. If that was the way she felt, why did she organize this kind of a trip? She was quite incomprehensible.

"Come on, Shu Zhen, give us another poem, just make it up."

Shu Zhen was surrounded by a group of youngsters who would not let him off.

"Let's do it this way," Shu Zhen suggested. "A joint effort. Everyone contributes two lines on the theme of river, sea, boat. Nobody should be exempted." After a pause he added, "What if someone tries to get out of it?" He hoped his proposal would force Diandian to join in with the others.

"Whoever tries to back out will have to have a drink," one young man swung the wine bottle in his hand.

"Drink wine? That's too easy. Drink cold water."

"All right, that's settled. I'll start." Shu Zhen swept a challenging look over at Diandian and presented his opening lines:

> For the first time I observe, ponder the world as an atom
>   outside self,
> I am but a small drop of water out of the rippling waves.

"Go on, go round clockwise," said someone.

> I am a white bubble of the foam, disappearing in a mere
>   second.
> I am but a breath of the surging sea.
> I am a seaweed buried thousands of feet below,
> I am a sharp, jaw-like crag just above water.
> I am a twinkling light at night on a float in the harbour,
> I am a seagull fluttering round the ship's bow.
> I am the small copper bell ringing out its warnings,
> I am a heavy lever of the crane in the ship's stern.
> I am a corner of the rusty iron sheet covering the deck,
> I am the greasy cable as thick as a man's arm coiled
>   and entwined in a heap.

It was now time for the girls to continue. "You've said it all," one of the girls pouted.

"There are plenty more," said one young man. In a shrill falsetto, he chanted:

> *I am the man whose glance caresses his wife's big belly,*
> *I am the lass hiding her face bashfully in her lover's arms.*

"We don't want to play the game with you. We won't allow such vulgar stuff," the girls protested, trying to back out.

"You don't dare to contribute even a few lines?" several young men pitched in.

"If you don't contribute I'll go and get the cold water," someone threatened.

"Hey, our Youth League secretary's slipped away," someone noticed. People looked around and they came to the same conclusion.

"I'll go and get her." Shu Zhen had already discovered her disappearance.

The river water slowly changed to a pale green-blue while the sky turned into silver grey. Night fell. Lightly-tinged sunset clouds brushed the far horizon as if etching it with colour. The clouds pondered heavily as daylight gradually dimmed.

Xiao Diandian sat alone in the boat.

"What are you thinking of?" Shu Zhen approached Diandian.

"Nothing at all. Sometimes I just like to be alone."

"It's your turn to contribute some lines."

"There's no poetry in my heart. I don't care for poetry."

"Why not?"

"You always want to ask why. You do everything you can to explore and probe into people's minds?" Her glance was penetrating.

"Don't you think this is a natural thing to do? Otherwise what point is there in contact between people?"

"Natural?... Curiosity, more like it. I used to be like that too. But no more." Her voice was low. "Why see things too clearly? Once you see through them, all warmth and feeling disappear."

"Not necessarily. There are always things good and beautiful to console, surprise and stimulate."

"That's what they tell you in books. You've still got bookish ideas."

"There's something to be said for bookishness." Shu Zhen was not a one to back out from polemic. "I've still got another why," he smiled doggedly. "Why did you come on this trip at all? I can see you don't seem much interested."

"You're quite right, I have little interest in this sort of thing. I come out only because I want to get away. I even feel as if I want to get out of myself so that I am no longer me, no longer Papa's daughter, or my elder brother's sister or the secretary of the Youth League committee..." Leaning against the railing, she seemed very tired. Her hair ruffled by the wind screened her quiet face. She was not really revealing herself, nor was she hiding anything.

What exactly was hidden in that small delicate figure? Every time Shu Zhen saw her, he felt as if he were approaching a deep, narrow underground channel which sent out gusts of cold air. For someone of her age, this was most unusual. Curiosity made him ponder and want very much to remove the stone opening to that deep channel. "Could you possibly try to bring yourself back and tell me something of that daughter of Papa and sister of the big brother...? You did promise me."

Herself? Diandian's mood frothed like the foam beneath the boat. She had not discussed herself with anyone for a very long time. She felt that only she herself was truly reliable and dependable. But she did make an exception of this young reporter of whom she knew so little. Why did she promise? She couldn't say. Sometimes one's actions were directed by a vague instinct which was hard to fathom.

Herself? Where was she to start? There were many facets. The vehicle of life went in all directions, not like the buses which stand obediently at bus stops and have their schedules. What was difficult for her was that when she started to find out about herself she was no longer so young...

In the dusk, she was a small, frail shadow, as slight as a papercut figure stuck to the big window panes round the stairway, waiting patiently. Papa! She dashed down without a word and took the small bag in Papa's hand. He bent down to rub her cold little hands. She had been waiting a long time, waiting like this every day. He gave to his daughter the only smiles he showed in those days. Yes, those were also the only times she smiled. There were only empty rooms in their home, a home where she was all alone.

One day when he left home he said to her, "Don't wait for me anymore..."

She asked no questions, like one who understood things. Gazing on her father's hair, turned grey overnight, and the dark rings perpetually round his eyes, she merely bit her lips.

When the time came for her to leave school before jobs had been assigned, she was summoned by the Workers' Propaganda Team. They told her, "You either stand firm on the proletarian side to expose the reactionary crimes of your father who was a fake Party member, in which case you'll be allowed to remain in the city, or..." Her heart trembled, just a slight quiver. How should she answer them? She had no fear of going to the countryside, but she was repulsed at having her fate arbitrarily arranged by others. Her father a fake Party member? In those days of White Terror when Party members ran the risk of losing their heads, why ever should anyone pretend to be one. What good would it do to pretend? It wasn't like now when people considered the Party card something of value... She loved her father, so kind though also stern. When she was small she loved to put her face against her father's thick palm, near the fingers stained brown by cigarette smoke and sniff the familiar smell. She hesitated as she pondered over her answer. Suddenly, she heard a static hum and realized it was a tape-recorder waiting to take down her answer. "How low down can they get!" She no longer hesitated but blurted out, "I don't know anything. Do whatever you like."

She did not escape being pushed around. She was sent to the poorest village in a mountainous area to do farm work. Before departure when she was in the midst of packing, she felt a strange sense of peace and consolation. She had passed the first test of life and came out victorious in body and soul. She had kept herself intact. Like the legendary Joan of Arc, she started to bear the cross of suffering for others. When it was time to leave she went to bid her father goodbye outside the tiny window of the isolation cell. She said nothing about her job for she found there were more white hairs on her father's head.

"And then what...?" Shu Zhen pursued like someone listening to a story. Although it was not a mystery nor like the fairy tales of childhood, to him it was more fascinating. After all, it was a real story.

Diandian said nothing more. Then what...she was sunk in unhappy reverie. Dark skies, floating clouds, the mast, the engine, the sound of waves...all seemed to have disappeared. Only the noise of the rushing wind seemed to have any appeal for her.

The two sections of the crane above sliced through a patch of light like a compass. A new moon appeared fluttering through hazy light clouds barely visible and the more beautiful because of it.

And then what...remained a mystery. Diandian was silent.

The boat moored near the lovely West Lake of Hangzhou.

At the Lingyin Temple, Shu Zhen took the group into a

restaurant. "My treat today." He announced. "What would you like to eat?"

"They've got crabs!"

"Let's eat crabs." It was unanimous.

More than a dozen of them crowded round the table. They had to sit sideways, allowing only one elbow each on the table. The day wasn't fine but rather overcast. The misty scene before the rains came was like a landscape painting. The crabs come on a large platter, their many legs all awry, the shells boiled a bright brick red. Small dishes of vinegar sauce with chopped ginger and sugar gave out a delicious aroma.

"This is really great," one young man cried as he broke through the shell of a juicy crab and the yolk appeared so that he had to put his lips to it to suck out the delicacy. Nudging Shu Zhen with an elbow, he remarked, "Isn't your paper running a column on the discussion of what is happiness?" Waving a handful of crab legs, he said, "At the moment, this is happiness."

"What a glutton you are. Is eating happiness?" mocked one of the girls.

"Then what do you call happiness?" the young man was not willing to be rebuffed.

"Aw, don't let's talk serious matters. Eating is eating," someone intervened.

Diandian, however, kept her eyes on the window. Suddenly, she ran out of the room.

"Where are you going?" asked the girls.

"To do a bit of shopping outside."

When she returned, there was a fine porcelain Boddhisatva about six inches tall in her hands as well as a Buddhist rosary which she rattled.

"Why do you want this sort of stuff?" The image and the rosary were passed from hand to hand as the youngsters examined them like curios.

"Why didn't the Youth League secretary buy a wooden fish so she could knock on it like a monk." Shu Zhen mocked.

Diandian only smiled without taking notice. "Hand me the camera. I want to take some pictures."

"Let me take them for you," Shu Zhen hung the camera around his neck.

Diandian did not reject his offer. She walked very fast, going straight towards the main hall of the temple.

In the solemn hall, the thick smoke of incense wafted upwards. Under the huge image of the Buddha several old women in neat peasant dress knelt with eyes half closed, their bony hands folded together, dry puckered lips moving in silent prayer. They seemed so pious, as if their souls were already saved by the incense which wafted them into another world.

Diandian kept her eyes on them for a long time.

"What do you want me to take?" Shu Zhen felt quite puzzled when he followed her into the hall.

"Take them," said Diandian, choosing an angle and pointing it out. "Do you know they have come up here on their bound feet prostrating themselves after every three steps. It took them seven times seven days to reach this hall. All this just to burn some incense and kowtow to the Buddha..."

Shu Zhen removed the cover of the camera. Diandian knelt down on one knee to watch as she said, "Try to capture their look." Then half to herself, she murmured, "It is a kind of happiness to be so devout."

"It's only ignorance."

"We are by no means so clever."

"What else do you want me to take?" Shu Zhen had no intention of getting into an argument with her at a place like this. Diandian made no reply but turned to go into the Heavenly King's

Hall. "Take this couplet!" She took over the camera. The two lines
of finely carved words in gold were reflected in the camera eye.

> Stand firm on your feet and the mountain behind will not
>   vanish,
> Hold fast the seal in hand and the Buddha appears in front of you.

Shu Zhen wondered if she really believed in this sort of
philosophy of life, but he pressed the button.

"Don't you want to have a picture of yourself?" Shu Zhen
suggested taking her to the famous cave to have a picture taken.

Diandian shook her head without interest. "If I take one who
shall I send it to?"

"Don't you have a friend?"

"Yes, I have a friend. But not necessarily a friend I love." Her
answer was candid. There was a sort of heavy-hearted tone to the
remark.

Shu Zhen could not very well go on asking more questions.

"Don't you want to know?" She kept her head half-turned like
a child.

"Of course I do...I intend to write..."

"Even if you weren't going to write anything I could tell you.
I said before that whatever I do I can talk about it."

Shu Zhen felt that with her he was often made to feel like
someone cutting with a very blunt knife.

In the evening, the young ones got some cinema tickets in
exchange for cigarettes. Diandian again wanted to be on her own.
She said she was visiting a friend in the suburbs.

"What friend?" asked the girls winking to each other.

"Someone very remarkable." In the knapsack on her back was
the porcelain Boddhisatva.

"I'll come with you. It's not a good idea for you to be walking about alone at night," said Shu Zhen. "I have some friends from my Forestry Centre days who live in the suburbs. I'd like to see them." Shu Zhen could be very considerate when he wanted something.

Diandian hesitated a moment before she agreed.

The night was very dark. It was only a little after eight but the lights were out in the houses along the small lanes. The people here seemed to be living in contentment. Like most people in China, they seemed to have nothing to do with the world outside themselves.

"Those friends of yours, how are they doing now?" asked Diandian as they trod the uneven pebbly paths.

"Since their return from the Forestry Centre things haven't been ideal," Shu Zhen sighed. "One of them took over his father's job in a horticultural nursery. He was a deputy chief of our Centre, a very clever and capable man. Now, he works on flowers and trees all day long. When I went to see him, he merely described to me the various colours and shapes of the chrysanthemums or discussed the weird holes and wrinkles of the rockery he was working on. He seems to have an easy life. Lost all that vitality and energy of the days we shared in the Forestry Centre. Another friend is an information officer in our propaganda group, a very sharp and learned person. Back in the city now, he was assigned to the sanitation bureau. His job is to cart around garbage. Last time I went to visit him, he was building his own house. The ground was littered with mud and broken bricks. He smiled at me wryly with a helpless expression. His glasses, turning yellow with age, were broken in the middle and stuck together with several layers of adhesives. Most of the others are workers. After work they practise calligraphy, or play chess or get on with household chores. Once we all climbed the famous Flying Peak together and got all

nostalgic at the sight of that poem written by the reformist Wang
Anshi. You know... 'Looking for the tower on the Flying Peak
where at cockcrow you see the sunrise; no fear of drifting clouds
hiding your view, for here you are at the very top!' Everyone said
they no longer possessed any of that immense hope and great
ideals." Shu Zhen paused for a few seconds. "In those early days
when we first went to the Forestry Centre in the Greater Xing'an
Mountains, we were all so courageous and full of spirit as if the
thousand hills and dales were in the palm of our hands."

"When we were in the mountain village, life was extremely
hard," said Diandian, hurrying her steps to catch up with Shu
Zhen's long stride, "But sometimes it was full of romance. You
seem to me to be still very romantic. You're an idealist."

"Because I write poetry?"

"You're a poetic person."

"But you're a person who dislikes poetry."

She was silent. They heard only the tap, tap of the nails on her
shoes.

Shu Zhen turned to look at Diandian. In the dark, he couldn't
see her eyes. He changed the subject. "How remarkable is the
person you're going to visit?"

"You guess."

"A great man with determination? A scholar with profound
knowledge? A brave communist with strong determination?"

Diandian shook her head. "She was a child-minder-cum-housekeeper
in our house. You're surprised?" She patted her knapsack. "I'm
taking this Boddhisatva to her. She was very superstitious, always
asking the Buddha to bring us blessings. She was good to us. My
brother and sister were all brought up by her yet her own children
were left in the village and fed on rice gruel as babies. During the
Cultural Revolution, when all our relatives and friends cut us off,
she alone often came from the village to see us, slipping stealthily

through our door. She'd leave a few fresh eggs, shed plenty of tears and go away silently... These last two years, our family situation has improved but nobody at home mentions her anymore."

"Is she doing all right now?"

Diandian did not answer. She hastened her steps as she went through a thick cluster of trees to come out in a desolate graveyard. The wind swept up pieces of paper, rustling in the tall grass.

Where was the child-minder's house? Why had we come here? Shu Zhen felt the cold morbid atmosphere of the graveyard penetrate his bones. His heart palpitated as they groped along in the dark. Beside a small earthen mound, with no wreaths, no tablets or any sort of monument, Diandian halted. Carefully, she took out the Boddhisatva, dug a small pit with a piece of loose stone and buried the porcelain image.

5

The Graduate Centre TV room was crowded. Before the feature film, there was to be a football game: Argentina versus the Netherlands. It was an exciting game. Many people stood on chairs, shouting bravos at times and roaring with disappointment at others.

"Come and sit here," Zhao Guokai managed to squeeze in and find a place in front for Yongyong. At first, she had no desire to watch the ball game. "You sit here. There are so many people." Yongyong wanted to back out.

"No, no," Zhao practically forced her to sit down. "It's terribly exciting. You'll find out the fun after you've had a few matches."

Yongyong had to comply, but she had never thought there could be much fun in watching a ball game. Back at the Forestry Centre, after wielding an axe or pulling a saw all day long, she had been so worn out after work that even getting up from her bunk to prepare food was a great effort. Sometimes while watching a newsreel, she saw bits of ball games and noticed that athletes sweated as much as she did at work and wondered why they bothered at such non-productive effort. She never understood the enthusiasm of sports fans. However, once she was in that crowded room as one of the spectators, she could not remain untouched by the general mood of the others around her. Technological development enabled the image on the screen to be carried across the Atlantic by satellite from London to Beijing, remaining clear and distinct in spite of the distance. The coming together of all parts of the world meant that the angular line of the ball, the jumping of the athletes and the roars of tens of thousands of spectators all became an artistic enjoyment of speed and vitality.

"Ah, fantastic!"

"Wow! Number Five take care." Suddenly everyone held his breath. Number five had tripped and tumbled on the ground. He was the Netherlands team's centreforward. The coach dashed forward. The broadcaster was silent. Number Five suddenly struggled to his feet. Limping just a little, he turned and began to run. The whole stadium burst out into thunderous shouts, "Hurry, quick, shoot!" "Number Five made it." The athlete jumped up to wave at the spectators and a thunderous applause broke out.

Yongyong was no longer a placid bystander. She felt as if she were on fire, wanting also to cry out like the others. She glanced at her friend, who, like a little boy, had wrapped himself over the shoulder of a schoolmate in front of him, and seemed on the verge of rushing out to put in a few kicks himself. Why was it everyone seemed bewitched? What was the motivating force behind this? It certainly was inspiring. Was it eagerness for victory, stubborn pursuit and vigorous struggle? In such atmosphere, Yongyong no longer felt burdened by the hidden pain and grievance in her heart. These were no longer important but very insignificant. She put her hands over her flushed face, warmed by the fervour coming over her. In the past she had rarely been touched by such strong, stimulating emotions.

In the arena of life, should not everyone be an athlete fighting for victory?

"Time for the film now, and it's even more exciting," Zhao returned to his own seat when the ball game was over and settled down.

"Too bad it's a film in English. I might not understand a single word." When Zhao came to tell her that the American film *The Dove* was being shown in their TV room that evening, she came eagerly though regretting that her English was still so poor. She was afraid she wouldn't be able to understand a thing but it would be a delight just to listen to the English dialogue.

The film finally started. *The Dove*.

Turbulent waves of the sea. A small boat, bounced and tossed like a little leaf. The story of a young man sailing round the world. Though there was no plot, it kept the audience spellbound from beginning to end. Two people whispered, "Wonderful film! I'd like to plunge into the sea too."

"Let's go on a cycling tour in the summer vacation."

"No, we should get a boat, too."

Yongyong had no way of expressing her feelings. She only wanted to get out somewhere, where there were spaces vast where she could dash around feeling free... She suddenly wanted to be free from something. From what? She couldn't quite make out. She had been living like a docile pony harnessed to a heavy mill, treading round and round only to find itself always at the same spot. But just look at that boat, the *Dove*. Like Pegasus, it flew across the oceans over such a distance. The young man also wavered at times. There was loneliness, difficulties, and endless battering by storms. But he eventually completed his round-the-world journey, a trip, something only a few were able to achieve.

He was no experienced sailor but a mere youngster of sixteen. He was a man who had full confidence in himself.

Yongyong felt that her life should also be developing like the courageous *Dove*.

Perhaps she had already entered the sea of life where the waves roar.

Early every morning under the trees on campus, by the basketball court, or along the running tracks, students paced, with bent heads, memorizing new vocabulary or sentences. At night when the lecture halls were quiet, many students still paced the corridors, loitering by the staircase with books in hand, reciting the rules of grammar or parsing sentences. Were they not making preparations to start out in life like so many little boats bound for the ocean? A hundred vessels competing in the stream, as the saying goes. Yongyong seemed to sense the vibrant force that was pouring out all around her.

Back in the dormitory, the other girls were all in bed. Yongyong turned on her desk lamp. She sat down but her head was so full of the scenes of the film she could not settle down to do more studying. An idea flashed through her head: "About time to write." She looked up.

On the little calendar over the bookcases was a date marked out with red pencil —— December 31. She said not to write in a year. Very soon, a year would be up. It was time to spread out paper and pick up her pen. But after a year of silence how was she to write this letter? She had thought about it more than once. At such times, yearning for her husband mixed with bitter grievance always overwhelmed her. "We'll not write for a year" had been said lightly while in anger. To live up to her own words she had had to swallow so much pain and bitterness.

The day her baby was born, a young mother in the next bed

read aloud the telegram her husband sent: "All my love and kiss our daughter for me." After the cheers of the other new mothers subsided, Yongyong put her head under the sheets to weep. There was no one to share her exhilaration and joy when she heard the first cry of her baby. Write to him immediately? Perhaps she really should let him know. Then she could get the happy response she longed for...

She finally received the examination board's notification telling her she had passed the entrance exam. It was time to leave the Forestry Centre. How she longed to tell him this wonderful news; she thought of it with a sense of pride. She even thought his letters might go to the Forestry Centre when she was gone. But no, she should not back out from her own words. She must wait patiently for the right time, she must be patient. Before leaving, she left the address of the college with a local girl who shared her room at the Centre. "If there's a letter for me, please forward it." She couldn't help hoping that he would be the first to write. But a year went by, no letter came. Before their estrangement, she used to look forward to every single letter of his, especially when she was at the Forestry Centre without him. The postman would not come up when there was torrential rain making the mountain paths impassable. She would put on her big rubber boots to scramble down the hill to the post office, appearing like a muddy shadow freshly fished out of a puddle. His letters were torrid, like a torch. If a forest fire had attacked her living quarters in the hill, the first thing she would have tried to save would have been the stacks of his letters which she kept filed neatly in chronological order. She wasn't able to imagine how she could possibly go on living without his letters. Now, a year ago it was she who said, "We'll not write for a year." Yongyong was thinking of writing to him now. After all there was that tenderness in her heart, like wisps of pure white clouds. Their days together in the big forest had left verdant dreams. Still the

months of not writing had made her feel quite strange. The many
things she wanted to tell him which surged and ebbed in her mind
seemed to have frozen at the moment she wanted to pour them out.
The changes in her life brought events which knocked hard at her
former existence, bringing things which had to be faced, pondered
and analyzed. Like a smooth peaceful river which flowed suddenly
into a rather narrow gorge, it was forced to rush through and run
ahead with no time to look back, to think or wonder how she had
got there. She was not able to describe clearly in a letter how she
had managed to get through this span of time, nor could she explain
lucidly the various impressions and feelings arising from this experience.
She couldn't help pondering over the tale of the "ugly girl" Zhao
Guokai had told her that day, encouraging her to make herself pretty,
affirm herself, appreciate herself and look into herself. Perhaps she
really should go and buy herself a proper mirror.

Yongyong chewed the tip of her pen as she tried to collect her
thoughts. Still, not a single word came out. Should she write about
the past year? It would be like a serialized story. Write about the
past twenty-four hours? She thought only of the scenes in *The
Dove*. Or should she pour out past sufferings and grievances? She
wasn't going to do that. She hated people who protested and
demonstrated self-pity. Besides these, what else was there to write
about? Might as well make it simple like a telegram: "I got into
college...also we have a baby..." No, better not tell him about the
baby at present. Who knew what he was like now? After a great
deal of thinking, she got out a postcard.

A most complicated problem had turned into something so very
simple.

6

Gripping the postcard he had just received, Shu Zhen rushed up and down stairs like a wound-up toy car shuttling between two walls. He did not know what he intended to do. He simply could not keep still.

There were only a few lines on the postcard and the words were rather cold. Was she still angry with him? Any way, she'd written at last, which brought her back to him like a lost kite blown back by the breeze. The message also included exciting information. There had been no word from her for a whole year. She had been like a lonely ship setting out to sea bound for no one knew where. Quite often he would think of her. In the long wait, which hadn't been easy to bear, he had had such misgivings about her. At the time when she was able to move back to live with him, he had imagined a life so closely bound together would be pretty tedious. He suggested that they should make a sort of contract involving "non-interference in each other's business and no strings to tie each other down." But once she had departed asking nothing of him, not even a letter, she was more frequently in his thoughts than before. Strange conjectures emerged in his mind which were disturbing. How would she handle everything? He was well aware that she would find the college examination very difficult. What if after all her hard work she still failed? Would she sink into despair? He realized that life at the Forestry Centre in itself had been trying... What if after a whole year, she would have to return despondently as a mere manual worker to settle down with him? What would he say? Repeat what he had said last time? Of course exactly the opposite might have happened, that she had got herself into college. Well, better not imagine things might turn out so well. Thoughts about her came up time and again. He tried to suppress them. It was like pushing down a fully-inflated ball into a tub of water, as soon as the pressure was released, it would bob up again. In a whole year of being apart, he could not achieve the peace of mind he wanted. Life was arranged that way; they were apart but they did not have the courage to separate. They would like to get together, but that was not so easy either.

It was getting close to the new year. Shu Zhen went to the mail room nearly every day. The man behind the desk always gave the same answer, "Nothing for you." Extremely frustrating. That was why he was overjoyed when he got the postcard. His heart nearly missed a beat. "She's passed the entrance exam." He wanted to shout, to tell someone the news. It couldn't have been easy for her. Not every one could get through. She did and she had managed it all by herself. Thinking of this, he felt a sense of guilt mixed in with his joy. He had a keen desire to do something as if to make up to her. Send a telegram of congratulation? It might be misinterpreted. Send her a present maybe? He felt that would be a vulgar thing to do. Write a really nice letter, that would be the right way.

Shu Zhen sat down at his desk and opened a drawer...

Old Zhao hurried into the room. "Shu Zhen, here is another assignment." Handing him a ticket, Zhao said, "Go to the Performing Arts School immediately. They are having a dress rehearsal of the play *Young Friends*. It's about some Red Guards who went to work in the forests. I am sure you'll be interested."

Shu Zhen had to stop the letter which he had just started. He was not much interested in plays as it was pretty hard to find a good one nowadays. However, an assignment was an assignment. Besides, the title of the play sounded attractive. It was about young people and a timber farm. "We were at the Forestry Centre for a few years. Why didn't I think of writing about life there?" he asked himself. He took the ticket, hoping the play would not be disappointing. Shu Zhen and his friends were those who had lived through such extraordinary times. They were very much alive and there were tears as well as laughter. He thought about himself and Yongyong. "I'll continue the letter after the play."

The theatre was not big. The rehearsal was already underway. There was no stage setting and the performers did not wear make-up. It was not actually a dress rehearsal. Shu Zhen sat down behind the small number of people there. The play reached its climax —— the Red Guards who used to fight on one side started to differ in real life. Shu Zhen had to bend forward to listen as two people sitting behind him talked continuously about the acting.

"They are trying to show their feelings. The feelings have covered the tension. They are not acting out the inner life of the roles... The way they talk is as if they're reading aloud. None of them are communicating. Just to communicate with the audience is not enough, the sound effects, the props, the environment, their vision —— they should react to all of these. They haven't done enough homework before the rehearsal and they don't understand the roles they are acting. That's the problem..." It was the voice of a woman. A very pleasing voice in standard mandarin, and a rather young voice though the words sounded like an expert expressing irrefutable judgement and conclusion.

Shu Zhen turned round to look out of curiosity. She was young, as he had expected, with long curling hair falling to her shoulders. She was in a light green pull-over with a silver gray anorak coat draped over it. She looked familiar. He had an impression that he had met her somewhere before. Maybe she was an actress in the provincial troupe? Shu Zhen's attention was distracted from the play itself.

When the rehearsal was over and before all the audience had left, the young woman went up on stage. She shrugged her coat down onto a chair. Raising both arms, she said, "May I have the attention of the performers, please."

She moved back a few steps. "You were all trying to perform by showing feelings and mood. To do that is like trying to catch birds in the trees which will fly away as soon as you reach out.

So all the feeling expressed today seemed faked. The point is that you've failed to have a deep understanding of the characters. We have stressed repeatedly that each character has its autobiography and file which has to be carefully studied. It's like using scaffolding in the construction of a building. When the building is completed, the scaffold has to be dismantled. But before that it is indispensable..."

"Who is she?" Shu Zhen asked a teacher of the Performing Arts School sitting beside him, for he knew quite a few of them. He had once accompanied teachers of the school to the Forestry Centre to select possible candidates for enrollment.

"She used to be a performing arts student. She graduated and became a teacher here. She would like to become a director. Right now, she is the assistant director of this play. This girl is quite something..." That sounded like a compliment yet there seemed to be an edge to his words.

Shu Zhen remained in the theatre, trying to find out why.

"Listen Chubby, these line of yours should be handled this way!" She started to demonstrate as she paced the stage.

Her movements also seemed familiar to Shu Zhen. "We must have met somewhere," he thought . He searched every corner of his memory. Suddenly, a blurred picture came back to his mind and slowly came into focus...

There had been a terrible snowstorm. A vicious wind sent big flakes of snow across the timber farm. Dry tree branches seemed to scream in the wind. Both sky and earth were a blur of white. All the roads and trails in the forest were blocked by heavy snow. In weather like this, who would dare to come out? The teachers who had come to the Forestry Centre to recruit new students had had to change their plans. With Shu Zhen acting as host, they stayed in the warm and cozy hotel of the Administrative Bureau of Forestry telling each other horrible tales of storms in the icy cold weather of the Northeast. Suddenly, someone knocked at the door.

"Come in, please."

A "snow man" staggered into the room. The mask covering the nose was frozen stiff. Frost was on its eyebrows, lashes, the wool of its cap and all the exposed fibres. It was difficult to judge whether it was a man or a woman. "I am freezing to death," the figure shouted, jumping with both feet to shake off the snow. "Please help me take off my cap and mask," the figure said going up to the visiting teacher, its teeth chattering. "My hands are frozen stiff."

Everyone rushed to help her remove the ice "armour."

"Good," the figure said as the cap was removed. With a shake of her head, two black plaits fell down. It was a girl. Her face was scarlet like the tiger lily in the wildness. Her figure in a thick sweater looked both full and slim. She warmed her hands near the radiator and rubbed them saying, "It's better now. How warm it is here!"

"How did you get here?" asked the teacher. "You didn't come on foot in such weather?"

"Of course on foot." She looked people straight in the eyes without a trace of shyness as if she were among old friends. "I'm from the Shengli Forest Farm," she said. Even local people would hesitate to go out in such weather. Shengli Farm was twenty kilometers away.

"You are teachers from the Performing Arts School, aren't you?" she said, tidying her hair tousled by the cap. "May I take the entrance test here? I didn't think you'd want to go to my farm."

"You'd better take a rest first." The teachers were moved.

"No, thanks. I have to hurry back," she said. "Can we start now?"

Shu Zhen still remembered that she had recited a poem "Ode to Lei Feng" written by He Jingzhi and also performed a short piece from a play, "A Family Visit." She was obviously very talented and she performed seriously and in a natural and bold style. He thought highly of her courage and eagerness. But he did not know whether she had been admitted to the school.

It was evidently her. Now she had graduated.

After her "lecture," the cast went back stage while still discussing the rehearsal. She put on her coat and hurried of the stage. "Well..." she said when she saw Shu Zhen at the door with the expression of a dim recognition. "Are you..."

"Do you still remember me?"

"Of course. It was in the Administrative Bureau of Forestry Hotel."

"Your memory is not bad."

"Only very famous people cannot remember others. We are only commoners," she said with humor. "I also remember your name: Shu Zhen. Am I right?"

"How did you know my name?" Shu Zhen was surprised.

"Who doesn't know the most famous poet at the Forestry Centre? Your writings were always on the bulletin of the Administrative Bureau of Forestry. I had once copied your poem —— Logging Song." She was still as she was years ago, looking people boldly in the eye. "My name is Qin Xin."

"So you have switched to directing now?"

"Acting is not so exciting. Directing is the center of drama." Her eyebrow danced and there was a flash of pride, as she asked, "Did you like the play?"

"Yes. But the conclusion seems a little unreal."

"Well, it has to be like this. Otherwise, the leadership would not approve."

"On the whole, the play is all right. It is inspiring, poetic, and reflects the experience of our generation," he commented.

"Then write a criticism of it, will you? Let's cooperate."

Shu Zhen wasn't prepared for this. He was surprised that she would make such a suggestion at their first meeting. She was really "something." "I am not a drama critic. You do the actual writing."

"You are a reporter. Writing is your speciality." She seemed to know everything about him. "I shall provide all the information about the background to the script and the whole process of staging it."

"All right. We shall have to discuss it some time." It seemed that he could only give in.

"What about tonight. You come and fetch me. We'll find a quiet coffee shop. It's too noisy at our school." She talked in the style of a director, ordering people around.

"Go to a coffee shop?"

"I like the special atmosphere in a coffee shop. Foreigners like sitting in coffee shops." Shu Zhen wasn't clear whether it was she who liked coffee shops or foreigners. "Wait, I'll get you a copy of the script."

Still thinking, Shu Zhen followed her as she hurried out. She had been "something" a few years back for her courage and boldness. What was she "something" for now? Five years had gone by...

Another new and mysterious "star" for Shu Zhen — like an "astronomer" forever seeking.

It was a very cold night. Shu Zhen put two letters which he just finished together with two envelopes and then put his hands into his sleeves to warm them. One letter would go to Yongyong and the other to Xiao Diandian. He wanted to make an appointment with Xiao Diandian again to learn about what happened "after that." It was clear that she wasn't superficial like a lot of girls her age. He felt that her coldness was there only to hide something about herself. There must be something behind the coldness. The other night at the graveyard, he did see tears in her eyes. Her heart was not cold...

He already had an opening of sorts for the article he was planning to write:

"Like looking for a mysterious and distant planet through a telescope, through the edges of the clouds, he perceived some light. He tried to imagine its interior. There must be more energy and more beautiful lights. It seemed that he was standing in a house by the beach. The wind blew up a corner of the curtains disclosing to him a limited view of the sea. He was convinced that beyond this there must be the vigorous waves of the wide ocean..."

Wasn't there too much imagination in it? He always romanticized people he ran into in real life. Maybe that was why he was always "poetic."

Sometimes he wasn't sure about himself.

When Shu Zhen woke up the next morning, it was already pretty late. He dressed and washed in a hurry and dashed out. Only when he was outside, did he remember the letter to Yongyong was still on the desk. He rushed back for it.

7

As soon as the class was over, Lili, who was in charge of the postbox keys, announced authoritatively, "Come with me for your letters." Several girls surrounded her immediately. Lili would never hurry at this point. Only after repeated urging from those anxious for letters would she lead the contingent to the mail room. This moment had become the most exciting time of the day as the letters brought to the campus information from the outside world. The next class would always be affected. Those students who had received letters would read them several times and their minds would be elsewhere.

Yongyong, who had never showed any interest in the postbox, felt somewhat anxious that day. Calculating the time required for a letter to travel there and back, by now there should be a response to her postcard. She couldn't help imagining in the past two days his reaction when he got her postcard. He must have been very happy and would light a good filter-tipped cigarette for himself —— the way he would always do when he had something to celebrate. He would be quite pleased this time. Wouldn't he? She had worked so hard for what he had wanted her to do. After she had sent the postcard, she had been so relieved and happy, feelings she had never had before. How would his two lady schoolmates regard her now if they ran into each other again in the tea garden? Now she could communicate with them on an equal footing and he would not be ashamed of her...

Yongyong almost stood up in order to catch up with the group going to the postbox. After waiting for a whole year, she couldn't wait any more. But she forced herself to sit still.

"Yongyong, here is a letter for you," Lili announced as she entered the room and jumped up on a chair, a letter in her raised hand. "For my darling wife: Yongyong, from her husband at the Newspaper Office." Lili read in a serious tone.

Everyone in the room laughed.

"Give it to me," Yongyong tried to grab it from Lili as she also jumped on the chair. Both of them fell off the chair as they struggled. What Lili read was indeed written on the envelope, but had been written by someone other than Yongyong's husband.

"I didn't do it," Lili said immediately.

Yongyong was in no mood to go after the culprit. She opened the letter as soon as she got back to her seat, but not before the bell for the next class rang.

Yongyong smoothed out the letter which was quite thick, several pages. She stood her notebook with the hard cover on her desk to shelter the letter and began to read... Suddenly, the notebook fell down with a plop. Yongyong was very much puzzled by the beginning of the letter: X. She looked at the envelope again. Her name was clearly on it. X must be the initial of a name. Whose name was that? Did he put his letter for someone else into the envelope for her? She had so looked forward to his letter to her. But who was this X? Yongyong read the letter in one breath. For a moment, her heartbeat seemed to stop.

What was the professor saying in front of the blackboard?

Yongyong's head dropped to the desk against her writs and her eyes were expressionless. The happiness that she had felt was completely gone. Her pleasant reveries and the exciting wait an hour ago were gone. Although from the letter it was hard to determine what the relationship was between Shu Zhen and X, the excerpt from Shu's notes, sentimental and romantic with its stars and ocean, seemed to indicate the X was quite a charming girl. It was obvious that she was attractive and he was interested in her. Women's intuition was often right. "In the past year, he..." His cold and unhappy look seemed to emerge in front of her. After a year's hard struggle when she thought she might win a smile from him, this X came out of nowhere and it was indeed an unknown figure. She gradually cooled down but felt her mind was a blank. How stupid of me. Why didn't I expect that?... Tears slid quietly down her cheeks.

"Yongyong, may I have a look at your notes?" Little Ou sitting behind her asked.

Yongyong wiped her tears away with her sleeves. She handed her notebook backward without turning her head.

"Where are today's notes?" Ou tapped her on the back with the notebook.

"I...I didn't take any notes." Yongyong turned halfway round.

"Are you all right?" Little Ou was disturbed by Yongyong's

pale face.

"Yes, I am all right." Yongyong tried very hard to concentrate on the lecture. However, the web of her mood was torn like a damaged fishing net so that her attention like the fish in the net slipped through the holes. She tried hard to stop those cruel thoughts from escaping. But she could not. How was she to relieve the pain? Tell someone of her distress? Maybe it would help a bit. Or perhaps she should go to the cinema. That would distract her thoughts for a little while, but only temporarily. She could not stop thinking. She longed for happiness and whole-hearted love. She had tried so hard to change herself all to no avail. "What is love all about? Is life so hard on everyone?" She could not understand. She had never given the question any serious thought. Last year when she should have been thinking about it she was too exhausted by her hard work. Before that, she just fell in love and got married and felt vaguely that she could not live without him. She just got carried along by life. "I must know everything, everything," she thought. She didn't understand everything about him. It was only because what he had said had hurt her self-respect that she had left him a year ago without saying goodbye. But he had made it very clear that they "had differences." Even now she didn't see where the differences lay. Some sober thinking was indeed necessary. Tears wouldn't help. Life was really hard.

The bell rang again. Streams of people came out of classrooms, dormitories, labs and library. Students went to the sport ground, to the canteen or the public bath house. People came and went. The loudspeaker was on. "Happiness" —— a piece of music played on traditional Chinese musical instruments —— was on the air. The whole campus was like a turbulent ocean, with waves of laughter, shouting and talking.

"Where shall I go?" Yongyong asked herself. She had no appetite and didn't want to return to her dormitory. She sat silently in the classroom.

She was alone there...

8

When Shu Zhen discovered that he had put the wrong letter in the envelope, he immediately wrote to Yongyong explaining his mistake and giving her a brief description of Diandian as he knew her. Would Yongyong be suspicious? That was inevitable in a woman. But he was not going to try to pacify her nor did he care to hide anything. He always considered contact with people, whether man or woman, as his window on life. He could not bear the kind of life that locked a person into a predetermined mode of behaviour.

After the lunch hour, Shu Zhen cycled down to Steel Five again. The article he wrote on the basis of the discussion the other day had been typed out. He brought it to be read over by the Youth League committee. The door of the Youth League office was only half-closed. He could hear Diandian's voice, apparently fiercely arguing with someone. Shu Zhen put up a hand to knock on the door, then thought better of it. He backed away to wait by a window round the corridor yet Diandian's voice came intermittently to his ears:

"...You needn't lecture me. Since the Almighty made me as I am I have to act according to my conscience."

"Do you think with your single piece of steamed bread you can give relief to all the hungry in society? You're more stupid than most."

"Others are others and I am I. If you only follow others, what's the use of being alive? All right, you can go now."

She sounded both indignant and severe. Who was the other party? Shu Zhen wondered whether he should leave. Before he could move, someone stormed out of the room and slammed the door behind him. Shu Zhen saw only his back as he went downstairs. Medium height, broad shoulders, solidly built. At the turn of the staircase, Shu Zhen got a glimpse of his profile. He had a straight nose but his eyes and brows seemed too close together. He looked like someone from the workshops.

"Who were you quarrelling with?" he asked Diandian as he pushed the door open.

"I wasn't quarrelling." Diandian was casually going over the newspapers without any expression on her face as if what Shu Zhen had just heard was only an old record.

"Is that man who just left a worker here?"

"No. It's him." That was her introduction. Her tone was still casual.

Shu Zhen understood at once the meaning of "him".

Diandian smiled wryly. "We usually speak in this sort of tone when we are together. He once wrote this verse:

*The normal form of happiness
Is enjoyed by lovers all,
Only for us there's something special —— quarrelling.
Quarrel —— love talk —— the burgeoning of a new life..."*

"That's rather quaint."

"No, it's not quaint. I don't like quarrelling but what can one do? We can't see eye to eye." Diandian leant against the filing cabinet, the expression on her face like one put there unwillingly. "We were talking about the Party meeting to admit new candidates. He told me it would do me no good to be so arrogant. I would only embarrass some people and make enemies of others. That would mean my never getting into the Party. To tell the truth, I'd rather never get into the Party than be a member like him, so timid and afraid of doing anything. He's too practical; always overwhelmed by circumstances and content to listen to the sweet talk of people around him. Last Wednesday when I called him with two tickets for an afternoon film, he told me that they were only allowed to leave in the afternoon and that was to go to the book fair. In the end, I got two book fair tickets as well. When we came out of the film it was nearly five o'clock. He still wanted to go though I told him it would be closing soon. Nevertheless, he went there all the same and came out without buying a single book. He was fooling himself really, as if he were telling the truth about going to the book fair. He couldn't tell a lie although the way he did it was really lying. What can you do with someone like that?...

"He shouldn't have come here to my office. It was our arrangement to meet only once a week." Diandian stood with her arms crossed, a cold light in her eyes.

"You shouldn't be so severe in matters of love," said Shu Zhen.

"There's no love to speak of."

"Then?"

"When we were in the countryside, it was terribly lonely... Life, you see, is more or less the result of history."

Shu Zhen was able to understand all that. But love is not something just to be kept going at all costs. He wanted to tell her that in this respect if you are too careful about hurting someone and yourself, you will end up hurting both yourself and others too. But if she asked him how one was to find love? Only by hurting? How was he to answer? Weren't there times in his own life when things had been a total mess? Was he still looking for the real answer? He kept silent.

Diandian seemed to have seen something in his face. "I still abide by my saying that happiness does not exist and it is not worth searching for."

"Have you really never felt happy?" Shu Zhen was very sincere as he asked. He genuinely believed that there was happiness for everyone or at least there once had been.

"Happiness?" She asked herself and also as if in answer. "No, when I was small I was very happy. Our family was a peaceful and happy one. Everybody loved me and I loved them all. Before going to bed, my father wanted me to kiss everyone on the forehead to bless them. I always did that gladly, blessing them with the wish that we would always love each other. But the Cultural Revolution started. The sudden change in our family was a terrible shock. The most painful thing was not only the calamity that struck us all but the distance that appeared between us. Friends and relatives who used to visit us often disappeared from sight. Brothers and sisters would quarrel or suspect each other over the slightest triviality. To preserve themselves, they even forgot about other people's interests. Of course, in those days it was possible that a decision of the moment could decide one's whole future life, work and career. Between my father and mother too there was estrangement. Mother was accepted by the rebel groups fairly early on and allowed to be one of their cadres. Because she was given a leading position, she honestly supported everything that happened at that time. Father's case was kept hanging in the air, he was not allowed to work. Every day, mother came home after work and quickly locked her documents, a thick package, into her drawer. Once, mother forgot to lock the drawer and father looked at them. Mother was very upset. 'You'd better not do that. There are regulations.' Father's face turned white, even his lips were white and quivering. He sighed in agony. 'Anyone else suspecting and distrusting me I don't really mind, but you... We've been through a score of years together.' That night, I felt the last trace of what I held sacred had collapsed. In the old days people were always criticizing the ugly relationships in capitalist society, but in that society everything was open. Disputes over inheritance, litigation, and other such problems were all open. Everything was unashamedly for money. But here with us high-flown words and reasons are used by selfish people to cover their ulterior motives. Isn't that hypocritical and therefore impossible to accept? What is love? Where is the happiness that love is supposed to bring? All these are illusions. I no longer believe them. In our family, though none of us left home and we continued to eat at one table there was no longer the love and harmony of before, though we have achieved some understanding now the Cultural Revolution is over." She stopped abruptly, too agitated to go on, her face pale.

"Here...have a drink of water!" Shu Zhen, forgetting himself, kept the glass of water in his hands though it was scorching hot. He didn't know what to say for indeed there was nothing appropriate for him to say, nothing which could help her to understand all those things. Where were his eloquence and his clever ideas? Maybe her cynicism was after all not far from the truth.

"Let's not talk about all that. No point!" Diandian seemed to have calmed down as she waved her hand as if to drive away something. The telephone rang. She picked up the receiver but only answered despondently with a "Yes, yes..."

Then, she told Shu Zhen, "They want us to start up that education by comparison again. What's the use?"

Shu Zhen agreed with her. "When the deputy editor of *Youth* came to our office for a seminar I expressed my thoughts quite frankly. It is now the eighties, the ideological problems of young people nowadays can no longer be solved by the formulas and slogans of the sixties."

"To tell the truth, I would much rather not be secretary of the Youth League. In units like this, it is the place only for people who talk in low tones, and are tame and obedient, people who care only about self-preservation. As for me, I have seen through a lot of people and events. I really do not want to obey certain people nor to command others." It was not often that she analysed herself so candidly.

"But what is the right thing for you to do?" That was the question.

"I really don't know myself. All I want at present is to learn a little English in my spare time."

"I've got some English textbooks which I could send you tomorrow." Shu Zhen appeared more eager than she. He was like that, always imbued with an extra eagerness and vitality. "But you shouldn't start something if you're not going to go far," he admonished.

"You're being rather severe," Diandian smiled. Nobody, including her father, dared to use a tone like that with her.

"You call that severe?" He had meant to continue, "And what is the purpose of learning English?" He checked himself though. He should not press a person too hard.

"Have you done your draft yet?" Diandian wanted to see herself under his pen and also to find out how well he understood people.

"Is there any reward when I finish it?" Shu Zhen said in jest.

"That depends how well it's written."

"If the draft depicts the person accurately?" His eyes glittered with confidence.

"I don't seem to have ever worshipped anyone."

She cast him an arrogant glance.

He lit a cigarette. "I've done half the draft already but there are still a few questions."

"What exactly? Perhaps I can tell you."

"Your weaknesses?" He put out the cigarette.

"Could you tell me some points you're already made?" Diandian's arrogance tapered off.

"You want to test me?"

She did not deny it. "I hope nothing has escaped your eyes." But her heart was pounding.

He thought a bit before going on candidly, "Because you

understand things too well you have lost all interest and joy in life's challenges and adventures. You are filled with ideals so that when you want to act decisively you are disturbed by feelings of irony in yourself, though you may not be quite aware of it yourself. You see through many things, but are unable to do anything about them. Instead, you feel as if you're in a mist-filled valley. That is why though unlike most women you seem to be very strong, when confronted by actual facts, you feel quite weak inside." Having said all that in one breath, he added the usual polite platitude, "Perhaps my observations are biased." Then he waited for her comments.

Diandian added nothing to what he said but thought for a while. She was surprised that he could see things so clearly and could not but admit that his words were fairly accurate. Some points were even more penetrating than she had expected for they touched on things she herself wasn't quite clear about, or rather things she dared not face. The friends around her were of all kinds, but most of them showed her only respects and compliance. None had ever pointed out her weaknesses to her. Nobody therefore was able to conquer her.

"Well, am I right or not?" he asked.

"Right or wrong you've said it all," Diandian smiled vaguely.

In a slightly melancholy tone, she said, "I'm very often miserable for I can find no way of devoting myself to society."

"Don't be impatient." Shu Zhen tried to console her. "The lava under the crust of our earth has so much heat and energy but doesn't have many outlets to burst forth from. Protracted motion and careful selection of something practical is what's necessary."

The telephone rang again. Shu Zhen stood up to go.

"Come and visit when you have time." Diandian told him, an invitation she rarely gave anyone. She laughed.

When he left, she stood by the window for some time letting the telephone ring on...

9

The sky was a dull grey, the cement ground was a dull grey. Those book-shelves covered with manuscripts were also a dull grey... Yongyong rushed along head bent, dragging her steps a little. She bitterly regretted having gone to that *Translation* office.

It felt like rain and the air was oppressive. Yongyong had a tightness in her chest. Every time she left the office along that grayish lane she felt like this. It was her third time. A car drove past stirring up a cloud of dust. Yongyong felt tempted to tear up the manuscript in her hands and let the pieces be blown away to distant corners like the dust under the wheels of the car... But once back in school, she would grit her teeth and try revising the manuscript again. "I don't know how you can stand it. If I were you I'd rather translate it all over again than revise it once more." Lili had told her. "I can't compare with you." Yongyong felt that she was not clever when she was with those brilliant girls in her dormitory. She was not clever and could only bear up patiently, trudging doggedly on, putting up with everything. Bear with things but do no despair. She understood herself. She found that was the only way she could go on. But putting up with unpleasant things was sometimes painful to heart and soul.

"Yongyong!"

Yongyong stopped in her track when she heard Zhao Guokai's voice. Like a child who has been bullied, she couldn't hold back her misery when she heard Guokai's voice, so close and dear to her.

"What's the matter? You look so defected." Guokai cocked his head to look at her, waving the blue notebook in his hands as if to a child.

Yongyong meant to wipe her eyes with a handkerchief but it

was too late. She turned her face away.

He had known she was going to the *Translation* office. He had expected her to be turned down again and would be feeling very bad. After he finished his class, he waited for her outside the school gate.

"It's all your..." Yongyong complained.

It was Guokai who had urged her to practise translation and then dragged her along to the office of the magazine to offer her contribution. "Whatever you do, if you try hard, there's always a chance of success, but just plodding along without making a splurge, you'll never get anything done."

The first time Yongyong went it was a sallow-faced thin editor who received her. Guokai took out her manuscript and said, "This is an essay translated by a student of our English department. Her first try..." He seemed to know the editors quite well.

"All right, we'll try to read it through quickly." The editor took the sheets, glanced through a page and placed them on top a pile of other manuscripts. Yongyong's glance followed his hands and noticed that her manuscript was on top. They would read it before the others.

Ten days later, Yongyong herself went to inquire. There was someone else there, a plump man who talked in a shrill voice but quite kindly. "Oh, it's an essay, is it? Let me have a look." He looked up and down and finally pulled her essay out from under a whole stack of manuscripts on the bookshelf. "Why has it gone right down to the bottom?" Yongyong wondered. The plump editor put the manuscript on top again. "We'll do our best to read it as soon as possible. We'll let you know our opinion as soon as we've read it. Leave your address with us." Yongyong, much hope in her heart, wrote down the postbox number of her college and department. Another ten days went by.

Guokai looked at the manuscript held tightly in Yongyong's

hands. "Did they tell you how you should revise it?"

"Yes, they did," Yongyong was very miserable.

"What did they say?"

Yongyong couldn't repeat it properly. She even wondered whether the two had really read her manuscript seriously. When she pushed open the door of the office this afternoon, the plump editor said, "The manuscript, uh...uh...we read it. Yes, we read it." Eyeing the thin, sallow-faced editor sitting opposite him, he searched around for some time before he dug out Yongyong's essay. Thumbing through the pages quickly, he scrutinized the last page, which bore no inscription at all.

At that moment, another person walked in, a man with white hair and an impressive air. "I sent someone yesterday to bring in my manuscript. Have you both read it?" His voice was loud and resonant as if there were loudspeakers in his breast.

"Yes, yes, we read it. Fatty Xu and I read it through last night. It'll go to press for this issue." The sallow-faced one smiled with satisfaction. "We were worried that we wouldn't have anything for this issue. You've sent us what we sorely need."

There wasn't anything? What about all those manuscripts on the desk and the shelves? Were they all going to be rejected?

The plump editor noticed Yongyong's glance and quickly introduced the newcomer. "This is the well-known translator. Mr. Hong..."

"Well, I'll be going now, you people carry on."

The editor picked up Yongyong's manuscript again with a pained look. "You see, this essay..."

"I'll take it back." Yongyong took over the sheets.

"The trouble is that you've failed to catch the style of the original so...uh the translation comes out a little too flat."

Outside the office near the entrance Yongyong saw the white-haired man again talking animatedly with another editor who was saying, "All right, we can keep it for a later issue..."

Yongyong was tempted to go up to him and ask whether when he was young and dying to be doing things it had been as difficult for him as it was for her now? Was it always like this that you have to strive desperately until your hair turns white before anything can be achieved?

"Give me that thing. I'll go over there tomorrow for you," Guokai stretched out his hand.

"Forget it. I didn't want to contribute anything anyway." Yongyong put her hands behind her.

"Forget it? You can't do that." He was not one to give up. In everything he realized the difficulties. He himself had come through this way. When there was only rough brushwood and gravel in the wilderness, much determination was needed to clear a path in order to get through. The first few steps were always the most difficult. He wished to bear on his broad shoulders some of the problems she faced, for there was so much that needed confronting in life... She had told him all about her husband, about their separation a year ago, about her baby and also that letter which was not meant for her eyes. Only then did he understand why her light-hearted gay laughter had disappeared but he had no intention of discussing or telling her how to face life and achieve happiness in an abstract way. He knew that life and happiness are meant for the strong. He wanted to help her learn to take the road of self-help. She must become strong, then life and happiness would be hers. He had the feeling Yongyong could become one of the strong ones in life though she was still far from that. There seemed to be some ingrained quality of strength in her but she had not yet been properly steeled. When he knew her a decade before he had discovered her purity and tenacity. He had treasured his discovery without showing her knowledge. When friends told him he was "cold" he thought perhaps they were right. These past years, he had not bothered to waste his time over his personal feelings.

There was too much he wanted to do. But he was only human, a full-blooded young male. Surging tides may be magnificent but hidden streams go deeper. If he ever got a chance to see Shu Zhen, he wanted to tell him like a brother, "Something of value should not only be discovered but also properly nurtured."

Guokai's hand stretched out stubbornly. Yongyong had to let him take the manuscript. "Don't quarrel with those editors."

He laughed. "Quarrelling or not depends on the situation." He opened the blue notebook in his hand. "I've finished that story you translated."

"How is it?"

"Not bad. Some of the dialogue was very humorously done. You've made progress."

"Really? Don't give me kind words." Yongyong's heart brightened. "The story's about a timber yard and the workers there. I know that kind of life."

"That's one of the elements." He pointed out the places he had marked out. "These sentences are not translated well, I've marked them for you to give them some more thought. I've shown your translation and the original to my teacher. He thinks your language is very smooth and shows good grounding."

"Oh, thank you!" Yongyong couldn't find anything else to show her gratitude though she knew there was no need for thanks between the two of them.

"How will you thank me?" he teased.

"You tell me."

"I want you to smile."

Yongyong chucked then like a bashful little girl. She opened his blue notebook and saw a picture. The sky was as black as ink and the sea was as black as ink. In the curve of the tall waves a small boat, its sails down, seemed about to be swallowed up by the waves. A young man was straining with all his might at the bow, his bulging muscles, hard as steel, showed his will and power.

"Ah, the *Dove*," Yongyong remembered the young man who had sailed round the world. There was a line of words underneath the picture also written in black ink.

> *If the wind blows the sails into bulging bags,*
> *If a tempest strikes us as soon as we leave harbour,*
> *We must be neither worried nor jubilant.*
> *Stand at the prow, hand right on the rigging*
> *Like a really good sailor.*

"Is this your creation?" Yongyong liked the picture and also the verse.

"Do you think I look like someone who writes poetry?" He did not answer her directly.

"Yes, you do. But you aren't the kind of poet who writes meaningless poems."

"So that's your comment, eh?" He was quite pleased. "If you like this, take it."

Cunning! Didn't he bring it along to give to me? Yongyong thought. She wanted to tell him she knew but instead only smiled sweetly, "Then let me thank you again."

The loudspeaker was broadcasting the weather: cloudy turning clear. Yongyong looked up. The sky was blue and translucent. She felt that her mood was clearing too as if ahead was a tempting oasis in a dry desert or a moist breeze coming from the ocean on a hot summer's day.

10

Another evening of smoke and ink.

Shu Zhen chewed at his cigarettes, putting one after another into his mouth. In spite of the cigarettes, his pen was not following orders. The ashtray was filled with an array of stubs, and ash littered the desk. The sheets of his manuscript had been so fiercely revised that there were hardly any of the original lines left. To write that criticism of the play had taken him two nights of deep suffering, every minute and second involving such deep thought that it was like binding himself with barbed wire. He was supposed to present a rough draft the day after tomorrow, yet he hadn't even got a proper beginning of a few hundred words.

Shu Zhen flung his pen down on the desk. Two drops of ink spattered his paper. What was the matter with him? His pen was getting more and more out of control. He leaned back against the back of his chair in irritation and despair. His head felt heavy but he was not sleepy. Cigarettes, tea and ink stimulated his nerves, making him both excited and exhausted. To others, an article in the paper was something so easily written and blessed with a halo of light. They wouldn't think every word was distilled from his heart's blood, filled with pondering, vexation and often with an agony of despair. Only after it was completed did he feel some satisfaction, which disappeared as soon as he spread out a new sheet of paper for another article.

Why had he promised to do this criticism? Shu Zhen regretted it very much. He was not used to doing literary criticism. What if his writing turned out to be a flop? He was getting worried. His desk was now like a small shop counter with ashtray, tea cups, keys, books, periodicals and banknotes, grain coupons, bus tickets lying all over it. Everything on his desk was in as much of a mess as his thoughts. He remembered the letter Yongyong returned still lying in his drawer.

He tossed away his pen.

The sky was no longer so dark. Dawn had not yet arrived but

a thin mist shrouded the new moon and the few twinkling stars. The house and the trees were shrouded in mist, the early mist between night and day.

There was a simple makeshift picture frame on his desk. Just two small pieces of glass, no bigger than pieces of pressed beancurd. These were clamped together by wires wrapped in plastic paper and in it was a small picture of Yongyong. She was wearing a bulky padded coat and loose slacks, leaning against a pine tree overhung with heavy snow. Perhaps due to the cold, her eyes seemed frozen so that they had lost their usual luster. Shu Zhen had taken the picture out from his old album after her postcard came, remembering that was the day of their wedding anniversary. They had been married four years, not such a short time. But he had rarely made an effort to love her. Love her for what? He did not care to deny that every conversation with Diandian always aroused some thoughts, giving him a special and unique sense of freshness. But with Yongyong, everything was calm and smooth. Shu Zhen's extraordinary ardour and vitality, stronger than that of ordinary people, were such that he could not help yearning for ever more unusual and fresher sensations. But he was constantly dissatisfied. "We will not write for a year." At first, he felt that it was just as well. When living apart, they could each develop independently. They could then make their decision when they saw the results. But what results had he been looking forward to? Was it merely to see the notice she received from the university saying she was admitted?

Shu Zhen's eyes fell on the picture frame again. She had sent back the misplaced letter without adding a single word... He seemed to see her moody, annoyed look. "We are too different..." he thought with a sign... But what about the time they came together? Her picture in the little frame seemed to grow bigger and bigger...

They were back at the Forestry Centre.

Smoke filled the Party committee conference room. Shu Zhen pushed back his chair. He could sit still no longer.

"Strung up a young man and had him beaten! Is that possible?" The last speaker was asking questions with disbelief in his eyes. "You people in the work team must be very careful about handling such matters."

"If you have any doubts about our report, I think the Party committee should move down to the brigade and convene your meetings there," Shu Zhen's eyes were blazing with indignation. He was ready to argue his case.

"Don't get so agitated. Sit down and speak calmly." The director of the Forestry Centre spoke evenly, rolling a cigarette as he spoke and suppressing a yawn.

What else was there for him to say? Shu Zhen could only sit down. He didn't want to say more. The No. 6 Felling Brigade was known as an advanced unit. Its leader was an important person in the Forestry Centre. The Women's Logging Team he led was a model within the whole province. No one would care to annoy such a man.

Suddenly the door of the conference room burst open and a girl rushed in. As soon as she removed her fur hat, she said still panting, "It happened like this. The brigade leader did it out of revenge..."

It was Yongyong! She was the leader of the Women's Logging Team. The whole discussion took a sharp turn at her entrance...

As they returned to her station in the snowstorm, Shu Zhen felt extremely touched. After the heavy snow, the forest was like a young maid wrapped in a white veil, so pure and serene. The gentle sunshine with imperceptible warmth poured down through the tree tops onto an open space covered in snow, with half a fir log buried in white. The whole silver-clad wood was occasionally brightened by penetrating sunshine. Shu Zhen wanted to capture this changing snow scene with a camera but he wanted more to imprint in his mind the image of the girl beside him whose gaze was as pure as the white snow and silver frost.

As the memories floated like a canoe out of a mist-filled lake, Shu Zhen's heart was stirred.

The neon light in the little cafe was not as dazzling as the commercial ones in the streets. Its dim blue and silvery light had a quiet, mystic effect. The lamps above the tables were pastel with a blue tint.

Qin Xin stirred the cubes of sugar in her cup enjoying that special aroma of hot coffee. "This is good coffee," she said after a sip. "Did you get my letter?" Her mind seemed to leap from one subject to another. They had agreed to meet in the evening, but that afternoon Shu Zhen got a letter from her. A rather strange letter quoting a verse by a contemporary Soviet poet titled *Not Necessarily*. Between the lines of the verse, she filled in with a pencil disconnected words and phrases, but when read together with the whole verse they seemed somewhat connected after all. Perhaps it was her "modern style."

Plums don't necessarily fall around the plum tree,
Why write letters when living in the same city?
Apples don't necessarily fall around the apple tree...
A long, long bamboo reaching into a serene world,
    Suddenly stirs up disorder.
Taciturnity and silence do not necessarily mean great wisdom.
Speaking of contact, why not be liberal, even with a woman.
Discussion and chatter do not mean frivolity.
Why say women are narrow-minded, narrower than a slit?
Beautiful women are not necessarily empty-headed.

I am so very greedy, greedy enough to swallow
The vast streams from the melting snow mountain.
A silly girl does not necessarily meet with a good fate.
Who says a woman's love is meant for one man only?
Lovers do not necessarily have smooth sailing.
Like the footsteps of spring, I will tread all over the world.
Bachelors are not necessarily always unfortunate.
Fate always loves to toss one out of one's tracks,
Real love may not necessarily be only once.
There's a thick, thick white cloud in the sky,
Twice or thrice real love is quite possible...
Like my heart which flutters and changes,
Truth may not always be in the hands of the experienced.
You ask: From whence do you come and where do you go?
Sometimes it's just as well to listen to the young ones.
There is no eternal love or hate,
Money does not necessarily brings misfortune.
Only the short time of meeting enters the heart,
It is worthwhile even with two empty hands.
We meet like flotsam, going different ways,
Life poses us many questions.
Just because of my never satisfied heart.
Can we necessarily answer? Yes or no...
Perhaps, therefore all talk is in fun
As we spin a beautiful fairy tale.

Quite unusual, it was also interesting. The original poem was
quite unconventional, presenting fresh ideas, while Qin Xin's additions
were very much like her person, revealing emancipation and liberal
ideas. She seemed to want to throw out all traces of convention
binding her. Amongst all his girlfriends in college, Shu Zhen had
never seen such a "Statue of Liberty." The young people who were

sent to the country like him had quickly tumbled down to earth from their idealistic clouds once they returned to the cities, becoming very practical. They lived without thinking much, eyes glued to everyday events, losing touch with their conception of the outside world and also the tide of strong feelings in their internal world. Placidly, they paddled peacefully as in a lagoon. This refreshing and bizarre "declaration" of Qin Xin's seemed frivolous and light-hearted, yet as he read it Shu Zhen felt as if a flock of wild geese was flying over azure skies making him feel that he too would like to leave the earth and soar upwards.

"Yes, I read your letter. It was rather refreshing," Shu Zhen smiled, leaning back in his chair. The leather chairs in the cafe had very high backs so that their two chairs formed a sort of world of their own.

"You mean the content or the form?"

"Both seemed original."

She looked rather pleased. "I appreciate some of the philosophical thoughts of the Western world. Sartre once said something like this, 'Other people are hell.' Too true. One must go after one's own values in life, go after things which are of worth. For such values, I am ready to give everything."

Shu Zhen believed her. He could not forget that stormy night in the north.

"You are married?" came Qin's sudden question.

"My wife is studying at college at present." "Why did you marry so early?" She asked the question in a very natural tone.

"Because it just happened." Shu Zhen had no wish to describe the events that led to his marriage.

"I had a boyfriend too. We started very well but when we talked of marriage his first words were: if we marry there will be no divorce. I told him: not necessarily so. I mentioned three conditions: firstly, the best thing is not to live together, secondly, no children, and the third thing was I would not want to become his family's daughter-in-law and he my family's son-in-law. He wanted to know what kind of a marriage that would be. I told him 'real love binds two people's hearts, there's no sense in sticking too close together physically.' Unable to do anything with me, he left. That was that." She spoke quite light-heartedly, with no trace at all of someone who'd lost something of value. She was just herself.

"That was your fault. You're much too unworldly." Shu Zhen thought her attitude rather ridiculous, yet lovable too.

"There's nothing out of this world about it. Didn't Chernyshevsky depict a new people in his *What to Do*? Didn't he pose a new way of living?"

The irony her words evoked left Shu Zhen speechless. A year before, didn't he himself quote the same ideas with righteous indignation to his wife? But now a year later when the same things were said by another person he felt strangely uneasy for no reason at all, no reason he himself could understand.

"Do you feel quite free and happy after marriage?" Her eyes were searching.

Shu Zhen did not care to answer. He had pushed off from his normal path in life out of dissatisfaction and disappointment. But after leaving the beaten track, in his heart of hearts he had never really felt much at peace. Sometimes, he even felt quite the opposite as if he had lost an anchor point from which he could use his energy.

Qin Xin was clever. She changed back. "How do you deal with life?"

"By being faithful to myself."

"Are there times when you try to hide or cover up from yourself?"

It was a question that probed deeply. Yes, there were times

when he did. To make himself believe deeply in something or to reconcile himself to something in order to achieve a sort of balanced satisfaction. What then exactly did he try to hide from himself? Shu Zhen felt himself on the defensive. Like a wooden toy at which Qin was rapidly throwing hoops one after another, he seemed to be completely encircled. Actually, Shu Zhen was rarely on the defensive when he talked to people. But as he faced this dazzling female whose thoughts flashed like sparks he felt as if he were standing in front of a splotchy old mirror from which he caught indistinct glimpses of himself. He tried to see himself clearly, and in the effort his own train of thought made no progress. He had meant to discuss his writing with her but instead there was this. Exchange of ideas and understanding was still pleasant. Good for him too. Besides, they did have quite a few things on which they agreed. Naturally, discussions like this were more interesting than talking of other things.

"You're not being frank enough," Qin wasn't quite satisfied.

"There are some questions I still need to ponder." Shu Zhen made no effort to hide this fact. True, the more he came into contact with life, the more questions life posed him, questions of his own, and of other people. Yongyong's, Diandian's and those of this young lady with no ties whatsoever now sitting opposite him. They were experiencing life in such different ways. And what about himself? Life was an endless flowing stream, bearing every willing vessel down new channels.

Shu Zhen was a vessel not willing to be anchored in a lagoon.

11

After receiving a number of letters from Shu Zhen, Yongyong was in a quandary: what kind of response was she to give him? It required a lot of thinking. Every letter was like an examination paper, demanding correct judgement and response. She was perplexed. She had come a long way in life but only recently had she awoken to the fact that "everything requires new understanding." If it were possible to start life from the beginning, she would certainly tell herself, "You must be very clear-headed when you choose love and happiness for yourself because you are really choosing the road you are going to take in life." But then, wasn't it usually only after a person had bumped her head more than once against a wall that she became really clear-headed? The path she struggled along was very bumpy and muddy, so much so that she actually stumbled and crept. Now that the pains were over she could see that the road ahead was easier. She had cleared a few paces for herself, but there were still plenty of ups and downs. Yongyong now felt that the burden on her shoulders was heavier, a weight pressing down on her all the time. Was it still those emotions that she couldn't untangle?

"Yongyong, are you coming to dance?" Little Ou flew into the room, timing her steps with "One, two, three!" She changed her shoes and told Yongyong that every one was in the gym learning ballroom dancing. Without waiting for an answer, she danced her way out again.

Dance? Yongyong went to the mirror to look at herself. There were fine wrinkles around her eyes. Could she still dance? When she was a little girl she had been very fond of singing and dancing. She had once given a performance in the Children's Palace where she was cast as an old woman. The teacher doing the children's make-up drew fine lines round her eyes with an eyebrow pencil. But those lines could be wiped away while the lines beginning to appear now would become deeper and deeper, quite indelible.

No! She would not learn dancing.

Yongyong tidied up her case. She decided to go to the graduate students' hall to practise English conversation with that Belgian girl who was studying Chinese here. It was Zhao Guokai who had introduced them to each other.

Tess lived on the second floor. She and her little boy Beck had a room to themselves. Beck's father was a Chinese student at present in the U.S. The boy was very bright. Only three years old, he spoke English and French and was also getting fluent in Chinese. Every time Yongyong went there she'd spend a few minutes with the child as if to pacify her own maternal instincts. If only it had been possible for her to keep the baby with her, like Tess, studying and being a mother at the same time... But how could that be? She couldn't hang nappies over the lines where the girls kept their face towels. Longing for her son sometimes kept her awake at night but there was no one to talk it over with. The girls in her dormitory were all young once still dreaming of life. Sometimes they would ask her, "Is it fun to be married?" That was a question no one could answer, somewhat like the question children ask of their parents, "Is it fun to be a grown-up?" So practical and yet so vague! The conclusion was like an unfinished formula with countless solutions. Yongyong herself hadn't really thought it out, what exactly was fun? Whenever these young girls who knew nothing of anxiety kept talking endlessly of their worries, Yongyong always kept quiet. If she didn't think of such things her heart could remain lighter.

Yongyong was envious of Tess who was always happy. In the summer Tess wore flowing silk skirts of gay flowery patterns, looking young and carefree. Were there times when she was sad and anxious? Once Yongyong asked Tess this question, "You study and have to take care of Beck, don't you find it hard?"

"Hard?" Tess blinked her brown eyes looking puzzled. Suddenly she smiled and spread out her hands. "No, no, I love studying. When we were working we both tried hard to save money, then we went off to study for a year or two like other people going off to travel. This way we learn about the world. When we go home we'll find new jobs..." Her way of thinking made everything sound extremely simple.

"Why did I come here to study?" Yongyong couldn't help asking herself. She was actually driven there by an invisible whip.

Yongyong went through Tess's open door.

"Oh, it's you. Please sit down." Tess was sitting by her desk reading. She turned to straighten her shoulder-length hair, "Beck is playing in Zhao Guokai's room."

Yongyong went over to the desk. "What are you reading?"

"*The Selected Plays of Maeterlinck*, English edition. He's a well-known impressionist dramatist in our country." She handed a well-bound volume to Yongyong. "Have you read his play *The Blue Bird*?"

Yongyong shook her head.

"Take this and read it. It's beautifully written. The Blue Bird is a symbol, crystallizing human happiness both in spirit and in body. The playwright wants to say that happiness does exist though it is usually not so easily discovered. The tale is about two little children who go out to look for the Blue Bird." Tess could already express herself in Chinese and had little trouble in telling the tale and its meaning and message.

Blue Bird...happiness...search. What a wonderful idea. Yongyong was immediately drawn to the play. She longed to know right away the secret of happiness. Whether in love and marriage or work and study what she experienced had been more misery than happiness. A year ago when she doggedly gave up the chance of a job in the city, it meant staying away from him instead of being near him. At that time she had a hazy idea that she was looking for something or other.

Was she looking for the Blue Bird?

In real life people dash around a lot, is it to look for happiness?

"I'd like very much to read it," Yongyong picked up the book and leafed through a couple of pages. It was full of words. "Will I be able to understand it all?"

"It's in very simple everyday language. You'll be able to manage quite well with the help of a dictionary." Tess leaned back against her bed. "Let's start. We'll read some of the dialogue. You translate into Chinese. It'll train your listening ability."

"All right," Yongyong sat down in the chair. She was a little nervous for though she understood general conversation in English, this was a play.

Tess read a section, her voice was clear and expressive.

Yongyong bit her lips in concentration as she started translating very slowly, stuttering as she went along, "The fairy said, my god...how stupid they are...stupid and timid..." She paused and quickly selected words she thought most accurately expressed the meaning. "Then you would rather remain in a stuffy little box or in the narrow water pipe instead of going with the children to look for the Blue Bird..." She was translating more smoothly now.

Tess clapped her hands. "Right, correct. You've got the main idea all right." She turned a page. "Come on, let's have another paragraph." Yongyong now felt more at ease. As soon as Tess finished reading a sentence she quickly translated. "Just empty words...misfortune lives in the neighbouring hole. That hole is separated from the garden of happiness only by water vapour, a very light curtain. Wind from the ridge of truth on the edge of eternity keeps blowing and lifting this light curtain..."

"You've only got one word wrong. Instead of ridge of truth, it should be ridge of justice." Tess closed the book and said, "You've learned so fast." She gave the book to Yongyong." I'm very fond of these two sentences. The fairy put it very well. The Blue Bird cannot be found by a single person all alone. Coming to China, I have the help of so many of you. I am very happy."

"You and Zhao Guokai have given me so much help. I'm also very happy."

Tess gave Yongyong a warm hug. "I think if human beings really could love one another, the Blue Bird would fly all over the world."

With Tess's warm white cheeks close to hers, Yongyong felt a rapture in her heart as if sunshine had poured into it. Though of different colours, and speaking different languages, they were not really separated and unable to communicate. The things they both wanted in life were after all the same.

"Mama, they are dancing out there," Beck called outside the door. "The uncles and aunties want me to fetch you."

Yongyong quickly opened the door to take Beck into her arms. "Give us a kiss, love."

Beck kissed her on the cheek.

"Come, let's go together," said Tess, digging out a pretty dress from a trunk. "After work, listen to music and dance a bit. All problems and fatigue will disappear."

"I'm no good at dancing..."

"I'll dance with you." Tess's warm offer was enough to melt all resistance. After changing her dress, Tess combed her hair, pulling it upwards and coiling it into a pretty black mushroom. She stood in front of the mirror carefully arranging herself until she was satisfied everything was in harmony. Ordinarily she wasn't fussy with her clothes, she wore simple casual costumes which gave an impression of relaxed comfort.

Yongyong admired Tess's figure in the mirror. Yes, she was making herself pretty so that people could enjoy looking at her. Beauty was something to be appreciated. A person should be nice inside and in appearance too.

The strains of a Strauss waltz were still ringing in her ears when Yongyong left the others. Strolling leisurely back to the dormitory, she turned back several times to look at the brightly.lit gym as if regretful of leaving it. She was not sure how many rounds she had made with Tess but she had the same sensation she had had when riding on a merry-go-round as a child. She was so happy, she wanted to cry with joy. Someone once told her dancing can become a craving. She knew she would not let herself be overcome by such a craving but at this moment as she left the dance, her heart and her feet were both ready to go on with the same rhythm.

In the dormitory, none of the girls were back. They were sure to stay on laughing and chattering till very late. She pushed open a window letting in the night air to cool her flushed cheeks. She found the sensation delightful.

Yongyong sat down by her desk. She should be writing to him. She no longer felt it so difficult to send him an answer. His cold, dissatisfied look and that unknown X now seemed unimportant. She only wanted to tell him that she borrowed from Tess Maeterlinck's *The Blue Bird*, that she had been dancing and that she had tried translating stories and essays... There were many things she should do and could do; there were plenty of things of interest.

As if sprouting wings her heart felt light and seemed to soar.

12

Bitter is the bloom of love,
Each blossom bitter to the core,
When can I cut the roots of bitterness,
Give me back my maiden moods.

Xiao Diandian pushed the chair back a little and leaned against its back as she declaimed the verse softly. "I copied that down in my diary," she said, draining her glass of red wine. Her face was paler than before she drank and her eyes were still cold like the moonlight.

Shu Zhen felt his heart quiver like the wings of the cicada on a summer night. Diandian had once said in such a scornful tone, "I don't like poetry. There is no poetry in my heart." Yes, she was chanting one of his poems now. He was surprised that this seemingly hard as steel woman harboured such fine, sad and yet such tender emotions. As he twirled the wine glass in his hand, he did not look up to meet her eyes. There were several dishes on the table, mostly untouched. They just sat opposite each other...

Yesterday he got a call from Diandian, "It is my birthday tomorrow. I'd like to take you out to dinner. Wait for me at the door of the Hongyun Restaurant at six." Her usual imperious commanding tone.

"Tomorrow evening...uh...I'm engaged...I have an appointment to discuss a manuscript with someone..." He thought of a reason to refuse. He wasn't sure why Diandian was asking him.

"Couldn't you discuss the manuscript the day after tomorrow?" She sounded unhappy. "Ever since our home was broken up, nobody remembered to celebrate anyone's birthday. This time I want to celebrate my birthday." Her tone was melancholy.

Could he still refuse the invitation?

By the time Shu Zhen rushed to the restaurant after work, Diandian was already standing at the door. "I'm afraid I've kept you and your friends waiting," He apologized to her. "I'm sorry but we had a meeting this afternoon."

Diandian's tone was casual as she answered, "There are only the two of us, so early or late doesn't matter."

"You only ask me?" Shu Zhen was puzzled but gradually began to see the light.

Diandian placed the wine glass against her lips, letting the wine flow into her mouth. Shu Zhen drank very little, trying to lead the conversation away from themselves. "How's your foreign language coming along?"

"I went through one volume and then stopped." With her chopsticks, Diandian tossed a shrimp into her mouth and spat out a whole shell.

"Was it too difficult to go on?"

"Not difficult but there seems no point. What ever is the use of learning a foreign language?"

No fun to be Youth League secretary. No point in learning a foreign language. Why does she insist on things like that? After all, fun and interest come from countless ordinary things. Such demands of life, and yet what had she herself ever done to deserve what she demanded? A sense of disappointment flashed through Shu Zhen's mind. He was like an explorer, lost in the desert, who sees in the distance an oasis flickering with magnificent promise stirring his excitement, but as he approaches discovers it is but a mirage. There are only lonely stretches of sand and gravel without a single blade of green grass. Although, of course there must have been cactus and other hardy plants here once... Shu Zhen became more reticent, lost in thought. He was unable to control his own sensitivity or his fickle mood, as fickle as the weather. Was he moody because of Diandian or was it due to something in himself? As if comprehending the laws of reflection, he seemed to see something of himself in her.

They let the food on the table turn cold.

After leaving the restaurant, they went to the park across the street and sat for a while in the tea room there. Few people were around as it was overcast with occasional flakes of light snow. As they strolled over the deserted path of the park, Shu Zhen's mind turned to the distant northern land and the rugged forests there. Once the Beginning of Spring was over, it would be time to prepare for spring ploughing. There would still be leftover snow drifts in the gullies and brown withered grass shivering in the chill wind but carts would already be busy carrying manure onto the land. The greyish dry land would be turning moist in the warmth of the sun and resuming its darkness. The seed drill would be planting seeds which would turn into crops. With the Beginning of Spring, everything was awakening from the winter. Men too would feel the familiar warmth of spring and the sense of life that comes with it. In this man-made environment of the park with its kiosks and groves and paved paths, all he felt was a sense of vapid inertia.

Diandian seemed also to be deep in thought. It was the first time he had seen her in a colorful stylish dress like a normal young girl, rather than the shapeless trousers she usually wore in the office.

"What do you think of that verse?" she asked him, staring into his eyes.

"It has a cold beauty," Shu Zhen said after a bit of thinking.

She smiled, "Men are born for happiness just as birds are born to fly." This was an unexpected remark from her.

"Didn't you once say that happiness does not exist and is not worth pursuing?"

"That was due to outside conditions when it was not possible to pursue what was wanted..." Her voice died in a whisper so that the last words were hardly audible. What was the thing she wanted? When they met before, her eyes had been cold and cynical. Since by a warm current which started waves and whirlpools? Was it the appearance of Shu Zhen in her life? She felt that her heart, untouched like the water in an ancient deep well, had changed. Every time there was a call from him, she could not calm herself down for quite some time. Was it because his piercing eyes seemed to look deep into her heart or was it that poetic ardour of his which generated steam and the heat of shock waves pounding at her heart? She did not care to think about the reason, all she wanted was to see more of him, to listen to him talk. Was it just her loneliness or perhaps there really was a need? That was the reason to celebrate her birthday with him.

They sat down on the stone bench amid the bamboo grove. There was a thin film of snow which Diandian brushed off with her gloves before they sat down.

"My father also remembered my birthday. He wanted the whole family to have a gathering but I...I came out alone..." She bit her fingers as if trying to restrain something.

Shu Zhen had a premonition that their conversation if it went one step further would stumble on a block which would prevent them both from going any further. It would then be necessary to find a way around it. He felt a slight tension which made him blurt out something quite unconnected with what they had been talking about, "My wife got into college...studying foreign languages."

"You told me that before...why do you say that now?" There was a very complex expression in her eyes. Her thin shoulders quivered. So his wife was in college...foreign languages. To her what he just came out with felt colder than the icy flakes floating around them. Suddenly she hid her face in her hands and burst into tears. "Why did you have to come to the plant to interview me?..."

Shu Zhen's hands, lying quietly on his knees, trembled. Her sincere emotions shook him to the core but he held himself tightly in rein...especially at a moment like this. How was he to explain things to her? He couldn't say his contact with her was only out of the curiosity of a reporter interviewing someone. Or that the meeting of their two young hearts had produced a common chord. He had expressed warm feelings for her, stirred by her unusual character, her extraordinary ideas and sentiments. Yes, there was a flash deep down in his heart. But then the flash was indeed bright and dazzling only because it was short and sudden. Had it gone on it would have become as plain as daylight.

He said nothing in spite of his thoughts. The snowflakes floated down soundlessly.

Her tears gradually subsided. Perhaps the cold snowflakes cooled her brows. She wiped her eyes. In a tremulous small voice, she said, "I really am a disgrace. You can laugh at me." Standing up quickly, she murmured, "I must go now." Practically running, she made her way out of the grove, her slim figure disappearing in the distance.

Shu Zhen stood there quietly for a while. The fluttering snow above cooled him though the flakes all melted as they landed on him, leaving only dark water marks. He stared down at the twisting footprints she left on the snowy ground. Perhaps roads were usually made this way by walking on them. He hoped that she would soon calm down.

The torrent had passed, there were no more waves but the shells washed up on the beach were beautiful and exotic.

13

"We'll be allowed to go home, to go home!" Little Ou rolled rapturously on her bunk. She was still a child and this was the first time she had ever been away from home.

"Don't you mention going home again," Wang protested. Actually, letters from her boyfriend, the tennis player, had been coming at an accelerated pace, from a letter a week to two or three now. Lili often resettled the postbox keys to say, "I'm becoming a private messenger for you." The little plastic tennis racket which used to hang by the bookcase had been moved to her bedside.

"I have to say it," Little Ou couldn't restrain herself. "My mum wrote to say she's bought two hens and is fattening them. She'll kill them for our table as soon as I get home..."

"Enough, enough, you're making my mouth water," Lili was already packing her things. Her desk was the most messy, with an array of toys: a little monkey with a red ribbon round its neck, a bearded Santa Claus and a funny-looking figure which refused to be pushed down.

Yongyong was the only one who seemed untouched by it all. Actually her longing for home was the fiercest. She would go and fetch the baby as soon as she reached home. How much weight had he gained now? He was seven and a half pounds when born and had given Yongyong such trouble coming into the world. He was full of smiles and laughing now, gurgling sweetly. Under her pillow was a whole stack of baby pictures. Babies change ever so fast, how she wished it were possible to retain every single change in him. But would he still know his mother after this separation of several months? When she imagined the baby finding her a stranger and pushing her away with his tiny hands, her heart was strong with a bitter pain. Still, the baby was an immense consolation. This time when she went home, it was the moment to tell Shu Zhen. He would be astonished and crazy with joy. That was for sure. The baby was after all their masterpiece. Whatever had happened between them it would be the sweetest sound to hear him calling her Mama and him Papa. Was there anything sweeter? The thought of the baby drove all pain and grievances from her mind like the sun dispersing the morning mists.

Yongyong couldn't help imagining how she would feel the instant she jumped lightly down from the train and he dashed over to meet her...then there would be the endless things to talk about, all the news to exchange, the interesting subjects, the tenderness... Yesterday, she bought a pack of good cigarettes. Although she had talked and talked in vain to make him stop smoking, she still liked to see the crinkling of his brows when he was deep in thought, a cigarette dangling in his mouth. She was also used to that slightly choking smell of his cigarettes. After all, they hadn't seen each other for a whole year and they had parted after a quarrel. Would they be very strange to each other? Would there still be unpleasant wrangling day after day? They had to talk properly, no matter what. Wasn't there a great deal she wanted to tell him? She now had her own demands on life and on him. But what was the most suitable thing to say when they first meet? What would they say to each other at that moment?

The lights were out. All the girls were in bed, their chattering dying away.

The moonlight coming through the window panes was like a projector casting white light on their celling. The night was bright with many stars. The two brightest stars on either side of the Milky Way were the Cowherd and the Weaving Maid while the row of scattered little stars were the kind-hearted magpies who would make a bridge for them on double seventh night so they could cross over to meet each other once a year. Yongyong searched the firmament for those two stars. How beautiful was this legendary tale of the separated lovers. For generations people had felt sorry for them, yet in modern times there were so many who also could see each other only once a year. Some, of course, were pressed into separation by work or other circumstances.

But what about Shu Zhen and herself?

The train rumbled on, its incessant rhythm flying over the steel rails. Leaning back in her seat, Yongyong pulled the curtains a little to keep off the piercing sunlight. Travelling alone was a lonely business. The open book in her hands remained unread for the words leapt with the motion of the train and her heart too was quivering.

Three days before Tess had gone home to Belgium with her

little Beck, Yongyong went with Zhao Guokai to see them off. Tess wept, hugging Yongyong's shoulders. "I wanted to translate that *The Blue Bird* with you. In Belgium we are very fond of this story. I'm sure people everywhere will like it for Maeterlinck wrote of something all human beings are keenly interested in —— happiness. I hope you will be able to translate the whole story..." She presented Yongyong with the English copy of Maeterlinck's plays.

Now, three days later, Yongyong had come to the railway station again.

A sweating Zhao Guokai squeezed his way out of the compartment. "All your things are on the rack above. I tied them together with a rope. You needn't worry about them," he told Yongyong.

"You're really not going home for the vacation?" Yongyong handed him her handkerchief to wipe his perspiring face.

He shook his head, smiling lightly. "I've not quite decided yet." In fact he was planning to remain in the dormitory throughtout the vacation for there was nobody waiting for him at home. He had had a reunion with his father recently when the old man had come over on a short mission.

"I'll write to you." Yongyong felt sorry for him. Why was there no happiness for him? It was so unfair.

"Don't bother to write, just enjoy your vacation." He produced a small package of pickled plums. "Here's something for you to nibble on the train to while away the time."

"Plums? Where did you get them?" Yongyong was very fond of tidbits to nibble at, a habit from her middle school days when she always had an olive or a dried plum in her mouth when school was out. Since that time, things had changed so much. Her husband had no idea what she liked or disliked, never bothering to observe or find out. Yongyong took the finely packed little gift, not sure whether it was a feeling of bitterness or joy in her heart.

"Just enjoy them. They're not stolen."

"You are giving me a treat?" Yongyong suddenly remembered. "What do you mean 'treat'?"

"Don't hide the reason why you should give me a treat." Yongyong brought out a small volume from her case. "I only saw this at the bookstore yesterday. Ha... Written by Zhao Guokai! At first I wasn't sure the author was the one I knew because you never mentioned it. After I read the postscript I realized you've kept some of your history hidden." She wouldn't let him off. "Why didn't you give me a copy of your book?"

"It was written when I was under criticism at the farm. It's very roughly done." Fidgeting like a small boy who has been found out, he said uneasily, "When I got the first copies, I hadn't the courage to read it through." He smiled apologetically. "Well, I'll tell you all about it later."

"Later? You'll have other excuses later."

"All right, I'll change that secretiveness and tell you everything frankly." A childish and merry twinkle flashed in his eyes. "For one thing, I want to confess that I have decided not to go home this vacation. I'm going to read up in preparation for an exam for foreign studies. My professor just told me the news. The state will be sending some students out to study abroad."

"Going abroad to study?" That was something Yongyong never even dared to dream about.

"I mean to do comparative literature. The key is comparison. Only through comparison can we really get a whole understanding of our culture. In order to compare, we need to know more about other countries. I want to try."

"Yes, do try. What can I do to help you?" Yongyong was excited. She was sure he could make it. Years of suffering had changed him into a clear-headed and determined person.

"You should do your own work," he patted Yongyong's case. "I finished reading *The Blue Bird* and can't help giving the author my full respect. He's turned a very abstract concept into something symbolic, alive and with definite characters and form. A philosophical idea, so simply explained and with such skill and charm. Remarkable!" Yongyong thought Zhao Guokai was a remarkable critic. "Put your heart into it, Yongyong. It's something really worthwhile. The blue bird, such a wonderful symbol. We should find the blue bird for ourselves and for our country."

Find the blue bird for our country. Yes, in a few words, he had brought out the soul of the tale and she was stirred deeply to the core of her own soul. She even felt like removing her baggage from the rack so she could go back to the dormitory and work on the tale immediately.

The train pulled out. Yongyong waved her hand at Zhao Guokai who stood motionless on the platform leaning against the cement pillar as if he were holding up the whole platform with his back.

The sun moved in an arc as it approached the horizon. The sunset was very bright and peaceful as it brightened the scenery outside the train: the trees and the sheep under them, the river and the buffaloes by its bank, the houses in the villages and the shadows nearby, the brown earth bare of crops in winter, the bunches of dried corn stalks stacked on it. All was enveloped in a serene, quiet sunset glow.

A few birds flashed hurriedly by in the dusk as if searching for a wood to rest their wings. "Are their feathers blue?" Yongyong's gaze followed the flying birds which disappeared in the distance. Blue bird?... Her thoughts were churning with the fast rolling wheels of the train. "Get home and let Shu Zhen read the play. Would he like it?" She was thinking of him... In the rumbling of the wheels she felt as if she were going north and further northward. Instead of the southern villages along the road, she seemed to see the vast northern wilderness and the stretches of rising mountains. The thick forests with many shades of green: new green, light green, dark green and brownish green...a variegated pattern of green colours forming the big forests. Deep in the forests was a bright little stream following a trail of light and darkness.

Shu Zhen and Yongyong walked along, following the bright stream. "Thirsty?" Yongyong offered him a big jar sealed with wax. Inside, bright red berries sparkling like gems were immersed in honey-sweet juice. There was nothing like chocolate or other sweets to offer her visitor who came over the mountains to visit her at her brigade. She had preserved the berries herself.

Shu Zhen opened the jar, swallowing down the sweet tart berries in big gulps. "Delicious. Much better than canned fruit." He had left his office at the Forestry Centre's administrative section before dawn, and walked five hours to reach her. He was parched and hungry. They had only a few hours to spend together, then he must walk back before sunset. Shu Zhen licked the last berry into his mouth and suddenly realized that he had not spat out a single pip. "There are no seeds in them..."

She gave him a very sweet smile. "There aren't any pips in our fruit."

He stared at her hands, roughened by the sawing and the cutting in the forests and imagined her holding a small needle to remove the pips from the small red fruit... How dainty she was really and so skilful. He tossed the jar aside and stretched out his arms. Gripping her tightly he kissed her wet lips with such passion that she became limp.

"Don't..." she protested weakly, trying to push him away. "We can't here..."

"Why not?" He looked into her eyes, his own bright and eager.

"No reason...but..." She blushed furiously.

"Don't be silly." He kissed her again until she had to break away to breathe. He laughed fondly. "There's no reason why not. We will have a sweet little baby as sweet as you."

"What are you saying!" She felt too shy to look him in the eye again, but turned away. A plump little squirrel hopped from one pine branch to another while merry sparrows darted to and fro, twittering loudly. Soft sunshine peeped in through the thick branches giving the forest a mystic beauty. Green scaly tree trunks glimmered like mother-of-pearl while the delicate pine needles were tinted red and blue like the bright feathers of mountain birds. The pine cones hung like bright little lanterns. How beautiful everything was! Yongyong's heart was still thumping with happiness. "A baby!" she whispered. For the first time after their marriage the great joy of being with her husband was so strong that it overwhelmed her. Leaning against his strong shoulders, she whispered, "If it is a..." she wanted a boy but she was too shy to say it.

"A bright little boy," he said it for her.

"Just like you?" Her eyes were on the blue sky in the distance.

"Yes, like me would be good."

Yes, it turned out to be a boy like Shu Zhen.

Now, they were due to meet again.

The stars came out in little clusters like red fruits hanging on bushes in autumn. Yongyong closed her eyes as if to let herself sink into the beautiful dreamlike reverie.

Nevertheless the golden sands of memory, washed by the current and however precious, were still cast-offs of the turbulent river of time as life continued ever changing...

More and more houses came into sight, chimney stacks, thick ones, sprouting black and grey smoke into the sky. On the highway parallel to the railway, bicycles appeared and occasionally a bus. Passengers around her began to stir. Some pulled gunny sacks or boxes out from under their seats; others brought down their bags or cases from the rack above. They were getting near their destination. Yongyong's heart began to thump again. How familiar everything outside was to her. In her ten years at the Forestry Centre, how many times she had gone through this station! She had been like the flocks of wild geese that flew north and then back south again year after year. Ten years! It was time to stop. Yet, here she was again approaching this station.

How many times more would she be travelling?

The train pulled into the platform, quietly, without a sharp whistle. The passengers were impatient to get off and surged to the door. Yongyong remained in her seat. She had marked the compartment number in her telegram and he would be waiting for her.

The train came to a stand still. Immediately a hubbub of voices rose as people looking for each other clamoured for attention. The loudspeaker outside also started. Everything was noisy and full of jollity. Yongyong stretched her head out of the window, her glance sweeping across the dark heads of people. He was nowhere to be seen. She looked around. She still could not see him. Perhaps there were too many people and he had not been able to get near her compartment. Or perhaps he was hiding behind a post, making her look everywhere for him. She picked up her things as she followed the queue down to the platform.

The platform gradually emptied as the long line of people moved out of the exit. Still there was no sign of him. Had he failed to get her telegram? Or was he sick? Full of anxiety and disappointment, she walked out of the station dejectedly still wondering what had happened to him.

At the exit behind the iron fence there were still people coming to welcome friends. Yongyong slowed her steps, hoping to hear his voice calling her. Again she was disappointed.

The bus stop was crowded with people. Yongyong backed away a bit, but down her things and rested her hands on her hips. Only then did she feel extremely tired. Her eyes roved left and right instinctively. Suddenly her gaze alighted on a sky blue bicycle, the wheels rolling slowly and glinting with a cold light. His hands held the handle bars gently, his head turned to a dainty-looking girl beside him. They were deep in conversation and he kept taking one hand off the handle bar to gesticulate as he talked. She was younger than Yongyong and listened attentively to Shu Zhen, her bright eyes were fixed on his face. Was she the girl named Diandian, the chief editor's daughter? They were coming nearer the bus stop. Should she call to him? Should she stop them? Yongyong suddenly turned around. Her steps froze. She heard the blue bicycle rolling and her husband's voice saying, "You should have second thoughts about this, Diandian..." Yongyong bated her breath as the sound of his voice faded. A chill seemed to rise from inside her. She stood transfixed, unable to do anything.

14

"I have already decided." At the entrance to the railway station, Diandian halted. "Go and meet your wife now. When is the train due to arrive?"

"There're ten more minutes." Shu Zhen looked at his watch. "We can discuss this further tomorrow."

"I've already decided." Diandian repeated. She was not one to be easily persuaded.

"You're too stubborn. One of these days you'll be sorry."

"Even if I should be sorry, I've still made up my mind."

"Let me know when you are going." Shu Zhen gave up trying and locked his bike.

Diandian turned and went away. Regretfully, Shu Zhen watched her hurried steps as she crossed the street before he went to the window for platform tickets.

"For which train?" asked the man as he took out a ticket.

"The 113." Shu Zhen fished out a few coins.

"That train arrived half an hour ago." The man looked at him with a yawn.

"Isn't it supposed to get in at seven?" Shu Zhen produced a timetable.

"A timetable for which year? Are you joking?" The man did not bother to give him a second glance.

Shu Zhen realized only then that the timetable was an old one. He left the ticket window thinking, "She should be home by now. She'll blame me for coming late." But, he had spent a whole morning tidying up their little room. That should exonerate him. She would probable be starting dinner by now. Their little paraffin stove, unused for a whole year, would be emanating a light blue flame at this moment. That lovely light blue flame.

On the way home the road seemed much longer than usual. The talk he just had with Diandian came to his mind again. It was such a surprising decision on her part.

They had been sitting on the stone bench by the river.

The wind over the river carried just a touch of chill. Mud-coloured water slapped noisily against the embankment. Diandian draped a short khaki army coat over her shoulders, her neck wrapped in a camel hair scarf.

Silence.

Shu Zhen lit a cigarette. A call had come from Diandian at midday saying she would like to see him as soon as possible. There was an urgency in her voice.

Diandian's eyes hovered over the boats on the river. A big ship, its whistle blowing, came by majestically, its ten thousand ton steel body moving smoothly with many coloured flags and banners fluttering merrily in the wind. Slowly, she brought her gaze back and said unexpectedly, "I want to tell you I'm going to return to the village."

"Going back for a visit?" Shu Zhen knew she had gone back to the village more than once to visit.

"No. I'm going to move back to live." Diandian gave a little smile, a rueful smile tinged with mockery for herself.

"You're joking!" Shu Zhen could hardly believe it. Of the many young people who went to the villages and state farms, most had returned, like a receding tide. They had quickly spread out like drops of water and were absorbed by the big city. Thought many of them were full of complaints and grievances about being assigned to small production groups in the city streets or not having their seniority counted for in their years in the countryside. None was willing to leave the big city again. Although most felt a nostalgic longing for that difficult, hardworking life which was also full of the joys of youth, who would want to go backwards? It was only natural to see life along the road ahead and not behind.

"Why?" Shu Zhen could not understand. "Have you quarrelled with him again?"

"I am not a child." Diandian's thin pointed chin was cupped in her hands. "He will not come to quarrel with me again."

Shu Zhen got the message. "You rejected him?"

"No, he was the one to raise the question. After he twice failed the exams for the post of editor, he was spotted by the Municipal Party Committee's Propaganda Department. They want him as a cadre. He'll be transferred over there soon."

"Merely because of a transfer of job?"

"No. He told me that quite by chance he met a girl who respected and admired him. She had also helped him out of the goodness of her heart. She made him see what love really was, therefore he..." Diandian paused for a long breath. "We parted company amicably. He is quite right. To tell the truth, I never really gave him anything, certainly not love. I only made demands on him. But I did not expect that he would be the one to decide on our separation. I felt relieved at getting out of an engagement that was a burden, but also depressed to discover that I proved to be inferior. From outward appearances I seemed superior, and he the weaker one. I did not look up to him and that was why we were always quarrelling. I knew quite clearly that we were not in love, but I was not determined enough to break our relationship. Perhaps I felt I was bestowing myself on him and in this way salved my conscience. What was more important was that I thought love and life were two different things and happiness was unavailable anyway. Now I can see he is the stronger of us two, at least he has the courage to get out of it, to make a change and to search further. I can only mock myself. Many stupid things in life have been done by those considered very clever." She shrugged her shoulders and paused.

Shu Zhen kept his eyes on the ground, unable to answer her. To him, it was not Diandian herself she was talking about, but Shu Zhen and his attitude towards Yongyong. Dimly, he felt rather uneasy. He knew that under the ice in Diandian's heart a warm stream still flowed. Hadn't it seeped through once? He remembered the footsteps she left as she hurried through the path in the park... What did she get out of their friendship? Only more snowflakes fluttering over the coldness in her heart, solidifying the ice even more.

"All because of him you want to go away?" At this moment, Shu Zhen wished she would say words of blame against him.

There were many reasons. When she told the family about her break with the boyfriend, the reaction was varied. Mother was in a hurry to introduce Diandian to another young man, son of her former boss. Elder brother grumbled and wondered about her not being married off already. "How long would she be living at home? I want a place to get married...this house..." Only father kept silent. Diandian felt there really was nothing to keep her at home. But she didn't want to talk about these things. They chilled her heart even without talking about it.

She looked up and gazed into the distance. Heaving a deep sigh she said, "I've been in the world more than twenty years but I have no idea who needs me and what I am able to do. I've had so many fine aspirations but I'm not clear really what I hope for. Being alive I shouldn't just consume without producing. I think, probably, in that little mountain village I can be of some use. I could teach the children." In her memory that little village was still dear to her.

A little thatched hut. In one corner were piled mouldy dried sweet potato slices and about a hundred *jin* of unhusked wheat. That was their grain ration for the year. There was a stone mill at the edge of the village where she often went with a patched flour bag to mill her grain. On the mud wall of the thatched hut there was a study corner where she had hung a little booklet she had sewn up with the first page being a quotation of Chairman Mao's: "Self satisfaction is the enemy of learning..." A neatly-copied composition with the title: "When the Whistle to Start Work Blows" was posted on the booklet. Once someone found a coin with a hole in the middle. A piece of coloured thread had been tied through it. This had been hung by the booklet and called the Literary Prize of the Mud Hut. There was much argument over which of the students should be included on the committee to judge the winner of the prize. Most of the life there was rather barren and poor like the barren earth of the land but there were also verdant fields and golden crops. When she left the village she missed the good honest peasants there. She missed the life of a homeless vagabond that was hers. She also missed the friends still there who had given her their friendship when she was in adversity. She had not gone there voluntarily, yet when she left it was not without regret and a lingering goodwill.

This time she would go of her own free will. Would she leave again? Her realization of her need for action showed her understanding of herself. But a remote mountain village is not the kind of Peach Blossom Vale of the recluse, such as Tao Yuanming in ancient times, or a Garden of Eden. Full of anxiety, Shu Zhen kept his eyes on Diandian as she pondered. He felt a sense of responsibility. As a friend, had he done anything to help her? He showed appreciation and excitement over the glow of life he saw in her character, but once he saw her weakness he expressed only disappointment and loss of interest. He was merely a person who observed new and interesting phenomena from a distance, like an astronomer using a telescope. "If I'd been able to help her find out about herself earlier, if I'd tried to help her overcome her weakness and find appropriate ways...if, if, if..." For the first time, he felt deeply that he was to blame.

Now all attempts to persuade her against going were too late. What was there for him to say? After a while, he asked, "Does your father know?" He seemed to see the moody look of the chief editor and heard his uneasy pacing on the floor.

"He doesn't know. He will not approve." Diandian's tone was cold. "It's no use his disapproving." She stood up to leave.

"Sit a while longer." He didn't want them to part like this. There was still a great deal to say. "We've known each other some time, do you think..." he wanted to hear her blame him, even just a little bit.

"You...what do you want me to say? Love or hate?" Diandian remained standing, her hands in her pockets. There was no animation in her glance. "Love has only turned out to be an illusion. Hate is something I can't manage, so now there is neither love nor hate.

I only want to go far, far away." She had no intention of blaming anyone. Life is one's own affair.

"You are too pessimistic. Life is usually unsatisfactory but in disappointment there is always hope." Shu Zhen tried to pull her back. "You should be able to see hope. To get away and escape reality is no way out."

"Say no more," Diandian stopped him. "You are you and I am I."

Shu Zhen stood up. "Of course, you are you..."

The wind over the river was cold but gentle, teasing the waves like a naughty child. The waves washed against the stones of the embankment, the brown, grey and whitish stones. The sound of the waves was vaguely disturbing.

Shu Zhen could only console himself with the thought that motion and surging is always beneficial. They signify life and vitality. Perhaps a typhoon would blow it somewhere it should not go and eventually it would return to the sea as long as it kept moving. He hoped to see such a day.

What was most terrible was stagnation.

The many bicycles along the two sides of the road went in opposite directions like fast-flowing roaring streams. Shu Zhen pedaled fast, cutting through several other bicycles, overtaking those in front of him. But however fast he went there were always more in front.

Home at last. Shu Zhen braked his bike and also his thoughts. He looked up at the windows. These were tightly closed and the flowery curtains pulled together, the way they were when he left the place. Why hadn't she opened the windows? He went upstairs carefully, treading gently to prevent the creaking of the boards. Would she be hiding behind the door to tease him? He could push the door back as soon as he opened it to squeeze her in until she cried for help.

There was no light in the corridor. It was very dark. He pushed at the door but only felt the heavy clang of the padlock hanging there. She wasn't back. His heart sank. Was she at her mother's? Just because he wasn't on the platform to meet her. Should he go to find her? He hesitated. A year ago after Yongyong left, he hadn't been there once.

He finally got on his bike.

The night was dark now. There were two very bright stars overhead, a little reddish in colour, like two hearts or two eyes.

15

He left, pushing his bright blue bicycle.

Yongyong leaned limply against the door.

The bicycle wheels rolled slowly as if sticking to the mud, unable to move fast, for Shu Zhen no longer felt like squeezing his way into the traffic on the road. He no longer needed to rush any where. He had no wish to go see anyone.

For this meeting with his wife, how eagerly he had waited. It was like sitting in a theatre waiting to see a drama which in his imagination would be an extremely good one. The curtain which was taking so long to lift was like the myriad stars at night, stirring so much imagination. Now, the curtain had finally lifted.

She was unpacking, a string bag full of small red and green apples in her hand. At the sight of him, she dropped the bag down under the table, letting the small apples roll all over the place like rubber balls.

Shu Zhen stared at her in surprise. "What's the matter? Just because I wasn't there to meet you?"

"It doesn't matter whether you met me or not, but you..." full of wrath, she shrieked in a voice hoarse and cracked from the fatigue of a long train ride and anger. Her face was flushed.

What else did she say? A whole string of unreasonable words spurting out continuously like a broken-down gramophone record out of control, repeating words at a speed making them incoherent. Without attempting to make explanations, he turned his bicycle around and went away.

After a whole year, that was the way they met.

Only last night in his dreams, he lived over and over again the moment of their meeting on the platform: she with her new school badge pinned at her breast, smiling radiantly, her eyes sparkling with ardor. Ever on the way to her mother's place to fetch her, a rosy picture lingered in his mind. At the familiar ringing of his bicycle bell, she'd jump out gaily like a happy little bird... What greeted him was the eruption of a volcano. Her eyes shot grievances and bitterness at him under brows tightly knit so that under the onslaught of her coldness and the cold wind he shivered. He knew that the suspicions first aroused by his putting the wrong letter in her envelope must have been reconfirmed. "Was it my fault?" He didn't think so. Life couldn't be just a single note and single symbol. Human sentiments are complex matters. "But I am in control of myself." His ideal and target in life, he felt, were things for him to decide. He also had his own values in his contact with people. He couldn't help grumbling against her again. Why was she so biased and narrow-minded? Why was she acting like an ignorant housewife who wanted to keep her husband under her control as if he were a button on her apron? Love could not be achieved by control. In comparison, he liked Diandian's composure and admired Qin Xin's liberal attitude.

Shu Zhen pedaled along silently.

A city night is a world of lamp lights with its riddle-like mystery and enchantment. He remembered a line from somewhere saying, "Night, the defender of the mystery of life." But what then is the mystery of life? Shu Zhen longed to delve into the haze mist of night to see himself clearly. He might be quite keen in observing others but he often felt unable to explain himself.

He remembered one vacation when Yongyong returned from the Forestry Centre to be with him. Again for no reason he could think of, they quarrelled again and again. One day after some bitter words, they lay down on the bed. He thought of turning round to say to her, "Let's separate!" But he dropped off. In a dream he was swimming in a big lake while Yongyong, not a swimmer, sat reading under a parasol on the bank. After spending some happy time swimming, he felt tired and turned to swim back to Yongyong. But however much he tried, he seemed unable to move from where he was. He could see her, a small dot in the distance. Suddenly the possibility of not being able to get back to her occurred to him. He felt lonely and desperate as he tried to struggle back, but his legs felt cramped. When he woke up with a start, his heart pounded and sweat wetted his brows, but there was Yongyong beside him, swinging a fan gently over his head.

"Did you have a nightmare?" she asked, her eyes tender with no trace of their quarrel. "What did you see?"

"A devil was trying to grab me," he lied and closed his eyes again. For some reason, he didn't want to see the deep love in her eyes. The cool breeze under her fan stirred deep ripples in his heart, deep like the tempest at sea.

Tenderness often seemed not satisfactory enough. But differences were not enough to start a break. This caused him suffering which others could not understand.

The night was so dark. The road home was so long. He was wheeling his bicycle along. "Tomorrow, will she come back? Will she be like before, calm and gentle again after a night's sleep?" he wondered. Although they merely exchanged letters twice around New Year's time, he sensed the changes in her. Changes in what way? She seemed to be standing far, far away, so it was hard to fathom her. He wanted to get nearer her but they were not opposite poles and therefore tended to repel each other until the distance grew again. How long would the stalemate last this time? Would it be another year?

When he finally got home, he discovered Qin Xin outside his door. She had donned a spring coat, ahead of the season, with a bright red woolly sweater underneath, wrapping her full breasts tightly under the coat.

She certainly knows how to dress, was Shu Zhen's first thought.

"Do you know that a seminar on drama is being convened by the Beijing authority somewhere in the south? *Ah, Young Friends* will be an important item for discussion. You and I are being invited to attend." Qin pulled out a letter with a self-satisfied flourish.

"Really and truly?" Shu Zhen tore open the invitation. He had not expected such strong reaction to the criticism of the play he wrote under their joint authorship. It was printed on the fourth page of his paper. Quite a number of readers and members of the audience had written in to give their support. A few of these letters were selected and published in the paper. Of course there were also opposite views, which only aroused more attention among the public.

"What do you mean by asking really or truly?" Like a magician, Qin produced two railway tickets. "We leave tomorrow."

"Tomorrow? I thought it starts the day after."

"We'll go one day ahead of time and have fun there first." She had decided and never asked him.

The chance to go out of town and to participate in a national-scale seminar was enough to make Shu Zhen feel excited. But the seminar would last more than two weeks. He immediately wondered, "Should I write and tell her?"

16

Yongyong had just turned a page in the dictionary when the baby crawled out from under the quilt again. He sat on the pillow on his bare bottom, gurgling happily.

"Do lie down, you'll catch cold!" Yongyong had to go back to the bed to coax the baby back under the quilted cover. "Go to sleep now, mummy has got to work. See —— there's so much to do." She talked in soothing tone as if speaking to someone who could understand. "Baby sleep tight now. Mummy will take you to the park tomorrow to see a big elephant and a tiger."

Baby's bright black eyes were fixed on her as if he heard and understood what she was telling him. In fact he just wanted his mummy to sit by him saying whatever she wanted to say, not really knowing what she was saying. Sometimes he just laughed at whatever she said. These days baby was not sent to the nursery but slept with his mother in her big bed. He became livelier and laughed a great deal. Unless he was asleep, he would not let Yongyong leave his side, not for even a few minutes, as if to make her compensate him for leaving him for so long.

Yongyong could not but try to do as her baby demanded. Even if during the whole of her vacation, she spent every single moment with him, it would be no more than a couple of weeks, after which there would be another long parting. Other children have the love of both father and mother but what about baby? She could only give all of her love to him making up for that of his father.

He was in her thoughts again. Was it their fate to go on like this, confronting each other with harsh words and angry looks? Smiles had no chance to light up her face before they were looking blackly at each other again. Perhaps she should have been more restrained, more patient. Hadn't she made up her mind to have a really good talk with him? Women should be more gentle, she'd been told. She admired some women who were able to deal with all unpleasant situations graciously. Letting troubles slip off like floating clouds. She knew a couple who were always harmonious. Once they quarrelled and the wife stamped her foot in rage, rushing to the door exclaiming, "I'm leaving, I'm leaving!" But when she was on the threshold, she paused, turning to her husband with a charming smile to ask, "Why aren't you pulling me back?" The husband couldn't help smiling and so the clouds were dispersed. Bright skies reigned again over their home. Men must prefer women like that who can compromise and are confident of their husbands' love. Yongyong probably did not belong to this group of model wives.

It wasn't as if she hadn't tried to give way to him. That, however, had not brought her happiness. It was a year before, when she stopped giving way and walked out that she was able to move forward a step. She began to find herself.

"Close your eyes, darling, mummy will tell you a story," said Yongyong as she stroked the baby's soft hair. Baby stretched out a chubby hand to grasp her mother's soft earlobe. He just loved to put a hand on the soft part of her mother's head. "Shu Zhen probably did that when he was a baby..." The thought of the baby's paternity stirred feelings which she tried hard to suppress.

Yongyong held the baby tightly in her arms. "There was once a naughty little boy by the name of Songsong. One day Papa and Mama took Songsong to the park, where he was very happy. Papa let him sit on his shoulders, which delighted him. Waving his hand, he cried: 'Giddy-up, my horse. Papa, please gallop.'"

"Pa-pa!" Baby compressed his lips and suddenly pronounced Papa very distinctly. Cheered by his own success, he also waved his arms and kept saying, "Pa-pa...pa-pa."

Yongyong kept her eyes on baby while her hand went on patting him automatically. The story couldn't go on, she was full of wonder for she had never taught him to say Papa.

Baby fell asleep. His lips parted as if still trying to say Papa. He'd not seen his father once. But a few days ago, his father had been standing outside Grandma's door together with that blue-coloured bicycle of his. He hadn't known or seen the baby as if this had been a plot arranged by some dramatists.

"If I had gone after him and urged him with a gentle look to stay, then the tension built up on both sides would have relaxed." Yongyong's eyes were still on the baby, as if she couldn't let him out of her sight. The baby looked like his father, as if cast in the same mould. The same good-looking forehead and the same bright eyes. Should she tell him? "A baby! We have a baby..." In many families, aren't conflicts smoothed out because of a child? No, what she needed wasn't that kind of outward peace and harmony. She must not muddle along in life anymore. Her intuition told her that his interest in others and his close contact with others showed that he was still not satisfied with her. Where is love when there is no satisfaction? She couldn't live under his look of frustration and try to make do. She had no intention of turning baby into a kind of psychological burden in their conflicts. Only when parents really love each other is there real happiness for the child.

"But will baby have such happiness?" Life was always a question mark with an unknown answer. Yongyong reclined against the child, her heart still stirred by his lisping of Papa. Though he slept soundly, she still could not settle down to work. In a baby's world there was only creamy fresh milk and smiling faces. How could he know that there were also contradictions, frustrations and grievances between his parents? He couldn't know that he had been born into this world at a rather inopportune time.

The white light of her room cast its beam on the picture on the wall of "A Hundred Birds." Were there blue birds among the hundred? Yongyong tried to find a pure blue bird among them.

There were a hundred birds in that wood with various coloured feathers: reddish gold, bright yellow, azure blue, pale green, ink black, snow white, dark brown, light purple...but none of them had a pure blue colour. Perhaps there was no blue bird among the feathered flock. Perhaps it really was a rare kind of bird and seldom seen.

But what about the happiness it symbolized?

"If I sit up I could still do a bit more work." Yongyong looked up at the little alarm clock on the desk. It was one a.m. Tied up with the baby all day long, she had not been able to check a single word. In her plan for the vacation, she had meant to get all the new words in the play *The Blue Bird* cleared up in her head so that when she returned to school she could start the translation at once. But a play of that length had so many words whose meaning eluded her. To look them up in the dictionary was such a terrific amount of work. "Now that baby's asleep I have some time to myself. Must go on working," she told herself. But drowsiness overtook her. Still fully clothed, she closed her eyes and succumbed to the sleep that was irresistible.

After goodness knew how long, Yongyong felt a gentle rocking and woke up to find the baby perched on the pillow again. He was in his flannel shirt, which made her sit up at once. "Oh dear, you must be wet again." She changed him and put him back under the quilt. She'd better undress and lie down too. As she unbuttoned her jacket, she glanced at the clock. "Dear, dear, it's four o'clock." She buttoned up her jacket again.

The schedule she made for herself during the vacation was to start work at four in the morning.

17

In the years since he had been sent back to study, this was the first time he had gone out travelling.

The drizzling rain finally stopped and the day was clear though the roads were still muddy. Qin Xin was in high spirits. The road to the Tian Temple was across a small stream. She took off her shoes. Rolling her trousers up to the knee, she bared her fine legs, dazzlingly white, to wade through the stream. After a walk of three kilometers, they came across a small Buddhist pagoda. Legend has it that in ancient times a giant boa dominated the place swallowing many on their way to worship at the temple. This so annoyed the Buddha that he turned the round stones along the way into steamed bread which the boa ate and then died. Qin Xin picked up a small stone by the road which she easily broke in two. Inside there was indeed a black center like black sesame filling in steamed bread. A passerby told them that these stones held certain ores and a plant would probably be set up to mine them.

"If these interesting anecdotes were written into a play, they'd make beautiful interludes," said Qin Xin, her eyes sweeping Shu Zhen's face as if watching him closely in order to find the right moment to say something to him.

The temple was surrounded by green hills coverd by bamboo and pine so thick that the eaves were not visible a few dozen steps away. There was a big pond outside the temple gates with a wooden placard saying, "The water does not dry in times of drought nor overflow in continuous rain." The pond was similar to the Heavenly Pond in famous Huangshan Mountain. They wondered how many such divine ponds there were in the world.

They went down to rest in the bamboo grove. The bamboos were a verdant green with leaves slim and fair.

"Shall we go mountain-climbing in the evening?" Qin Xin was still fresh and vibrant after a day's excursion.

Shu Zhen was so exhausted he just collapsed on the leaf-covered ground. "There'll be a discussion tomorrow morning. We should consider what we are going to say."

"Does it need much consideration?" Her eyes shone with confidence.

"Good, you will speak on behalf of both of us." Shu Zhen was glad to rid himself of responsibility. He was worrying about how to show his opinion at the meeting the next day. *Ah, Young Friends* was a controversial play, with divergent opinions regarding its theme of young intellectuals being sent down to the countryside and descriptions of the cadres committing mistakes. Was that to be called a distortion of the Party's image? These were extremely sensitive questions and it was hard to say whether they should be dealt with lightly or in depth.

"All right," Qin Xin said, decisively. She enjoyed playing the main role on whatever stage. "Tomorrow, I shall just say that I think the movement that sent young people to go to the countryside should not be pronounced totally wrong. There are always two sides to a question; for instance, it is generally agreed that war is a crime, a judgement not to be refuted, but war also generates a force which pushes society forward and improves it. If it had not been for the Second World War, it would not have been possible for so many scientists to get together and develop nuclear science to such an extent within such a short time, enabling humanity to enter a new era." She spoke with emotion and cadence as if declaiming a monologue from some Shakespearean play.

Shu Zhen was surprised at her opinion, which was not the ordinary expression of what everybody was saying but rather original. Such a fresh approach was not common among people he generally went around with. He wondered from which strange book or magazine she had gleaned these views which helped her to make such a speech. She was always bold in words and in actions, sometimes quite unexpectedly bursting out with something fresh.

"Do you agree with my views?"

"I reserve my opinion towards such ideas, though I do admire your unique stand for what is new at the expense of the old."

"I dislike opinions repeated over and over because they are something everybody says," said Qin Xin with emotion and rather smugly. "As for the way the cadres are portrayed in the play I don't think it is right to confuse one or two men with the whole Party. We live in the actual world, so the situation in society is always more convincing than propaganda on paper. Of course, politicians have their ideas about real situation while writers have theirs..."

"Please be careful with the terms you use," Shu Zhen reminded her. He guessed that her radical and fresh expressions would win some approval and smiles, but if overdone it would make people think she was exaggerating in order to get applause.

"You are too careful and timid, just like a scholar."

"It is you who are the scholar. Once aroused, you're all sharpness and behave just like some demagogue."

"I hate lukewarm water. I dislike slimy round pebbles, so smooth and slippery."

"I hate noisy slapping waves, which are really shallow and won't last." Shu Zhen mocked.

"Never mind, I'll argue with you some other time." She was sueing for peace. "Anyway, we've plenty of time to do it." There was a hint of something in her words.

After the argument, there was a moment of silence.

Qin Xin leaned against a thick bamboo, as if deep in thought, a long bamboo leaf between her lips. Suddenly she looked up, tore the leaf in two and gazed passionately at him: "A woman friend of mine fell in love with a man but he is already married... She asked me what to do. What would you say?"

Shu Zhen was very sensitive. A young woman's eyes could keep no secret, though Qin Xin thought she was being clever. But he didn't want to discuss such things in a general way. What is really love? He had thought fairly deeply about this already. As for himself, he wasn't able to judge whether he loved or did not love his wife... "I can't answer you," he said lightly, "for I do not know or understand your woman friend."

"Someone told her, if you really loved him you should go after him boldly, courageously. So-called moral standards are..."

"Is it someone or is it you?" His sharp glance pierced the thin veil that covered their exchange.

"You might say it is I," forced to admit her involvement, Qin Xin smiled.

"Not *I* might say, but it's you who are saying it." He pursued.

"Then what?" She turned her gaze slightly. "What if it is me who has happened to fall in love with you?"

Her sudden confession put him in a quandary. He wasn't sure what she meant by love. According to her own proclamation, her love was generous, like the "footsteps of spring" which roamed all over, arriving suddenly and disappearing equally suddenly. Still he was surprised that she would reveal herself like this without subtlety. Did he love her? Contact between man and woman did not necessarily produce love. Wasn't friendship more beautiful, purer than love? The important thing was mutual understanding. He merely smiled without saying anything.

At times, silence can be more beautiful.

Qin Xin suddenly said, "I'm just a little worried for you..."

Her words were enigmatic.

"What do you mean?"

"I feel the establishing of a family depends mainly upon mutual understanding and communication. It relies on mental and emotional interflow, instead of on a legal certificate. Some people have self-respect; once they discover they are not equal to their spouse, they voluntarily withdraw. Your Yongyong? You really should not let yourself be pushed, bit by bit, into a tragedy...in the end you'll be the one to suffer."

At these words, Shu Zhen felt very uncomfortable. Why did she put on an act as if she just felt compassion. Behind this concern and consideration, were there real demands? This seemed so very out of step with that proclamation of hers. When she first appeared she brought a breath of fresh air with her attitude of the new woman. She went for generous love, she seemed out of the ordinary, like a person bathed in some immortal pool and steeled in a furnace of purity. But why did she want to stretch a foot out from that pedestal, covered in glass, and devoid of all mundane vulgarity?

Perhaps she was merely a comet flashing past in the night sky and fading into darkness.

The beauty of the landscape now seemed dull and uninteresting in his eyes. "Let's go," he said casually. He did not want to hurt her with strong words.

Qin Xin sensed that what she had said just now made him uncomfortable. She became very careful and considerate.

He walked very fast, feeling a little cold. Spring, after all, had not yet arrived.

That evening participants at the seminar were given tickets to a ballgame in an open-air stadium. It wasn't a very exciting game and by half-time it started to rain. Qin Xin undid the pink plastic raincape she was wearing, put it up like a big mushroom and moved towards Shu Zhen. "Come, we can share this."

"You put it on. This bit of rain doesn't bother me."

The rain was coming in a thicker stream, driving quite a few people away.

"Let's go too." Shu Zhen felt out of sorts. His clothes were half-wet.

They reached a small road where the lights were dim. Qin Xin halted. Pointing to a low house with overhanging eaves by the road, she said, "Let's shelter there for a while." Her voice was like a command.

"Come on, we're wet already anyway."

"The rain's too much. I'm cold." She moved under the eaves.

The rain was indeed pelting down. Shu Zhen followed her reluctantly. The space under the eaves was very narrow. Water streaming down from the edge formed a sort of translucent curtain. There were practically no pedestrians or cars on the road. It was quiet, the only sound was the sloshing of the rain. At the corner of the house, a silhouette of two people was dimly visible. They were clinging tightly to each other, making a romantic picture in the rain. Suddenly Qin Xin declared. "There are other people here, let's go."

"We might as well remain here, out of the rain."

"Come, there's a small park between the streets, which has a big shady tree."

"I don't want to go."

Qin Xin turned round and ran off, her raincape flying out like the gauzy wings of a dragonfly.

Shu Zhen was uneasy to see her go off alone on such a dark night...he followed slowly behind.

Qin Xin reached the big tree in the corner park. She spread her raincape against the tree and half-reclined and leaned against it. She kept her raincape half-empty in expectation. With a glance at Shu Zhen sauntering over, she hid her face with one hand as if waiting.

Was it romance or passion? Shu Zhen wondered. He stopped, his feet could not move, as if the rain water was gluing them down.

Fifteen minutes passed. One of them stood half-reclining against the tree, the other stood in silence.

Suddenly, she turned her head and started to sob.

The rain and wind lashed them. Shu Zhen shivered as if he'd been dropped into a freezing gorge after a balmy day. He thought of his wife Yongyong. "She's so much more solid..." This girl standing beside him who had appeared so unusual was not a bit superior to the common lot. Like other women she made her demands, and could also cry for them.

"We'd better go," he said coldly. Only the dripping of the rain answered him.

18

The old man at the post office with his "on duty" red armband appeared with broom and dustpan at intervals to clear the bits of paper and cigarette butts scattered on the floor. Every time he reached under Yongyong's feet with his broom, he eyed her with a puzzled expression, for the table before her was not covered with stationery or forms for mailing parcels or money orders but stacked with books of foreign words. One book in particular was as thick as a brick and filled with words so small they were like mosquito legs. Yongyong herself sat there muttering under her breath, looking more diligent than the monks in the temple chanting sutras. He was on duty and had the right to tell her to move on, for this was not a library but a post office. The kind-hearted old man turned away without saying anything, for he could guess that her home must be over-crowded. He also knew that the library was always full up, fuller than a theatre on a good night. Unless you actually stood outside waiting for the library to open its doors, it was impossible to get a seat. The post office was by no means an ideal place for brainwork, since people kept streaming in and out and the bell of the long-distance telephone booths kept ringing every few minutes, really disturbing one. Anyone with somewhere proper to go would not choose such a place to study.

Yongyong felt the old man's eyes on her. She had also feared he might drive her out. Once or twice she thought he was going to speak out. But he had been most tolerant, never uttering a word to show his disapproval. She was grateful from the bottom of her heart. She was there because there was nothing else she could do. She had left the baby at home.

A few days after the holidays had begun, Guokai wrote to her, enclosing an offcial letter from the Students' Union. A national drama festival of college students would be held next semester and the contestants were to present plays edited or translated by the students themselves. When the Students' Union learned from Guokai about the *The Blue Bird*, they were immediately interested. The official letter stamped with the Union's official chop was to ask Yongyong to make use of the holidays to get the play translated.

She could hardly refuse the assignment, although it meant less time with her child.

Yongyong had discovered the post office with its nice chairs and tables quite by chance. Her mother's house was so crowded that it was not possible to sit there undisturbed. The post office lounge was indeed noisy, but once accustomed to the hubbub around her, she could get on with concentrating on her task.

The old man was coming round with his broom again. Yongyong put down the book in her hand, longing to say a few words to the kind-hearted old soul. She was going back to school the day after tomorrow so she would not be there the next day. This was her last time and she felt like expressing her gratitude. He, however, went past her seat quickly and lightly as usual as if afraid to disturb her. Yongyong said nothing. She felt tongue-tied. What was there to say? The best way to show her appreciation was to get that play quickly and properly translated.

The ringing of the telephone in the long-distance booth sounded so urgent. Should she call to tell him she was leaving in two days? She hadn't returned to their home and he hadn't come to see her. After all, she was going soon... Every day she worked so hard and her head was so full that she had no time to think disturbing thoughts.

Was it really possible to forget these thoughts?

The day before, when her bus had passed the central crossroads, the road had been packed with cars and people.

"What's happened?" Passengers stretched their heads out of the windows to look.

"A man's been run over. Someone on a bicycle."

"On a bicycle!" Yongyong jumped up from her seat, "What colour bike?" she asked inadvertently.

Someone looked at her in surprise. Shu Zhen's blue bicycle was still in her eyes. She was seized with a strange premonition which urged her to get off for a look. Just then, a passer-by outside the bus window sighed with compassion saying, "What a shame, the poor man's not yet fifty." Yongyong sat down again. "It wasn't him. No, not him." She told herself with relief. But he...she had to force herself to forget the longing and concern that disturbed her peace.

Well, the day after tomorrow she was going back to college. Baby would return to the nursery. Life would follow the usual pattern and then after another six months, tossed out of her orbit like a comet, she would return to earth.

Another six months.

Yongyong went to the telephone and slowly dialed his office number. Line busy. She tried five times before she finally got through. The newspaper was certainly a very busy place. Her heart pounded.

"Who's calling?"

"May I speak to Shu Zhen?" Her voice wavered.

"He's out of town on a mission..."

"Is there any message for him?"

No message could be relayed by a stranger. "Never mind," she said and hung up. She was relived and yet bitterly disappointed.

19

Shu Zhen had returned the previous night. Their seminar had gone on only a few days longer than planned. When he got to the office, there was a call from the chief editor asking to see him in the afternoon.

The chief editor's desk was always beautifully tidy. The various documents, materials and manuscripts were all neatly filed in hard covers of different colours. On a small oval cork pad was a glass of steaming tea, wafting a strong aroma.

"The seminar finished yesterday..." Shu Zhen was very excited as he related the news, the views of various government leaders and the arguments of different types of people.

"I have already had some reports," said Editor Xiao listening attentively to Shu Zhen's concise but well-analysed summary. There was a gleam of approval in his eyes. "Would you like to do more studying?" he asked suddenly at the end, with an abrupt change of subject.

"Study?"

"The Academy of Social Sciences will enroll postgraduate students in journalism this year." He produced a circular. "The tutors will be noted personalities in the field."

"I'd certainly like to have a try." When Shu Zhen finished reading the circular his heart was hammering with excitement. "Do you think I could make it?"

"What do you yourself think?"

"I'll take the risk —— it's a wonderful chance." His mind was made up. Only by fighting hard could he feel keenly alive.

Editor Xiao put away the circular. From a green covered file, he brought out a few sheets of a manuscript. "Take a look at this." His eyes suddenly looked somber.

It was a news item about Diandian, praising her for high ideals and dedication in planning to return to the countryside. "This is an exemplary model for youth at a time when so many young people have lost their ideals and their sense of purpose," said the item, elevating the theme to a pinnacle of high thinking.

"Does she know there such an article is going to be printed?"

Editor Xiao shook his head. "I'm not quite sure. She hasn't even discussed with me her plan to return. I'm afraid..." Then he asked Shu Zhen, "What do you think is the real reason for her decision to go back? Is it really as the article says?"

"They don't understand her at all. I even suspect..." The door burst open at this point and Diandian rushed in.

"Where is that wretched news item, papa?" She confronted her father.

"What item?" The editor seemed to be testing his daughter.

"Don't pretend innocence. The editorial room downstairs said it was sent up to you yesterday. It's not gone to the printers, I hope."

Editor Xiao remained expressionless.

"The article bypassed me in our plant," Diandian told them. "Some of the secretaries of the plant's Party Committee started the idea and had the new item written up." Her eyes were busily searching all over her father's desk.

Shu Zhen, who had the sheets, involuntarily put his hands behind his back. Diandian's glance promptly swept to him. "Give it to me."

Shu Zhen looked at her father.

"Are you helping to hide it from me?" she asked accusingly.

Shu Zhen had to produce the sheets.

Diandian snatched them. Without a further glance, she tore them into pieces. "You should understand me and not do this sort of thing." She thrust the torn pieces into the wastepaper basket then, as if an important mission had been accomplished, went and sat down on the sofa with a tired sigh.

"They want to give me a farewell party at the plant. What a bore. I refused to let them. Why make such a fuss? The best thing is for everyone to forget that I ever existed. Don't either of you come to see me off."

Her father puffed at his cigarette, blowing rings of smoke, his brows tightly knit.

"Papa...I didn't tell you earlier for fear..." Her voice softened. "You should come to the village for a visit when you're exhausted by office work. It's quiet out there."

The editor, his hands behind his back, stood by the window.

No one spoke. Diandian knew her father would not say anything. He never tried to force his will on her, no matter how much he might worry about her. Ten years back, when she went to say goodbye to him outside the little window of his cell, he had only smoked with intensity like this. She had not told her father of her decision, for she hated to see his moody eyes and worried look. Even the thought of it made her heart ache. But she was so stubborn, it was not possible for her to change. During those days in the village, he had gone once to their little thatched hut. When he shared a meal of mouldy dried sweet potatoes with her, his eyes were wet with compassion, though all through his own trials he had never shed a single tear. Just before leaving, he had asked her, "Could you go on living here?" She nodded. Actually when he came to see her, he wanted to tell her that he was no longer under a shadow. Under the new policies she could easily make arrangements to return to the city. Many other young people were doing everything they could to do just that, so there was no need for her to go on living there.

"Let me take you to the hospital for a check-up tomorrow. You've forgotten to go and the doctor said..." Diandian bit her lips. She stood up suddenly, "I must go." Without looking back, she rushed to the door, hating to let them see the tears in her eyes.

The door slammed shut again. The chief editor moved his legs slightly...cramped by his tense posture.

"I'm going," Shu Zhen also stood up.

The chief editor stood there woodenly as if not hearing his words.

After work, Shu Zhen got on his bike and headed for Yongyong's place. "Her vacation should be nearly over by now. I wonder what she's been doing these past weeks?" He felt rather remorseful. "I should have told her about going to the seminar." But then he was often willful like this.

As soon as he turned into the lane, a neighbour's child told him, "Are you looking for Aunt Yong? She's just left for the railway station."

"Just left?" He got on his bike and shot off like an arrow towards the station.

At the ticket office, the blue-uniformed attendant heard the bell announcing a train's departure. He slammed the window shut.

All Shu Zhen could do was to peer out from the waiting room window to see the last carriage of the train disappear out of sight.

20

The last scene of *The Blue Bird*, the "Awakening", was finished. Yongyong had spent another sleepless night.

She quietly left the dormitory.

Early morning light seemed to have wrapped the awakening

morning in a translucent, light blue cellophane. The campus, in light mist, was cool and fresh.

Not a soul was in sight on the sports ground. Yongyong walked light-heartedly along the oval sports track as if she were going somewhere. No, she was not going anywhere, though she felt so happy her heart seemed about to burst out of her. Too bad there was no one to share her joy. Wasn't this her happiest moment? Wasn't happiness right there by her side? The two children in the play went first to the "land of memory" to look for the Blue Bird from their dear ones who were dead. They burst into the "palace of night" to ask for the Blue Bird from darkness. They went into the forest, exploring the graveyard and travelled through the "garden of happiness" and the "land of the future", but wherever they went they failed to catch the Blue Bird. But after going through a thousand trials and difficulties, they found that the feathers of the turtledove in their own home had turned blue like a Blue Bird. So, "some birds can change their colours." As she translated *The Blue Bird*, Yongyong too seemed to feel a kind of change, as if such a Blue Bird were actually flying towards her from afar.

She had finally finished the translation, a thick stack of pages. There were also the many sheets twisted into little balls that filled the wastepaper basket like a heap of snowballs... When she finally remembered that she should comb her dishevelled hair properly in front of the mirror she discovered that she had obviously lost weight. She had bought the mirror when she first started translating the play. The oval shape of the mirror was just right for her thin oval face.

The morning star was still in the sky, as if waiting to disappear with that crescent-shaped fading moon. The east was turning red. "I want to see the sun jump up into the sky." Yongyong gazed with joy at the magnificent changing scene before daybreak, her mood just like the bright morning, fresh and jubilant. After giving her whole heart and soul to her task, once it was finished, it didn't matter whether it would be successful or not, there was only joy and a relaxed peace. Hard work and persistent struggle made life busy, fulfilled and extremely comforting.

As she put the last full stop on her manuscript, Yongyong did not dare to believe it. "Was it really me who translated all this? Such a lot..." But by then she had completely forgotten all the trouble of looking up the meaning of new words, the vexation of searching for the right phrase in translation, the fatigue of repeatedly checking against the original and revising and certainly the many nights of exhausting work and pondering under the desk lamp. All she felt was the satisfaction after hard work and the exhilaration in seeing herself able to finish a task... She wanted to thank those thousands of giant trees which she had felled at the Forestry Centre which endowed her with tenacity and will-power. She wanted to thank the impetus that flowed from China's new surge of life which had provided her with new targets and a new starting point. She must also thank friends for their sincere help and solicitude; they had given her confidence and strength. She also wanted to thank him —— her husband who gave her pain. Without that kind of suffering, there probably would not have been today's new life.

The dialectics of life were just and rational.

Back in school Yongyong had not written to Shu Zhen, not because she was too busy doing her translation... When she first arrived back in the dormitory still carrying her travel bags, Lili brought her his letter: "My, my, here he comes chasing the train. You two sweethearts do stick closely together." Yongyong only smiled. If she had told those gossipy girls, "We didn't see each other at all during the vacation..." it would have become top news of the class within half an hour. Well after all, he was the first to start writing and the letter contained apologies and said how he missed her... Like frozen streams in March, her icy heart was thawing rapidly.

Who could tell what this matter of love really involved?

Yongyong did not write a reply. She was no longer the Yongyong of a year ago. When translating her play she had discovered a logic, something so ordinary but which had aroused her deepest pondering. Yes, happiness required searching and the process of searching is also a time of giving. She asked herself, "Did you give?" She also thought of him, "What did he give?" She loved him. He was a person who thought deeply and felt deeply. He had his own ideals and demands on life. This made him constantly dissatisfied, continually urging him to upset the old balance. But to cease being dissatisfied with the old ideals and to cease one's demands for more would not establish new balance.

What they needed in order to be able to live together again was a "new balance".

Would a new balance appear?

At the thought of all this her heart, as light as if she were able to soar into the sky, plummeted down to earth.

There was a feeling of deep apprehension and anxiety...

21

"A person by the name of Zhao to see me?" Shu Zhen wondered as he came down stairs. Among his friends and acquaintances there seemed to be no one by that name. "Perhaps it's a new author bringing in his writing for review." Shu Zhen's eyes swept over the occupants sitting in the waiting room wondering whether Zhao was a man or a woman. He stood by the door, waiting for his visitor to stand up.

"You must be Shu Zhen," someone behind him slapped him lightly on the shoulder.

Shu Zhen turned sharply. A stranger, strongly built like an

athlete, a dark blue cap on his broad brows, was looking at him with a gaze so penetrating it was like a searchlight at night.

"You are...?"

"My name is Zhao Guokai, a schoolmate of Yongyong's."

"Do come in and sit down." He noticed only that the man had a school badge pinned to his breast.

Guokai took a quick look at him, trying to gain a first impression. "We'd better go outside and walk about," he suggested casually.

Shu Zhen hesitated slightly, unable to gauge his visitor's intentions. "Is he here because of a manuscript or because of Yongyong?" But he quickly agreed. "All right. Just wait a second till I go up to get a scarf."

"Here," Guokai unwrapped his woollen scarf. "I have this," he said pulling down his cap. His tone was warm, natural and friendly.

Shu Zhen accepted it gladly.

If only their conversation would be as easy.

They walked along aimlessly down a narrow street. There were many pedestrians and people kept bumping into them. Passing cars in both directions kept honking, piercing their ears. It was hardly the kind of place for conversation.

"I have three days' leave from university to look for some material. I'll be boarding a train in two hours." Guokai cleared up in only a few words practically the whole reason for his presence.

So why had his visitor come to see him in such a hurry just before leaving? Shu Zhen pondered. Maybe he wanted something done for him? "Is there something I can do for you?" he asked.

"There is something I want you to do." Guokai smiled and added frankly, "I hope you'll do it." There was no time for him to beat about the bush; there were only two hours left and that squeezed out from his tightly arranged schedule after much planning. But the fact was that what he wanted to say was far too long to be said in just two hours although he had turned it over and over again in his mind.

"No problem. I'll do my best." Shu Zhen used a man-to-man kind of tone but in his heart he thought, "As I expected. He's someone who'll come straight to the point."

"Then pardon me for speaking so abruptly," Guokai was looking him in the eye as he hesitated.

"Go ahead. As long as I'm able to do it."

"I think you are quite able to do it," Guokai's eyes softened. Very sincerely, as if expecting a favour from his listener, he said, "What I want you to do is not difficult. One sentence only: You must love Yongyong properly."

Shu Zhen stopped in his tracks in utter surprise. His eyes were on the alert as he looked the man over anew. "Did he come to see me just for this? How strange. How did he know? What has it got to do with him?" Shu Zhen knew nothing about the man's background. A series of questions came to his mind; there was hostility in his eyes.

"Yongyong and I were classmates in middle school. By coincidence we are now again at the same university." Guokai hoped to dispel Shu Zhen's enmity with a simple explanation.

Shu Zhen felt irritated and somewhat humiliated as if some scandal connected with him was being exposed. "This is our private affair," he had no intention of continuing this conversation.

"It is your own affair but you haven't managed things very well, have you?" Guokai pursued further. He knew beforehand that touching on this matter openly at their first meeting would not please Shu Zhen. It might even end up so awkward that he would not know what to do. Shu Zhen could very well reject his concern and walk off in anger. But Guokai was confident in his own ability to manage the situation. He would at least be able to gain some ground. He had thought a great deal before arranging such a role for himself. He noticed Yongyong had become much thinner when she had returned after the vacation. There was also a sadness in her eyes. She tried bravely to keep it from him but he had discerned it. After questioning her twice, she finally blurted out what had happened during her trip home. He immediately felt that he had a duty he could not ignore.

Shu Zhen remained silent, his face dark. "Why should I let a complete stranger intervene in my affairs like someone from the civil court mediating a divorce case?" His vanity was hurt. He stopped, unwilling to walk on. He was obviously telling the other man, "This is all I want to say. You go your way."

Guokai did not mind his hostile attitude. He stopped too, one foot on the curb. "We are not acquainted with each other and don't understand each other. Perhaps it's inappropriate for me to come to see you like this, completely out of the blue. But because of this strange contact, we may be able to get acquainted very quickly." He glanced at his watch —— he must get to the heart of the matter right away. There was no time to beat about the bush. "You haven't seen each other for over a year. Life is difficult enough for a husband and wife to tackle together. One can't just put all the blame on one side."

Shu Zhen listened half-heartedly. The reason he didn't march off rudely was because he wanted to see how this character meant to finish this episode.

"Yongyong has certain weak points, but she has changed a great deal in this past year. You probably don't know much about her at present." He slapped Shu Zhen on the shoulder jovially. "To tell the truth, old chap, you shouldn't let the good fortune you possess slip away, though it may not seem that satisfactory right at the beginning. After all, where can you find anything ready-made that's absolutely perfect? You won't find it anywhere. One keeps having to change and adjust in order to make things better. And only such things as these are solid and belong to you. For such changes, Yongyong made a lot of effort, endeavours beyond the imagination of ordinary people and ordinary tenacity."

Unconsciously Shu Zhen's hand went to his jacket pocket. He was longing for a cigarette, the stronger the better.

Guokai produced a pack from his pocket and handed it to Shu Zhen, who took out two cigarettes. Guokai shook his head. "I don't smoke." He had bought the pack for Shu Zhen knowing that their conversation would mean tension. He also did not expect that their two-hour talk would have much effect. To him, an understanding of life could never be achieved by one person's sermon or lecture. It takes life itself to teach people to understand life.

Shu Zhen took a deep drag on his cigarette. He seemed to have calmed down a bit, though emotionally he still would not let himself be convinced by what the man was saying. That this man, whom he had met for the first time, could speak so frankly and sincerely with him had dissolved some of his hostility. After all, hadn't he himself already been pondering new ideas about himself, about Yongyong and about their relationship? Wasn't he hazily aware too of the problems they faced? His strong rational mind made it impossible for him not to admit that what this uninvited visitor was saying shook him like a strong tempest. At the same time it also helped to dispel those vague and blurry feelings in his own heart. Yes, it was true that he yearned for something better but had done nothing to help create it.

"Oh yes, there's another thing. Yongyong wants me to tell you that she is translating Maeterlinck's play *The Blue Bird*. Our university drama club is preparing to stage it for the national festival of university students." Guokai said this with pride. "Her classmates tell me that Yongyong hardly goes to bed properly. She works through the night, snatching a few hours of sleep only when too exhausted to keep her eyes open. It wasn't easy for her because she's never had a proper basic education."

"She's translating *The Blue Bird*?" Shu Zhen could hardly believe his ears, yet he had no doubt about what he heard. He didn't know how to express his reaction but he was quite able to imagine how Yongyong would work. At the Forestry Centre, when there had been big battles in their logging campaigns that was the way she had worked. He tried to appear quite unmoved; he had no wish to reveal the turbulence in his heart to this stranger.

"I must go now," Guokai stretched out a hand. "Don't be offended. I want to be your friend."

Shu Zhen did not offer his hand.

"All right, goodbye then." Guokai turned round smartly, military fashion, and dashed off across the street like an athlete to catch a bus that was just pulling up.

Shu Zhen followed the bus with his eyes as it drove off.

It started to rain, the first rain of early spring coming later than previous years. Rain drizzled down while the people on the street quickened their steps, keeping close to the houses along the sides. Shu Zhen continued at his usual pace, walking silently, welcoming the refreshing rain drops of spring, which were like small new shoots that had just popped their heads out in the fields.

The rain was gentle but it brought a slight chill.

"Oh no, his scarf." It suddenly dawned on Shu Zhen that the visitor's scarf was still around his neck. He started to run as he chased after a bus going towards the railway station.

Would his train have already left?

22

The lunch break and rest hour.

Girls were still chattering animatedly over this and that, things Yongyong had no wish to listen to. She would have been still asleep if it had not been for their shrill voices. Relaxing after working hard made her feel very tired.

The door burst open as if blown by a gale. "Telegram!" Lili ran in panting. "Yongyong, your telegram."

"Telegram?" Yongyong sprang up from her bed like a puppet pulled by a jerk of the string, her every nerve tense. "Is mother feeling unwell or something wrong with baby?"

The girls all came round, sensing her anxiety.

Yongyong's out-stretched hand was trembling.

"Let me," Little Ou took the telegram. Half a dozen heads peering at the telegram exploded together in a shout. "Yongyong come and look quick." "Your Zhen..." and "This too..." Wang Ping's hand touched her lips and swung out in the gesture of blowing a kiss.

Yongyong never expected a telegram from her husband.

"Congratulation on your *The Blue Bird*. Kisses. Zhen"

A few short words epitomized everything and signified so much more to come.

Besides pleasant surprise what else was there? Yongyong's feelings were so mixed it couldn't be explained in a few words.

"It's certainly nice to have a husband," Ou said in envy, her eyes on the telegram in Yongyong's hands which was already folded into a small square.

"That depends whether you choose the right one. Do you think all husbands are so considerate?" Lili was much more mature.

"At any rate our Yongyong has found such a one." Wang Ping put her hands on Yongyong's shoulder. "How lucky you are!"

The telegram aroused the desire of all the girls to find good husbands. Yongyong really did not know how to answer them. Their wishes were just wishes.

After putting the telegram under her pillow, she could not go to sleep. She just could not accept as a matter of course the strange way in which he had so suddenly expressed his warm feelings. She wasn't sure whether she felt glad or a little bit sad. She wanted to discover in that little square of paper the underlying meaning of those few words: "Congratulations on *The Blue Bird*..." The words danced in her head. *The Blue Bird*. How did he know about it? A sudden question appeared. She had not told him about her translation of the play, not because she wanted to surprise him with her achievement but because when she first started she had never thought she could do it. Then who had told him?

Suddenly Little Ou cried, "Someone's coming, guess who?"

The girls all turned to look at the door. Lili after listening carefully, announced, "It's Zhao Guokai," His footsteps were heavy, like two sand bags pounding the ground. He was a constant and extremetly welcome visitor here, bringing with him each time an atmosphere of merriment and interesting news. Lili crept like a mouse towards the door and suddenly pulled it open, catching Guokai in the act of raising his hand to knock.

"Ho, you sensed my coming eh? Must be telepathy."

"Go on with you. I have no relationship with you, so where's the telepathy?" chided Lili in her charming Shandong dialect.

The girls laughed.

Yongyong put on her coat. "Do you want to see me about something?"

"Yes, there's something I want to talk about."

"Can't you talk about it in front of everybody?" Little Ou was a sly one.

"Mind your tongue," Guokai was already at the door, but turned to Ou with a threatening wave of his hand. "One of these days the weasel will get you."

"Oh, it won't dare." Ou pushed Guokai out of the door. "If you go on telling secrets like this don't you come back."

Another burst of happy laughter.

There was a stretch of purple wisteria at the west end of the campus. The young buds appearing after the spring rain stuck to the brown branches like artificial plastic leaves. Sunlinght cast a fine pattern on the ground.

"What is it?" Yongyong sensed that Guokai had something important to tell her. She also wanted to tell him right away about her husband's telegram, for she wanted to hear what he thought about it.

"I went home for three days to get some materials I needed. I was granted permission by the department very suddenly and left promptly. That is why I had no time to let you know about going," he sounded a bit heavy-hearted.

"Is your father all right?" Yongyong thought something had happened at home.

"He manages his life quite well. He does a lot of gardening and also exercises regularly," he paused. "There's only one thing very much on his mind."

"What is that?"

Guokai smiled ruefully. "Worried because his son hasn't found a wife."

"You are a one. You should have thought of this long ago instead of making your old father worried." Yongyong mocked with kindly concern, with no inkling as to why her friend had not bothered about his matrimony prospects. A dozen years before, at a mass meeting of their city's Red Guards, Zhao Guokai was a prominent figure on the rostrum when he stood in his khaki uniform with a Sam Browne belt at his waist. His good looks and his powerful build had aroused the admiration and reverence of so many young girls. During the past decade he had pondered deep, studied hard and matured into a thoughtful, serious man, though the power and vitality of his younger days seemed to have disappeared. In Yongyong's mind he should have found a beautiful, gentle and clever wife, worthy of his intelligence, long ago.

"Have you really never fallen in love with anyone?" As soon as she said this, Yongyong's heart missed a beat. Oh dear, she was being dumb.

He only smiled a little, but in his heart he answered her. "You were too innocent thirteen years ago, a little girl pure and glowing like crystal..." He put his hand into his breast pocket, groping for something. "My father was worried and asked an old friend of his who works in the city's cultural bureau to find me a girlfriend. This is her picture."

A three-inch photograph, very well-printed. A rather unusual young woman. From her costume it was obvious she knew how to dress. But there was nothing vulgar about her. She wasn't exactly pretty. There was just a certain flair. Her eyes, especially, looked out boldly with a very warm appeal.

"Not bad at all. Has she agreed to be friends?"

"She said...she loves me..." Guokai's brows were puckered and he gave a whimsical smile.

Yongyong was surprised. "She knew you before?"

"We only met this time at home. The uncle introducing us told her about me. Said I would be leaving to study soon and asked if she was willing to wait. She expressed her admiration for someone with brains and talent and said she would be willing to wait ten years."

"Where does she work?"

"She's a teacher at the school of drama. Graduated from the performing arts department and is now learning to be a director."

"Is she called...Qin Xin?"

"How do you know?"

"Shu Zhen mentioned her in his letter. She seems to be quite liberal-minded."

"She did say she meant to go on pursuing things in life..."

Guokai's expression was grave, with no indication of interest. "She also said she loved modern drama and would like to learn how to direct drama abroad..."

Yongyong said nothing more. After seeing her photo she had a more realistic impression of this woman named Qin Xin. She certainly was an unusual character. What Chinese young woman would be so bold as to say, "I love you" to a man she had met for the first time! She herself would never dare. Naturally Guokai was the sort of man worthy of a girl's love, but this girl in the picture, would she know what to love about him? He was much more than what his friend would say in an introduction: a research student, going to study abroad soon.

"I've come to hear your opinion." Although from Yongyong's eyes, he probably knew already what she thought, he still wanted to hear her say it.

"Quite nice..." the words slipped out easily, but Yongyong realized right away that she wasn't quite sincere. "You are much sharper than I. What do you yourself think?" Yongyong found that the "opinion" Guokai was soliciting from her was very difficult to express. Someone who was going to live with Guokai as his mate shouldn't be someone like the woman in the picture. As to the reason why she wasn't at all sure. It was only a feeling, a feeling derived from her own understanding of him.

"I..." Guokai took up the picture to scrutinize it once more. In appearance, she was more dazzling than Yongyong, who was very ordinary in every sense, but the source of that dazzle needed questioning. Did it come from inside her or just something on the surface? He knew his hesitation wasn't superfluous.

Yongyong watched him in silence. She knew he would not deal lightly with his emotions. She felt he really deserved more happiness than any other person she knew for he was always sincere and good to other people. But where was the girl who could give him happiness? Imperceptibly, a feeling of regret floated like the morning mist to her heart... How many people like the two children in *The Blue Bird* urgently aspired for that happiness which was so difficult to achieve!

"Try to find out more about her," Yongyong said casually.

Guokai put the photo back in his pocket and with a wry smile, muttered, "All my own fault, much ado about nothing." Then he seemed very cheerful again, as if the hesitation and doubts were all pocketed like the picture.

"What do you mean?" Yongyong didn't hear what he said.

"No meaning at all." Guokai concluded the subject, leaving his words a nuance.

"Oh, you..." Yongyong sighed. She understood him, but there was nothing she could do to help in this matter.

"How have you been recently?"

"I got a telegram from Shu Zhen today."

"What happened?" Guokai's tone was casual.

"Nothing. Just congratulations on *The Blue Bird*. I don't know who told him about it."

"Why bother about who told him? He should know. Isn't that right?" His tone was light-hearted.

Could he be the one? Yongyong's eyes followed him closely, but Guokai had already walked out from under the wisteria.

23

Shu Zhen recalled the three weeks of reviewing for the exam as living with a constant effort to keep exhausted eyes from closing. He'd finally done the research student exam for the department of journalism.

How had he got through those three weeks and more? The days before the exam he lived for nothing else; the moment he tore

open the exam papers there was worry and anxiety; the first look
at the questions brought both joy and despair; the rapid flow of his
pen as he wrote out the answer; the desperate trembling of his
limbs when he realized he had to race against time to finish...all
that was over now. He could not bear to remember that nightmarish
feeling which left him still trembling. He remembered the long
hours of studying till late at night, till his brains felt numb. After
crouching long over his desk, everything in front of his eyes
appeared dark in the white light of the lamp, but when he opened
the window the splendour of spring confronted him: budding peach
blossoms, lightly fluttering willow tendrils...how he longed to walk
out into the green world of spring. He could only sigh and return
to his desk, piled high with notes on the various subjects of his
journalism course, foreign language textbooks, geography and history
and little index cards with closely scribbled words. In those days,
if he were asked what would be the happiest thing he could
imagine, he would immediately reply, "To walk out of the exam
room and plunge deep into a swimming pool and not to come out
until it was necessary to take a good, deep breath. Then toss the
books, materials, notes and all into the wastepaper basket...better
still into the ocean."

Naturally, the books were returned neatly to the bookshelves.

He finally got through this passage in life. It left him with a
sense of consolation and gladness. In this small but significant trial,
he felt as if driven by an invisible force which enabled him to
endure.

This invisible force! Was it Yongyong and her efforts over *The
Blue Bird*?

He felt ashamed of himself. After Guokai's visit, Shu Zhen had
not felt at peace. "She worked with such intensity, she tried so
hard to change herself, but what about me?" He wanted to write
her a long, long letter, write about himself...but the pen in his hand

was heavy, weighed down by the heaviness of his heart. Even if he tried, he could not express all that he felt...and so he thought of the quickest and briefest way of communication...

When he passed the telegram form to the operator, a man in his forties, the man looked up at him with curiosity. This type of wording, not commonly seen in Chinese telegrams but more the way a foreigner would express himself, was strange to the man though those few words had taken Shu Zhen a whole night to compose.

He also told her of his preparation for the exam. He was beginning to make a start. In this respect, even if he failed to be accepted at least he had not been defeated.

Perhaps a letter from Yongyong would come tomorrow.

His disturbed heart was slowly returning to normal.

"Shu Zhen, your letter."

He had just reached the entrance of the office when the mailman put his letter and papers on his bicycle rack.

"Thanks." He was very glad, for he saw at a glance that the top envelope was addressed in Yongyong's handwriting. After he had locked his bike, he opened her letter. Her pen seemed inspired; the letter was not only fluent, flowing like a bubbling fountain, but intricate and fine, not just a flat narrative of her life. She told him she was revising the translation of the drama which was going to mean hard work. He felt for her, knowing that there was nothing more tedious than revising something. At the end of the letter, she mentioned Qin Xin and Guokai, "Qin has expressed her love for Zhao Guokai. Do you know much about her? Tell me in your next letter..."

Shu Zhen walked slowly upstairs to his desk. He couldn't help thinking of her bold assertion of her love that rainy night and how she had sobbed with emotion. Was it strange? Perhaps this was her kind of "generous love." Her unscrupulous pursuit of all good things...but how was he to tell Guokai about his contact with this female. She had told him, "I love you," and now she was telling Guokai, "I love you..." Perhaps she did love both of them. After all, they each had their distinct character. Perhaps she loved neither of them, and was merely playing with them to satisfy her own ego. He felt that Yongyong posed a difficult question for him to answer.

He had barely reached the turning of the staircase when the gateman called up to him, "You have a visitor, Shu Zhen."

When he looked down, he discovered Qin Xin standing at the foot of the stairs. He hesitated a moment.

"Why, don't you know me anymore?" She hopped up the stairs, vivacious as always. She had on another costume, a smart black leather jacket which made her look very chic as she stood with hands in her pockets. "Here's a cinema ticket for you for this afternoon. A documentary which we've organized with our teaching."

"We have a meeting this afternoon, I can't go." Shu Zhen did not take the ticket.

She looked a little dejected. "Then I'd better go," she said though she did not move her feet.

"Yes, go on then," Shu Zhen went down the stairs to see her to the door.

She became lively again. "I want to learn poetry writing from you." She glanced at him. "I haven't too much to do right now and I've written a few lines." She produced a piece of paper.

Shu Zhen glanced at it.

Where do you find so much happiness in life?
I come to you in utter loneliness.
......
I do not blame the dripping rainy night

But would like to become crystal drops of rain
Seeping into the leaves sheltering us...

"Is it poetic enough?" Her eyes were hot and passionate. "This is really what I felt in my heart."

Shu Zhen said nothing, just returned the slip of paper to her. After they got to the entrance, he walked out a short distance with her.

"What are you thinking?" asked Qin Xin timidly. She seemed to sense that something was not quite right.

"Nothing much."

"You don't seem to be in a very good mood."

"I just finished my examination. I'm rather tired."

"No, you're still displeased with me."

"Still displeased?" He thought that was funny. He walked on a few more steps then suddenly halted. "Zhao Guokai wrote and told me about you."

"You know him?" She changed colour and asked tensely what Zhao said.

"Nothing much," his tone was flat. "He talked about you and him."

She was silent. After a while, she laughed awkwardly, "I don't suppose you mind, do you?"

"I do mind," he said this coldly. He did not consider love something to be taken lightly.

"You should understand me..." She looked like a very pretty but deflated balloon, flopping limply down to earth.

Shu Zhen longed to tell her, "It's not very hard to understand you. You heard Zhao Guokai would be going abroad soon. You might very well be walking into another world, breathing in another kind of atmosphere..." How very romantic and also how very practical she was. All those proclamations of hers were after all only flowery wreaths to decorate her own head till she herself was taken in by them. What she called "searching for herself" was nothing more than a wish to satisfy her own desire. Perhaps he should not be so hard in judging her. Hadn't he thought highly of her before and even fantasized about her?...

"I'm surpised that even you don't understand me." Qin Xin nervously pulled the zip of her jacket up and down.

"There's no difficulty in understanding. Everyone with the imprint life has carved on him tries to discover what he considers to be his happiness."

"Towards you I have been sincere." Suddenly she cried out hysterically, "But when I needed you so much what did you give me? You were not willing, you were scared, weak..." She lowered her voice now. "I don't really blame you, I only blame myself..." She turned and left without finishing the sentence.

He felt he was stumbling over hidden rocks. "Perhaps I shouldn't have said so much. I have no right to blame her." He suddenly felt very upset, as if the sky had turned grey and overcast as on a snowy day. He was always wanting to see the beautiful side of life but there was so much that needed to be changed in his life, including himself.

The light-hearted feeling he had felt after coming out of the exam had evaporated, as if swept away by a gust of wind. He had entered another exam to be tested in the trials of life.

24

The wisteria on the campus was in full bloom, purple clusters hanging down like ripe grapes among the green foliage. Amongst the tall branches of the plane tree were small white flowers while the oleander was bright with big white and pink blooms. On the bare branches of the magnolia creamy, white flowers looked pure and sedate. None of these were very fragrant, but they had brought spring so close.

Time left its mark on every branch and every blade of grass. For Yongyong, time was speeding ahead of her every page of manuscript. The school group that was to take part in the student drama festival had already been formed and was all ready to start rehearsing at once. *The Blue Bird*, because its imaginative scenes vary so much, was a play most drama troupes dared not put on. The students, however, felt that the flimsiest of props could be used as symbols in the drama. They were convinced that the audience would not mind, so long as the dialogue and performers were good. Revision and polishing of the script was vital therefore. Yongyong spent practically all her time and energy on the revision, pondering over every sentence in an effort to make the dialogue fluent, vernacular, easy to understand and yet without losing the artistic and philosophical sense of the original.

The revised play was ready to be mimeographed. Then she had to analyse the play with the performers and give an introduction to Maeterlinck's life and works and present his artistic views. After that her mission would be complete.

With white silk thread, she carefully bound the loose sheets together into a thick volume. Holding it in the palms of her hands, she felt an immense satisfaction. When she was copying the revised version she had often paused to imagine the scenes when staged, where each character should stand, how each should manoeuvre himself and the actions that should go with each dialogue... As a matter of fact, she had had little experience with literature and art and no contact at all with the stage. In the old days the only times she had gone up on a platform was to make a speech about her logging work in the forest, about her determination to be even better and so on. But in the past year a change had come over her thinking and perspectives which was like a fountain which flowed gently down a deep gorge and then suddenly burst out into the broad plains after the collapse of a mountain in front. The world now seemed so rich, so varied and magnificent. Her feelings had changed, her views had changed and her thinking about life had also changed, together with her moods.

Change is, after all, the law of life.

"Yongyong, have you finished the revision?" the girl in charge of propaganda in the Student Union came in, her pretty dark eyes dancing as if she had some happy news to tell her.

"Here your are," Yongyong handed her the handbound manuscript. "Let me know when you need me to analyse the play. I have to go back to my studies now."

"Hold the studying for the time being," the girl said, snapping her fingers. "You must first come with me."

"Where to?"

"The drama festival for university students has already started in some cities. The National Federation of Students has decided to get people in charge of production and the editors of the plays to be put on to go and watch performers in other cities. When the notice arrived our University Party Committee agreed to send two deputies: you and I."

"Where are we to go?" Yongyong was delighted.

"Well...that's a secret for the moment."

"So you won't tell me, eh?"

"All right, I'll tell you. It's your hometown. You can stay on there for the summer vacation. Great, isn't it?" The girl was full of spirit, her eyes dancing merrily all the time. "You should write to tell *him* ."

"It's not all that important. I'll be going home for summer vacation anyway." Yongyong put on an appearance of nonchalant calm.

"I don't believe you," the girl shrugged and dashed off.

When Yongyong was alone, she couldn't calm down at all. "Go home early to take part in the city's student drama festival..." Even in her dreams she never had such extravagant fantasies. Now she started dreaming: The newspaper would send reporters and very likely Shu Zhen would be sent so that she could be with him every day going round the theatres to college auditoriums. Perhaps she would go to his old college, to exchange views with his college drama group... She'd never been to his college. In those days, he hadn't been eager to take her... Now she was a student representative she would be welcomed there. She was rather startled by thinking of the change in her status. Could it be true that a turtledove like her could also change the colour of her feathers to blue?

Was it *The Blue Bird* that was bringing her all this joy?

No. Before she had seen him in person it was not really time for her to say she had the happiness the Blue bird brings people.

Him! Yes, they would be meeting again. But the hopes and excitement she entertained on the eve of winter vacation no longer gripped her. She could be very calm about life now. She had replaced the blind fervour and hope of yesterday with deeper thinking. Was it possible for them to rebuild their life properly? Hadn't he said that time, "...Cannot imagine the two of us in our present state just living together...we haven't got anything done yet..." What about now?

Like all women, there was love deep inside her heart.

But this love is often tinged with bitterness. Just because they had both achieved a little, would it mean that they could get along now? To build a good life together is like building a house. Besides the foundations and the central beam, there is the main structure and the bricks and tiles which all have to be closely welded together into a whole. No simple project, this. Would he and I be able to pile up the bricks and tiles one by one properly? She seemed to lack the

necessary confidence. She had persevered in the hard work of getting
the play translated. It was something that could be accomplished by
her determination alone. Now their life together was something that
required the cooperation of both of them.

She had stuck it bitterly for a long time. She had longed for
him and waited for a long time. Would it turn out to be again only
a beautiful bubble, a dream from which she must wake up, an echo
to reverberate over the river?

25

Tough luck.

The exam results arrived. He was not among the successful
candidates.

Shu Zhen walked to work that day. He wasn't in the mood to
ride his bicycle. Although everyone in the street was rushing along
on this early morning, some on foot, some in cars or bicycles, he
went slowly. People jostled him in their hurry but he was not in
the least aware of the hubbub and traffic all around him, so deeply
was he sunk in his own thoughts. He felt as if he were alone in
a small, narrow lane with its exit invisible, while his black mood
was just like the lane, without an end. His despondency in failing
the exam, his disappointment in the halo he fancied round his
friend's head and the discord in his personal life due to his wish
to break through something...all this made him think deeply about
himself, going over every detail like rereading an old novel. There
were a number of positive elements in him: his vitality of youth,
his desire to search for the new and his dissatisfaction with
traditional mores and prejudices. All this meant he was not destined
to enjoy peace and serenity in a sheltered harbour. Sometimes he
might even reject ordinary modes of life which would have enabled
him to see things he would never catch sight of otherwise. But at

the same time, the sharp edge of life whose extraordinary ways had exposed him also dissected him like a scalpel so that he got to see himself clearly. He pursued the "new" fervently with keen curiosity. He followed his own ideas, hoping to reap the good and the beautiful in his contact with people, but he only made demands on life and other people while giving little of himself. He was conscious of the fact that he sought to perfect himself in a one-sided way, not realizing that for a self to be wholesome he must always be imbued with a very strong sense of responsibility, able to shoulder voluntarily all that he should carry. Only when you give as much as you can will you feel happiness.

He wanted very much to talk to a friend. After thinking so much all by himself, he felt rather lonely.

"Hey, Shu Zhen," Old Zhao came running up from behind. "It's nearly time and you are still strolling along."

"What's your hurry?" Shu Zhen looked at his watch. "There're ten more minutes to go."

"Oh, it's better to get there early rather than late," Editor Zhao was dubbed "slippery eel" in the office although he was a good-natured person. Unfortunately he was always getting caught up as a target in most political campaigns so that he acquired a kind of self-protective veneer.

"You seem to have something on your mind," Editor Zhao could see it at once.

"Not at all," Shu Zhen denied it.

"Why are you looking so downcast then? Just at the time when your life is taking a turn for the better." The older man smiled meaningfully. "It is rumoured that you will be sent to the capital to get your internship at one of the national papers."

"It can't be true. Just a rumour."

"Absolutely reliable news. Chief Editor Xiao said at a meeting of section leader: We must give our attention to training young reporters and editors with talent..."

"What talent do I have?"

"Believe it or not as you will. When the time comes, you'll have to treat us." Then Zhao seemed to remember something else. "Do you know the city has mobilized a group of middle school teachers to go to Tibet to help in improving the education in border areas. Our paper will be sending two reporters to go with the group. It'll be a two-year mission. A fine mission. Who knows on whose head it'll fall? Supposed to be a voluntary thing, but who will want to volunteer for that area? Older people will not be able to adapt to the altitude, the middle-aged have difficulty in leaving children and household cares, as for the young ones, most of them have just been recalled from the countryside and border areas, they can't afford another two years in Tibet." He was a veteran editor who knew everything about people in the press.

"Go to Tibet?" Shu Zhen's heart stirred.

"You won't be the one. You just wait to go to the capital."

Go to Tibet, Tibet, Tibet! The idea had plunged into his head and seemed difficult to dislodge. Shu Zhen told himself to consider carefully, to keep a sober head. "Going to the capital for an internship on a national paper was of course a wonderful chance but such opportunities will come again in the future. After all, I am still very young. Go to Tibet to experience a hard life... Have to change myself...should be putting myself in the service of others...need to do some solid work. It'll be only two years, won't it? It will have a good effect on me over the next twenty years or even for the rest of my life." Ideas were tossing and turning in his head, and suddenly he felt that he had stepped out of that wretched endless lane and entered a broad open road.

"When's the mission due to depart?"

"In about a month or so." Zhao eyed him in surprise. "Why, you..."

"I'm just asking." He did not voice his decision. Decisions such as this cannot be taken lightly...

Night. Everything was in deep sleep. Even the stars on high seemed to be blinking their eyes coldly with a dim light. The night was deep, dark and very black.

Shu Zhen sat staring at the blank paper in front of him. There was only the beginning of a letter: Yongyong, my beloved... For the first time, he felt it difficult to write to her, more difficult than writing his essays. Should he tell her about going to Tibet? They'd not seen each other for nearly a year and a half. Now there would be an even longer separation... He was still hesitating. All was silent in his room, the silence broken only by the little clock on the bookshelf ticking away indefatigably. Did the ticking say: "Tell her, tell her!" or was it: "Wait, wait a little!"

The clock would not answer.

Who could answer him?

In the deep of the night, how many people were looking towards the sky, looking for the "star" able to understand his call. Was she such a star?

No, he should not demand this of her. She had already done all she could. If he had had thousands of ideal standards, then now there was only one left. He wanted to understand her, to be considerate to her. He only wanted to have a good, long, talk with her, starting from the first day they had met...

He took up his pen again.

...You finished the translation of The Blue Bird, *I couldn't sleep,*
  Night. Rain beating against the window, frogs croaking,
  For a year and more, like this incessant dripping rain,
  How much piled up grief, bitterness and perhaps tears...

And I also harboured infinite conflicts of soul.
Looking back and thinking of the time since we went down
How big the steps I had taken.
As if driven by some strong whip,
I can't help wanting to start on a road to happiness,
A bigger stage, more spectators...
But I only expect, I'm always expecting
Rarely being tender and considerate, criticizing much
But you only looked at me puzzled and bewildered.

Gritting your teeth, you finally took a step forward,
Tasting the fruit with its sweetness, sourness and bitterness.
Not having planted, I plucked only a leaf
Of my renewed understanding of self.
Please forget, I can only say this to you,
Let it be swept away like snowflakes by the wind.
...There will not be another such winter.
How I hope that we'll both be quite new when we meet again,
The warning is: we must continue to change ourselves
Like molecules accelerating motion
But never wait for the day when the water boils up...

He used verse form and endowed it with the sentiments of a poet,
but he was not satisfied. Should he send it off? Was he to dissect
himself like this in this kind of a garrulous way? He was fed up
with his own habit of reasoning all the time. Hadn't he said
enough? It was action that was important.

Shu Zhen locked the unfinished letter into his drawer.

26

"When are you going?"

"Tomorrow."

"What time is your train?"

"Ten in the morning."

"I have a class."

"No need for you to see me off at the station. This is all I have." Yongyong put her bag down, not quite filled, in front of Guokai. "See how light it is if you don't believe me." Like a customs officer, Guokai picked it up before putting it down reassured. "Have you written to him?"

Yongyong shook her head.

"Sent a telegram?"

She again shook her head.

"Why not? Are you afraid he'll get the time wrong again?" Guokai laughed.

Yongyong smiled ruefully. "Since I don't need anyone to see me off, I don't need anyone to meet me either."

She did not tell her husband about going back for the drama festival. She didn't want to disturb her mind prematurely like last time. Let things develop quietly in a natural way. As she thought about their impending meeting, she dwelled more on the possibility of their not getting on well. As she imagined the moment when she would knock at their door, she had only a sense of uneasiness as if she'd be entering a maze, not sure what would be awaiting her at the end. She had not been back home for more than a year. Were the desk and wardrobe still arranged the way she had left them? She had a feeling of strangeness, yet of familiarity, also. Perhaps it would turn out like last time when she arrived at the door but did not enter, like the Sage Yu, who did the same thing three times in his mission to harness the rivers. Unpleasant thoughts filled her with anxiety before the start of her journey.

"Did I tell you I had a letter from Tess? She asked about the play you were translating." Guokai appeared very jolly for he

sensed her anxiety. "I told her in my reply that *The Blue Bird* was
in the air." He was trying to cheer her up.

"You shouldn't have said that." Yongyong replied moodily.
"Where is my Blue Bird?"

"You should know yourself." He was leading her like a patient
teacher helping a wayward pupil. "I still remember the conclusion
of *The Blue Bird*; the blue-coloured bird in the children's cage
struggled out and flew away. A neighbour's little girl began to cry,
but the children told her not to cry, for they would get the bird
back. Wasn't that what you yourself wrote in your translation."

"I'm just worried that..."

Guokai cut her words short. "You should believe in him.
Everyone is trying to change himself. If you're both doing that
you'll get the bird of happiness back. But the Blue Bird has wings
and will fly away, it'll never stay still. You'll have to look for it.
Isn't life a perpetual search?"

Yongyong's eyes brightened a bit. She admired Guokai's ability
to open up one's heart without much effort and yet he was so good
at controlling himself. He was not touched by circumstances and
never distressed over his own affairs. In contrast, she felt her own
weakness and instability. To her, life continually posed new lessons.
She should be like him, attack life with confidence and composure.
Her smile was bright now. "You certainly have a much deeper
understanding of that play."

"I'm only talking. If I really meet with a problem I can be very
stupid."

"I don't even know how to talk."

"This time when you go home, you should have a proper talk
with Shu Zhen and straighten things out. Don't act like a child any
more."

Yongyong blushed. In her heart she felt very warm. He was like
a real brother, so considerate, and thought of everything for her.

About himself, he was so casual as if not caring about anything.
"What about yourself?"

"What about?"

Yongyong realized that Guokai did not care to have other people bother about him so she said, "You know about going abroad to study."

"By the time you come back from the summer vacation, I'll probably be gone."

Yongyong suddenly felt the weight of these words. Her smile disappeared. "Didn't you say you wouldn't be going till winter?"

"Just got a notice saying the date has been moved forward..." He had not intended to mention this when he came to say goodbye. He would have written her a letter before he left.

"Then..." Her eyes clouded as if something was amiss and a look of sadness crept in. Guokai had always been like a brother to her but at this moment a sentiment stronger than losing a brother smote her like an underground courrent. "Then...it looks like I wouldn't be able to see you off just as you can't see me off..."

His eyes on Yongyong, Guokai felt his heart quivering so sharply it was like a blade of grass swirled by a gale. He wanted to say something and restrained himself after great effort. He moved his eyes away. Silence. The soft tinkle of a bell wafted over from afar.

"Want to hear a story?" Guokai began pacing around in the room. A gleam of merriment and humour flashed in his eyes.

"Tell me again the story about the ugly girl looking into the mirror?" Yongyong also did her best to hide her feelings.

"Didn't the ugly one become beautiful?"

"Yes, because a kind-hearted old woman gave her a lesson."

They both started to laugh.

"You'd better go now. Aren't you having a discussion session this evening?" Yongyong urged him to go.

"All right. Say hello to Shu Zhen when you see him."

"When you come back from abroad, I'll introduce you to him."

"We don't need any introduction," Guokai winked knowingly.

Yongyong suddenly remembered the telegram her husband had sent her. "You've seen him?" She looked at him, feeling certain it was him.

"Well, goodbye," Guokai evaded her question and stretched out a hand. "Have a good trip."

Yongyong felt she couldn't put out her hand to say goodbye. "Let's not..."

"Well, I'll just go." He turned decisively and walked out.

Wait! Yongyong longed to cry out. She ran to the door but stood still.

Guokai walked out of the dormitory building and went straight to the Students' Service. He sent a telegram to Shu Zhen: "Meet the 113 train on the 5th, Yong."

27

Shu Zhen stood woodenly in front of the placard with the timetable in the railway station. Was he afraid to get the time wrong again? He fished out the telegram from his pocket: "Meet the 113 train..." He was pleasantly surprised. "Why is she coming back suddenly? Can it be she learned about my going to Tibet?" But his application to go had only just been approved. Never mind the reason, she was coming home. He was exhilarated for a whole day and night. This time he must not miss meeting her.

That morning, as soon as he arrived in the office, a call came from the chief editor. "Diandian is leaving this morning..." The old man's voice was very sad. She was leaving, keeping the news from all his friends. Her father had learned about it only that morning.

"I'll go and see her off," he told the chief editor, remembering

Yongyong's telegram only after he put down the telephone. But he had to see Diandian off. She was finally going. He felt sort of responsible.

Two trains, one coming, one going. Luckily they were thirty minutes apart at the same station so he could do both without any trouble.

Both women were of significance in his life.

The trains were like magic boxes appearing or disappearing after a roar of the whistle.

"Xiao Diandian..." Shu Zhen called as he walked from window after window.

"Shu Zhen!" Diandian heard his call while she was standing on her seat, arranging her bags on the overhead rack. There was a startled look of gladness in her eyes as she stuck her sweaty face out of the carriage window. "Why are you here?"

"Why didn't you tell us about your leaving."

"I said before that I don't need anyone to see me off."

"You are really going like this?"

"Why are you acting in such an old-womanish way?" Diandian smiled disapprovingly. Then she asked, "They tell me you'll be going to Tibet... Is that true? I don't believe it."

"Why not?"

"You seem able to enjoy life with a light heart more than anyone. What's happened to cause you to make such a decision?" Her tongue was as sharp as ever even at this parting moment.

Shu Zhen had nothing to say. He did not feel like explaining. Her judgement of him was probably right because he had rarely thought of his duty to life and that was why he always appeared to be light-hearted. At this moment, as he stood in front of the green carriage, his heart felt heavy indeed as if the wheels of the train were crushing down on it.

Diandian appeared as jolly as if she were going to a meeting in the capital as she told him, "I bought some play things for the children in the village and slates too for writing."

Shu Zhen found it impossible to smile for he knew that she wasn't really feeling so jolly inside.

"Why are you acting like a dumb-bell?" Diandian asked, leaning over the windowsill of the train. "Haven't you anything to say?"

Shu Zhen smiled slightly. What could he say? He pulled out a nicely bound portfolio from his satchel. "Here are the notes I made for the sketch about you. I mean to keep it as many things I wrote about were really about myself. Also because..." He had considered for quite some time before deciding to bring this to her. In his notes, he had portrayed her as two women; one was the actual Diandian, the other a Diandian of his ideal. His portrayal contained a real silhouette and also visions touched up in idealistic hues. In actuality it was of course very difficult to preserve the vivid colours of her character as described in the notes. Still he wanted to present her with the notes. The page after page he wrote did record a period of history for both of them.

There was a thundering blast of the whistle rolling into the station from afar. A long train pulled into the neighbouring platform. Shu Zhen couldn't help turning round to look.

Diandian was aware of his unrest. "Are you going? Perhaps you should go now and not wait for the train to start..."

"No, it's not that. Yongyong is coming home today."

"On vacation already?"

"No," Shu Zhen spoke quite naturally. "I don't really know why she is coming back suddenly."

"She didn't write?"

Shu Zhen's silence was an admission.

"You should be good to her..." The crisp ringing of a bell broke through Diandian's words.

Why was she saying that?

Two more minutes before the train was to depart. The last two minutes.

"You go now. Go!" Diandian suddenly pulled down the window.

Shu Zhen saw that her eyes were wet... He did not leave but felt as if his feet were cast into the cement of the platform.

A corner of the window was hidden by green curtains. Dinadian's face was no longer visible to him.

Two short minutes. The train pulled out.

Another platform.

Only a few people loitered about. Were they wives and husbands? Walking past them, Shu Zhen noticed the joy and impatience in their eyes. He could understand their feelings though he wondered who would be able to notice his own feelings.

This was not the first time he had waited at a train platform to meet her, but never like this, impatient and slightly tense and flustered. He felt like a shy young man waiting for his first date, not quite sure what kind of a gaze the girl would turn on him so he felt restless and anxious. For no reason at all as the minutes and seconds ticked by and his wife's train came nearer and nearer, her image became more and more blurred and unfamiliar as if she had existed only in his dreams. He did think a great deal about their meeting when he first received her telegram. He had put their quilt out to sun early in the morning and puffed up their two pillows side by side. When translating the play she had not slept properly and throughtout the past year she had been having a hard time, now let her... Before coming to the railway station, he had gone to the cosmetics counter to buy her a bottle of pearl cream for her face. He could imagine that fatigue and worry must have added lines around her eyes but if the ads were true about the pearl cream, he was willing to massage her face for her a thousand times. In the past, he had done too little for her, hardly considering her comfort at all... But, when she was really there, standing before him, would he let some of his irrepressible disappointments flush all this tender feeling out of sight?

No, it could not be like the year before. Besides, he himself would be leaving very soon.

More people were waiting on the platform now. All looked eagerly in one direction. A green mail cart and the flat baggage wagon were lumbering onto the platform. Uniformed railway workers appeared. Leaning against a pillar, Shu Zhen watched the changing scene in front of him, his mood also changing. He was more at peace now. A young mother carrying a toddler in her arms brushed past him. He heard the interesting exchange between mother and son.

"The train's coming bringing your father. Do you know papa?" The mother's eyes glowed with happiness.

"Is it the papa in the picture?"

Obviously the son had never met his father. "If we have a child, then after two years, she would come to meet me with our child who would also talk like this..." A thought which never occurred to him before flashed into his head. "Is it possible?" he mocked himself. "That would be in the distant future..." What he needed to think about now was how to tell her of his decision to go to Tibet. He had imagined a conversation with her when they would be strolling beside the ink black waters of the river accompanied by the splashing of oars and lamp light. He would talk of a simple algebra formula on his mind: if A plus B equals C then when A and B remains unchanged C would be the same. An extremely simple formula, perpetual and solid. But the reverse of unchanged also holds, that is if A changed and B changed then C would also change. That would be something more vital, such being the law of life. Only change would make people feel life's leaps and bounds.

Could she understand this?

Suppose she was rushing back so very suddenly only to try to stop him from going to Tibet. Suppose her hasty temper, which could burst out explosively would, like before, emit bitter fumes?

No! It could not be like a year before. From the few letters she sent him, he'd already felt her change.

The dream he had at dawn just before he woke up came back to his mind.

The station platform again. The train whistle sounded, he leaned out of the coach window while she rushed towards him through the crowd to clasp his hands tightly, bright tears bursting out of her eyes... The wheels were beginning to move while the crowd followed the moving train like a tide, making it seem as if the whole platform was moving. She still would not relinquish his hands, but held on tight so that she seemed to be flying with the train as it gained speed. He was frightened that the train would throw her under its wheels. "Let go your hand, quick." She unclasped his hands and fell on the platform as the train pulled further and further away. She became smaller and smaller in his tearful gaze while he still gripped the windowsill, trying desperately to say something to her only to wake up in the effort. He felt the salty taste of his own tears in his mouth. Did he really shed tears? No longer able to go back to sleep, he pondered over the dream, feeling a deep regret that he wasn't able to say a last word of parting to her.

"What would I have said if I could utter the words? When we were really saying goodbye what should I say to her?..." As Shu Zhen backed away from the rails with the other people on the platform, he was still wondering about the words of goodbye he should have said with as much intent as he usually did for one of his verses. Suddenly like the flash of a white seagull, flapping its wings, a sentence came into his head: "Yongyong, the Blue Bird is flying overhead, do you see it?..." He became very excited.

Immediately, his steps felt lighter. "Yes, those are the words I should say to her." Then he mocked himself, "We've not yet come together, why am I thinking of saying goodbye?"

The loudspeaker overhead rang out: "Attention please, train 113 will be five minutes late..."

A hubbub rose from the waiting crowd. Was it to exclaim that fortunately the delay was only five minutes or was it to criticize the station for making them all wait an extra five minutes longer?

Shu Zhen paced up and down, impatient. Five minutes seemed so very long, for he had already waited so long... Yet five minutes is such a short time, she would be here any moment, arriving with the speeding train. He felt unprepared for their meeting, he wasn't sure what his first words should be. In the distance, two red lights blinking like a beacon at night became brighter. A bell announcing the approach of the train broke the quiet hush on the platform. Shu Zhen's heart pounded as if a mortar were working it.

He could hear the rumbling of the wheels. The air quivered slightly.

The waiting crowd lined up along the platform, all eyes turned toward the coming red lights.

Gradually, the blurred silhouette of the engine appeared together with a trail of white smoke slanting across the horizon. Wheels rolled in the steel rails.

Translated by Tang Sheng

The Mountain Flowers Have Bloomed Quietly

You might forget the people who laughed with you, but you'll
never forget those who cried with you.

——A girl's words to me

1

IT was her first time on an aeroplane.

The sky was a dazzling bule. Huge clusters of white clouds drifted back and forth. Occasionally a few small, wispy clouds floated southward quickly and gracefully. On the surface of the earth, the endless ranges of mountains stretched, alternating bright and dark, in layers of deep green.

Xiaoxiao stared quietly out of the window. But, as the plane took off, the joy and the novelty made her hold her breath. As a little girl, she had watched the toy-like aeroplanes mysteriously passing through the clouds, one after another, over her head, so high up and so far away from her, within sight and yet beyond reach, and she had always felt that those who travelled by aeroplane were all "high-class" people.

Now she was on board an aeroplane. Had she become high-class too?

The Great Northern Wilderness had invited them to come back

for a visit —— a group of young intellectuals —— in the old days they had been nothing but an ordinary group among several million high school graduates, a few inconspicuous drops in the ocean.

Now that she was really flying, the feelings of joy and novelty soon disappeared. She didn't quite approve of flying. It was too stylish. After all, they weren't going abroad, just returning to the Great Northern Wilderness. In the past, when they had gone home to see their families, they had always crowded together in the train passageway, leaning against a water cistern full of rubbish, dozing off like drowsy insects. When they saw passengers swaggering in and out of the sleeping car, they felt that those were the "high-class" ones.

"We're going on business, so we'll all go by plane. I can't stand the train." Huang Meng, who was a director at the film studio, picked up the receiver with determination and ordered twelve plane tickets.

The plane rose higher and higher and the mountains, rivers and fields became smaller and smaller. Looking down, it seemed as if the plane were circling the huge globe. Everything changed as time and space shifted. And life wasn't an exception.

She had spent nine full years in the Great Northern Wilderness and it had been almost four years since she had left. And now she was closing in, at high speed, on that place again. Close and then far away and then close again, she couldn't describe the variety of feelings that the fluctuations of time had stirred in her heart.

"Go to the Great Northern Wilderness, they're inviting you!" Her friends were all very excited, they had all said that they wanted to go back for a visit.

And her?

At night, when she was exhausted, she would have a recurring dream: she returns to that part of the country —— she left a major part of her life there —— and even though it doesn't belong to her anymore...she just could not cut the ties.

Dreaming, always dreaming.

She'd never expected that she'd really be able to go back. And, by aeroplane...

The plane flew over clouds and through fog, it was as if it were towing an endless roll of colour film that laid bare a singular, most rarely viewed scene. She was fascinated. "What if we are never going to land again, if we just keep flying, in between the blue skies and the white clouds, unstained by the dust of the mortal world..." She was, after all, grateful for Huang Meng's "determination," which had allowed her to leave the surface of the earth, leave the world and achieve a sense of tranquillity.

She hadn't felt so "tranquil" for a long time, even the moment she stepped onto the ladder, her heart was stung by a look from behind.

"Don't go, think it over again..."

"I have thought it over and I want to go back to have a look."

"Then don't go by plane. Haven't you heard about the recent crash..." Ling Zhi shot a glance at her unhappy expression and then swallowed the rest of his words.

Still, she sensed what was on his mind, "The policy group of the Institute for Literary Research is looking for a secretary. I've recommended you. It's a great opportunity! They're going to come over to talk to you about it in a couple of days..."

Was it spite or was it resistance, did she want to break away or was it a faint kind of longing that she wasn't willing to admit to herself?...

"Why upset yourself?"

She had never been at peace with herself.

"You have to weigh the advantages against the disadvantages and give priority to what's most important."

He was so calculating, the quintessential accountant.

She didn't know how to "weigh." The value of different sorts of things could not be measured on the same scale.

"Think it over again, calmly, the Institute..."

She was standing at the end of the line. He kept on urging her.

"You'd better go back." The look in her eyes softened, she was moved. After all, he meant well and they had only just met.

She was the last person to board the plane. But as she stepped through the cabin door, she wished that the plane had taken off right away and freed her from his gaze.

The plane took off on time. The little "No Smoking" sign lit up.

She took a deep breath and right away she felt lighter, just like the white clouds outside that drifted unhurriedly past the cabin, brushing the wings ever so slightly. It seemed that everything had turned into a very long dream.

But, after all, nothing is really a dream!

"Xiaoxiao, what's on your mind?" Huang Meng nudged her. He couldn't stand the silence.

"What's on *your* mind?" she asked him back.

"I was thinking about my son," Huang Meng answered straight away.

"You must have been thinking about your wife." Someone from behind joined in.

"Honestly, I was thinking about my son. As soon as I boarded the plane, I thought: what if we..."

"You are hopeless." Yali, who was sitting in front, turned her head, and a look of ridicule shone through her thin, crystal-like glasses.

"Madam journalist, wait until you have kids of your own, then there won't be any hope for you either."

"I don't want kids!" Yali tilted her face defiantly. "Don't I have my own life to lead?"

Xiaoxiao didn't like Yali's attitude. Does one appear refined and uncommon by not wanting kids?... But, do you love children? The deep self-reproach that suddenly welled up in her cast a shadow over her heart like unexpected bad weather.

"They say that nothing could be more tragic for a man than to find himself a woman who doesn't like children." Huang Meng was merciless. "A woman should be willing to bear children for the one that she loves and she should do it joyfully, regardless of the circumstances. It is an emotional investment that you can never count on being able to realize. It is the kind of love that humans cannot do without!"

"Your standards come from the last century." Yali turned to Xiaoxiao and asked, "Isn't it nice to be carefree and single? What do you say?"

Xiaoxiao didn't feel like saying anything. Am I qualified to discuss this topic?... From the minute she started on her trip, she'd been deliberately trying to keep her mind free of confusion. The great dam nevertheless collapsed. What's more, they absolutely had to talk about children...

Her hand unwittingly touched her bag, stopped, and then reached inside. In her wallet, she kept a few photographs of her son, those that *he* had sent to her. On the back of each photograph was always the same line of character: "The mountain flowers are blooming again." Year after year, the mountain flowers were always so bright and colourful: red, yellow and purple...

That's right, it was in the early evening at the time when the mountain flowers were in full bloom.

Once again she heard his voice by her ear. It was low and deep, yet full of joy, so pleasing to hear, so intimate, like a warm spring breeze, "Did you like it? I'll tell you another story..."

...Death took away the child unexpectedly. In order to find her child, the mother had to carry thistles and thorns against her chest, she had to give up her eyes to the lake-bottom and sacrifice her beautiful, long hair. She gave away everything that she had, and finally the mother found her child in Death's greenhouse. The child had been changed into two small, blue early spring flowers.

"How did you find this place?" Death asked the mother angrily.

"I'm a mother." The mother's hands were shielding the delicate flowers.

"Of these two flowers, one is the world's greatest happiness. It is full of joy and celebration. The other one, however, is the embodiment of worries, poverty and bitterness. Go ahead and pick one —— it will be your son's fate, his future!" Death roared.

Full of terror, the mother started to wail...

"The end is no good!" Having heard the story to the end, Xiaoxiao held her child tightly in her arms. She could almost hear Death knocking at the door.

"Well then, change it a little." His eyes glistened with expectation.

She did change it but still it wasn't very good. The mother in the story didn't take her child with her after all.

And what about her own child?

Are they still living in the little mud cottage pieced together out of adobe bricks? Once she had mixed the mud and made the adobe in bare feet. In the winter time, the little mud hut was warm and cozy. The double windows were never covered by frost...

"Xiaoxiao, come on, say something!" Huang Meng tapped on the back of her seat.

"Oh..." Xiaoxiao was very confused. "I'm not participating in your debate."

What could she say? She had once experienced that kind of "human affection," but only an impression remained...

The plane ticket was light blue, it resembled a little slice of the clear sky. Xiaoxiao was even more excited upon getting in than she'd been when she got a copy of the magazine in which her first story was published. She couldn't help but take it out to show everyone, though they responded with silence.

Why do you have to go to find what you already have right here? Ling Zhi's pressure was getting slightly annoying.

She wasn't trying to find anything, still she did have a wish, like a child longing for its hometown. The stream just outside of the town, the little wooden boat in the stream, there was a pure, unaffected sort of gentleness about it. After graduating from middle school, she felt like visiting the reed pond in the countryside where she had gone down to work. Every day, she'd row the little boat on the way to work, and play hide-and-seek in the midst of the snow-white reed flowers, it was fun —— an ephemeral sort of happiness.

What about the land she remembered?

There wasn't just gentleness and happiness, there was love and hate, there was enthusiasm and reluctance, celebration and grief. And what else? Much, much more...

"And what's the significance at all. She just wanted to go back and see the place. No matter what, she wanted to see if the little mud cottage that she had built with her own hands was still there...

What kind of urge was it? She really couldn't say.

Unexpectedly, the plane shook and abruptly began its descent.

Xiaoxiao grabbed a hold of the armrest. Suddenly she felt empty inside, there was absolutely nothing left, not even that "longing."

What have I come for? She was nervous, like a student that rushes into the examination hall, totally unprepared, just as the exam questions are being handed out.

The plane landed and the droning of the turbines got even louder.

2

The main building of the Central Farm stood silent and erect, right across from the bustling train station. Its walls were still the greyish colour of cement.

The multi-storeyed building seemed lower. I must have grown taller, she thought.

The first time she saw this tall building, Xiaoxiao was still a young girl, not quite sixteen, standing in the back row of the team. The flagpole had broken on the train, so she had to roll up the flag and carry it on her shoulder like a gun...

"You will go back on the same train that you came on. We only accept people in an organized way." An old PLA soldier met them, he was frighteningly solemn.

"Now that we have arrived, we are not going back." None of them were afraid, they simply stood up to the collar badges and red star insignias. They invited themselves to sit down, the tables and radiators were all occupied and Xiaoxiao had to make do with the armrest of a worn-out sofa.

"This is unacceptable!" The PLA soldier was forced to leave.

"Why isn't it acceptable?" Their leader blocked the entrance. "We are fully qualified. It's just that we're a little young that the school refused our applications."

"Even if you're only one day too young, it's no good. We have regulations."

"So we're too young this year, but next year and the year after that we'll be all grown up!" Xiaoxiao jumped up from the sofa with a childlike expression on her face. "Uncle please accept us."

"He's the director of the military supplies department." She was reminded by the young person next to her who was also wearing a military uniform.

What makes you think that you're so special, you don't even have any badges or insignias yet! "Uncle..." shouted Xiaoxiao unaffectedly.

"Uncle!"

"Uncle!"

They all gathered around him, all talking at once, dancing for joy, like a pack of quick-witted monkeys descending from the Mountain of Flowers and Fruit. Even the solemn director couldn't keep a straight face.

They were jubilant when they came out of the building. The banners were jerked open and the line of characters "Fifth Battalion, Eighteenth Company" was added in chalk.

Xiaoxiao suddenly turned her head and shouted, "Wow, our building! Look how tall it is!"

She used the word "our" so naturally and so proudly.

In fact, the building was no more than four storeys high.

As soon as they entered the big building, the small window of the reception opened with a "bang" and two faces, a boy's and a girl's, appeared next to each other. Like children leaning over a balcony to watch a big demonstration, they stared with curiosity at the guests who had just got off the train. Huang Meng was wearing a round, white plastic hat like an overseas Chinese from Southeast Asia; Yali was pulling a bright red suitcase with four wheels; Little Li was dressed in his Hong Kong suit with four little bronze buttons glistening on his shoulders. Xiaoxiao examined herself. She was okay. Dressed in a blue skirt and a white blouse, she still looked like a refined student. Only the heels of her sandals had got a little higher, "tap, tap, tap," they resounded on the cement floor.

She lightened her step.

There was a constant stream of people climbing up and down

the stairs and walking back and forth in the corridor. The door of the office opened and closed, the phone rang and stopped and then rang again. The atmosphere in the administrative building was largely the same. Xiaoxiao remembered it well. During her three years as editor, she had spent every day in this kind of atmosphere. At first, she couldn't stand it. As soon as she was off work she'd hurry out. But the streets were also very narrow, with all sorts of vehicles passing by continuously and people jammed everywhere. Houses side by side, buildings upon buildings, and such a small piece of sky. She had been used to the wildness of the Great Northern Wilderness, a much more spacious world. In the morning, she could watch the sun rise, in the evening, she saw the sun set. It was as if the sun was somewhere close by and if you walked toward it in a straight line you'd bump right into it...

After she had left, the memories that remained were all happy ones. Many things appear more beautiful from afar than close up, this is probably what distance does.

A circle of leather armchairs had been set up in the conference room, in front of which a finely woven, white-coloured straw mat was laid out. On the light green wall hung an oil painting several metres long: *Today's Great Northern Wilderness*. The entire painting was of a golden, tempestuous, billowing wheat field, with just a thin line of clear blue sky showing far off in the distance. The brilliant, warm colours, the vast perspective and the powerful emotions gave it a certain majesty, which inspired and elated the viewers.

On the coffee table, curls of vapour steamed up from the delicate porcelain cups. Cigarettes, sweets and fruit were neatly arranged on the gold-rimmed silver platter in perfect symmetry.

All of this just to greet us? Xiaoxiao felt uneasy. Since she had begun to make a name for herself, she had often enjoyed sumptuous entertainment in first-class conference rooms. But upon entering this particular building, she once again became reserved, as if she was still part of that remote, isolated company at the foot of the mountain.

Her hands clutched the chair's cushion, her body was tight and she sat awkwardly. She was as nervous as she was the first time she attended a meeting at the editorial department. Her first work had won a prize and she was supposed to talk about the creative experience —— she had written about an elementary school in the Great Northern Wilderness, about a group of kids in the hills, she would always remember them. She had lived there for nine years —— that was the heart of the matter. She had spoken rapidly, her heart thumped and, for a long time, her face still burned.

Gradually, she had learned to talk cheerfully and even humorously in these sorts of conference rooms...

Her destiny's sudden change seemed effortless.

"You're doing very well," they all said.

She couldn't explain it. When you're successful, the only thing that other people see is that dazzling halo.

"Can I have your autograph?" With both hands, a clerk offered her an ornately decorated autograph book with gold and silver threads that glistened on its satin cover. Xiaoxiao accepted it, how heavy it felt. Gingerly, she opened it and saw that the writer Ding Ling had signed her name on the title page. Last year, she had come back to visit the place where she had stayed during troubled times.

Xiaoxiao took the brush but hesitated. How could I sign my name in such a book? I didn't accomplish anything when I lived here or when I left. She handled the autograph book to Yali, "You sign it first."

With a few quick brush strokes Yali signed her name the way she had practised, naturally and unrestrained. Wherever she went, a young, stylish journalist must leave her name in other people's address or autograph books.

The autograph book went round and ended back in Xiaoxiao's hands. She leafed through it, cover to cover, and then closed it quietly.

They waited for their interview. The senior cadre was to arrive at eleven o'clock.

Still half an hour.

Xiaoxiao pulled out her note pad with the attached pencil. What should she note down? Her head swam, she was tired.

"Waiting for an interview?" Still thinking about it, she recalled a long, long time ago she'd also been waiting like this...

"Forget it, everybody, go home!" he roared furiously.

The rain became heavier. It was pouring. Xiaoxiao couldn't make out his face though she could feel his sharp, hawk-like eyes were on fire. The deputy-chief of the company normally didn't say very much, but when he got angry, everyone was afraid of him.

The entire company stood silently in the pouring rain and the cold wind.

"Didn't you hear me? Have you all gone deaf?" He jumped onto the tractor and opened up the throttle. The engine was dead, the exhaust pipe was mute. The "putt-putt" sound was gone and, except for the hooting of the wind, an absolute stillness covered the bean fields.

"Deputy-chief Li, let's wait a little while...the political instructor did go to phone somebody, right?" The old platoon leader pleaded cautiously.

Still wait! Xiaoxiao was shivering with cold, and her clothes were soaked. But no one dared move. The Bureau Chief was going to come out to the company to inspect the autumn harvest, and a few days ago, the Farm Headquarters had sent out people to prepare. "The whole company must turn out, harvest as much as possible, take action and strike hard..." The political instructor mobilized everyone as he did at all the meetings, "We must take the class struggle as our guiding principle..." Early in the morning, the whole company acted promptly and, except for the dining hall staff, everyone went out into the fields, classes even stopped at the elementary school. A powerful momentum had been built up.

After lunch, it began to rain. One after another, the little kids who had come along to gather the bean stalks found their way under the jackets of the grown-ups. In the field, there were no trees to shelter them from the wind and the rain, so they were all drenched. Half an hour went by and then another half an hour.

"Go home, everybody, go home! I'll wait here myself." He tugged at the sleeves of the two platoon leaders. "If we all catch cold, will the Bureau Chief come out to do tomorrow's work?"

"Well then, go ahead!" The platoon leaders cowardly issued the order.

When they were finally allowed to leave, Xiaoxiao almost ran. But they hadn't yet gone half a mile when they ran into the political instructor.

"Who told you to leave? The Bureau Chief will be here any minute now. Quickly, go back."

"It started raining..."

"The Bureau Chief tackles his job in spite of the rain...and a reporter from the provincial newspaper is coming too." As if he was shooing away sparrows, the political instructor drove everyone back to the fields.

They finally arrived. Three small jeeps stopped on the road. The Bureau Chief and the others who got out of the jeeps were all wearing super-waterproof raincoats.

"Quick, go and get Company Deputy Chief Li to give an account of today's rate of progress." The political instructor was so anxious that he ran all over the field.

"It can't be? He's gone," someone cried out.

Xiaoxiao immediately stood up straight and she saw him just as he strode by the three jeeps, without looking back.

"He's got a panther's courage..." one of the platoon leaders whispered.

What would happen to him? Xiaoxiao worried.

The first thing the next morning, there was going to be a company mass meeting, the Bureau Chief was going to make a speech and no one was to be absent.

Before dawn, Old Liu, the stockman, rushed in. "Medic, Deputy Chief Li has fallen ill."

"Just a minute, there are no more syrings." Xiaoxiao frantically checked her medical bag. In one night, ten people from the company had taken ill, each of them with a high fever. She hadn't slept the whole night, her head felt as if it were going to explode and she was filled with indignation. "Why did it have to happen like that, why did they have to stand in the rain?..."

"Are you sick?" She pushed open the door to the small room in the stable. He had already fed the horses and had squeezed in with Old Liu on the small *kang*. He hadn't moved, even after he was promoted to deputy chief of the company.

An oil lamp was burning in the room, its long glass chimney was blackened by smoke and the light was dim.

"No, I'm not sick." Crouched beneath the oil lamp, he was flipping through a book.

She stood there without moving, the medicine box on her back.

The loudspeaker on the clay wall resounded, "Mighty officers and men of the Fifth Company, work and study vigorously...give your all for the revolution, defy the rain..."

He jumped up and "Pa!" it souned as he ripped out the wire. The wire snapped and the speaker fell silent.

Suddenly the room was quiet. One could hear the sound of the horses chewing grass in the shed next door.

"How come you're still sleeping in the stable?" She had to ask even though she knew the answer. It had nothing to do with being ill.

"I still have to feed the horses every morning and evening."

"Your temper is going to get the better of you," she said what she had been feeling.

"I'm not a business person and I'm not looking to sell a bill of goods." His voice was cold.

Old Liu came in with a lantern. "What's he got?"

"Eh...he's got a fever..." Xiaoxiao swiftly opened the medicine box. "The mass meeting...you'd better help him get sick leave." She tore off an official sick-leave slip.

"Do I get a shot too?" He lifted one eyebrow.

"Mhh." She smiled mischievously, then took off the lamp chimney and wiped it clean with gauze...

"Sorry to have kept you waiting," Bureau Chief Zhao greeted them as he entered the conference room. "I've just come from receiving an American agricultural delegation and we got delayed for half an hour."

Sitting in an armchair, drinking tea, smoking cigarettes, chatting about this and that, before you knew it half an hour had gone by. Standing in the rain in autumn, however...

Bureau Chief Zhao leaned back in his chair and leisurely lit a cigarette. As Xiaoxiao watched the chief attentively, she felt indescribably moved. During her nine years on the farm, she had never entered a room like this and she had never seen the chief. Now, only after she had left, was she cordially invited back for a visit and the Bureau Chief himself came to receive her.

Exactly what was it that had changed?

"They've all become editors, journalists, they've written quite a lot." The clerk brought forward a stack of magazines tied with red ribbon. "You'll find all of their published work in here."

Without paying attention, the Bureau Chief glanced briefly through them and then waved them away. Xiaoxiao's heart sank. Oh yes, a few magazines, a few novels, they just weighed too little in comparison with the hundreds of thousands of hectares of land that filled the chief's heart.

"After leaving the farm, you've all been quite successful, eh?"

Was he praising their success, or was he still upset about their leaving the farm? Xiaoxiao was very sensitive.

"Group after group of you came here, then you all took off again and left us in a tight spot. You complained that you were wasting your youth, your future, but we had complaints too. With no one to teach, the classes stopped at the school. With no one to do the accounts, wages couldn't be paid. Without drivers, we could only fill the tractor with water... Of course, we don't blame you. No one was able to escape this historic tragedy, no one can escape it..." The Bureau Chief lit another cigarette.

"Nevertheless, your staying in the Great Northern Wilderness a few years had its advantages too." Bureau Chief Zhao's tone of voice lightened up a little, he leafed through the autograph book. "Well, let's find out who everyone is."

One after another, they introduced themselves. At last, Chief Zhao settled his eyes on Xiaoxiao.

"You haven't signed your name?" The clerk was quick to act and hurriedly brought the autograph book over to the coffee table in front of Xiaoxiao.

"Watch out, it's wet!" Huang Meng cried out on purpose. Xiaoxiao had no choice but to take the book in her hands, then she looked at the chief again.

"Forget it."

"Why?"

"What are we worth?"

"Worth? You're worth a page in the history of the Great Northern Wilderness." The Bureau Chief sat back in his chair and sighed. "Your experiences, your destinies are also bits of the entire country's history. I have very mixed feelings about seeing you..." He turned around abruptly and lifted up the stack of magazines with the red ribbon fluttering. "Last night, I went through them all. I never got to sleep. Very well written! You feel for the Great Northern Wilderness, you write about your own lives in such a way that truly moves other people. You're very gifted. It's a pity that, in the past, you only worked as labourers..." He squeezed out the cigarette butt forcefully into the ashtray. "If we were given another few million young intellectuals, I would work to boost their morale and we would certainly be able to do more to modernize our farm!" He got up, his coarse, black eyebrows trembling with emotion.

Everyone was surprised.

"Naturally, you wouldn't return now." The Bureau Chief had calmed down, he waved his hand.

It's true, once you had been there, you wouldn't want to go back...

Xiaoxiao's heart suddenly ached.

The door opened and someone poked his head in. "Chief, a staff member wants to see you right away. You?..."

Bureau Chief Zhao left the room immediately, but soon the door was pushed open and he returned mumbling to himself, "He was from the Seven Star Farm, it's about the dam again...?"

Seven Star Farm? Dam? Xiaoxiao couldn't help asking, "Which company?"

"Were you at the Seven Star Farm?" Chief Zhao looked at Xiaoxiao with interest. "That's a good area, mountains and rivers.

With proper management, it could become extremely fertile... Of course you'd have to manage it well," he repeated.

But it never was managed properly. There were always mountain torrents. They were flooded several times...though Xiaoxiao didn't say that. Perhaps this was already history. They've got a dam now, haven't they? At last they had a dam.

"Do you know a fellow by the name of Li Juntang?" Chief Zhao asked casually.

Him... Xiaoxiao's heart suddenly stopped beating. She wanted to nod her head, and then again, she felt like shaking it.

"He used to be the deputy chief of a company and now he's the chief of the Seven Star Farm. He's very capable. Recently..."

Had he become the chief of the farm? She hadn't known. She had written to him, she'd written several letters. He never wrote back. "Forget about him!" she told herself over and over.

Had she forgotten?

Gradually, she believed that she had.

But, as soon as she heard his name mentioned, it was as if in the midst of darkness, a lamp had suddenly been lit, all of the memories stood out as clearly as a printed picture.

When the reception was over, Bureau Chief Zhao shook hands with each of them, "All of you go take a look around your old homes. If you find any problems, report them directly to me."

Xiaoxiao retreated to the back of the crowd.

Chief Zhao nevertheless walked up to her, "If you want to go back to the farm, I'll talk to Chief Li about it. He's here in the Central Farm for a few days to attend a meeting of the propaganda department of the provincial Party committee.

"I...I'll find him myself."

Would she really go look for him? See him immediately? Was that what she most desired or most feared? Coming back to look around to see everything that she had left behind her, and to see him and her son. She had brought a small electric car for her son as a birthday present. He was just about to turn five.

Her son's birthday!...

"Pa! Pa!" The cracking of the whip in his face, cracking the whip. His open shirt flapped about him like two flags, the back of it was soaked with sweat.

"Hold a little longer, a little longer..." He looked at her anxiously. She gnashed her teeth, her hands appeared. She tried her best not to cry out, because if she did, he might thrash the horses to death. But she couldn't help herself.

"Pa!" The whip whistled as it ripped through the air, and then it died.

"Damn!" He struck the whip against his knee. It was broken.

"Don't..." She didn't have the strength to talk.

He took off his shirt, held the sleeve and lashed it desperately against the backs of the horses, "Gee-up! Gee-up!"

Like whirlwinds, the horses' hooves kicked up clouds of dust.

They never made it to the delivery room. Right there on the floorboards, the doctor delivered a rosy-coloured, healthy-looking little baby whose wailing alerted the entire hospital.

She lay in a pool of sweat. The date-brown horses snorted, they too were dripping with sweat.

He wiped the perspiration off her forehead with a towel, then he used his clothes to dry the horses' backs.

"Come..." She lifted up her soft hand and wiped away the blood from the whip-sores on his face. One of the date-brown horses bent down to lick his still slightly trembling foot.

"Wait a minute." He turned around and ran off.

She lay there very quietly. There was no wind, the sky was extraordinarily blue.

He returned with an armful of mountain flowers, red ones, blue ones and purple ones...

"All the mountain flowers in the fields are in full bloom."

She buried her head in the bouquet of scentless flowers.

"Wah! Wah!" Still crying...their son!

Afterwards, every year on that day, he never failed to send her a photograph of their son. But never any letters. They had broken up so completely.

But she nevertheless remembered his words, "All the mountain flowers in the fields are in bloom."

3

"He's staying in Room 203." The attendant checked the registration book.

Room 203.

She stopped in front of the door and knocked very lightly. "Tap, tap." It was a hesitant sound.

"Come in." It was a man's voice.

Was it him? Her heart pounded in her chest.

The door opened, it was a stranger.

She quickly cast a glance inside through the half opened door. "Excuse me, the chief of the Seven Star Farm..."

"He has gone."

"To a meeting?"

"He asked to be excused and left in a hurry, it had something to do with the dam."

Now the dam again!...

"On which train?"

"The 10:30 train."

It was already 9:30.

She was very familiar with the northeast station. A distinct smell, a blend of tobacco and fresh garlic always lingered in the waiting room. The long benches along the walls were forever fully occupied. A huge crowd of people were crammed together in the corners, some sitting, others lying down.

"Still ten minutes to check in for Train 302," the loudspeaker announced.

Xiaoxiao looked around impatiently but she still only saw unknown faces passing in front of her.

Suddenly, her eyes lit up.

He was lying on his back on a bench right next to the ticket window. His hands were folded underneath his head, his legs were bent and a hat covered his face. She couldn't resist walking over to him. She didn't want to disturb him. She just wanted to see him. Were his eyes still sharp and expressive? She had loved to guess what was behind those eyes, which appeared to conceal so many mysteries. Sometimes, however, his eyes could frighten her too.

He rolled over onto his side and the hat fell to the ground.

No, no, that wasn't him. She halted abruptly. It had really looked like him. He used to lie in a similar position, like a sculpture. A worn-out, dirty, old leather hat with drooping ear flaps that resembled the wings of a hawk would cover his face. It was a winter day, the New Year was approaching...

"And where did he go?"

"He went to the station to fetch fertilizer. He was up at dawn harnessing the animal to the cart." Old Liu was sifting feed.

"That kid..." He gave a rough sigh.

Xiaoxiao was disappointed. She was going home to see her family and was just about to leave, she would have liked to let him know. He really was back in the stable because he had offended some work team again.

The midnight train. It was dry and very cold. The ground was frozen solid. The walls of the waiting room were covered by a thin, shining white layer of hoarfrost. The passengers who were waiting for the midnight train were all crowded around two small stoves, huddling themselves, rubbing their hands. The ceaseless sound of stamping feet seemed to have a definite rhythm to it. On a bench next to the ticket window, someone was lying on his back with a worn-out leather hat over his face. His elbows showed through the ragged, quilted blue overcoat, a whip-lash was tied around his waist and fastened to the whip-lash was a handle that lay obediently on the ground. He was fast asleep, as if he was lying on a warm and cozy *kang* .

What an odd person. Xiaoxiao curiously kicked the whip handle very lightly. The handle tugged at the whip-lash tied around his waist and, like a puppet on a string, he sat up with a start.

"It's you!" Xiaoxiao was both surprised and happy. "What are you lying here for?"

"I got sleepy." He grabbed the hat and put it on.

"Why don't you go home?"

"The goods didn't arrive, they'll be here on the first train in the morning. It's too cold outside for the horse to go back and forth."

"If the horse can't stand it, what about a human being?" Xiaoxiao was touched. "Are you cold?"

"I'm okay." He folded his arms around his knees without looking at her.

Xiaoxiao took off her overcoat and tossed it at him, "Put it over you, after all, I'm on my way home now."

"I'm used to it. Growing up in the snow, I won't die from the cold." He threw the coat back to her.

"Are you going home for the Spring Festival?" His home was in a different company.

He shook his head. "My dad is studying at the Party school."

"And he's not coming back for the holidays?"

"There's no one at home."

"What about your mum?"

"My mum's dead. That was also during the Spring Festival... My dad and a group of 'capitalist-roaders' had been sent into the mountains to build roads, they wouldn't allow us to notify him..." he spoke with a dry voice.

She wanted to comfort him. "You shouldn't be all alone."

He interrupted her at once. "I've got the horse." He grabbed the whip handle and bent it into an arc, then he let it go and the tensile handle straightened out again.

"But a horse can't talk."

His lips moved slightly and a bitter smile drifted across his eyes.

He was in bad mood; she understood.

A sharp whistle melted the almost frozen solid waiting room.

People rushed toward the ticket check, hustling and shouting. The doors opened and a white mist of cold air came howling in.

He lifted up her bag and marched forward with vigorous strides.

The train window was stuck, welded shut with ice, and the glass was covered by a layer of white frost through which it was impossibe to see. Xiaoxiao put down her bag and went back to the door.

"Here take it." She threw him the overcoat. "It's too cold, you better hurry on!"

He turned around and walked away.

She wanted to call him back. She had hoped that he would stay until the train started moving...

Grudgingly Xiaoxiao went up behind a small group of passengers and followed them onto the platform.

The train came to a complete halt. It stopped here for seven minutes. She ran from the first car all the way to the last one and then back again. She looked through each window but he wasn't there.

"Maybe he didn't go to the station? Just to avoid me..." Xiaoxiao's hurried pace suddenly became so weak she could hardly take another step. She turned around.

I can't blame him, after the way I hurt him.

Afterward, he did insist that I leave. He couldn't stand people who didn't value that land.

"Xiaoxiao, Deputy Chief Li is looking for you. He's over by the school."

"I'll go right away." Xiaoxiao had just returned from giving injections and was still carrying the medicine box on her back.

The school had been set between the dining hall and the communal kitchen, on what had originally been a threshing ground. They had taken the old, dilapidated shack for drying the grain, plastered the walls with mud, packed the roof with straw, and partitioned it into four small classrooms. The threshing ground became a pretty decent playground.

"Over here." Xiao Fang pointed up. She was the only properly appointed teacher in the school. She had taken a year of teacher's training and, as soon as she got to the Great Northern Wilderness, she volunteered her service: "I'll make a good teacher." At least this was the rumour around the company.

"What does he want me to do?" Xiaoxiao asked Xiao Fang.

"You ask him."

He was squatting on the roof, stroking his chin with his hand. The small, wooden ladder that leaned against the walls of the house wasn't far from falling apart. Xiaoxiao climbed up nervously.

"This is our school!" With the tip of his toe, he brushed away the straw on the roof. The roof looked like the unkempt nest of an old hawk. A couple of spots were covered by asphalt felt held down by stones.

"No decent classrooms, no decent teachers." The stones rattled as he threw them down and the felt flapped in the wind.

What was his point? Xiaoxiao carefully stepped up onto the roof, it felt as if just a little force might cause the entire roof to collapse.

"It's been discussed in the company that we want to bring in two more teachers, in the meantime, we'd like you to step in."

"And do I continue with this?" Xiaoxiao tapped the medicine box on her back.

"Do that as well."

"You should try doing them both." Xiaoxiao made a long face, like a little girl who easily takes offence. In fact, she could do them both. She just didn't want to be a teacher. The kids here had never seen a train, they had never seen a multi-storeyed building, they were as stupid as...she almost said it out loud. What's more, the universities were about to begin recruiting students from the workers, peasants and the soldiers and that was what interested her...

He got a very anxious look in his eyes, it simultaneously embodied hope and disappointment. "Will you do it or not?" he asked her.

"I won't do it," she answered softly.

"Get down from here!" With his back to her, he squatted down again.

She stood there without moving. She seldom lost her temper with anybody, she was always obliging. What had happened today? She wanted to explain. But, all of a sudden, he leaped up and jumped off the roof.

"You!" Xiaoxiao's face turned white.

He landed on the ground with a "bump" as if a sandbag had tumbled down. He shook off the few pieces of straw from his hand

and strode off.

Xiao Fang ran up to him, held him back and said something to him. For a long time, the two of them stood off in the distance under a big tree.

It looked as if he was smiling slightly.

Xiaoxiao felt sorry. She rushed toward the ladder, but her body felt light as air, like an inflatable doll that would fall over with the first puff of wind.

"Let me hold it for you." Xiao Fang rushed back to hold the ladder. "Don't be afraid, it's steady now."

He turned his head and walked away.

Xiaoxiao leaned against the unsteady wooden ladder. "Wouldn't you like to go to university?" she asked Xiao Fang.

"That's up to the group to decide."

"I asked: wouldn't *you* like to go?" Xiaoxiao tried again.

"Either way is okay with me," Xiao Fang answered calmly. She seemed completely self-confident.

Xiao Fang was a year younger than Xiaoxiao, but it appeared that Xiao Fang was more mature; she always talked and worked unhurriedly.

"Go and talk to Deputy Chief Li," Xiao Fang urged Xiaoxiao.

"No, I won't," Xiaoxiao kicked away the small stone under her foot.

"You may not know, but the sub-committee had quite an argument over the teacher issue. The chief recommended two convalescents who can't work in the fields. He thinks that teaching is an easy task. Deputy Chief Li strongly disagreed, he suggested you. But you..." Xiao Fang pulled Xiaoxiao into the classroom, "Think it over again."

The classroom was very primitive. The coarse mud on the walls held together strands of straw, the dark, broken planks formed a makeshift ceiling —— it looked like a shack. Xiaoxiao dared not even think about standing there...

There was no one in the stable. Two light grey foals licked at each other affectionately in front of the door to the fodder room. By the trough next to the well, the date-brown horse was drinking water.

Behind the stable, Old Liu was walking a couple of emaciated, sick horses on the feeding ground. Xiaoxiao made a gesture, Old Liu understood and shouted back, "He's gone to the woods to cut some poles. He hasn't eaten yet."

Xiaoxiao walked toward the woods.

In spring, the roads were particularly difficult to walk on. The earth was frozen, the snow had melted, there were mud puddles and water-logged depressions everywhere. A cart loaded with poplar trunks was moving slowly along the path by the river.

Xiaoxiao crossed the bridge and ran along the river bank up to the cart.

The cart wheels turned with difficulty in the mire. Sometimes it was necessary to go backwards a little to be able to continue going forwards. He was wearing only a thin corduroy shirt, his body bent forward, his hands gripped the handles, and the hemp rope that was wrapped around his shoulders had become deeply embedded in the muscles around his shoulder-blade, as if they were bound together. The young, slender trunks that extended beyond the length of the cart jolted up and down like a raft rising and falling with the waves.

Xiaoxiao stopped.

Bent forward at the waist, he spotted a pair of rubber boots covered with mud, though still revealing a bit of green. With much effort, the cart continued rolling. Slowly, it rolled by the green mottled rubber boots.

"Can I help you?" she followed behind.

"Push." His voice was dry.

The cart stopped at the bridge. He sat down on the handles and caught his breath. She wiped the sweat off of her face and leaned over the bridge's railing.

"Who are you doing this for?"

"Last night we lifted that old broken roof off the school."

Only then did it occur to Xiaoxiao that Xiao Fang had returned to the dormitory around midnight, filthy and weary, washed herself in the doorway and soaked her dirty clothes in a basin. She couldn't help feeling guilty, "I didn't know that the sub-committee..."

"It doesn't matter whether you knew or not." His eyes were fixed upon the congealed water, the tone of his voice was cold, as if it too was filled with splinters of ice. "Don't think that by nature we country folk are more stupid than you. Don't think that the kids from the countryside won't be able to attend university." He stood up. His shoulders shivered. The sweaty corduroy shirt cooled as the wind blew. Slowly, he rolled himself a cigarette. "In 1954, I came with my father to reclaim the wasteland. A few families lived together in a dilapidated stable. Where could we find a school? Every day, we travelled tens of miles back and forth to go to school in a neighbouring town. In the winter, we got blisters on our faces from the frost. Every day, the girls would cry themselves home. However, we couldn't not study, could we? The Great Northern Wilderness is not really wild, the earth is so rich, the natural resources so plentiful. If you must talk of wasteland, it's our minds that lack the most. We can't continue like this!" He was silent, only then did he take a deep puff and exhaled large clouds of smoke.

Could she still refuse?

This was the first time she truly saw the contents of his heart; it was like the rich, black soil beneath his feet.

Go on, accept his suggestion, she thought. But her lips replied, "I'll think it over again, if that's allowed."

"There are no despots here." He suddenly threw the half-smoked cigarette into the river.

The rest of the way back, he didn't smoke again.

When the cart got to the bridge, the wheels turned effortlessly.

On the first day she entered the classroom, she noticed him sitting at the back.

"How was I?" she asked after class was over.

"I was right about you." His face was expressionless.

"How come you thought that I could be a teacher?" She'd wanted to ask that all along.

"My eyes told me so."

She wasn't satisfied, not able to let it be, so she asked again. This was like a key with which to probe into his heart. Just like some girls who never tire of hearing the answer would ask again and again, "Why do you love me?"

He didn't volunteer an answer, but only said, "It's a reaction of my spirit."

This was more powerful than a direct answer, and she was satisfied...

A bell rang, the train was about to leave. Xiaoxiao couldn't stop herself from looking once more. The next moment, she felt as if she had been electrocuted, her body went numb. As if by some miracle, he appeared, sitting up against the window of the car right in front of her, his head tilted and a weary look on his face.

She wanted to wave to him, she wanted to rush up to the car and knock on the window, but she remained motionless, and stared blankly at him. Clearly, he had got thinner. He seemed lost in thought, as if surrounded by countless difficulties. Gradually, her line of vision blurred.

Xiaoxiao took a step forward, then another. But he turned his face spontaneously toward the interior of the car.

Didn't he see me? Didn't he want to see me? The hand that she had raised to the level of her chest now dropped down again.

The train started moving.

A string of questions was left behind.

Xiaoxiao quickly left the station with some beautiful memories and a heavy heart.

4

It was called an informal discussion with amateur writers but, in fact, they were giving lectures. "The use of montage in movies, time montages, space montages, emotional montages..." Huang Meng spoke very eloquently, and went on for an hour and a half before he wrapped up the first point, then there were the second and third points. He knew how to please the public with claptrap.

Pair upon pair of eyes, full of concentration and sincerity, looked on. Most of the audience were members of the farm staff and had never been out of the land. Meeting someone from outside and hearing about what went on there could keep them excited for a long time, but made a lot of them jealous too.

Didn't we use to look through eyes like those? Xiaoxiao thought. One winter day, when the mountain pass had been blocked by the snow, she and Huang Meng had walked sixty or seventy miles to meet a seasoned writer who had come to visit the Great Northern Wilderness... We were all together, yet our lives had gone in such different directions, it's as if we were from different worlds. Was it because of these differences that I left this place?...

As soon as her foot touched the soil, her heart sent out many delicate feelers. A whole range of thoughts spun around like a merry-go-round.

Huang Meng was still reading from his voluminous lecture notes. Xiaoxiao, however, hadn't prepared anything. Her topic was

"Your Work and Your Life's Path." Where should she begin? She didn't think that her life amounted to so much. Two of her novels had won prizes and had been rather highly praised, "The author's love and attachment to the land flow from each character in the novel..."

Was it really like that?

She always wished that she could look back on her life and remain detached, but she was never able to calm herself. She couldn't tell if her experiences had given her "impetuosity" and "inspiration." When writing "Summer's First Thunderstorm," her heart had been immersed in the torrential rain, the rumbles of thunder and the flashes of lightning...

Summertime. It was the middle of the night. There was a great thunderstorm. It seemed as if the raindrops were pounding on a drum. From all directions, only the never-ending barking of someone's dog.

Suddenly, the entire company was woken by the sound of wild beating on the gong.

"Quick! Wake up! Mountain torrents! Floods!..." The old guy who beat the watches went from house to house banging on the windows with more urgency than a call to arms.

Soon after, everyone in the company was gathered in front of the dining hall. None of them had brought an umbrella, they were all soaked by the rain.

"All five companies at the foot of the mountains to the south are flooded," the political instructor shouted hoarsely. "The Farm Headquarter has sent out an urgent message. They want us to start up all of our tractors and go out there as soon as possible. All the carts must be brought into action. Attach the trailer to the tractor. Party member, follow me!"

More than ten people came forward from the team.

He walked by right in front of Xiaoxiao, as always with big strides. At that time he still wasn't a Party member, he had only just filled in his application form.

For the first time she really envied them. They were members of the Party.

"Comrades from the Party, we must prepare our minds amply." The political instructor lifted his head and looked at the sky. The southwestern corner of the night sky was blacker than ever. "The flow of the water is enormous... Count off." His short body moved to the very front of the team.

Xiaoxiao followed him with her eyes. Never before had she observed this short, uneducated political instructor with a feeling of such deep respect. At ordinary times, in the dormitory, they would mock his incoherent manner of speaking when giving reports, they even picked up his Shandong accent, "Tanaka has come from Japan, Kakue has come too, the two brothers have both arrived..." But the thunderstorm flushed it all out, leaving behind it that lofty image of him standing in the front row of an emergency squad made up of Party members.

"One! Two! Three!..."

Silence reigned over the crowd, it seemed as if the several hundred people had all stopped breathing.

"Fourteen people altogether. Get up on the vehicles!" The political instructor draped a towel around his neck.

Several hundred pairs of eyes followed their footsteps, saw them off.

"See you tomorrow!" someone from the squad said lightly.

But everyone else felt their hearts sinking even lower under the pressure of an ominous presentiment and deep anxiety.

"You're not coming." The political instructor held him back by the side of the tractor. "We have got to leave one cadre here..."

He leaped onto the vehicle.

The main road went through to the mountains in a straight line. Silence reigned over the surrounding country, only the tractors roared in unison, resonant, yet solemn and stirring.

The steel caterpillar tracts started rolling, running through puddle after puddle, spattering mud all over. Raindrops strafed the wind screen of the driver's cab, the wipers moved endlessly to and fro in the shape of an arch, forming one after another shining fan. Everybody followed the tractors a long way to send them off on their way.

At midday, the dining hall only sold half the food.

In the middle of the night, the lights were on in all the houses in the company, they looked like pairs upon pairs of widely opened eyes.

One o'clock, two o'clcok...

"Tractors!" A faint sound of motors could be heard.

Everybody swarmed out to the mouth of the road.

On the main road the tractor lights sparkled and moved. The motors sounded hoarse, as if they were consuming their very last drop of gas.

Everbody hurried up and surrounded the tractors. But the drivers remained silent in the cabins. Suddenly, the throttles of four tractors simultaneously started turning, the exhaust pipes emitted columns of pitch black smoke, and the smoke enveloped the long sorrowful blows of the whistles, it was even more heart-rending than the warning sirens in the mines.

They all held their breaths.

The political instructor jumped down from the trailer. Then followed one after another. "Three, four, five..." All were counting to themselves, "eight, nine, ten."

Ten! Why were there only ten?

There were fourteen of them when they left! Fourteen!

It was much too dark, impossible to see who was missing.

"Four...comrades..." The political instructor's voice trembled with pain as if someone had pulled a sticking plaster from a wound.

And he? Had he come back? Regardless of anything else she made her way up to the front. The crowd grew tighter, it was like a wall too hard to drill through. How she wanted to ask those around her.

"Have you seen Vice Chief Li? He?..."

"Where"s my husband?"

"My husband!"

"The child..."

Voices of despair rose and fell. Xiaoxiao put her tightly clenched fist in her mouth, she couldn't stand it any longer...

"Four youngster: Wang Qiang, Wu Huanhuan, Jiang Ping, Song Yuzhen..." The political instructor's voice was too light to hear now.

Somebody broke down crying.

Xiaoxiao's legs went soft, her head was like a ball of lead, so heavy that it was about to fall to the ground. She immediately squatted down, held her forehead in her hands and the teardrops fell into the hollow of her palm.

The whole company held a meeting, two journalists were present too.

"What were your thoughts during the emergency?" They were probably eager to spread the news. "A couple of words from each of you will do."

"I thought that since I'm not yet married, my death wouldn't matter, but then again, it would be a pity..." Yuan Yuan the carpenter wasn't very convincing.

"I thought of my mother, she worked so hard all her life to bring me up, but I..." Big Wang, the blacksmith, was a very filial son: in order to be able to look after his blind mother, he had never married.

Then the journalist approached him, "You're the deputy chief of the company, you..."

"I didn't think of anything," leaning against the wall he spoke with indifference. "When you're supposed to live, then live well; when the time comes to die, you just die."

The journalist flipped a blank page in his notebook.

"Must I say something?" He saw that the journalist was having a hard time. "Could I raise some questions?"

"Sure, sure." Full of hope, the journalist twisted off the cap of his pen again.

"In one flood, four young people have died from our company alone, what are the leaders thinking? Honour rolls replace the wreaths and elegiac couplets, is this a way to solve the problems? And the newspapers make a great story out of it, advocating the revolutionary spirit of not being afraid to die. In the future, couldn't you perhaps write the kind of article that calls for measures to be taken so that people won't die for nothing?" He waved his fist, agitated, as if he could only work off his anger and calm down by punching a hole in something.

The page in the journalist's notebook remained blank.

A solemn silence fell over the meeting hall.

Xiaoxiao's eyes never left him. She wished that he would go on speaking, go on speaking endlessly. This was what everyone felt deep down. It was the truth. It was the truth that no one dared to utter. He said it, and perhaps he would be sent back to the stable. What was there to fear, people had died, how could one still worry about losing a little something?

The seat behind him had remained empty all along, how she felt like moving up to that seat...

Two days passed, it seemed that the flood waters had washed out her heart too.

Xiaoxiao was always very excited at the opportunity to go to the stable to give him his medicine and injections.

"This is the last injection... You're almost okay now..." She shut the medicine box. "I'll be off now." But in her heart she was still thinking: the last injection...she hesitated.

"Wait a minute." His tone of voice had changed.

"Is there something else?..." She didn't turn around. He was leaning up against the stacked-up quilt, his eyes focused on his bundled legs.

"Is there something else?...

"No, nothing, just go!" Suddenly irritated, he waved his hand, turned onto his side and pulled out a book from underneath his pillow.

She left, feeling uncertain, and closed the door quietly. But as soon as she was outside, her heart curiously began to throb, there was no stopping it. Does he... It had crossed her mind, but she hadn't dared to think anymore about it...

The door opened again, she stood silently against the door frame.

He turned towards her, the book slid out of his hand down onto the *kang*.

At the time of the emergency, did you really not think about anything? Didn't it occur to you that there were things on your mind that you had never had a chance to tell anyone? Would she have the courage to approach him like this?

"You'd better leave now, you shouldn't delay giving other people their injections." His hand rested heavily on the *kang* as if he was doing his utmost to hold something down.

"Did you really not think of anything that day?" she asked him after all.

"Actually, I would have liked to think of something, but there was just no way I could. With the torrent rushing towards you, all you could do was to charge back like a crazed lion. In the heat of action there was no fear at all, even if you were about to die, you were happy. Fully exposed there is nothing to worry about. When you returned alive, however, there was just that much more to think about." He smiled self-mockingly.

"Like what?" she asked in a light voice, pretending to be unperturbed. She wanted to hear him say it, and yet she was afraid that he should really say it...

"Everything."

"Can you tell me about it?" She blushed.

"Okay." He thought for a minute, then said, "But not today."

"But when?" Right now. At this moment. She didn't want to continue tugging at her own heart so that it wouldn't jump out.

Obscurity is wonderful. Then again, nothing is as unbearable as obscurity.

He paused, then suddenly he sprung it on her: "I've been thinking...I've been thinking that it's about time we build a dam, if not..."

Like a drifting, buoyant balloon, Xiaoxiao's heart burst with a "bang." She responded unwittingly with a "yes...a dam..." She got up. She wanted to leave.

"I've also been thinking..." he continued, "I've been wanting to ask you whether or not you plan to settle down here?" His body was completely relaxed now, as if he had finally got rid of something.

"I've never really thought about it seriously," she said frankly, and slowly sat down again. For a long time she had been sad because she couldn't go to university. She had cried when they saw Xiao Fang off. Had she been sad about parting, had she felt sorry for herself, or was it that he had only recommended Xiao Fang at the Party branch meeting?...

"Are you willing to think it over? Seriously..."

She panicked a little and yet, inexplicably, she nodded her head.

She ought to say that the greatest happiness would be to live together with the one you love.

She had given it a lot of thought. She loved him, she loved him so much.

"As long as you are here, I'll stay and build the dam together with you..." she wrote on a small piece of paper.

He solemnly folded the little piece of paper and placed it in the gold-plated cigarette box that he always carried with him.

Eventually, she left anyway. Nobody had time for the dam, one campaign followed another...

Having left him, having left the land, she focused all of her cherished memories, her feelings, her guilty conscience and her thought into the tip of her pen. She wrote a lot. Every time she had something published she rolled up the magazine and wrapped it neatly, wrote his address on it in regular upright characters...but she would hesitate, and the rolls of meticulously wrapped publications kept piling up on her bookshelf.

Shortly before boarding the plane, she finally stuffed all of them into her suitcase...

Huang Meng finished his lengthy speech, Xiaoxiao couldn't hide herself any longer. She improvised and talked about her novel *Summer's First Thunderstorm* which had won a prize. The oppressive thunder often rumbled in her heart, along with his "I've been thinking...I've been thinking that it's about time we built a dam..." She wrote down his words at the end of the novel.

"Certain things stir you up emotionally, and if you don't write them down, you feel like you owe something and you're never quite at ease." This was indeed her experience. She didn't want to betray her own feelings, to let down her own life. "Write about the things in life that touch you and move other people to live their lives well."

"What do you think should be emphasized in creative writing?" a girl, who appeared to be a middle school student, got up and asked. She was in the front row.

"I emphasize my own feelings." Xiaoxiao immediately felt kindly disposed towards the young girl who asked so courageously.

"She's a fan of yours. She's read all your stories several times," the clerk whispered to Xiaoxiao.

Xiaoxiao was touched, and yet she smiled rather regretfully. "Fame," "reputation" and "admiration" used to excite her, but very soon she became indifferent towards it. It was all nothing but the stuff of illusions. When you have it, you have it, when it's gone, it's just gone, there was no need to bother about it. She was very clear-headed. In the past, she had been able to write because there were still passions in her heart. In the course of time, however, certain feelings were lost. She began to feel an emptiness in her heart, like a tree about to wither, unable to spit out a green leaf, incapable of making people feel fresh and new, or feel uplifted.

"...Think it over again, the timing is crucial..." After she had obtained her plane ticket Ling Zhi still wanted to take her to see Director Zhang from the Institute for Literary Research.

"How come you know so many people?"

"When you want to get to know them, you can." He was truly remarkable, he socialized so easily.

"You're really good at mixing with people..." She wasn't sure what to make of him.

"It didn't come naturally to me either." He smiled wryly. "What can you do? You get transferred from the countryside to a factory, from there you struggle to get into university, when you graduate you worry about job assignments, once in the work unit you have to open up new prospects. Step by step, if you can't rely on yourself, who else is there? What is 'opportunity?' It's making sure that all your efforts won't be wasted."

They had met at an art exhibition, and when they talked about Picasso, Van Gogh, Renoir, and contemporary western literary trends, Ling Zhi was never at a loss for words. But, as soon as they stepped into the home of Director Zhang from the Institute for Literary Research, he refuted everything:

"Western culture, with its high level of materialism, has drowned the people as well as their spirit, and this is the kind of foundation upon which these schools of art have been built..."

She was stunned.

"What exactly is your opinion?" she once asked him earnestly. Sometimes he was very clear, at other times he seemed shrouded in mist.

"To be too extreme and too pure is, on the contrary, to be too fragile, you'll collapse at the first blow. If you want to get a footing in life nowadays, you have to stick close to those who grasp the real power." He exposed himself, without hiding anything.

She had been about to stroke him but couldn't help withdrawing her hand, as if there had been a strong repellent force that might have instantly pushed her back a few steps. She had to admit that he was truly powerful. But as a friend, or even something more than a friend, she preferred someone who had maintained a real purity of heart.

"Life is motley, you can't make a clean break with the past, nor can you completely accept whatever's new. We are always patching up our lives with what's new and what we have inherited..."

"There's something else I have to attend to..." She didn't feel like listening anymore, so she crossed the street and walked away.

Whenever they spoke it was never very joyful. Sometimes she really wanted to find a peaceful sandy beach, and just lie there comfortably and calmly think it all over. Then she wouldn't have to listen to the constant noise of honking cars...

When the meeting was over, each of them was surrounded by several enthusiastic amateur writers.

"Hurry up and eat, otherwise there'll be complaints from the dining hall," the clerk shooed off each of the "surrounding groups."

As they were leaving, Xiaoxiao inadvertently looked back and saw the girl who had raised the question. She was putting the tables and chairs in order, her movements dexterous and efficient.

"Go on and get something to eat." The clerk took the broom from her hand and spoke to Xiaoxiao, "These kids just don't get to read that much, they're good people, enthusiastic and eager students. Some of them had to travel a day over the mountain by foot before they could catch the bus, so that they could be here to listen to your talks. They want to learn, but it is not so easy."

"I'll talk a bit more in the afternoon." Xiaoxiao suddenly felt some kind of responsibility: she must tell them all about what she had seen, heard and learned. They could write of their lives in the Great Northern Wilderness. This was a very special stretch of land. Numerous people who devoted the energy of a lifetime to develop the area lived here.

Him!

5

"Miss, let's take a walk by the river." The young girl came looking for her after dinner.

"Okay, let's go!" Xiaoxiao agreed, she felt like going for a walk too.

The young girl amicably took Xiaoxiao's arm.

The Songhua River is magnificent, gentle, clear, as it quietly flows through tall mountains, over fields, through forests and through the developing cities. It possesses inexhaustible life and yet remains perfectly silent.

Xiaoxiao was very fond of this river. Here on the beautiful, still river bank she had spent three of her life's happiest days and nights, together with him...

There days of marriage leave, no banquets, no bridal chamber, no well-wishing guests, just the two of them. By the side of the river they broke off a few branches and set up a small green shelter in the grass. There they lay, completely relaxed, thinking about nothing, just listening to the splashing of the water. Now and again they'd take a walk down towards the river's lower reaches, all the way down to where there weren't any more boats, or human habitation, down there the mountain flowers were in full bloom, red, yellow and purple...

Along the way, she picked flowers and hummed a tune, "In that far-off land, there flowed a beautiful river..."

He started singing, too, his voice bold and vigorous, "Oh, the Great Nothern Wilderness, we got rabbits and wolves...but not enough gals."

"Shame on you."

"But it's true, in those days they really treasured you women." In the shabby stables he had grown up listening to this song.

"And now?"

"Now, we need to get the women to treasure the land."

"Nobody treasures this place!" She lashed out at him with her bouquet of mountain flowers.

"Of course people treasure it. Xiao Fang insisted on returning after she finished university!" The breeze from the river was playing with his open shirt, he straightened his broad, firm chest, "After all, the Great Nothern Wilderness has a certain charm."

She suddenly stopped talking, she walked ahead of him, the bouquet of mountain flowers dangling from her hand.

An orange light shone timidly next to the dike.

"Which farm is that?" Xiaoxiao brought her thoughts back to the present.

"The Seven Star Farm."

"I'm from the Seven Star Farm."

"Really?" The girl raised her brows in surprise, "too bad when you people were here I was still at school. Our company is the most remote one, people seldom came to visit in the mountains and we hardly ever went outside either. Later on a batch of young intellectuals came and it was as if a big department store had just opened in the company. It got much livelier."

They felt much closer now.

"What are you doing in your company?"

"I'm a teacher."

A teacher? Xiaoxiao couldn't imagine it, this young, childish looking girl, her hands behind her back, seriously and solemnly walking up and down between the rows of school desks.

"You don't think I look like a teacher, do you?" The girl was sharp. "Did we have any choice? After you people left, the elementary schools in all of the companies were short of teacher and, as soon as I graduated, I was assigned to teach. My legs were shaking all through my first lesson, I couldn't speak without stuttering, my throat went dumb, and the pupils murmured that they couldn't understand. I was so nervous that I started crying. But it was no use crying, I had to go to class again the next day..." Like a child who felt wronged, she pouted.

Xiaoxiao pulled out her arm, put it around the girl's skinny shoulders and hugged her tightly. Such a young age, such a small body, already carrying a heavy responsibility. Was it painful? She stroked her lightly, she felt slightly guilty...

"You should come to visit our company, to see our school —— the famous 'Tent School' —— it's green inside, pitched halfway up the mountain and the mountain is green too." The girl's words were poetic and picturesque. "Now we have built a small house and we have painted the doors and windows green as well."

Xiaoxiao had heard that it was a newly established company. To begin with they only had a few tents.

"Teacher Fang set up our Tent School all by herself."

"Xiao Fang? She..." Xiaoxiao hadn't left when Xiao Fang came back to the farm after her graduation. Xiaoxiao saw before her the picture of someone very common looking, a round face, small eyes, a flat nose. No one was likely to notice her in a group of good-looking girls. But she wasn't like everyone else, her attitude towards life made people remember her. Like the day the Farm Headquarters had prepared a welcome party, they made red flowers, mounted frames for awards, but when the party was about to begin, they couldn't find Xiao Fang... All along Xiaoxiao had admired Xiao Fang's self-reliance, she couldn't be like that herself.

"Do you also know Teacher Xiao Fang?" the girl asked, as if feeling a bit mutt. "A few years ago someone said that she was a typical example of the extreme 'left,' and she was made to write a self-criticism...but I felt that she was genuine and sincere."

"Has she been teaching all along?"

"Immediately after her return the Central Farm appointed her to deputy secretary of the Farm Party Committee, but she declined. She insisted on going out to a company to work as a teacher and chose this poorest and most remote company of ours. We were sixteen pupils, spread over six grades, and she taught all of us. I'm a student of hers myself. At the beginning of the year, Farm Chief Li nominated Teacher Xiao Fang as dean of the school in the Farm Headquarters, and everybody endorsed his nomination."

"What's your Farm Chief like?" Xiaoxiao couldn't help asking.

"In terms of what?"

She wanted to know everything about him.

"Were you in the same company?" The expression that suddenly swept over the girl's eyes was full of suspicion. Obviously, she knew everything about him...

"No...just asking..." Xiaoxiao avoided the girl's focused eyes.

"I've written a story about our Farm Chief."

"Has it been published?"

"I never sent it in. I'm not satisfied with it myself, it's not very realistic. He has weak points too..."

She's more mature than I, Xiaoxiao thought. At her age I only saw life from an idealistic perspective.

After the wheat harvest, the entire company had three days off.

"Let's go down to the riverside." Xiaoxiao pulled a bright red swimsuit out of her case. She'd brought it along but it had been sitting in the trunk. She had long wanted to return to the Songhua River, to immerse herself in the clear, cool waters...but they'd been busy all the time from the spring sowing up until the wheat harvest. When they returned home in the evening they were so exhausted, they'd collapse on the *kang*, and before she had time to even imagine what colour the water in the river was, she would hear the sound of him snoring. "We should just take it easy, relax a bit now."

He was sitting on the door step, his head bent over the pail that he was repairing, and he didn't respond.

"Did you hear what I said?" She draped the swimsuit over his back and its two straps dangled in front of his chest. "Stop working, let's go enjoy ourselves."

"Don't do that." He whisked the swimsuit straps over behind his head.

"What, are you afraid they'll say that you, too, harbour 'sentimentalism of the petty bourgeoisie?'" Xiaoxiao was disgusted with this vague label that had been attached to her. But each time there was a session of "fight selfishness, repudiate revisionism," someone always had to bring it up.

"Of course I'm not."

"So are you coming or not?"

"How could I go now? There's a pile of work to be done, the courtyard fence needs mending, the private plot has to be tidied up, the toilet needs cleaning...and tomorrow I must go to Huangdian to do a survey, the tractor is soon going up there to open up the wasteland." He knocked on the pail a couple of times.

"Well, so much for you!" She flung the swimsuit onto the pile of quilts.

He didn't humour her. She wasn't quite sure when exactly he'd stopped humoring her.

Xiaoxiao fetched an armful of willow twigs and angrily began mending the fence. It was after all a small yard. Eggplants, cucumbers, tomatoes, the more the better, and yet they couldn't replace her interest and keenness in reading novels, watching films, hiking up the mountains and fooling around in the water. In middle school, she'd been like a small bird, flying all over the place. In the summer, she'd be rowing a boat on Kunming Lake; in the fall, she'd be hiking up Xiangshan Mountain to see the red leaves; in the winter, she'd be admiring the snowy scenes in Beihai Park. Despite the fact that she'd made up a resolution: to forget about "her" as she was in the past, to "thoroughly remould herself," it seemed as if her "resolution" wasn't in the least reliable. It wasn't easy to get three days off and she wanted to change into a wild goose so she could fly out of the little courtyard, fly to distant places, see something new. But he...

As soon as darkness fell they lay down on the *kang*. No films, and no TV either.

"I'll sing a song for you." At lunch she'd had a lovely meal of two egg-and-onion pancakes that he had baked, and her anger had disappeared. She rested her hand on the pillow and began humming the songs that she used to love singing:

> *Let's begin pulling the oars, and plough the waves in the little*
> *   boat...*
> *The sun has set behind the mountain, the peaceful sound of the*
> *   bell is ringing.*
> *Girl I've always loved to sing, let me sing you a basketful...*

One song after another. She recalled the rehearsals with the Red Pioneer Choir in the Children's Palace; she thought of the solos accompanied by an old organ in the music class; and she thought of how the fluttering flags on the way to summer camp had drawn a choir of mighty singing voices.

"Did you like it?" she asked him. She was intoxicated by her own singing. It was a long time since she had last sung like this. "Did you like it?" she turned and asked him again.

He was asleep, he'd fallen asleep long ago. He was already sound asleep.

Suddenly, she felt hurt. Not that she needed his praise, she only wished that he would have listened quietly to the songs that she loved so much. Of course, he was very tired, he had finished up all the work in an afternoon.

He was reclining on the pillow, breathing very regularly. She looked at him for a long while, she had never watched him this carefully before. She used to feel that beyond her little mud cottage was loneliness, and apart from the slogans like "Fear neither hardship nor death," "Resolve to not be afraid of sacrificing yourself...," nothing was allowed. The little mud cottage gave her a different type of life. In this moment, however, with him lying next to her, she felt indescribably lonely. She needed more than a few sweet words after a quarrel.

One of the most painful experiences of growing up is probably the discovery that nobody is perfect, especially those you love. Furthermore, no particular way of life is as beautiful and happy as you imagine it to be.

She walked on the long stone dike. A sculpture of a young girl is standing tall and upright next to the tower, she seems to be running towards you on tiptoe to greet you, her eyes are narrow, a soft gauze scarf flutters from her raised hand. Her skin is smooth and white, it makes you feel that countless live cells, the heart and blood are all jumping for joy.

Once upon a time she, too, had run towards life in this way. But life was grim.

"You're still awake?" He switched on the light.

"No, I just woke up." She rolled onto her side with her back to him. For several nights in a row, she hadn't slept much. Each minute seemed to drag. Everyday someone came by to say good-bye. They were all leaving.

Back then, when they had dashed out here with the red banner held high, they touched a lot of people with their vow to "take root for a lifetime!" But who had ever thought about what "a lifetime" really meant? Those three days of happiness by the Songhua River, she had immersed herself deeply into the beauty and mystique of the river. Now, the mystique had been shattered, the sole contents of their lives were contained in the little adobe cottage and a vegetable garden. If they wanted to eat in the summer they had to plant in the spring.

If she left, her life might take on a different look —— broad vistas, profession, heaven and earth, the future...

That was also "a lifetime!"

"Here you go, eat." That morning, he had fried three eggs for her. It was obvious that she had lost weight.

She forced herself to have a bite and felt like throwing up. She pushed the bowl away. "I'm not hungry, you eat it."

He looked at her, with his chopsticks he pushed the three eggs to the edge of the bowl. "There's no point in worrying so much."

It wasn't that she had gone looking for "worries."

"Get some sleep." That evening he laid out the quilt for her.

She just sat next to the window, expressionlessly. She didn't talk much anymore.

"Come on, sing me a song. Back then..." He sincerely tried to cheer her up.

"My throat is sore." She silently went out, leaning against the gate to the little courtyard she watched the cold crescent moon with terror.

He walked to and fro inside, fidgeting. His shadow flashed back and forth on the window pane.

She saw him. She commanded herself to go back inside.

"Get some sleep, your eyes are all bloodshot." He turned her around, his hands on her shoulders.

"It's because of the lamplight."

"In three days you have only eaten two bowls of porridge..."

"I have no appetite, my schedule is too tight, we're approaching the mid-term exams."

"No. Yesterday afternoon you were alone in the classroom, crying."

"No, I wasn't. Don't listen to people's gossip."

"I saw you myself." He looked at her full of concern and expectations. "You wouldn't..."

She was afraid of the look in his eyes. "I would like to sleep now." She quickly slipped under the quilt.

He lay down too.

They were silent for a long while.

"Just tell me the truth!" Suddenly he got up on his arms, looking down at her. He could sense it, everything. But he so hoped that he was mistaken. He wasn't willing to move the lever that was still able to hold up the little cottage. Even though the fulcrum had started moving.

She closed her eyes, two teardrops moved between her lashes and she ground her teeth into the quilt. "I want to leave." "I'd like to leave." "Should I leave or not?" "Do you approve of me leaving?" Which phrase was the better? None of them clearly expressed her state of mind. Before she knew it, nine years had gone by, and what had they achieved? No trace of any dam, the school was still as backward as before. They worked their butts off at sowing and harvesting the fields, and still they incurred losses year after year. She deeply regretted that her fleeting youth had been so colourless and that it had been wasted without accomplishing anything. Life went by so fast. What else was there for her to do? She was afraid of answering her own question. She simply had one wish: she wanted to change. If she made a go of it now, it might not be too late. It was so difficult, such a simple sentence and still she hesitated uttering it.

"Say something!" His heart was burning, as if it had caught fire. At the time of the wedding, someone had warned him: "I'm only afraid that she's not dependable!" He had been very certain of himself, believed that his own strength could overcome all of her qualms. But in this he had been mistaken.

Xiaoxiao sat up. Just tell him, he has to be told anyway. Leaving or not leaving, both ways would hurt. She thought that he ought to forgive her.

"I've been at the company to ask for an application to leave the farm because of family difficulties." She wanted to look at him while talking, like when they normally discussed their family affairs. Yet she lowered her head.

"Why didn't you discuss it with me?"

"I thought you would approve."

"I don't approve!" he roared.

Her heart trembled.

"Didn't you say that you'd stay here forever?" In his eyes there was reproach, appeal, hurt and a thread of hope.

"But...you and I are so different. I...everyone else has left!" No, that wasn't important. She had so much on her mind, couldn't express it clearly. She just clung to his arm.

"That's enough." He brushed her away. "Why couldn't you have made it clear before that you and I are not alike! Not alike!" He could endure all kinds of inequality, only he couldn't accept that people's personalities were unequal. Especially when it came from her eyes and mind.

"You...I never expected you to..." Xiaoxiao lost control too, she bit her lips and spoke out through the crack between her teeth. "You, you're so selfish!" It was the first time that she stared at him with the eyes of a stranger, her hands grabbed even tighter onto his arm, as if she'd fallen into the river and, while struggling, suddenly caught hold of a floating log.

"Selfish?" He waved his arm violently, his tightly clenched fist flew up. "Just go! Just go to hell!" His fist hit her right on the nose.

She immediately fell down. As if welding, sparks burst in front of her eyes. Drops of blood trickled out between the fingers that she held up to her nose.

He unclenched his fist and quickly went over to help her up. Full of hatred, she pushed him away. She felt like crying, crying really loudly. But she just clamped her teeth firmly together.

The baby started crying.

He jumped off the *kang* and pushed the door open.

She lifted the baby up into her arms, buried her face in the small quilt, and tears began streaming.

The late night wind from the mountains swept up the withered leaves which rustled as they whirled about in front of the door.

She sat silently by the baby that was soon fast asleep again.

He smoked one cigarette after another. "Ritsch, ritsch," the matches lit up and then died out...

Next day after class she went home and threw herself on the *kang* .

He came in with a basin full of hot water and sat down by her side for a while.

She wanted to push him away again but didn't move.

He wrung the steaming hot towel and gently put it over her black, swollen nose.

She didn't want to open her eyes and look at him.

"Does it still hurt?" He stroked her hair.

Tears trickled down from the corners of her eyes. Love, it's the world's purest reconciliation.

He fumbled about his pocket and pulled out an application form. "Go on, sign it, the company is going to submit another batch to the Farm Headquarter."

She didn't take it.

He took out a pen, "I'll help you sign it!"

"No," she threw herself to his shoulder and began crying, "I, I..." She hadn't explained to him how she felt at all. She was a small goldfish who could swim out into the great ocean. She was yearning for the ocean. Did he understand that?

"Don't say anymore." He stopped her.

"What about the baby?..." It was another difficult matter to bring up. She wanted to take the child with her. She was his mother. The child would grow older each day, he would smile, he would learn to grab hold of things, turn over, sit up, he would learn to talk...like a comic book printed in her heart, so vivid, so funny, so very fascinating and absorbing.

"The baby will stay with me. You can only change your own residence this time. That's the rule."

"No." She covered the form with both hands.

He removed her hands, "I can take good care of the baby."

She clutched the form tightly. Her hand trembled.

"Give it to me."

"I'll think it over again."

Nothing was as painful as thinking this over.

How long did it take? She couldn't remember.

One day she'd decide upon something, the next day she'd change her mind, would she decide upon something else the day after?

One day, the political instructor handed her the crumpled form. "It's been approved, you'd better get ready to move." In the last couple of years he repeated that sentence countless times.

There were a few red stamps on the form, her fate had been decided upon.

He had signed the form.

Now that she was leaving, she longed to hear him say something.

In silence, he helped her nail up the luggage trunk, he packed down the dried fungus, mushrooms, hedgehog hydnum, hazelnuts...when everything was in order he finally said to her, "I'm going to attend a short-term training course at the agriculture university, so I won't be able to see you off."

"What time do you have to register?" They were really going to part. Suddenly she felt as if she had only just moved into the small mud cottage and life hadn't quite begun yet...

"I'm leaving tomorrow."

"Can't you put it off two days?"

He shook his head. Obviously he could choose not to take the short-term training course, or he could start next semester. But he insisted on going...

He didn't let her see him off. As soon as the day broke, he slung his small school bag over his shoulder and leaped into the front seat of the tractor which was just starting up.

She pushed open the paper-plastered window. The early spring wind was still piercing. A thin layer of frost remained on the window. She could see the tractor stopping at the main road but she couldn't see him. The tractor windows were also covered by frost.

Suddenly, a clear spot about the size of a fist appeared on the tractor window, and gradually his face became visible, then his eyes. But the warm air that he breathed out soon blurred the clear spot on the window. He wiped it with his hand, his face and his eyes became visible again.

Had he discovered that the window was open in the little cottage? And had he seen her standing there by the window?...

It was completely dark now. The cars on the road drove faster and faster, one after another, like motor boats skimming over the water. There were no motor boats on the river, and no ships either, just layers of fine waves, light bouncing movements.

The movements of the waves were blind. In the end, they led nowhere...

Xiaoxiao watched the slow flow of the river, she felt lost. After she went away, she had worked very hard and gradually she had found a niche, she had made a name for herself, she had a new world...she had everything, yet she had neither worries nor delight, grief nor joy, nobody needed her concern, nobody needed her care, and nobody needed her to contribute. Still, she sometimes felt that she had nothing. The only things she had to leave behind were the few magazines which published her work.

Her work, the magazines, could they really be left behind?

"You don't like smiling, do you?" The girl was very perceptive. Xiaoxiao smiled without any comment.

"Something is weighing on your mind." The girl looked at her. "I can read people's hands, let me see yours."

Half-believing, Xiaoxiao put out her hand.

The girl carefully examined all the lines in Xiaoxiao's palm, as if they really indicated something.

"From reading your hand I can see that you are a person who is hurting deep inside, your life-span isn't long. You have a brilliant career but your life is not a happy one. You're very intelligent, but too much intelligence often carries with it a great deal of worry..." The girl's way of speaking and her judgement were like those of a grown-up, one rich in experience.

"Will I make a fortune?" Xiaoxiao asked as a joke. Her stomach kept tightening. Did all of this really show in her hand? "Tell me how to do it, will you?" She unfolded her palm.

"No, I won't, it's a family secret that's been handed down from generation to generation," the girl said mischievously.

"I don't believe you." Xiaoxiao withdrew her hand. "It's all your own feelings. You're very clever, too."

"You don't believe me?" The girl got very excited. "While looking at your hand I was thinking, why all this pain with such a shining career? If I could write something and get it published I'd be enormously happy."

The girl was, after all, just a young girl.

"Wait till you do publish something and you'll learn that happiness is not being published."

"What is it, then?" The girl was bending over the railing on the dike, then all of a sudden she asked again, "Miss, do you like this river?"

"Yes, I like it."

"Why?"

"The surging waters can wash everything, just like the earth can bury everything. No matter who, everyone is insignificant and equal before this river, and status, wealth, a moment of great renown and influence, they merely seem worthless. The only valuable thing is the throbbing heart inside your chest." Xiaoxiao actually felt much better, as if she really had been cleansed by the river.

"You express yourself so well."

"Those weren't my own words."

"Whose were they?"

"Your chiefs." Xiaoxiao blurted out. He had said that, by the side of the river...

"Oh, you..." The girl seemed to realize something, she fixed her eyes on Xiaoxiao.

"We were...quite close." Xiaoxiao mumbled.

The girl knowingly withdrew her gaze, then suddenly, "It's not easy to be the chief," she added sadly.

"How come?"

"As soon as he was appointed, he reorganized the leading body, from the Party organizations to the various companies, he replaced quite a few people who would neither shit nor get off the pot. Then, he turned to the dam. He got rid of the original temporary Party committee at the site, dubbed "loafers on the job" by the Shanghai intellecturals, and thus offended a group of people who should not be offended. Most recently, he has been on site to personally direct the work on the dam. The rainy season is approaching and if they don't finish the dam in a hurry, a series of mountain torrents will cause a lot of hardship among our companies at the foot of the mountains. I listen to the weather forecast each day, the probability of a rainstorm is high. But building the dam in a rush is also not so simple..."

The dam. The dam. Always the dam!

He'd wanted it for so many years. But how many difficulties and obstructions could there be? A rather faint premonition made her uneasy.

Furthermore, they might get a rainstorm!...

Xiaoxiao quickened her pace, her heart was in a turmoil. "I'll take the night train back to the farm. I won't participate in the reception and the banquet!" So she decided.

"I would really like to hear you talk some more." The girl was so eager.

Xiaoxiao wasn't in the mood any longer.

"Let's go, let's walk a little faster." She seemed to be pushing herself.

There were fewer pedestrians in the street.

A car drove by, its lights swept over them...

6

She climbed onto a horse cart.

Three big brown horses, like three brothers, holding up their long necks, running with even and straight steps, the rhythmic sound of their hoofs was relaxed and lively. Xiaoxiao was fond of going by horse cart, jolting and swaying at a regular pace, listening to the driver singing ditties with the whip in his hand, and making small talk with the grannies and aunties in their kerchiefs, or guessing the shape of the changing clouds above: doesn't that one look like a sika deer? No, it looks like a muddle-headed sika deer...what a treat it was.

She was really back now!

The sky was still so blue and the earth still so black. The corn with its white tassels towered over the soy beans in the furrows, kids were herding sheep along the dirt roads in between the fields, then there were the little girls, covered with bits of straw, running barefooted around the fields, and the bright red tractors roaring close by and far away. Everything was so very familiar, nothing had changed.

She sat to the right side of the horse, the driver was a spry old fellow.

"Where are you from?"

"Beijing."

"Visiting relatives?"

"En..." she answered with difficulty.

"Oh you're here on business!" A content smile appeared on the old man's dark brown face, revealing a mouth full of extraordinarily white teeth, just like his horses.

"Was it a good harvest this year?"

"The wheat was scorched, the soy beans grew well, we should get about two tons per hectare. When it's all been harvested we should easily make a profit of about 700,000-800,000 yuan." He had an account book at the back of his head.

"The dam must be finished now?" Xiaoxiao couldn't help asking.

"Oh...the dam..." The old man hummed and hawed and looked back vigilantly.

At the back sat a man dressed in a dark-grey dacron coat, his face was as yellow as his two nicotine-stained fingers, and he held tightly on to the black artificial leather bag in his lap.

"Director, why didn't you have a car pick you up?"

"What car? They're all at the construction site. We almost send the pigs and dogs there." He put a cigarette in his mouth and struck a match with repressed anger.

"This dam...you've been working on it for two years and not a drop of water has flowed from it, but a whole lot of money has sure flowed into it..." The old man's eyes rested resourcefully on the little black artificial leather bag, and then he changed the subject,"Did you go to the central farm?"

The other man pretended not to have heard him, but instead turned towards Xiaoxiao, smiled and asked, "What sort of business are you in ?"

Director Dong! She suddenly recognized him. When they had experimented with the "Criticize Lin Biao, Criticize Confucius" campaign in the company, Director Dong had been the leader of the work team and everybody called him the "smiling face Buddha" behind his back. Whenever he met sombody he would be all smiles and if you asked him about something he would readily promise, "That should go smoothly. That should go smoothly." And that would be the end of it. But if anybody provoked him, things would really move "smoothly" and no time would be lost. Therefore, all the old workers would be careful not to ask him for anything and not to provoke him. Li Juntang had gone against him and consequently had been sent back to the stable. Apparently, the open strife and veiled struggles had never ceased...

"I'm going to the Farm Headquarters." Xiaoxiao was a bit nervous. Does he remember me? she wondered.

"Who are you going to see in the headquarter?"

"I'm going to see...the chief." She couldn't lie and remain calm.

In an instant the smiling expression vanished from Director Dong's eyes.

"You've come from Beijing, how are all the youngsters who moved back there?" The old man interrupted and, seemingly carelessly, he poked Xiaoxiao with his whip.

"They're fine! Fine..."

"To be honest, those youngsters haven't had it easy. When they arrived at first and I saw that each of them was so delicate and fragile, I said to myself: will they be able to stand all the hardship? I watched them as they knelt on the ground to cut beans, levelling the ground with their bums in the air. When they were thirsty, they

drank from the little lake; when they were sleepy, they dozed off
with their hoes; when they were cold, they jumped up and down
around the fire; when they were hungry, they wolfed down three
steamed cornbread buns at once, it was a pitiful sight. Back then,
there was a blackboard by the gate of the company, and though I
can't read I still used to enjoy the bright colours of the characters.
When we had a festival, there would be song and dance performances,
everyone would share in the fun. My little girl used to love
running over to the big dormitories, she had her eyes on things
from Shanghai, one day she wanted someone to bring her a dacron
gown, next day she wanted to buy a pair of fancy leather shoes.
Nowadays, the atmosphere is less friendly." The old man got more
and more agitated.

Director Dong's eyes moved away from Xiaoxiao.

Xiaoxiao was relieved. "When they returned to the city, they,
too, missed this place a lot..."

"People's hearts are all made of flesh, when you have spent
time in a certain place, how can you not have some feelings for it?
Don't say that this is a poor area, some people swear and curse:
'This damned place!' Ha, this very 'damned' place has fostered
more than a few talented people. I hear there are people from our
farm everywhere."

Xiaoxiao would really have liked to write all his words down,
so honest and so kind, so proud and yet so sound.

A truck drove up from behind, Director Dong waved his hand
and immediately the truck was brought to a halt. The driver rolled
down the window, "Director Dong, come have a seat inside."

An old, stooping man made his way out of the cabin and with
much effort he climbed up on the back of the truck and pulled his
collar further up around his neck. With an easy conscience, Director
Dong took a seat in the cabin. The driver winked at the old fellow,
took off his hat and waved, and then sped off.

"Go to hell, bastard!" The old man shook his whip as if he intended to go after the truck.

Xiaoxiao laughed, she felt happy.

"Is he still the director of the political section?"

"The political section doesn't exist any more, so he went down to the construction site and busied himself setting up a temporary Party committee with himself as Party Secretary. This 'Party secretary' did everything but real work. This year, Chief Li took charge of the dam and completely reorganized all the sites. They nevertheless lodged a complaint with the Central Farm."

"Does Chief Li know that?" Xiaoxiao couldn't help but worry.

"I think he expected it." Wielding his whip the old man sighed. "These people are hard to get to, like the ancient trees in the forest, their roots go really deep."

If you couldn't get to them, then what? Wasn't there another attitude towards life? "We're still young and have no power. In order to protect ourselves, we must take advantage of all our connections to develop ourselves. So what if we must compromise our principles? Keep looking at the future..."

Two so completely different attitudes!

Once again, her thoughts went to that bleak autumn rain, that ice cold bench...it was at that moment that she fell in love with him —— such an indomitable heart.

Indomitable. He was still the same.

And she?... She very much wanted to hear more details about the four years since they had parted, especially this past year when he had become the chief...

"Ginger gets hotter with age but a calf is most fierce when born." The old man sounded optimistic. "This chief of ours really likes it hot. At the first enlarged Party committee meeting after his appointment, he raised some points about reforms on the farm. Director Dong wasn't interested and he purposefully kept on talking to the head of the production section who was seated next to him. When Chief Li had finished his speech, he asked in front of the crowd, 'Director Dong, did you understand what I said?' 'Yes, I understood it very well,' Director Dong replied. 'Oh good, then you can repeat to the others each point I just raised.' Chief Li dealt him a head-on blow. Director Dong hummed and hawed and his face just dropped."

She could imagine it. That was just like him!

"Have you come from the Central Farm?" Only now did the old man take a closer look at Xiaoxiao.

"Yes."

"Chief Li also just returned from the Central Farm. I was going to the station to fetch some goods and bumped into him there. If you want to see him, you'll have to go to the construction site."

"And how is his son?" Finally, she could ask what she had wanted to know for several years now.

"He takes care of the kid himself," said the old man, "he could have let the kindergarten take care of him, but whenever he is at the farm headquarters, no matter how late he works, he always comes to take the kid home and looks after him himself. When he goes out to the work team in the company he takes the kid along with him. And he is a good kid too, anywhere they go he never causes any trouble. When they go out into the field and he feels sleepy, he simply crawls up into the tractor and sleeps there; when he's hungry, he goes to the cook and asks him for some steamed, stuffed buns. He's been around to all the companies in the farm. They're very close, father and son. If you ask the kid, 'Where is your mother?' he says, 'my father gave birth to me.'" The old man smiled sadly, "She was a youngster from Beijing, she left a few years ago." There was no reproach in his voice.

"Does the child know his mother?" Xiaoxiao shivered.

"The child has a sense of propriety, he never talks about his mother in front of him."

"What if I want to see the child?"

The old man looked at her suspiciously.

"I, I'm in the same work unit as his mother."

"Oh..." The old man, seemingly lost in thought, gave the horses a couple of lashes. "You can't blame her either. At the time, a whole bunch of them left." He waved the whip, "shooshed," and the horses obediently slowed down. "We're almost there." He pointed ahead.

On the gentle slope of the mountain, a dense stretch of green foliage set off the limitless blue sky, and little spots of red brick sprung up, it was like a small, magical, beautiful island in the big ocean.

She sighed deeply and tried to control her intense heartbeat.

Like a green screen, the thicket of trees linked up with two perpendicular rows of red brick houses and surrounded a small square courtyard. It was quiet in the courtyard, nobody was on the move.

"Xiaoxiao!"

Old Ye, the manager from the office dining hall was pulling a cart full of vegetables. Xiaoxiao rushed over and helped him push.

"When did you get here?"

"Just now."

"Go attend to your business and then come back to eat soon." Old Ye used the same sentence with everyone he met.

In the past, Xiaoxiao regularly came to the Farm Headquarters to eat. Her classmate Little Bao had been transferred to be a clerk in the security section, and whenever they had a day off in the company, they would gather in Little Bao's office, where they pushed the desks together to make up a dining table. Each blue rimmed bowl of crude porcelain was filled with "shredded potatoes," "fried beancurd," "vinegar sautéed cabbage," and then there was a large pot of clear "out of the sleeve" soup to share. They would open up a couple of bottles of "Great Northern Wilderness Liquor," pour it into a mug and take turns drinking —— they had to down a real mouthful too, just like a bunch of forest outlaws.

How happy they were! Bold and unrestrained, boorish, sincere, affectionate. Back in Beijing, Xiaoxiao had tried to find these buddies so they could once again eat out of crude porcelain bowls and drink out of big tea mugs. But none of them had the same capacity for liquor anymore.

Without the collision of laughter and noise from each glass window, the small courtyard of the Farm Headquarters had become still and lifeless.

The switchboard room had been moved to the low-rise club building, the only storeyed building on the farm. Originally this was a small library. Xiaoxiao came here every time she was at the Farm Headquarters but despite that there weren't any good books to speak of.

As she stepped onto the building's wooden staircase Xiaoxiao halted, she seemed once more to hear those footsteps, dong dong, particularly heavy and noisy...

"How many steps can you take in one stride?"

"Three."

"I can take five."

He seemed to have springs underneath his feet, "dong!" "dong!" three bounces and he was at the top.

In the beginning she came to borrow books for herself.

"I'd like to borrow *How Lenin Took Reading Notes* ."

"Li Juntang from your company has it."

"I'd like to take out *Marx in His Young Days* ."

"Li Juntang from your company has it."

......

He had taken out all the books that she wanted to read. After having flipped through the entire card catalogue, she noted a few books down but even those weren't available. She felt depressed. She had had a whole box full of her own books that she had shipped out wrapped in her quilt. But the box had been searched, the political instructor looked at a page in Mao Dun's *Midnight* and upon reading a few words he patted the book and yelled: "Pornographic, obscene!" A whole box full of books had been confiscated...

"Deputy chief, are you going to the Farm Headquarters to return some books?" Eventually she couldn't bear it any longer, she had to ask him.

"Why?"

"You've occupied all the good ones."

"Let's go tomorrow at lunch." He smiled.

For the first time, they went together to the Farm Headquarters library.

"Aren't you distressed about all those books of yours?" he asked on their way over.

"I've forgotten them all!" she said feeling wronged.

"Not a single one is missing, I've taken care of them. When you want to read them just come over to my place to pick them up."

"Really? You, you're not afraid..."

"I was afraid that they would be burnt as cigarette paper." He smiled cunningly. "I've read them all..."

The books were hidden in the stable, nobody went there. She was very grateful.

"Are you going to the library?" From then on she would ask him whenever they were off in the company.

"I'm going this afternoon."

They didn't go to borrow books. There weren't any books to borrow.

"How many steps can you take in one stride?"

"Three."

"I can take five."

In their eyes the small building already wasn't a library any more...

The small building was still there. The library wasn't. And there were no more sounds of footsteps... Xiaoxiao slowly walked up the stairs, "I've come to see my son..." She made an effort to dispel those memories.

"Who are you looking for? A tall girl with long braided hair came out. She was probably the switchboard operator.

"Is Little Tie Han here?" She pronounced his name stiffly, he had changed their son's name. She had just been at the kindergarten and the teacher had told her that Little Tie Han was in the switchboard room.

"No, he's not here. But he will be soon. Chief Li let him make a call every day at noon." The girl whisked her braids away from her face and stepped aside. "Please have a seat."

Over by the window, there were two old-fashioned telephones, above and beneath which two rows of sockets for the phone connections. Several black wires crisscrossed like small, thin snakes and were pugged into the sockets, small copper plates were popping noisily. The indicator lamp lit up.

"This was originally the library, wasn't it?" Xiaoxiao said as if talking to herself.

"Look over there where they're building that high-rise." The girl pointed outside. "That's where our farm's cultural centre is going to be: the theatre, the film projection team, the library, they're all going to be in there. This was one of Chief Li's first initiatives."

With her slender fingers, she plucked at one of the crossing wires. "Chief Li is talking to someone from the production section. Just to get started with the building, he went over to the production section to make his case. The head of the production section and Director Dong..." She shut up. She probably realized that she had already said too much.

Xiaoxiao stared at the earphones hooped around the girl's head, it seemed she could hear his voice, full and deep each word pronounced clearly and without repetition.

Does he still remember my voice? She wanted to put on the earphones, ask about the dam, ask about other things...though he wouldn't talk about himself on the phone...

The door opened, a small boy strode in like a little tiger. "I'm here!" He announced loudly, his voice sounded natural and self-assured.

"Little Xiaoxiao!" Xiaoxiao immediately fixed her eyes on him. In her memory, there were only a few photographs and they couldn't speak, had no voice and only showed a certain expression. But here, in front of her, was a child —— alive and kicking —— who seemed to have stepped right out of those photographs. He looked the same: the eyes, the nose, the mouth and yet he seemed so much like a stranger. He'd grown a lot, his wondrous eyes now had the expression of someone who could observe and think.

She just stared at her son. In her dreams, he would always open up his arms, run over to her and intimately bury his chubby face in her bosom. But this wasn't a dream.

Her eyes moistened. She really wanted to give him a big hug, to kiss his thin lips, to kiss his broad forehead and his pudgy cheeks. She wanted to say to him, "Tomorrow is your birthday, here is a little car for you, it's electric, it'll run by itself." He had loved cars ever since he was a baby. Whenever the big bus from the Farm Headquarters came out to the company and blow its horn, he would cry out that he wanted to go see it. She still thought of bringing him back with her to Beijing, to take him to the zoo to see the elephants and the panda; to take him to the planetarium to see the stars and the moon...she wanted to repay her obligation as a mother.

Little Tie Han's eyes swept over her and then he went straight to the telephone. "Is my daddy still at the dam today?" The clever little thing crawled up on the woman's knees and dialled the familiar number of the line that went across the room. "Is someone phoning the dam?"

"It's your dad."

"Hurry up and tell him that I'm here! I have something to tell him."

"He's talking business with someone from the production section." She took off the earphones. "Listen."

Little Tie Han held his ears closer and blinked, "Auntie, are they fighting?"

"They are not fighting, they are discussing. There's some divergence of views."

"What is 'divergence?'" Little Tie Han's eyes opened wide.

"Divergence..." The girl couldn't think of a good explanation. "Go ask auntie over there."

"Auntie ——" Little Tie Han cordially dragged out the tone.

Auntie! When she left, he was only a year old and was able to mumble mama. It sounded so sweet.

"Auntie ——" Little Tie Han called again.

"Divergence..." It was as if she couldn't think. She wanted to say something that would appeal to her son's dim memories, even if it should only feel vaguely familiar.

"Aha, aha." The girl spoke lightly on the phone, "Chief Li, your son is here..." She couldn't help feeling a little worried since she had just heard the violent conversation.

"Oh good!" The voice coming from the phone sounded exhausted but, at the same time, it sounded peaceful, as if it had just been soothed.

"Daddy!" Little Tie Han shouted as soon as he grabbed the phone, "my tummy ache is all gone, I took some medicine, one yellow pill and two white ones, the auntie at the clinic says I'll be fine tomorrow."

"......"

"Really!" Little Tie Han smiled contentedly, turned his head and said, "Daddy says that when they finish the dam, he'll take me there to swim."

"......"

"Listen to this, Little Ming's mum and dad had a fight and his mum was so angry that she ran off, she doesn't care about him any more, she'd been gone for two days. Little Ming was crying. What do you think I should do?" Little Tie Han sat straight up as if he was giving a work report.

"......"

"O.K., I'll tell Little Ming a story." Tie Han was happy again, he swung his legs back and forth. "Should I tell him the story about brother dog?"

"......"

"Right, okay." Little Tie Han jumped down on the floor.

"What story did your father want you to tell Little Ming?" The girl removed the line.

"The Mother's Tale." As if revealing a secret, Little Tie Han added in a low voice, "My dad really likes that story, he's told it to me lots of times. I know it all by heart now."

"Did you like it? I'll tell you another one..." Xiaoxiao seemed to hear that joyful voice again, so gentle, like a warm breeze in spring.

"I'm off!" Little Tie Han said loudly. "Bye, bye auntie!" He waved at the girl.

"Bye auntie!" Then he waved at Xiaoxiao.

Xiaoxiao slowly lifted her hand, it was stiff and heavy.

"Weren't you looking for him?" The girl reminded her.

"Oh...yes." Xiaoxiao mechanically walked toward Little Tie Han. She had been looking for him, just to see him.

Now she had seen him. Her son looked like him, his contours, his bearing, his temper, even his expression. The boy was his.

"Auntie, were you looking for me?"

Xiaoxiao nodded. Then, as if to deny it, she shook her head. She wanted to take Little Tie Han's hand.

Her own hand was trembling.

7

This was where he lived now.

The yard, enclosed by a fence of branches, was very big, but deserted, there wasn't even a chicken coop. In the northwest corner was a bird cage on top of a pile of uncut birch logs. But where were the two pretty orioles? She had caught them in the woods over by the mountain. At daybreak, they would start twittering and they sounded even better than playing "Skylark" on the flute. But the cage was empty. Had the little orioles starved to death or had he let them out? Originally, this was meant to be an excellent vegetable plot, a few rows of vegetables could last them through the summer. When autumn came, they would be able to hang up strings of the best red peppers under the eaves together with bunches of dark green bean stalks for drying and clusters of golden corn cobs too.

But now, there were only two birds' nests under the eaves.

The small bamboo gate was broken and half open. Xiaoxiao stepped onto the little path paved with grey bricks, which led straight to the door of the cottage, just like their old home. They had also had a path of grey bricks. In the summer, the beans, which loved to climb up the little poles, turned the little path into a green corridor with their dense dark leaves.

Xiaoxiao stood in front of the door. On the darkgreen door was a group of blurred characters written in chalk. What naughty student would have used someone's front door as a blackboard? She was curious, so she tried to make out the characters.

"Little Tie Han is staying with me for a couple of days." The writing was vaguely familiar.

"Please help him with his homework." That was his message.

"Little Tie Han isn't well, I'm taking him to the clinic."

"I have to go down to the fourth company in a hurry, please phone and let me know how he is."

......

"Whose writing was that?" Xiaoxiao tried to guess, she felt faintly jealous, as if she was still the lady of the house. "What is it with you?" She shook her head vigorously, and smiled self-mockingly.

There was a small iron lock on the door. The paint on the lock was peeling off and revealed dark specks of the original colour, the two characters for "Yonggu" stood out in the centre. Xiaoxiao recognized it. It was the old lock that they used to use, so she quickly took out her key ring, picked out a key and fit it into the keyhole.

"Click." The lock opened. She pushed the door open, just like she used to.

With the door ajar, she felt uneasy: can I still use this key as I please? She was also afraid of revisiting that "home" —— the bowls, the chopsticks, the spoons that they had used together...so mundane and yet so intimate, her memory of them was still so clear. She wouldn't be able to avoid bumping into them. She wondered whether he still kept the *kang* in the middle of the room like she used to, with two book shelves that he had made on either side, which doubled as bedside cupboards.

She gently lifted the curtain to the inner room and looked around. She was astonished everything was different. A dilapidated table from some unknown office, an old bookshelf made up of four wooden planks stood against the wall. And where were her little toys? A crafty Mickey Mouse, a good-natured black bear and a clever little squirrel? There were absolutely no decorations in the room except for a picture frame on the wall —— a photograph of him and Little Tie Han. Underneath the photo a few characters were scrawled, "Me and Daddy."

He had replaced all of the things they had had together. He was probably right to do so.

She calmed down.

"Don't go, don't go, think it over again..."

Maybe she should have listened to this advice.

"The Institute for Literary Research...they'll be coming to see you one of these days..."

Maybe she had chosen the wrong time to come, after all.

No, she hadn't come to revisit a dream that had died a long time ago!

As she walked past the farm gate, she saw the trees that they had planted to symbolize their "taking root." They were already fully grown. The thick trunks, the dense foliage, so full of life. It was rather ironic: the people who had planted these trees were all gone...nevertheless, it was a phase of history, a record of their ideas, enthusiasm and courage. Even though it wasn't very substantial, it had its admirable aspects.

Taking-root trees, do you still remember the people who dug you holes and watered you?

They didn't need anybody to support them anymore, their

numerous roots already penetrated deep into the soil. They could rely on their own strength to grow and flourish, they could rely on their own strength to resist rainstorms and hurricanes. They were already fully grown, or would be soon.

Xiaoxiao felt relieved. No matter how they had been planted, they would eventually "take root." And no matter where you moved them, they would continue to branch out and flourish!

She had come to see them, even though looking back into the past always meant a lot of regrets that could never be made up.

The kindergarten was to the west of the farm's Northern Mountain Elementary School. Inside the sky-blue painted railings was a square patch of bare ground. On the ground, underneath two rows of red and green benches were a few patterned plastic balls.

The parents were waiting outside the railing. Xiaoxiao had been the first to arrive. She stood at a distance, underneath a large tree, holding the box with the electric car.

Not long after, the excited children rushed out of the building and straight into the arms of their mothers —— hugging them and calling "mummy, mummy!" As they walked past her, their affectionate whispers hung in the air,

"Mummy, today I got a red flag."

"Mummy, auntie says my paper boat was the best."

"Mummy, tomorrow we're going to put on a show."

......

She was the last to enter the yard.

"You're here to fetch Little Tie Han?" The auntie was locking up. "He left quite a while ago.

"Who came to get him?"

"Xiao Fang." The auntie was looking at the big box in Xiaoxiao's hands. "It's his birthday today."

Xiao Fang! A round face, easy to forget, though Xiaoxiao

remembered her well. The big box seemed to get heavier, it weighed down her arms...

"Quack, quack, quack."

As she walked by the window of the teachers' dormitory, Xiaoxiao heard the sounds of a toy duck.

She stopped underneath the window.

"Quack, quack, quack." The sounds of a wooden duck.

"Di-di, di-di." That was Little Tie Han's voice.

"Watch out, we're turning a corner." Xiao Fang's voice.

In the dormitory, half of the room was taken up by a long *kang* and a row of desks was lined up in the remaining space. A row of lunch boxes was lined up on the desks. A row of wash-basins was lined up underneath the desks. On the window sill were a few mirrors, round, oval, rectangular and square, as well as all sorts of combs, hairpins and curlers, the kind of things that girls can't do without.

Little Tie Han was running back and forth on the *kang*, pulling a small wooden car behind him. It was painted red and when its wheels turned, it sounded just like a wooden duck.

"Auntie, the car ought to say 'di-di'." Little Tie Han squatted regretfully beside the wooden car.

"They don't sell these in the shop, your daddy made it himself. Yesterday evening, he had a meeting which ended very late, and he still made a car for you." Xiao Fang was busy doing something over by the table.

"How do you know that, did daddy call you?" Little Tie Han asked, tilting his head.

"I ran into Uncle Fatty, the driver. The wheels came from his tool box."

"Daddy says that when I'm grown up, he'll teach me how to drive a real car." Little Tie Han's eyes shone with pride when he

talked about his father. "I'll let all the kids have a ride for free."
Little Tie Han began pulling the wooden car again. "We're going
up a hill now!" he stepped up on the folded quilts.

"Little Tie Han, let's celebrate your birthday!" Xiao Fang had
put five small pieces of cake on the table. Each piece was
decorated with flowers, and in the centre of each was a thin red
candle.

Xiao Fang lifted Tie Han down from the *kang* and made him
sit down on a chair next to the table. "Little Tie Han is five years
old now, so auntie bought five pieces of cake. What do you say,
should we eat them?"

"Let's wait until daddy comes, then we can eat them together."
Little Tie Han folded his arms and looked at the cake with
temptation. "Why isn't daddy here yet?" he pouted.

"They are very busy at the dam, your father..."

"He promised to come home for my birthday." Hurt and feeling
wronged, Little Tie Han jumped down from the *kang* and walked
toward the door. "Tell daddy to stop working. People say bad
things about him."

Xiao Fang grabbed hold of Tie Han. "Who's been saying bad
things?"

"Niu Wa. He says daddy is a 'careerist.' I grabbed him and
asked 'Who says so?' and he said that he had heard the grown ups
say it." Little Tie Han frowned. He was worried about his dad.

"Don't be afraid of what people say. We all know better.
Right?" Xiao Fang put her arms around Little Tie Han. "Let's go
give your father a phone call."

Xiaoxiao hastily stepped back and walked over behind the
corner. She was thinking that when she saw him, she would
definitely tell him that even the children were talking about the
dam. It was truly a major undertaking, the benefits of which bound
the tens of thousands of people on the farm with a common cause.

He was finally doing what he had always wanted to do...

Fatty the driver rushed up huffing and puffing.

Little Tie Han hurried forward to meet him, "Uncle Fatty, has my daddy come home?"

"Your daddy can't make it after all, they're having an emergency meeting at the dam." Fatty now held out the hand that he had kept behind his back. "Look here."

A bouquet of brightly coloured mountain flowers, red, yellow and purple.

"For you. Happy Birthday!" Fatty stroked Little Tie Han's head. "Your daddy said that as soon as they let water into the dam, he will come and get you and take you into the wilderness to play." Then he said to Xiao Fang, "Would you take Tie Han to have his picture taken, I haven't got time."

He had changed. In the past, when he got caught up in something, he would forget about everything else... Xiaoxiao also wanted to pick a bunch of mountain flowers and bury her face in the sweet smelling flowers.

Tie Han hung his head silently.

Five small flames brightened up the room, which had become dark with the sunset.

"Auntie, why do we light candles when we celebrate birthdays?" Little Tie Han was happy again.

"You're five years old now, so we light five candles to represent your life. Like the red candles, people's lives should shine in the darkness and be ready to burn themselves up." In the orange-red candlelight, Xiao Fang's eyes were gentle and touching.

"Auntie, you must give me red candles every year on my birthday. Will you?" Little Tie Han implored her. He liked the thin red candles, he liked the small orange flames.

"Okay, auntie will buy them every year." Xiao Fang kissed Tie Han and then looked at her watch. "Auntie has to go now, you'd better go to sleep."

"Auntie, don't go." Little Tie Han rubbed her collar, reluctant to let her leave.

"I have a class tonight, and I also have to go to see another auntie."

"What auntie?"

"From Beijing." Xiao Fang answered knowingly.

"Beijing —— Tian'anmen!" Little Tie Han drew the characters with his fingers.

"Come on, go to sleep now." Xiao Fang lifted him up on the kang and brought out a pile of children's books. "Are you frightened? Auntie will lock the door..."

Xiaoxiao fled from the small room. For some reason, she didn't want to meet Xiao Fang.

Xiao Fang hadn't changed. She was resolute, yet gentle; punctilious, yet friendly; prudent, yet original. In spite of everything, she had remained here, even though many people didn't understand her.

"Do I understand her?" The dark green door and those faint characters scribbled with chalk rose up before Xiaoxiao's eyes. Xiao Fang had written those characters! All of a sudden, she felt as if something had been taken from her. She leaned weakly against a huge tree.

She had cried back then when she had left. But at the time a kind of reverie about her new life had dispelled the gloom of parting, and she was never really aware of how important and precious all of it had been to her. When she couldn't sleep at night, she always found comfort in the thought of her son's sweet smile, which was imprinted deep inside her. The smile belonged to her.

No, it doesn't belong to me any more.

The tears fell quietly down her collar...

She stood for a long time underneath the big tree. When she

had calmed down a little, she gently pushed open the door to the little room. She put the big box with the electric car next to Little Tie Han's pillow, then she took out her note pad and, in the dark, wrote out a few characters, "Happy Birthday." She ripped off the note and put it on the box, then she put the bouquet of mountain flowers on top of it.

Little Tie Han slept soundly. The pale moonlight shone on his sweet smile.

She got up to leave, feeling sad. At the threshold, she turned around abruptly and gazed once more at Little Tie Han. "I'll take him with me. My son!" Her heart beat fiercely. The child needed the love of a mother, she needed to love the child too. That kind of love was all too rare in her life.

She went up to Little Tie Han again.

Would he agreed to this? She thought about it. She would talk it over with tim. She could always send the child back in a few years.

But he was at the dam.

They were really struggling at the dam.

She hesitated again...

8

Three tractors loaded with cement culverts stopped in front of the store. The two drivers were packing a few boxes of "Great Northern Wilderness" liquor into the cabin.

"Are you headed for the dam?" Xiaoxiao went up and asked.

"Yep," said one of the drivers without lifting his head. "But there's no more seats left."

"I don't need a seat."

"There's no standing room either." The driver resolutely threw a bunch of dirty cotton yarn on the ground.

"I'll sit in the culvert." Xiaoxiao drew a circle with her finger. "When it rolls, I'll roll too, I won't get cramped."

"Why bother, there's a bus in the afternoon."

"That's no good. This is an emergency," she pleaded.

The driver looked her up and down.

Xiaoxiao was wearing a cream-coloured, trim, polyester suit, which really wasn't appropriate for crawling into a cement culvert. She had hurried over. That morning, she had bumped into the old man with the horse cart; he had begun talking about the dam as soon as he opened his mouth:

"Last night, they phoned him from the Central Farm and ordered that work on the dam be stopped temporarily and that all the Party members leave the site and return to the Farm Headquarters to get new directives. In the middle of the night, all the leaders had come back by jeep except for Chief Li, who refused to leave and refused to stop working." Heavy-hearted, the old man let the cigarette droop from his mouth. The smoke rose feebly. "The Central Farm is going to send somebody out to mediate anytime now, it's still unclear who they'll side with. The bad guys always complain first, from ancient times until now, the good guys have always got the worst of it." He forcefully knocked the ashes off his cigarette. "They're having an animated discussion in the office, every one has a different opinion. I really feel bad for him. After all, he's not building the dam for his own family. If you see him, urge him to be careful, to take it easy for a while and not to be too stubborn..."

Would she be able to influence him? Xiaoxiao wished that a word from her would still have some impact.

She fidgeted at the thought of seeing him in a short while.

The tractor started up.

Curled up inside the culvert, her body arched like a shrimp. As the tractor started moving, the culvert rolled back and forth, it was like lying on a crescent-shaped, wooden board.

Xiaoxiao shifted her body and tried her best to find a more comfortable position.

"It wasn't easy coming here to see you," she wanted to tell him.

One winter, he had gone into the mountains to log. At Chinese New Year, all the loggers, except for him, came back from the mountains. They brought back a letter:

...Everybody has left, the mountain is even more peaceful, the pure white snow is everywhere. Walking around in the snow is like having landed on the moon, the world's troubles seem to have vanished. I want to remain here by myself for a few days, to stay in the old forester's hut. Don't worry, there's a shotgun here..."

She was worried anyway. What if he came across a bear and had forgotten to load his gun?...

A horse-drawn sleigh passed by on the road, the old villager in the driver's seat swung the whip leisurely.

"Grandpa, are you headed for the mountains?"

"Sure am, I'm going to get some firewood." The old man's beard was as white as snow.

"Could you take me along?"

"Have you got one of these?" The old man patted the leather overcoat he was wearing. "Have you got this?" Then he patted the wine bottle that was tied around his waist. "It's a tough ride."

"I'm not afraid." With a small bag underneath her arm, she climbed up onto the sleigh.

As the horse trotted along, the bells around its neck jingled and two deep ruts appeared on the snow-covered ground, as if they were pulling two long ribbons up into the mountains. The snowy scenery was enchanting, a world of ice sculptures and jade carvings.

Before they were half-way there, Xiaoxiao's feet were frozen stiff, the two layers of face masks stuck to her face like a thick slab of ice and pricked like needles. The leather hat and collar were white from the air she breathed out.

"I'll get off and walk."

"You won't get there before dark." The old grandpa untied his wine bottle. "Have a drink."

Xiaoxiao lifted the bottle with both hands and took a sip. "I would still rather walk."

"Where are you going? I'll go ahead and leave word from you."

"I am going to see someone named Li at the old forester's hut." Keeping in the rut that the sleigh made, Xiaoxiao ran along with quick, short steps.

It got dark after she crossed the first range and the hut was on yet another range. Tired and cold, hungry and frightened, she wanted to cry. Suddenly, in the woods beside the road, a spot of light gleamed like a firefly. She ripped off her face mask and, heedless of everything, she started shouting:

"Whoa, hey!..."

He emerged from the woods carrying a lantern.

She leaped across the snow-filled ditch, threw the bag at him and started crying.

"Oh, it's raining, it's going to freeze!" He teased her.

She pounded his chest with her frozen hand. "It wasn't easy coming here to see you."

"If it was easy, you wouldn't remember it, you wouldn't treasure it." He shook the powdery snow off his leather overcoat. "I thought you might show up."

"Why?"

"The woman called Meng Jiangnü* went all the way to the

---

*The reference is to a story that took place during the Qin Dynasty. A woman called Meng Jiangnü travelled all along the Great Wall in search of her husband who had been forced to help build it.

Great Wall to see her husband."

"Who says that you are..."

"The great mountain is our witness."

"I want your heart as a witness."

"Of course." He put her hand on his heart. "We'll get married in the winter."

"It's too cold in the winter."

"There's snow in the winter. On a snowy day..."

"I love summer, mountain flowers bloom in summer!" Deep in the mountains, with no one around, she felt at ease holding his arm tightly.

Suddenly, with a deep sigh, he said, "The mountains are the best place after all, aside from all the trees, there're just you and me..."

It was then that she realized why he had wanted to stay alone in the mountains for a few days and why she, regardless of anything else, had come all the way up here. Xiao Song the shepherdess and Er Huzi the carpenter had become quite friendly. The foul-smelling sheep pen was the only place where they could sit and talk quietly. Of course, they were discovered by the combat-alert group on duty, reported to the company and criticized at a mass meeting. Xiao Song appeared to have done something improper and, for several months, she couldn't face anybody...

The light was on in the small hut. Embedded in the valley, it resembled a star fallen from the sky.

"You must be tired. We're almost there." He slowed his pace down considerably.

"I'm not tired." Her pace was much lighter now, she could have crossed another mountain top...

The culvert kept bumping against the sides of the carriage and each time, small bits of cement sprinkled down. She covered her face with a handkerchief and only left her eyes exposed. She wanted to see something, she was bored. She turned her head but was only able to see a little patch of sky at the end of the opening, and there weren't even any clouds.

When they met this time, it wouldn't be as joyful as it had been back then...her state of mind was like the waves, now up, now down. Again she recalled the ceaseless autumn rain and the solitary bench. Now the pressure was even more intense and there were many more difficulties, what would he be like?...

She pulled up the handkerchief to her forehead, so that it covered her eyes.

The headquarters of the construction site was in the largest tent. Each of the small, square windows was open and, with the wind blowing through from the gorge, it was nice and cool.

There was no one in the tent, but obviously it had been recently tidied, the tables, the shelves, the instruments and the tools were all very orderly. And on the smooth plank bed lay five or six neatly folded quilts. On the wall hung a large sectional drawing of the dam, covered by a thin sheet of clear plastic.

Was this the headquarters? It was too spick and span, too well organized, it had none of the urgent and grave atmosphere she had imagined.

Where was his space on the plank bed? Which one of the desks was his?... Xiaoxiao's eyes searched about.

"Who are you looking for?" A girl came in. Her hair was wet, her trousers were rolled up to her knees and she was wearing a pair of black plastic sandals on her bare feet.

Xiaoxiao fixed her eyes on the bouquet of mountain flowers in the girl's hand, red, yellow and purple ones...

"I'm looking for Chief Li."

"They've all gone for a swim." The girl put the mountain

flowers in a white enamel tea mug. She had clearly just come back from the river herself. "Have a seat, he'll be back soon."

Xiaoxiao didn't sit down, she went over and stood in front of the bouquet of mountain flowers that had just been picked in the wilderness.

"It's been a good year, there are lots of flowers out there." The girl smoothed out her hair till it shone and tied up two pigtails with elastic bands.

"You like mountain flowers too?" Xiaoxiao touched the delicate petals lightly.

"I like everything and nothing." The girl laughed coarsely. "Chief Li likes mountain flowers, it was he who picked them. I was afraid they'd start wilting in the sun, so I brought them back to put them in water."

He still liked mountain flowers.

"So work on the construction site isn't all that busy?"

"Not busy? The past two days, we hardly have had time to breathe. Today at noon, Chief Li ordered everyone to take an hour off and go for a swim. You should see them down by the river, it's so funny, it's just as if someone had released a flock of ducks, they all waddled in. It was great to soak in the water!" The girl spoke cheerfully. She was very candid.

Xiaoxiao felt like stretching her arms and taking a few strokes in the clear, cool water too. But the bright red swimsuit was still packed in her case. Perhaps she had kept it as a souvenir, or perhaps she'd left it there in order to forget it.

He on the other hand, had come to love swimming, especially at stressful moments, like the present.

"I'll go down to the river and take a look."

"Let me get him for you." The girl looked at Xiaoxiao amiably. "The sun is too strong at mid-day, your skin is so white." She laughed heartily again.

Xiaoxiao unwittingly touched her own face.

As she was waiting, she began to feel a bit nervous. She had thought a lot about seeing him again and, curled up inside the culvert, she had imagined what it would be like at the moment they saw each other again...

"Chief Li, she's waiting for you at the headquarters."

Xiaoxiao heard the girl shouting and took a few steps forward. She spotted him. There were two other people with him, a boy and a girl.

"...They've run out of meat in the dining hall and the Supplies Section won't send any more. They say that the decision was made by the Party committee." The girl was small and skinny but very bright.

"If I get a hold of him I'll break his damn neck." The boy looked like a pillar —— tall and muscular, with a thick neck and a loud voice. "Chief Li, let me go. I'll get eight or ten pigs from there. I'll stick those pig heads at the entrance to the Supplies Section."

He didn't respond but walked on with big strides. A big, old straw hat hid his face. He was wearing a blue undershirt and his bare neck and shoulders looked as if they had been covered with a layer of deep brown oil paint.

"You keep out of it," the girl was very direct. "Chief, let me go. I'll go straight to the company and ask."

He stopped at the entrance to the tent. "Forget about it —— nobody is going." He was very composed. "So what if we have no meat to eat? Tonight we'll have a meeting and I'll inform everyone. Save you anger for a while. The tough part has yet to come."

"Fuck, they're going too far!" the pillar mumbled.

"Stop cursing, if you want to say something, say it straight to their faces." The girl was even tougher.

He laughed. "You two really are a couple! After we've finished the dam, you're going to offer me candy, aren't you?"

"Candy? You still owe me," the pillar said, "you lost our bet in the river."

"Let's go, no more nonsense." The girl turned around.

The pillar followed immediately behind her.

He didn't enter the tent right away.

Xiaoxiao stepped back from the door. Coming towards her, he seemed very calm, less hot-tempered, less impetuous. It was him, and yet he didn't seem the same as he had been back then —— stranger, yet more familiar.

As he entered, he took off his straw hat, his wet hair had been flattened.

"So you're here." He didn't look her straight in the eye, he walked right across to the corner and hung his straw hat on a hoe.

You made a mistake, she felt like saying. The rack for clothes and hats was right beside the hoe. She followed him with her eyes and, all of a sudden, her heart was calm, not a touch anxious.

So this was how they met.

Life was always more dull than the imagination.

He turned around, sat down, bent his head and began rolling a cigarette, but all the tobacco fell out.

"The paper's torn," she said in a soft voice.

He crumpled the paper and the tobacco together, lifted his head abruptly and looked at her a long time in silence, though his eyes seemed to have a whole lot to say.

She bowed her head. She wanted to wash her face, which must have been full of dust from the culvert.

He brought a basin full of hot water. He still understood her very well.

Should she say "Thank you?" It sound too formal. Should she

smile to express her thanks? She couldn't smile. Like an impolite child, she took the washbasin, without looking up, and immersed her face in the water. The water was a bit too hot, her face burned, the blood welled up.

He had carefully rolled a cigarette and was smoking, taking deep puffs.

She spread out the towel and put it to her face. It smelled familiar. She took a long, deep breath.

He poured out the water for her.

She hung up the towel.

He came to straighten up the towel a bit more.

"You've improved," she smiled slightly.

In the past, whenever she went to the stable, his quilt would be lying on the bed in a big bundle. His dirty clothes and ripped socks were heaped in a messy pile, it looked like a corner of a salvage station. After they were married, she made a rule: each of them had to clean up their own things. He had abided by it, though she often had to remind him.

"I guess I had to!" He, too, couldn't help but smile.

The ice had been broken. It was as if the electricity had suddenly been reconnected.

"Let's go take a walk," he draped his shirt over his shoulder.

She walked over to the door, then she turned her head again and looked at the headquarters that he had arranged in such perfect order, at the white enamel mug, at the multi-coloured bouquet of mountain flowers.

They walked along the bank of the Aogen River. The rushing current was like children running in an endless quest for fun and games. The sky was a deep blue, the large clusters of clouds were even thicker than those on a painter's palette. The sun seemed coy, one minute it would reveal its red face and the next it would hide behind a cloud.

Their conversation was, like the sun, rather evasive as well.

"Have you come out to experience life?"

She smiled bitterly.

"Are you well?" She saw that he had lost quite a lot of weight.

"I won't collapse," he said casually. "So, you're doing quite a bit of writing?"

"It's not very good. How about your dam?"

And then they'd walk on for a while in silence.

"Why don't you return to the Farm Headquarters to attend the Party committee meeting?" She hadn't wanted to touch upon this subject right away, but she asked anyway.

"Now is not the time to hold meetings, we mustn't delay the project, even for a day. We might get a rainstorm any day now. If we get mountain torrents, more than ten companies will be flooded." He had a few blisters on his lower lip and the corner of his mouth was festering. "Do you remember that year when we had the mountain torrents and four people from our company alone died?"

She hadn't forgotten. Though it ought to be said that the event had faded in her mind.

Her eyes rested on the blisters on his lower lip, an inexplicable awareness was stirring. "You should eat more fruit and vegetables..." She knew that it wouldn't help the matter, a fire was burning in his heart.

"They are going to send someone from the Central Farm..."

"Let them come. Let them look at the construction site." He had a well-thought-out plan. "The dam should have provided benefits at the same year, but we've been dragging our feet for three years now. The labourers assigned to the job have been taken out for subsidiary production. Their pockets are bulging; they can lead an extravagant life, eating and drinking every day. Even when there's a meeting at the political department, they bring in people to the dam to eat and drink, that's how profitable things are here. I wanted to bring them back a long time ago, but I just don't have the power."

"You've only been in this position for a year..." She was a bit worried.

"But I have no alternative. We've got to finish the dam in a hurry to protect the autumn harvest."

"They won't give up."

"I know. They've sent people to the Central Farm to lodge a complaint." He was magnanimous. "At worst, I'd be removed. But it's not going to be that easy."

"You're still the same..."

He was more experienced. He understood a lot and he was so bold. That was commendable indeed.

"I would like to change. But it's very hard to change one's self."

You've changed, I can see it. She felt like telling him. She stopped underneath a gnarled tree on the river bank. "Do you think that I've changed?"

"You've become famous," he smiled knowingly. It wasn't flattery, it wasn't irony either.

"Famous? That doesn't mean anything." Now that she'd met up with him, all the words hidden in her heart rushed out, like a spring long buried underground. Once it found a way out, there was no stopping it from gushing. "My novels have been published, a collection of my short stories has been printed. Fame and gain, a reputation —— at a time when I have more than ever before, I find that I've also lost more than ever. People envy me, that's what I find the most tragic..." She stared dejectedly at the trunk of the tree. She bared her heart. In elementary school, she'd been the big brigade leader. In the eyes of her classmates, she was talented, extraordinary. But when she got home and took off her badges, she would act like a spoilt little girl around her mother, or she would talk about how unhappy she was. After all, she was just a young girl who needed other people's support.

She still needed that kind of support.

"You can't calculate gains and losses in such a simple way." His eyes left her and moved out to the river. He tried hard to calm his speech, to make it just a bit calmer. He had also hoped that they'd be able to meet, since he had a lot that he wanted to say to her too. But he didn't want to send her back with more regrets. He didn't want to add any more pain to her heart or to his own. So he calmed himself a little. "If you could get everything, life would just be a string of dull successes. When you lose something, it's hard to avoid feeling pain, but this kind of pain can lead you to unexpected experiences. I must say, I think you're stronger than you used to be."

Their eyes met for a moment.

The four years they hadn't seen each other, she appeared to have become younger, her skin had become whiter, more delicate, her face prettier. Her shoulder-length, permed hair added a touch of style. In those days, she had worn her hair in braids that went down to her waist. When she worked, she would tie them into a knot at the back of her neck, but the ends would still swing back and forth and touch her shoulders.

"I'll just have them cut off," she said when they were married.

"No, leave them. I like them."

He liked the two small braids swinging to and fro. After she left, they would still haunt his dreams after a day of hard labour. She had still chosen to cut them off.

At first he couldn't get used to it, but when he looked a little closer, he felt there was something touching about her permed hair.

She was stronger than she had been in the past! He had always trusted his own eyes. Yet he just spoke calmly, "'When water is too clear, there are no fish.' This proverb makes a lot of sense. In the past, we were too pure, like pieces of glass. In the real world, we shattered as soon as we bumped into something, because life isn't pure at all. Still, we have to maintain our basic principles."

"Maybe you're right."

"Not maybe, I *am* right."

She looked at him and couldn't help smiling. When they were together, she always trusted him and yielded to his self-confidence.

"I've brought all the pieces that I've written with me..." She had kept a complete set for him.

He had already read them all, without exception. Every day, when he read the newspaper, he would first flip to the fourth page where the contents of all the magazines were published. He hoped that he would often come across the name he wished to see. Even though there was no way she could have felt this sincere and subtle concern, every day he searched, every day he went on paying close attention. It was as if he was trying to make up for some kind of fault. After she had gone, he woke up to his error —— he was responsible for her leaving. He would dream of her often, wake up and feel as if something was weighing down his heart. He was depressed and unhappy and he would go out and work hard for a long time. Only when he was soaked in sweat, would his mind be at ease. Gradually, the dreams became less frequent. When he did dream of her, the dream was always long and complete. But the dreams couldn't replace her after all.

He didn't say this, he could never say this to anyone.

"Wonderful, I'll give them my fullest attention." He reached out and picked up a big handful of jade green hazelnuts from the hazel tree next to them. She liked to eat them raw, they tasted like fresh, tender lotus seeds. She used to be able to eat a scoopful in one go. "Greedy cat," he used to laugh at her. She didn't care.

He gave her the hazelnuts.

"Don't speak to me like a bureaucrat." She was upset. "When

you read them, you'll find out that they aren't very well-written. Nowadays, I feel as if there isn't much more to write about." She poured the hazelnuts from one hand to another. One by one, the nuts fell to the ground. She wasn't that "greedy cat" anymore, she wasn't a wife anymore, and not a mother; on the contrary, she had completely cast off her girlish innocence.

He had his own opinion about her writing. You might say that he liked it. It was only that some of the later novels were rather vague in ideology and content. He wanted to ask her, is there still "anger"...is there still rage in your heart? Do you still care for other people as much as you care for yourself? But he only said, "Let me read them first and then I'll tell you what I think."

"How have you been?"

She asked him.

"The same as usual."

"Why didn't you write back to me?" She had been wanting to ask this from the moment they had met again.

"What could I write?" he said rather hesitantly.

"You could write anything, about yourself, about our son, about your lives..."

"There were times that I wanted to write, but I was too busy..." He changed the subject. "Have you seen little Xiaoxiao?"

"No I haven't." She had seen "L:ittle Tie Han." With her arm resting against the tree trunk, her face was partially hidden. On the surface of the river, the waves were shiny and crystalline, as bright as the red candles... Gently, she kicked the round cobblestone by her foot into the river and her heart sank as the stone did.

"I didn't make it back for his birthday..." He squatted and feddled with the hazelnuts on the ground, one but one. "I left him with Xiao Fang," he said frankly. He lit a cigarette, but kept it between his fingers. A wisp of silky blue smoke curled up and gradually faded away.

"Is Xiao Fang married now?" she asked purposefully.

He shook his head.

"How is she doing?"

"You ought to go to see her."

"You're really quite concerned about her." She was still like that, she liked to irritate him.

He fell silent...

His first day on the job, he had set out for the most isolated company in the whole farm. It was already dark and had begun snowing. The small jeep's shining lights swept across the sloping mountain road and explored everything on each side.

"Look, over there by the woods..." He tapped the back of the driver's seat.

In front of them, to the left, a dark shadow was moving.

"It's a person." The driver signalled by turning the lights on and off.

The dark shadow stopped moving.

The car halted.

The person turned her back to them, stuck her arm under the rope that was tied around the firewood, and by supporting her hand on her knees, she tried to stand up. The bundle of firewood was too big, it was impossible to move.

"Tie the wood to the back of the car," he instructed the driver.

"That's not necessary, I can carry it myself."

"Xiao Fang!" He recognized her voice.

"Chief Li," Xiao Fang addressed him politely.

"Who did you cut it for?" He let Xiao Fang sit in the car first.

"For myself," she rubbed her frozen face.

"Have you married?"

She smiled.

"Do you have any kids?"

She closed her lips and a kind of contentment spilled over the corners of her mouth.

"Boy or girl?"

"Both," she laughed.

Suddenly he realized what she meant. "Have you got a building for the school now?"

"At the moment we haven't, we're still using a tent. But the company has agreed to build two classrooms next spring."

"Are you still taking a lot of ideological pressure?" he asked straightforwardly.

She bent her head and twisted the tassel of her mohair scarf and, without answering, said, "The mountain kids are very lovable."

He didn't ask any more questions.

The car drove on quietly.

That night Xiao Fang was preparing her lessons at a large chopping board in the dining hall as he came in and so they met again.

"I got hungry and came to get a steamed bread."

Xiao Fang helped him cut the steamed bread into thin slices and toasted them over the stove cover.

"You're a college graduate and you've still come to stay in the ravine, don't you feel..." He stubbornly began asking questions again. He wanted to hear her talk about it, she was doing something very difficult and he was hoping that he could be of some help to her. For several years now, he had never been able to forgive himself for having punched Xiaoxiao...

Xiao Fang carefully turned over the small slices of burning hot steamed bread.

"Won't you tell me about it?" He tilted the stove cover, moved closer to the fire and lit up a cigarette.

"I would tell anyone about it," she grumbled a bit. "It's just that no one is really willing to listen." She passed him the crisp steamed bread slices. "They've all got their opinions about me. But to me, it's really quite simple. As a little girl, I was sent to the country and was brought up there. My parents were geologists and were away most of the year. They didn't bring me up. I am not nostalgic about my family but I do have a special kind of feeling toward the countryside. That's why, after my graduation, it didn't take me long to decide to come back here. The Great Northern Wilderness is richly endowed and a very fertile area, but it is so backward. The children here are earnest and simple, they're good-natured but they lack education. I would like to teach them something." She looked at him, her eyes were very sincere. "Have you seen *The Teacher in the Village*? I loved that film. Since I was young, I've longed for the kind of life Warwala had..." She lowered her head and looked at the stove cover, which was slowly becoming red-hot. "People criticized me, I couldn't take all of their deliberate misinterpretations, I couldn't stand the freezing satire and the burning irony... I thought to myself, it's not as if I have nowhere else to go, I'm going, I'm leaving this place..." She stopped.

"Did you really leave?"

Xiao Fang nodded.

......

She had, indeed, been prepared to leave, she had packed her things quietly.

The children were practising their lessons in a tent just across from hers, their undulating voices drifted through the air and tugged at her heart. "Hurry up and leave," she pushed herself. "Go around the tent and out to the mountain road and this will be over forever."

Xiao Fang ducked her head and dashed out, but the curtain of the tent facing her was drawn apart and the children swarmed out, squeezed together in a crowd and stood looking at her in silence.

"You... I..."

The children just stood there anxiously, their eyes full of sadness over her leaving.

"Go back. Go back to your studies!..." Xiao Fang muttered. She felt like herding the kids back in the tent and, once again, placing her book and her slate on her knees...but the bus had arrived, she turned her head and jumped on.

The children scampered up to the bus door but it closed in front of them.

The bus started moving and the children ran after it as fast as they could. Then, slowly, they began to fall behind, one by one, dot after dot, like an ellipsis with boundless implications. Xiao Fang squeezed up against the back window of the bus and the warm tears began to roll.

The mountain road was tortuous and the children fell out of sight as the bus took the first turn. All of a sudden, Xiao Fang felt her legs get weak and her body started to sway like a withered leaf about to separate from the branch.

A withered leaf. Oh yes. She'd lost all of it —— the green mountains, the green tent —— her heart was empty like a withered leaf...

When the bus stopped, before going on through the pass, Xiao Fang jumped down. She threw the suitcase up on her shoulders and began walking back into the mountains.

From a distance, she spotted the green tents and saw her children again. They were still standing silently at the bus stop in front of the tent.

When someone suddenly pours out their heart to you, you may be at a loss as to what to do, you won't know how to repay their confidence in you.

At that moment he was frustrated too, and kept on smoking one cigarette after another.

The steamed bread slices had been flipped over and over but had finally turned into coke...

The cigarette in his hand burned up, he remained silent. Just tell her. In his heart, he had often told her everything. But now the woman of his thoughts was actually there next to him and he found himself face-to-face with those eyes —— so full of emotion —— that he became even more clear-headed. He didn't want to say anything at all. He just hoped that when she left, her mind would be at peace.

"Why don't you say anything?" Xiaoxiao couldn't stand it any longer. "Is it because we were talking about her?..."

He couldn't answer her and yet, he couldn't avoid it. "I don't understand what you're getting at?" was all that he could say.

He knows very well, she thought. Should she just put it bluntly? But she was still being evasive, "Now that you have her...can I take Little Tie Han with me?"

He was stupefied. He crushed the cigarette butt on the ground and then pulverized it.

"I was thinking..." she couldn't express what was really on her mind. "I was thinking that the child should go to school in Beijing. The quality of education here..."

He was still squatting and had arranged the hazelnuts into two straight lines.

"Maybe I'm being selfish, but I..."

"The quality of education here is poor because we don't have qualified teachers. Do you think that you could send all the children of the old workers to school in Beijing?" He looked up at her like a stranger. "Did you just come to take the child away?"

How should she answer him? Her feelings were scattered like the hazelnuts on the ground and she was unable to sort them out.

"Let's go and ask the child," he relaxed his tone.

They were very close to each other. All at once, he felt that his breath was even colder than a snowstorm. She seemed to sober up a bit. I don't have the right to take the child with me. He has put all his energy into bringing him up.

"Okay, we'll ask the child," she nevertheless agreed. "I have to go now, the afternoon bus leaves at five."

"There's another one tomorrow morning." His eyes urged her to stay.

He had really become much thinner. "You must take good care of yourself..." Her thoughts jumped about randomly.

"Another two days and the dam will be finished." He sighed deeply and repeated in a light tone. "There's another bus tomorrow morning, it doesn't leave until nine."

She didn't want to change her mind. You'd better go, now that you've finally seen him.

She shook her head.

9

It was a dark night, there was no moon, just a few button-like stars far, far away. The vast expanse of fields was like an ocean in the black night.

The bus was extra fast that night.

Xiaoxiao sat next to the door. The wind made its way through the crack in the door and stirred the bottom of her slacks. It blew energetically, though it wasn't cold.

"Have you decided where you're getting off?" The conductor came up to her.

She still held the money to buy her ticket. As she was about to leave the dam she had phoned her old company, "...I'm coming tonight." By a lucky coincidence, it was Uncle Liu who answered the phone. When she got on the bus she hesitated again: leaving just like that? She hadn't said anything. She still had a lot on her mind that she wanted to say... They had been separated for four years and yet they had met for less than four hours. And then? Maybe four years, maybe eight years, maybe they'd never have an opportunity to see each other again... She regretted her decision. She should have taken the bus the next morning, then she would have had all night to listen to him talk. Talk about the dam, about himself. He hadn't said anything about himself, not one sentence. Even if they wouldn't talk about anything, they could just sit together silently...

But eventually she would have to leave.

Flowing water cannot be cut in half, the only solution is to build a dam.

The night breeze gradually calmed her down. Then she discovered that she had taken the magazines that she intended to give him. She hadn't given him anything. She felt even more remorseful.

"So where are you going to get off?" The conductor came up and asked her again.

"At the Fifth Company." She handed him the money.

The bus stopped and then continued.

Xiaoxiao walked over to the gate of the company. The chalk characters on the small blackboard next to the gate had been smeared by the rain and looked like a big flower. Were the basketball stands and parallel bars still over at the back? They had been built by a few Youth League members who had gone to the woods on a Sunday to collect the timber. She seemed to be able to hear waves of uninhibited laughter and shouts. At midday, when no one was playing, colourful quilts and clothes from the girls' dormitory would be hung out to air on the basketball stands and the parallel bars.

She walked by all the pitch-dark windows. On the ground by the company chief and political instructor's small room, there was always a layer of cigarette butts, every day someone was called over for a chat...they all loved to get together in the account's room because there was a phone in there. And the mailman always dropped the letters on the cashier's desk. The cashier was a girl who smiled whenever she saw anybody... Xiaoxiao stopped when she reached the third window. This was her clinic. It was bolted firmly. Was it still tidy inside? A small, snow-white cupboard, medicine bottles, large and small, were lined up straighter than exercising soldiers. The little table next to the window was covered with a white cloth. On it was a white vase which sometimes held lilies and sometimes held mountain flowers.

The large dormitory was empty, weeds were growing in front of its door. The glass in all of the windows was broken and the paper that had been pasted over was torn and rustled when the wind blew. Inside, in the space between the two long *kangs*, was the "basin area." At the peak, there had been twenty people to a *kang* in the large dormitory. Their mattresses overlapped, their pillows lay on top of each other, during the night, when someone wanted to roll over, they all had to roll at the same time, with one of them counting down, "One, two, three..."

What fun it had been!

The door creaked open and a small dog crept out of the empty building. What colour was it? Xiaoxiao wanted to find out, but the dog became frightened and ran off. She had once kept a dog she called "Beggar." It had had a few black spots on its snow-white hair, a very handsome animal. She had tied a copper bell to its neck with a red satin ribbon. It was fond of running behind his horse cart and its bell would jingle pleasantly. When she left, he had been transferred too, but what had happened to Beggar?

"Wah! Wah!" another dog scurried out from behind the building.

"Beggar!" A reprimand followed.

Beggar? She went forward and took Beggar in her arms and rubbed her face against its long shiny fur.

"...The bus arrived a long time ago and we still didn't see you. Your auntie got worried and urged me to look for you. Beggar came along too." Uncle Liu was carrying a flashlight, a dim, white light shone on the ground.

"Uncle Liu, how are you?"

"Fine. This year we had five more foals, I'm still looking after them all by myself. The date-brown horse and the big, black one are both going to foal again."

"Can't your grandson help you?"

"He left. He left last summer."

"Where did he go?"

"He went to Shenyang to study. He was accepted at the Forestry College. Since he was the first university student from our company, our family had to accept the consequences, and your auntie invited a round of people to dinner."

"Are there many who are accepted at universities?"

"No, only two from the entire farm. The other is one of Xiao Fang's students. We finally got two." Uncle Liu waved the flashlight. "If all of you hadn't left, our farm would have produced quite a few university students."

She walked into the circle of light from the flashlight and slowed her steps.

"Have you seen him yet?" Uncle Liu's tone changed. "One year on the job has already caused him an awful lot of worry. All these years, we've had the same group of people and horses on the farm. We've always done things in this manner but he wants to turn things around. It's not so easy. First he took charge of the dam, he was desperate. If we didn't finish the dam, there wouldn't be any future for the farm. Just for the dam, he ran around trying to find means, to gather materials, to invite technicians...they say he's become all skin and bones. Your auntie is very fond of him, so she had someone bring him a few dozen eggs, but he took them to the dining hall, where they fried all of them up at once."

I never paid attention to any of this when I saw him. I was only concerned about myself, I only cared about my own feelings... Xiaoxiao felt deeply guilty.

"Go wait at the door." Uncle Liu kicked Beggar.

Beggar darted forward.

"Your original Beggar died just after having this puppy. He buried the little bell along with the dog. He spoon-fed and raised this little Beggar. He always said how fond you had been of Beggar."

I'll give little Beggar a bell too, Xiaoxiao thought.

"He's already so big."

"Little Tie Han is already five..." Uncle Liu coughed lightly.

Oh yes, it had been four years.

The small gate to the courtyard was open. Auntie was standing there with her arms around a child.

Uncle Liu raised the flashlight, "Little Tie Han!"

His eyes were still very bright.

Xiaoxiao unwittingly rushed forward. Uncle Liu followed her with big strides.

Little Tie Han broke free from auntie's embrace, threw himself at Uncle Liu and began to cry loudly.

"What's the matter?" Uncle Liu hugged Little Tie Han tightly. "Who's been bullying you?"

"Look at this child. He came all by himself and he didn't take a bus, he walked over ten li." Auntie patted Little Tie Han lovingly.

Little Tie Han leaned up against Uncle Liu's shoulder and

continued to cry heart-breakingly.

Xiaoxiao longed to embrace him and to console him with a mother's voice: Don't cry, it's all right, my child, tell mummy...

"Tell me, who has been bullying you?"

Little Tie Han wiped off his tears with the back of his hand, sobbing, "Little Ying was missing two biscuits, I sit next to her, she said that I took them, so the auntie got mad at me. I didn't take them! I'm never going to go back to kindergarten..."

"He's like his dad, when he grows up, he'll be a real iron man." Uncle Liu patted Litte Tie Han on the back. "It takes a lot of courage to be an upright person."

"Didn't you tell Auntie Xiao Fang?" auntie asked anxiously.

"Go and boil the dumplings," Uncle Liu interrupted her.

Xiaoxiao took Little Tie Han in her arms. One of his trouser legs was wet.

"I went to see Auntie Xiao Fang, but she was in the middle of teaching the teachers." Little Tie Han looked at Xiaoxiao. In the darkness, he couldn't distinguish her face clearly. He rubbed his trousers, "A truck forced me into the ditch."

"Did you hurt yourself?"

"No." Little Tie Han swung his legs. "The big trucks are the worst!" Suddenly he cried out, "Where's my car?"

"On the *kang*," Auntie answered from the inner room. "As soon as the child walked in, he asked me to put the car in a safe place."

The little car had fallen into the ditch too, there was a little mud on the front end and on the wheels. Xiaoxiao wiped it clean with a wet cloth, then she cut a garland out of red paper and fastened it to the car so that it looked like a float. "Do you like it, Little Tie Han?"

"Yes." Little Tie Han followed behind the moving car and shouted "di-di."

"Little Tie Han, how would you like to drive out to Tian'anmen in Beijing?" Xiaoxiao sounded him out.

"That would be great!" Little Tie Han jumped up and down singing, "I love Beijing's Tian'anmen. The sun rised over Tian'anmen..."

"That's really good, sing another one." She carried Little Tie Han over to the *kang*. "This is the stage, now you can perform for everyone."

"Little Tie Han is very good at telling stories," Uncle Liu said.

"All right, I'll tell a story." Little Tie Han tilted his head, thought for a minute, then unaffectedly pursed his lips and put his hands behind his back. "I'll tell 'The Mother's Tale...'"

It was late at night and the wind forced the snow around. By the candlelight, the mother was watching over her sick child. Suddenly, the door opened...

Little Tie Han seemed to have learned it all by heart, each beat of the rhythm, every pause and transition, he hardly left out a single word. This story had been his wish for her when she had just become a mother. And now, as Xiaoxiao heard it from her child's lips, it became a kind of profound condemnation.

...The mother was very persistent, she said to Death, "I have sacrificed everything, I only want my child back, even if endless hardship awaits us, we still want to be together and to depend on each other for survival."

Death was moved...

He had changed the end of the story, Xiaoxiao thought. Oh yes, God's heaven doesn't exist. A child's heaven is its parents' love. What about Little Tie Han's heaven?... Xiaoxiao lifted Little Tie Han and held him close to her heart —— could he feel a mother's heart filled with love and guilt?

Auntie brought in the dumplings.

Xiaoxiao ate the dumplings with her head down, one dumpling after another, her mouth was stuffed but she didn't taste the type of filling or the flavour they had.

The door opened.

Little Tie Han put down his chopsticks and shouted with happy surprise, "Auntie Xiao Fang!"

Xiao Fang stood in the doorway, short of breath and with a sweaty face.

"Auntie, have some dumplings." Little Tie Han took his own plate over to Xiao Fang and rubbed his greasy mouth against her.

"You naughty child!..." Xiao Fang's reproaching eyes also held deep affection. "Auntie was worried sick."

"Have a seat, auntie." Little Tie Han knew that he had done something wrong and sensibly pulled Xiao Fang over to the *kang*. Only then did Xiao Fang see Xiaoxiao and she put out her hand happily. "I heard that you had come, I went to see you the other night, but I couldn't find you."

"I was at someone else's house," Xiaoxiao remarked casually.

"Little Tie Han, come over here, do you know who she is?" Xiao Fang warmly put her hand on Xiaoxiao's shoulder. Xiaoxiao held her breath and didn't move. She felt as if there was a piece of glass on her shoulder that would fall to the ground at the slightest touch.

"Yes I do, I even told auntie a story."

"No, she's not your auntie..." Xiao Fang pulled Little Tie Han closer.

"She is auntie, she is auntie." Stubborn and affectionate, Little Tie Han snuggled up to Xiao Fang.

Xiaoxiao held a pair of chopsticks between her fingers, and with her head down, she used them to draw circles in the vinegar that had spilled onto the table top. She felt sick at heart. Could she blame the child? He didn't know anything...

Xiao Fang took Little Tie Han's face in her hands. Might she not tell him, "She's your mother." Might she not let him say mummy. He would certainly make the proud announcement to his friends, "I also have a mummy now!" Nothing was as touching as the sound of a child calling for his mummy.

Xiao Fang looked at Xiaoxiao as if to ask her opinion. Xiaoxiao lifted her head abruptly, the look seemed to be connected to an electric current and it made Xiaoxiao's heart spark in a frightening way. "No!" She grabbed Xiao Fang's arm. Don't make the child say mummy to someone who's still a stranger, it might bruise his heart. His heart is too fragile.

Xiao Fang just kissed Little Tie Han's face.

"Let's eat." The child is here in our home and you can all relax!" Uncle Liu brought in two plates of dumplings.

Xiaoxiao wasn't hungry any more.

Xiao Fang ate slowly, counting the dumplings on the plate...

"I have to go now." Xiao Fang was anxious to leave. "I have another class tonight."

"What kind of class do you have tonight?" Auntie blocked the door. "Tonight you'll stay over at our house."

"I'm teaching advanced mathematics to the teachers." Xiao Fang rolled up her trousers. "I biked over, it'll take me a half hour to get back." She turned toward Xiaoxiao, "Are you staying here for a few days?"

"No, I'll be leaving in a day or so."

"Auntie, I'll come with you." Little Tie Han pushed forward.

Xiaoxiao rejoiced in her heart.

But Little Tie Han tugged tightly at Xiao Fang's clothes and pleaded, "Auntie, I want to go with you."

"It's too dark outside." Uncle Liu came up and pulled Little Tie Han back.

"I'm not afraid!" Little Tie Han rushed up to the door and buried his face in Xiao Fang's clothes. Like a crab, his two little hands clasped to her jacket.

"Be good now, auntie still has something to see to. I'll come and fetch you tomorrow..." Xiao Fang urged Little Tie Han softly.

Upon seeing Little Tie Han nestling so closely to Xiao Fang, Xiaoxiao was instantly overcome by an uncontrollable feeling. No mother could bear seeing her own children treat her like a stranger and transfer their affection to another woman.

"Auntie, I want to go home, let's go!"

Xiao Fang looked at Xiaoxiao as if to ask, "Should I take him along?"

"I'm taking Little Tie Han with me," Xiaoxiao burst out.

"You're taking him with you?" Xiao Fang asked stunned.

"Has he agreed to this?" Uncle Liu asked in a worried voice.

"I think...I think I'll take him with me." Xiaoxiao just stood there with a blank expression.

"Auntie, let's go!" Little Tie Han was still urging her.

Xiao Fang stroked his head.

"You'd better leave!" Uncle Liu pulled Little Tie Han away from Xiao Fang.

"Would you see me on the way?" Xiao Fang asked Xiaoxiao hesitantly.

Xiaoxiao walked out first.

There was no wind and the air was dense. The clouds got thicker and they hung low enough to touch the tops of a few tall elm trees in the distance. The button-like stars had disappeared, heaven and earth were black and heavy, as if they had fallen into an abyss. A few frogs croaked in the puddles.

The two of them walked in silence, separated by the bicycle. Its wheels pressed against the bits of sand and pebbles on the road and they crunched reluctantly, as if they were fidgety too.

"Am I the reason you want to take Little Tie Han with you?..." Xiao Fang asked bluntly, even though she didn't really want to ask like this.

Xiaoxiao's heart shivered slightly. Xiao Fang's directness embarrassed her.

"I can understand you. If it was me, I'd probably do the same." Xiao Fang's eyes were fixed upon the bell on the handle bar.

Xiaoxiao walked with her head down, she was very upset. She hadn't wanted to say those words, why had she done it? She couldn't sort it out now.

"I'm very fond of Little Tie Han," Xiao Fang said with certainty. "From when I was small, I did not grow up by my mother's side either. I know what it feels like to long for warmth. I've tasted the grief and disappointment that follow from not getting any affection. These kinds of feelings and emotions can cast a shadow over a bright heart. I want Little Tie Han's heart to be forever bright. The child is lovely and extremely sensitive..."

Xiaoxiao remained tacit. She was filled with contradictions. She ought to have been grateful to Xiao Fang for having been so affectionate toward Little Tie Han and for caring for him. But when she saw the result of this affection and concern, she just couldn't stand it...

"Perhaps he would agree to your taking the child with you. But you can't imagine how he has raised Little Tie Han the last few years. He couldn't live without Little Tie Han." Xiao Fang paused, should she go on? He had always shown concern for her. Once, when they were talking about each other's lives, he said that he'd introduce her to a friend. Half-jokingly, she asked, "Is he anything

like you?" That's right, half-jokingly. Because she half-meant it.
She respected him and admired him profoundly. But she also
understood him very well, his feelings were like a well, they ran
so deep. He had never forgotten Xiaoxiao. She understood that she
had to respect his feelings, she understood that she had to get a
grip on herself. Sometimes, she would feel sorry for Xiaoxiao,
sometimes she would feel sorry for him and sometimes she would
feel sorry for herself. People's emotions were like their lives, so
very complex. Of course, she would never expose these sympathetic
feelings. They belonged to the innermost part of her, to her alone.

She walked a few steps forward, then turned her head and
looked at Xiaoxiao. Almost begging her, she said, "Don't take
Little Tie Han with you. You must think of him..."

"He must think of me too." Xiaoxiao stopped.

"He has thought of you, he thinks of you in everything. He has
suffered the most." Xiao Fang was still walking. "The business
with the dam has already given him a lot of trouble. And when the
dam is completed, the story isn't over yet. At a time like this, you
shouldn't..."

"This has nothing to do with the dam." Xiaoxiao caught up with
her.

"Yes it has. Apart from his work, there is only the child in his
heart. They are complete together, you mustn't break them apart."

"No, you are in his heart too..." Xiaoxiao finally said it. She
said it very quickly, very lightly, like a swift current carrying away
a leaf.

Having said it, she immediately felt relieved.

"You are wrong!" Xiao Fang's feelings became heavy. "You are
quite wrong!" she repeated, in a hard voice that seemed to crash
down from somewhere high above them. She had thought that
Xiaoxiao might mention it, but she had hoped not to hear it. It was
something she couldn't explain, and something she didn't want to

have to explain. She pulled the brakes.

Like two small trees in the darkness, they stood there facing each other. For a long while, neither of them uttered a word.

"I'm running out of time, I have to go now..."

Xiao Fang stepped down on the pedal. "Let me just say one last thing, no matter what, please do not take Little Tie Han with you! Goodbye!" She mounted her bicycle and rang the bell. In the still of the night the bell sounded clear and resonant...

The night was frightfully black like the skin of a whale. A faint sound of thunder rolled through the clouds, it was oppressive, like someone hitting a drum with restrained blows.

It was about to start raining. Heavy rain, thunderstorm, rainstorm?

Xiaoxiao watched the sky for a long time, unable to see a thing.

10

What a rainfall. It rained for two days continuously. The thatched roof was leaking and the water dripping down from the eaves formed a small river in front of the door. The roadbed was washed away, the mud from the turbid water trickled into the ditch and the water from the ditch in return flooded the road. All over there were shining white water-logged depressions.

"When is the rain going to stop!" Unable to go outside for two days, Little Tie Han got so anxious that he almost cried. "I want to give daddy a phone call."

Xiaoxiao also wanted to phone him. Two days and two nights of heavy rain had cleansed her heart. She was calm now, and clear.

"How could I, prompted by my own feelings, let myself be drawn into such a tight whirlpool?" she reproached herself shamefully. To be fair, he wasn't in the wrong, Little Tie Han wasn't in the wrong, neither was Xiao Fang. It was all so natural, fair and reasonable, and beautiful.

Was she in the wrong?

She hadn't dreamt that her own peace-seeking heart could cause such a great disturbance. At the moment she got on the plane, she had believed that, already, this land was far away from her. Going back for a visit was nothing more than the fulfilment of a long-cherished wish. But she had misjudged herself. Her heart had never left the place at all.

And yet she had left after all!

"You must think of him!" Xiao Fang had been right in reminding her. He was at the construction site, in the midst of the rainstorm... She thought of him, two days and nights in a row: had they managed to finish the dam before the rainstorm? Were the mountain torrents very fierce?...

There wasn't the slightest news.

The phone had been disconnected long ago. The wire poles along the road fell over one by one and dragged the long phone lines through the puddles.

Xiaoxiao was standing by the window watching the water splashing against the window pane. Her heart seemed full of rain water too. She felt suffocated. She dared not think of the conditions out by the dam in the middle of the rainstorm, and yet she couldn't stop imagining how it must be: the cold, hard rain lashing like a whip, they'd be gasping for breath up against the wind. Rubber boots hard to pull out of the mire...lumps of slurry, heavier than stone, would stick to the shovels, and bits would only come off when they had exerted enough strength...the canvas bags on their shoulders would be saturated with water and weighing down heavily on their bodies... he'd be running around shouting himself hoarse, his dripping wet hair sticking to his temples, his eyes sunken and bloodshot...

"The rain has stopped, the dam is finished, you must take a good rest, you're so exhausted..." she spoke to the drenched window panes.

"Take a rest? They're still waiting to hold the Party committee meeting to investigate me..." The dripping water answered on his behalf.

"Di-di!" Behind her, Little Tie Han was playing with his car.

I have no right to take him with me! She became more and more clear about this. Little Tie Han, however, had become close to her. When eating, he wanted to sit next to her, when sleeping, he wanted to snuggle up to her and listen to her singing tirelessly and tapping gently, with his eyes half shut he was fully at ease, as if he was back in his swaddling-clothes only wanting to sleep when his mummy coaxed him. It had only been two days! Experiencing a warmth that no one else had ever given him, Little Tie Han seemed to be trying to make up for lost time. A child seems to be particularly sensitive to motherly affection. It was probably nature's message.

Endless worrying, like continuous rain. Concerned about him, far away out at the construction site, and fully occupied by the thought of the child at her bosom. Worried and uneasy, her heart was nevertheless calm. She'd experienced this sort of feeling before when she'd gone through all kinds of hardship while filling page after page of writing paper. Like the love for one's profession, the love for one's husband, for one's child and for everyone else who should be loved could make one a richer person.

People can't do without love, just as they can't do without air.

"Auntie, the rain stopped, the rain stopped!" Little Tie Han was jumping and shouting. "Let's give daddy a call, let's call him!"

The rain had stopped!

The sky was a light greenish-blue colour and the air was damp with a strong refreshing scent of water. The eaves were still dripping, the leaves were still dripping. The waterlogged depressions in the road were glistening and sparkling like fish scales.

"Let's go!" She also couldn't wait.

"The lines can't have been reconnected so fast." Uncle Liu came back from feeding the horses, he had bits of straw all over him.

"They're reconnected, reconnected!" Little Tie Han was too impatient to wait.

They wouldn't be reconnected so fast, but Xiaoxiao, too, wanted to get outside and walk around, trample about in the clear, unsoiled rainwater, breathe in the fresh, clean air.

Everybody had come outside. The windlass on the well was operating noisily once more. A long line of buckets stood next to the well and a bunch of men, leaning against their shoulder poles, were laughing and joking. In front of and behind the houses, wet clothes were once again hung out on the iron wires. The women, separated by the bamboo fences between the small yards, were busy running in and out while constantly chatting with each other. Two days of rain made it seem as if people had been locked up for two years.

Xiaoxiao stood in the doorway of the company office, and the people coming and going on the road greeted her without stopping:

"You've come back!"

"When are you leaving?"

......

When would she leave? The rain had stopped, the bus was running again, maybe it was time for her to leave now...

"Xiaoxiao, a phone call for you," the old accountant was calling her from inside.

"The phone has been reconnected!" Little Tie Han ran faster than she.

Who would be calling her? The lines had just been reconnected...

"Is it daddy on the phone?" Little Tie Han stretched his neck, tilted his head and without blinking stared at Xiaoxiao as she picked up the receiver.

It couldn't be him. The rain had just stopped, there were so many things to be done at the construction site.

"Hello," she said effortlessly.

"......"

"Speaking." At once her voice became agitated.

"It's daddy. Give it to me, quick!" Little Tie Han was so alert.

She immediately handed the phone to Little Tie Han as if she'd answered a call that she didn't wish to answer. But she had been waiting for this call for two full days!... She suddenly heard his voice again, and even though it was very faint, as if they were separated by innumerable mountains and valleys, her heart began beating violently. She wanted to think, to think over again what she ought to say. She took a few steps towards the door.

"Daddy, it's me, Little Tie Han. I guessed that it was you on the phone. You must have missed me. It's been raining here. Did it rain out where you are?" Excited, Little Tie Han pressed his mouth to the mouthpiece. "I'm staying with Uncle Liu, I went there by myself and I took my little car with me. When are you coming back?"

"......"

"All right!" Little Tie Han rather grudgingly handed the receiver to Xiaoxiao. "Daddy wants to talk to you."

There was a lot of noise on the line and his voice had become hoarse too. "... The dam is finished. We braved the heavy rain and stood next to the dam for two hours, waiting for the mountain torrents, but as it turned out the torrents never came..."

"We were very worried about all of you..."

"You should have been here to see the site in the rainstorm, to feel the kind of excitement and happiness of risking one's life for the struggle, then you'd be able to write another good novel..."

"You didn't ask me to stay," she said deliberately.

"I couldn't make you stay..."

No, I have regrets, and I'm sentimental, whether it's about the moment I left the dam or the time that I parted with the little mud hut... She felt like saying but didn't know where to begin. She paused.

"When are you coming back to the farm headquarters?"

"For the time being I won't be able to come back."

"Why?"

"I want to go to the Central Farm right away." His voice was very low, she could barely hear him. "They are preparing to call the Central Farm Party Committee's attention to my punishment, there are many charges against me; number one; ignoring the farm Party committee's collective leadership; number two, presumptuous defiance of the higher leading body's orders; number three, since there weren't any mountain torrents, my directions to finish the dam in a rush were arbitrary and impracticable, it's just an excuse to criticize me..."

"So because the mountain torrents didn't come, it was a mistake to finish the dam?" She was outraged. "I'll wait for you to come back." Could she leave without feeling uneasy? How would the Central Farm handle this suit? Those "charges" were sufficient to send him back to the stable. Of course, feeding the horses was much easier than being the farm chief. But he wouldn't give up. So what would the outcome be?...

"I won't leave." She was determined. When he needed her in the past she had left. Now he could do without her. But he was faced with a difficult situation, she felt she ought to stay.

"No, you must leave!"

"Why do you want to chase me away?"

"You'd better leave, but I'm not chasing you." He was very sincere.

"For what reason?"

"For no reason."

"Then I won't leave."

"What if I ask you to..."

Xiaoxiao sensed that his voice sounded unusual. "Is it because of 'her'..." She could only explain it this way.

"Don't say any more." He forced the sounds out of his burning throat.

For several minutes there was only some noise on the phone.

She thought he had walked away in anger, but she hadn't hung up. Why had she mentioned "her" again thus bringing up a sense of wanting to control him? He had a right to a new life!

She had no idea how long it had been when she heard his voice on the phone again: "What date is it?"

"The twentieth."

Then another pause.

"Could you do me a favour and see Xiao Fang on her way tomorrow..."

"Where's she going?"

"To the hospital."

"What's wrong with her?"

"You ask her." Sweat seeped out of the hand in which she held the receiver. Xiao Fang hadn't mentioned a word about her own situation the other day. Why didn't I show some concern for other people?...

"You'd better leave, don't be swayed by your emotions." His voice sounded as calm as water without ripples. "Don't always look back. 'The past' that's left in your memory has been sifted and selected and only a few beautiful things remain. The everyday, the unhappy and even the bitter events have faded from your memory. Your new life will inevitably be full of contradictions but, after all, it is a new life, and it holds many new things in store for you. Most important is the present. The path has been cleared for you, it is wide, and once you're on it you can go a long way..."

What more could she say?

"Little Tie Han...you may take him with you. I've thought it over, you need him even more than I..." His voice suddenly became very unclear.

"No, Little Tie Han belongs to you..."

"Don't argue." With his hoarse voice he then requested, "Give the phone to the child."

Little Tie Han sensed that something had happened. Why was auntie's face white as if she was sick? "Auntie, what's wrong?"

"Oh...nothing..." She passed the phone to Little Tie Han.

Little Tie Han took it suspiciously, his voice sounded rather worried too, "Daddy..."

"......"

"What? What are you saying, daddy?" Little Tie Han's expression changed from suspicion to surprise. He swiftly turned his head and stared at Xiaoxiao, questions, judgments, contemplation, apprehension, hesitation, all of a sudden numerous complexities gathered in his clear eyes. Then gradually, they became clear again and full of joy, "Daddy says you're...you're —— mummy?..."

No? She wanted to grab the phone and loudly call him to account, "Why tell the child?" But she just took Little Tie Han's head between her hands and held it up to her chin, and her tears, like dewdrops rolling down the tip of a leaf, fell on his thick, black hair. She slowly reached for the phone and said full of emotion, "Thank you..."

Little Tie Han ought to know that he also has a mother who loves him very, very much.

"The other day I came back with all the magazines that I'd wanted to give you. I'll give them to Little Tie Han..." She really felt like going on talking like that with the phone in her hand.

"But..."

"What?"

"Actually, I've read most of them," he said after all.

"I'll leave them for you anyway..."

He took over immediately, "I can't see you off, I hope you'll forgive me like you did back then."

"No, let's see each other once more. Can't we get together once more?"

He didn't respond.

"Otherwise I'll just wait for your return before I leave..."

"How about this, we'll meet midway. Wait for me in the woods by the small bridge behind the brickyard." He finally consented. "Wang Qiang, Wu Huanhuan and the others are buried there, we moved the graves earlier." He was thinking about something. "Please pick some flowers for me..."

The wire attached to the receiver quivered.

"Let's go back!" Little Tie Han was tugging at Xiaoxiao's clothes as he bashfully called, "mummy——"

She lifted Little Tie Han up in her arms and the tears welled up again.

"Little Tie Han!"

"Auntie!" Little Tie Han opened up his arms.

Xiao Fang was standing in the doorway.

"Auntie, she is mummy!" Little Tie Han pointed at Xiaoxiao a little embarrassed.

"You..." Xiaoxiao gave Tie Han to Xiao Fang. "I was just going to see you."

"I wanted to see you about something too. The teachers' advanced class wants to invite you to teach a class, to talk about your writing and your life. One of my students just came back from the Central Farm, she praised you endlessly." Xiao Fang was so warmhearted. "Or you could choose your own topic..."

"Let's not talk about that now." Xiaoxiao interrupted Xiao Fang. "Tell me, what's with your illness?..."

"How did you know?..."

"He told me. He asked me to see you off."

Xiao Fang smiled slightly. "Actually, it's really nothing. But Chief Li brought it up at a Party committee meeting and demanded that the Party committee take care of me, so then things seemed to become more serious."

"What's the matter with you?"

"It's possibly cancer of the uterus, they'll have to remove it. And then there's rheumatism, the legs, the heart..." Xiao Fang spoke very lightly, as if it was nothing but a regular cold. "Do you remember the second year after we came to the Great Northern Wilderness, the mountain torrents flooded the wheat and we waded in to the water to harvest the wheat. My period had just started...I didn't understand and didn't care..." she gave a light sigh. "The doctor says it's too late to cure..."

"That's impossible. Come to Beijing and I'll help you contact a hospital."

Xiao Fang shook her head. "Don't worry. These illnesses of mine can perhaps never...that's okay too, unmarried, I won't be a burden to anyone. I'm used to living on my own, when I started elementary school I lived on campus. If my parents were going away to look for minerals, I wouldn't even go home on Sundays."

"Who says you're not fit...wait till you're well again..." Xiaoxiao felt profoundly guilty.

"You don't have to comfort me. As for myself, I've thought it through long ago." Xiao Fang smiled. "Let's not talk about these depressing matters." Then she blurted out, "To tell you the truth, I am very fond of Little Tie Han. If you take him with you, we'll all be very sorry."

Xiaoxiao embraced Xiao Fang tightly, it wasn't just to ask her forgiveness. No, her heart needed to be close to another heart and feel that special kind of warmth between two hearts as they silently melt into one. These past few years, she had been like a small, solitary goldfish in a glass bowl and, though she had busied herself swimming around in endless circles, she remained on the inside of a miserable glass bowl. The people around her, the world around her was separated from her by a layer of glass. In the past, however, she had been to the "ocean", together with her buddies. They'd gone through thick and thin together, when thirsty, they shared a jug of glass. In the past, however, she had been to the "ocean," together with her buddies. They'd gone through thick and thin together, when thirsty, they shared a jug of water; when hungry, they split a steamed bread between them. When the *kang* in the men's dormitory caught fire, the women vacated a room, spread out half of their quilts and everybody slept sitting up back to back... The hardships of those days were gone, and so were the joys of sharing each other's sweat. When she thought about it, it was close and yet so distant, like the land underneath her feet.

She squeezed Xiao Fang's hand tightly.

The rain had washed the mountain flowers. The petals were more brilliant than ever, red, yellow and purple, bloomed in the midst of the thick, green grass, waving merrily in the wind.

She picked a large bouquet and divided it into four.

In the woods next to the small bridge, people had trodden a meandering footpath. Next to the path were clusters of golden yellow cornflowers and many greyish-coloured mushrooms. In the wood were white birch, poplars, northeast China ash, small Korean pine, and though very different from each other, they grew harmoniously side by side. She hadn't been in the wood for a long time and as she watched the thick, green area from afar, Xiaoxiao once again felt a certain freshness and mystique. In the past, when she'd gone to the woods with her buddies to play hide-and-seek, she'd circled around all the big and small trees, agile as a loach, no one could catch her...

Her steps got heavier.

Graves. Four cone-shaped small mounds, and four upright rectangular stone tablets. There were no inscriptions on the tablets, just some blurred characters, the grooves of the carvings filled with dust. The mounds were covered by dense weeds. There were no flowers.

Just lying there, forever silent, nobody asked about them anymore. If he hadn't reminded her, would she have thought of coming here to see them? Her heart was burning from feelings of remorse and emotion.

She stood silent for a moment in front of each gravestone. Then with her nails she scratched out the earth that filled the grooves of the characters on the tablets: Wang Qiang, Wu Huanhuan, Jiang Ping and Song Yuzhen. Their vivid, smiling faces floated towards her. She wanted to tell them, "The dam has been completed, now there's no need to fear the crazed and the wanton destruction of the mountain torrents."

If the dam had been completed ten years earlier, would they have?...

She leaned up against a white birch, facing her four companions. The small, round pastel green leaves shaded her intimately, like a huge parasol. They had once stood quietly like this, facing each other, resting up after a game of hide-and-seek. If their hearts were still able to beat, if they were still able to speak, they'd certainly ask her questions from all sides.

"What are you doing in Beijing?"

"Is it fun to be an editor?"

"You're so fortunate!"

"How's everybody else doing? Big Horse, Olive Head, Long-footed Egret..."

In her heart she was asking about them, "How are you all? You must be a bit lonely?"

"Sometimes it gets lonely. You've probably all forgotten us."

"No, we all miss you, we miss the land that we once lived on. It's true, I've asked a lot of people, they all would like to come back and see you. After all, our lives began here. We come here on foot, and the road was very long, we strode with our youth, but you offered your lives..."

"You're doing well now, you have everything."

"That's what everybody thinks. If you could really understand me... I've left many valuable things behind here and, just like I've lost you, I will never be able to take them back..."

"We, too, have only come to understand this stretch of land gradually after we'd really remained behind. People still farm the land, they still have a hard life, they still have to spend a great deal of energy and pay a high price just to make a few changes. But they are indomitable in their work, and bury their lives in this land. Therefore, the earth here is always fertile. They still remember to come and visit us. In the summer, they pick a few wild flowers; in the winter, they break off a couple of pine branches. This is a great comfort to us, nevertheless it also makes us ashamed that we never really did anything for the land!"

"No, you've made the biggest sacrifice of all."

"Our sacrifice was for nothing. If we had died while constructing the dam, it would have been worth it, then it would have been in an effort to improve the land. But..."

"Maybe, the dam was built because of your sacrifice."

"You're just consoling us."

"It wasn't easy to build this dam. In a little while, he'll be here too, he can tell you all about it." Suddenly her heart began beating fiercely: write all of this down!

"We're happy to see you. Don't forget us when you go back home."

"I'll send you a copy of every piece that I write." I won't go to the Institute of Literary Research. I won't become the secretary. I must write diligently. I've got a responsibility to write. I can do it! She decided in an instant.

"Would you like to see what I write?" Each time that she had a piece published she'd felt anxious and fearful. She knew: Wang Qiang was fond of detective novels, he had kept a hand-written copy of *Collected Cases of Sherlock Holmes* on him (it was buried with him); Wu Huanhuan loved lyric poetry, Pushkin and Lermontov; Jiang Ping used to "steal" the company's *Reference News* and take it back to the dormitory every evening; Song Yuzhen, like a child, would go out and buy comic books to read. "But I'll definitely write well..."

She was confident.

"We'll give you a title..."

"What?"

"'The Distant Land'."

The distant land!

Oh yes , she would soon be leaving and the soil underneath her feet would again become so distant to her...

No, hadn't she become closer to it? It was in her heart.

Xiaoxiao pulled the weeds from each mound, cleared the space around, and then she placed a bunch of colourful flowers in front of each tablet.

"I won't be able to come and see you very often, but when the mountain flowers bloom I'll write to him, 'Go and sweep the graves in the woods by the small bridge, and please leave a bunch of flowers from me, too!'"

They all fell silent.

He ought to be here by now. Xiaoxiao woke from her deep thoughts and looked at her watch. It was long past the appointed time.

She walked out of the woods.

It was peaceful all around her. The water in the small river flowed quietly.

She walked up on the bridge and looked in the direction of the main road. Suddenly, at the turn of the road, a cloud of dust whirled up with a momentum, like smoke spurting out of a rocket. She watched the farm headquarters' little army-green jeep roar past, like a bullet out of a barrel. Were the higher-ups already coming to punish him?

At the road-fork the jeep turned down the big road to the dam without halting.

He wasn't going to come.

He wasn't able to come!

Xiaoxiao suddenly became aware of something and hurried back to the woods to pick up her bag.

"I'll go to the dam. I'll go to the dam, too!" But as she slung the bag over her shoulder and halted once again next to the white birch, all of a sudden she recalled the words of the bureau chief:

"If you have any troubles at the lower levels, you can come to me directly..."

Go and see him?!

Xiaoxiao slowly circled around the white birch, looked back once more at those erect grave stones, looked at the few bouquets of brightly coloured mountain flowers.

Reds, yellows, purples...

Translated by Anne-Marie Traeholt and Mark Kruger

One on One

"SISTER Huishan, why don't you call for a taxi? You're not so young any more."

The youths in the office were all so sure of themselves.

"Because it'd cost me twenty or thirty yuan, which means forty or fifty round trips."

Song Huishan couldn't bear to waste money. It would only be fifty or sixty fen a ride on the bus, and if she caught an early one, she might still find a seat. There was no reason for a taxi.

It was almost five o'clock. Far off in the sky a few stars still twinkled as Huishan got ready to leave. She had put on a sombre outfit, greyish-white and new, made especially for his anniversary. Last night she had neatly packed together a box of fruits that were available year-round: peaches, oranges, apples and bananas. "He was basically a vegetarian, and though he's now in another world, he still needs his fruit and vegetables," she thought to herself, forever thinking of him.

Song Huishan had been a widow for three years now. Today was her husband's anniversary. Once again she had hardly slept a wink last night, thinking back on their lives together from the very beginning. She had had to go to several florists before she had found his favourite, a bouquet of light white roses, which, though lacking in fragrance, were in full bloom. Even under the harshest conditions, when they were most poor, she had managed to scrape together enough money to buy some roses to put in the big vase before the window.

The sky remained dark. The breakfast she had prepared began to cool on the table. Twin bowls of grey porcelain filled with thick, golden millet gruel and red dates and kidney beans lay across the table from each other, a pair of carved chopsticks lay by the side of each, while in the middle, four dishes —— spicy turnip slices, sweet and sour cucumber, pickled beancurd, and a beancurd-skin salad completed the picture. It was said that these four dishes were Confucius' favourites.

Her husband had researched it. The porcelain plates with their antique colour and flavour were all very authentic. All of this had been his hobby. Probably because they'd had no children, their life together had been substantiated with his hobbies, which had made it quite interesting at times. Song Huishan knew him inside out; she could manage everything to suit his taste, even the tiniest detail. Alas! He had departed so quickly, without leaving behind a single word.

The house was very dark, lit only by a small incandescent lamp which grew dimmer with time. Extremely frugal, he had been against a brightly-lit house mainly to conserve electricity, and she had gradually been influenced by him, saving every penny. On her annual trip to the cemetery, she always squeezed into the packed city bus, and then waited for a transfer to the outskirts of town. It took four hours roundtrip, so she always had to take a day off from work. Fortunately her colleagues were very understanding and did not deduct from her bonus.

All was ready. Song Huishan was just about to step out when someone knocked on her door, so softly and delicately that it sounded like kitten paws patting the door.

"Who is it?"

She thought it odd anyone would come at such an early hour.

"It's me."

The voice outside the door also sounded soft and delicate. "You?"

What's she doing here so early in the morning, Song Huishan wondered.

Hua Jing, the one waiting outside, was Song Huishan's neighbour. Though they lived across the hall from each other, one in apartment 301 and the other in 303 with the stairs between them, they never interacted much save an occasional nod or smile when passing each other on the stairs. Actually, they had both been cadres at the same place, the district textile bureau, where Huishan had been a model employee in administration and Hua Jing had been the best in design. The two departments also happened to be across the hall from each other with the stairs between them, one on the right and the other on the left as one went up the stairs to the second floor. But even then, the two women had never really been on friendly terms. Hua Jing had been quite pretty when young. With her trim figure and delicate features, she looked a typical southern belle. Though she had a shy demeanour, she was quite aloof and never said much. Even when she walked, her footsteps were as light as a kitten's and made no sound.

"Such haughtiness! Why put on airs?"

Song Huishan didn't like self-admiring people. She herself was amiable and got along with everyone except Hua Jing. Before the Cultural Revolution, there had been quite a scene in the design department. The wife of Engineer Yin had crashed into the office and overturned Hua Jing's desk, all the while crying and screaming profanities. The entire bureau had been in an uproar; everyone had buzzed with talk. Stories involving Hua Jing and Engineer Yin became alive with repeated telling. After that, Hua Jing was temporarily transferred out of the design room. Before long, she left the textile bureau altogether. From then on, Engineer Yin had to see his wife off to work every morning and wave goodbye to her until she was out of sight. They acted so lovingly that his office often praised them as "the perfect couple."

All the while Hua Jing never married.

"Is it worth it?"

Song Huishan couldn't imagine. She had asked for it, trying to break up someone else's home, Huishan thought contemptuously. Even if a third party had tried to cut into the life she had had with him, she couldn't imagine that person causing a crack or even a crease, but then, they had been truly close.

Before she left the textile bureau, Hua Jing had been allocated new accommodation and lived there alone. All who saw it said her place was decorated quite tastefully and comfortably. She installed a telephone at her own expense and was also the first in the whole building to move in a refrigerator.

"Sister Huishan, go see for yourself. Telephone, refrigerator; everything's modern."

All the youths in the office were so admiring.

"Hmph!..."

Song Huishan had disdained to even go look. She thought that if one loved and was loved in return, then life was happy and complete and made sense. But three years ago he had left, and left her to be alone also. "I'm different from her, absolutely different," she would tell people she met, and repeated it often to herself.

In any case, everyone in the building knew that in 301 and 303 lived two single women who, though neighbours, never associated with one another.

Song Huishan would never have expected Hua Jing to come and tell her that there was a car to the cemetery.

"You don't need to leave that early. I've reserved a car for myself. We can go together."

Hua Jing wore a silver wool skirt. Impeccably pressed, it looked refined and natural.

"I...I'd better take the bus." Song Huishan bluntly refused. On his anniversary, she just wanted to spend a quiet and peaceful day with him. Besides, she and Hua Jing never associated much...

"There's a marathon today. No more buses will be in the suburbs after seven this morning."

"Oh?"

Song Huishan had to admit that Hua Jing was more thoughtful than herself. She hadn't even known about the marathon. He had read the papers and listened to the radio broadcasts regularly each day and relayed any and all exciting news to her. When he left, their newspaper subscriptions had eventually stopped.

"We can leave at six."

"Who are you going to see?"

"A relative who passed away just last year. Come to my place for a while; it's still early."

"No, thanks."

Song Huishan had set three rules for herself during the week of his anniversary: no visiting, no socializing, and no receiving guests. This was to console him. She was used to it; she had to think of him in everything that she did.

But with no other choice that day, she ended up riding in Hua Jing's rented car, chatting randomly along the way. This pretty much broke the silence barrier.

Not long after that incident, Xiao Wang of the design department came to ask her help:

"Sister Huishan, could you please tell Designer Hua that we'd like her to design some cloth patterns for us? Several countries in South America will be placing an order. You two live so close, and it'd save me a trip."

"Your design department just can't do without her, can it?"

"She was responsible for designing our export products before and was very popular."

"Let your Engineer Yin ask her," Song Huishan said intentionally.

"Sister Huishan, you know how formidable his wife is. Once she's offended, our department will never have any peace. Please, I beg you just this once in my life."

With his glib tongue and persistency, Xiao Wang really knew how to get to people.

Song Huishan gave in. After work and after making dinner, she walked over to Hua Jing's. She only planned to stay a little while and leave as soon as she relayed the message.

Hua Jing was just getting ready to eat. In the middle of her carpet sat a low, square table around which were placed several legless rattan chairs with high backs, in Japanese fashion. A salad with potatoes, sausages and peas lay on the table. With its red, white and green, it looked quite a refreshing mix. On another plate was a pork chop with fried eggs on the side. Between the two dishes stood a tall glass filled with fresh orange juice.

"You...eat like a Westerner."

Song Huishan had only seen this in movies. All had been as he wished. Since he only ate Chinese food, she had never set foot inside a Western-style restaurant.

"Come and join me. There's plenty."

Hua Jing was quite warm-hearted. Opening the refrigerator, she bustled about taking out this and that.

"Don't bother. I've already made dinner."

Song Huishan stared at the refrigerator as it opened and closed. With its insides full of assorted, colourful edibles, it resembled a treasure chest. All she had was a cupboard for dishes; leftovers were left to hang in a bamboo basket.

"Come on, it's more cheerful to eat together."

Hua Jing placed a similar set of dishes on the table.

"Well, in that case, I'll join you then."

So Song Huishan folded her legs and sat. She felt awkward yet excited, because this was all so new.

Though only a casual meal, she took it seriously, chewing thoroughly and swallowing carefully as if to savour every last bite. For the greater part of her life she had been used to his tastes alone. Outside of that, she had hardly tried any other tastes. Besides, for the past three years she had often dined in solitude, with a place setting for him as always...

Eating and chatting, Song Huishan only then began to relax. Drinking the Longjing tea that Hua Jing had prepared, its light aroma filling her senses, she began to talk more.

"Hua Jing, why didn't you get married?"

"You're single also."

Hua Jing smiled, a smile that showed no regrets. She was also nearing fifty, yet her figure remained delicate and trim.

"But I'm different. For this life, I'll love only him."

Song Huishan spoke from the heart. But the year that he had passed away, she hadn't been able to talk about the love between them without grieving for several days afterwards; she couldn't help it.

Their topics gradually widened, naturally revolving around that office building they were both so familiar with. They exchanged gossip and anecdotes about their bosses and their employees. Song Huishan's interest heightened. At the office she had kept the same routine day in and day out for several decades, easy-going yet controlled, and discreet, never talking about anything she shouldn't for fear of causing trouble. And now that he was gone, there was no one to talk to at home either.

Before they knew it, twelve o'clock rolled around.

"Oh, no, it's so late."

Song Huishan was filled with contentment, yet also thought it strange: how had she ended up staying for dinner and ended up saying so much? Returning home, lying in bed, she was still keyed up with excitement and replayed once more in her mind those fresh new tastes. That night she slept soundly, without those vague dreams and vague visions of him.

For courtesy's sake, Song Huishan returned Hua Jing's invitation at the end of the week.

"Try my cooking. He always used to say that not even the best restaurant tempted him after eating my food."

Using her lunch break, Song Huishan excitedly went off to the supermarket and bought chicken, fresh fish, half a catty of shrimp, a box of quail eggs. Busily stewing, deep-frying and stir-frying, she efficiently produced a full course in a short time. For dessert, she even made an "eight-treasures dish" with glutinous rice.

Hua Jing brought liquor. Every bite was tasty and scrumptious.

"You really like it?"

"Yes, it's delicious."

Song Huishan was happy, as happy as if he had praised her.

"I can't cook. I eat Western stuff only because it's convenient, so I sometimes buy it to go. I haven't the time to cook either; my freelance assignments keep me tied up."

After Hua Jing had transferred to the industrial art design centre, she had become its mainstay also. Unconventional yet appealing, her creations combined traditional folk art with modern drawing techniques, a style that became uniquely her own.

"At least you have something to show for it. I too keep busy all day, and yet I don't seem to achieve anything."

Song Huishan rarely showed such humility.

"We all have our shortcomings and good points too. As long as we try our best, that's enough."

"That's what people say, but..."

Song Huishan thought Hua Jing was quite understanding, not proud and aloof as she had thought. As for that "story" involving Engineer Yin, well, it was all in the past; people seemed to have forgotten it, so of course she wasn't going to bring it up.

Once again, the meal lasted until midnight. Only when Song Huishan was clearing away the table did she realize that for the first time in three years she hadn't placed a setting for him. Had she forgotten or was it just too inconvenient?

In this way, coming and going, apartments 301 and 303 that faced each other no longer seemed to be separated by the stairs; in fact, they seemed to be interlinked. Whenever Song Huishan prepared anything delicious, she would invite Hua Jing over. "Come, it's more cheerful to eat together."

She discovered that she enjoyed feeling needed, in the way that he had made her feel needed. But Hua Jing was too busy, often eating dinner at her office and returning home late. She also went on endless business trips, if not for this conference then for that exhibition, once even taking her products to Canada. Whenever she had to leave for these trips, she always gave her apartment keys to Song Huishan.

"Watch it for me, will you?"

"Don't worry."

Hua Jing's trust gave Song Huishan a feeling of comfort and a sense of responsibility. Everyday she would take the keys, open Hua Jing's door and fastidiously check the gas lines, the electricity meter, the faucets and such. Sometimes she would sit on those legless rattan chairs and reminisce over that novel feeling she had first time she came. Hua Jing was quite thoughtful; if her business trip was a long one, she would be sure to write. The first time she received such a letteer, Song Huishan's hands shook, she was so moved. Reading it over and over, she felt all warm inside. He had never liked to write; when he went out of town, unless an accident occurred, she would never hear from him. She cherished Hua Jing's letter, tucking each one under her pillow, never tiring of pulling them out and looking at them again and again.

Thereupon, everyone in the apartment building knew the two single women in 301 and 303 were now the closest of friends, like sisters.

Two years quickly passed. Song Huishan was fifty-five, while Hua Jing, four years younger, had also passed the half-century mark. All was as before, except a new wool-covered sofa had been added to Song Huishan's apartment and a valuable Hetian tapestry to the wall of Hua Jing's bedroom. The day the tapestry was delivered, Song Huishan had been incredulous: "Over two thousand yuan? Over two thousand yuan?"

Song Huishan's new sofa set, priced at almost five hundred, had also been bought at Hua Jing's insistence. Once home with the set, she had still agonized over it; tossing and turning, she slept fitfully all that night. When he had been alive, they had never squandered; the only thing they had gone to any expense for was his collection of porcelain. Their most valuable possession, a three-door wardrobe, had cost no more than two hundred at the time. In the middle of the night, she climbed out of bed and tried out the new furniture. It was soft, she had to admit, but then felt even more uneasy: he had never sat on anything so luxurious.

"Why save all that money when you can enjoy yourself?" Hua Jing frequently spoke sense.

"There isn't that much..."

Song Huishan had more than ten deposit books; together they accounted for five or six thousand yuan. This amount was substantial, and yet it wasn't really much. She rarely touched these savings. She had to think of the future: in a few more years when she retired, with decreased benefits and increased spending, she had to have enough set aside to hire an attendant in case she ever fell ill. With no one to rely on but herself, how would she get through hard times if she didn't save now? Years ago, with him beside her,

Song Huishan had never suffered for the lack of children. He had filled up her life, the way a bamboo basket sunk to a river bottom was suffused with water. When he left, the bamboo basket had been cruelly jerked up, only to be found empty. That year they had consulted several doctors and discovered that she was infertile. She had secretly cried many times. "We'll separate so you can find another." She was sincerely thinking of him. But he wouldn't. Later, his sister had wanted to give them one of hers, but he had also refused. "There are plenty of childless couples in this world." She knew he was consoling her. She didn't know how to repay him, yet she was constantly repaying him in every way possible. A few well-intentioned co-workers tried to persuade her to remarry, but she turned a deaf ear.

Only Hua Jing never pushed her. Occasionally, they talked of the times ahead.

"Hua Jing, you really don't plan to marry?"

"No."

"But the future..."

"Will be the same as now."

"Don't you feel incomplete somehow?"

"Marriage and family don't guarantee happiness. A meaningful life doesn't need to be lived a certain way."

"You feel that way now because you're keeping busy. But wait until you retire..."

"When I retire, I can still draw and design, or we can work less and go travelling."

Hua Jing was very optimistic.

Song Huishan thought travelling solved nothing. Besides, she wasn't interested in such diversions. Never active when young, she found it even less appealing now that she was getting on in years.

Their views seldom coincided during these discussions. Luckily it was only talk, and neither took offence. But one day their

difference of opinion almost erupted into a falling out. The trouble
seemed to be over a telegram.

"Hua Jing, what should I do?"

Song Huishan threw the just-received telegram on to the table in
frustration. His sister had sent it, writing that she was sending her
son over to spend his summer holiday.

"You don't have to do anything. Let him come. He'd be good
company."

"I don't need company. I'm used to living alone!" she cried out
in exasperation.

"Why are you making such a fuss?"

Hua Jing couldn't understand Song Huishan's agitation. The boy
was, after all, her nephew, and he was only going to stay a month.

"I'll go tell him not to come!"

Song Huishan whirled around to go.

"You can't do that!"

Hua Jing anxiously blocked the door.

"I can do what I please."

Song Huishan was quite stubborn.

"Don't you get along with his sister?"

"She's deliberately trying to provoke me. Why's she pushed that
child on me when she knows I can't handle it?"

Song Huishan's eyes reddened; she was so vexed. The boy
planned to stay a whole month when she didn't even have a place
for an extra bed. In the living room that also served as his study
were a few curios and pieces of porcelain, untouched since his death.
Even the bronze paper-weight, ink pen and inkstone on his table
remained sitting where he had left them. She was reluctant even to
part with the trash in his wastepaper basket, so how could she put
in another bed, much less move in a person? That left her room. But
no, she was used to solitary living. Just a new sofa set had cost her
several nights' sleep, so what would an extra person do to her? The

telegram alone wreaked such havoc on her nerves.

"Sister Huishan, why not give it a try? If it really doesn't work out, he can stay with me."

"It's not just for a day or two. I can't trouble you like that."

"I don't mind. We'll each be busy with our own things, but for fun we can go out together. I like young people. The kids at the office always invite me along when they go swimming, dancing, to the movies or whatever."

Hua Jing was determined not to let Song Huishan back out of this.

"All right, then."

Song Huishan yielded, but the very next day she still wired an excuse and declined the company.

Hua Jing didn't pursue the matter. For several days running, she returned home very late. Song Huishan knocked on her door every night, but she was never home. On Saturday Song Huishan left work early and waited in the reception room at the design centre. Not until almost everyone had left the building did she way-lay Hua Jing. The words didn't come as easily as before.

"What have you been doing these days? I never see you any more."

"A conference is coming up. I have to get the materials ready."

"I bought a chicken today, the kind you like."

"I can't leave just yet. I'm coming back to work as soon as I grab a bite to eat outside."

Song Huishan hurriedly left. The chicken had been left to stew over a slow fire, but it still got overcooked. She couldn't eat, couldn't watch television, just felt plain restless. Her heart would start to thump strangely whenever she heard footsteps outside on the stairs. She knew Hua Jing's footsteps, and lying in bed she still listened for them, but with the dead of night no further sound was heard on the stairs. Song Huishan had only dozed for a bit when the sky began to lighten and people began rushing off to work. During that catnap she dreamt that Hua Jing joyfully brought home a kitten.

Why a kitten?

Song Huishan didn't understand the dream, nor did she know why she had felt so worried or had such a dream.

It was autumn once more. His anniversary again.

"Are you going to the cemetery tomorrow? I've already reserved a taxi for us and prepared lunch."

Song Huishan asked Hua Jing this time. She seemed to have changed quite a bit. A couple of months ago she had even bought a refrigerator.

"Yes, yes, of course I'm going."

As before, Hua Jing wore a skirt, a pale pinkish-grey one.

Hidden behind a poplar grove, the cemetery was peaceful and solemn. In a few places incense was burning, its hazy smoke curling up like silken wisps.

Song Huishan stood in front of his tombstone in silent tribute, then sat with him for a long time. Four plates of fresh fruit lay in front of his tombstone. Colourful and luscious, they gleamed with vibrancy. She had specially asked someone to pick these fruits for her from an orchard. She had also given some to Hua Jing.

"I'll take them with me tomorrow, too."

Hua Jing wrapped up the oranges and peaches one by one in keep-fresh paper.

"Who exactly is it that you're paying a visit to?" Song Huishan queried. She vaguely felt that Hua Jing was holding back some deep secret.

But Hua Jing only gave a mumbled reply.

The sun rose high until it was hanging directly overhead. Warmly shining down, it was gentle and pleasing. Time for lunch, Song

Huishan thought. She circled the grave once, her hands caressing the rough stone tablet. Silently she told him, "I'll return this afternoon." She was following a meandering footpath out of the poplar grove when, suddenly, she saw a familiar back flashing past in another part of the grove. Shocked, she looked again to be sure and, no mistake, it was Engineer Yin. Who had he come to see?

Hua Jing was already waiting by the entrance to the memorial hall.

"I got hungry a while back but didn't want to disturb you."

"I like to sit with him a long time. A moment ago..."

Song Huishan wanted to say something but stopped herself.

They sat at a stone table underneath the shade of a tree. The four marble-topped stone stools felt cool and slick to the touch. Song Huishan set out the lunch she had prepared: a vegetarian diet of beancurd, gluten and such.

"Hua Jing, do you like it?"

"It's delicious."

"What time do you plan to leave this afternoon?"

"I want to leave early. I still have business to finish at the office."

"Oh, business..." Song Huishan thought for a moment before she slowly said, "I saw Engineer Yin just now..." She watched for Hua Jing's reaction.

But Hua Jing showed none, as if she hadn't heard.

"Hua Jing, did you see him?" Song Huishan asked.

"I saw him before you did."

Hua Jing calmly smiled.

"Was he embarrassed?"

"Not likely."

"What do you mean?"

"Sister Huishan, the person I came to pay a visit to was Engineer Yin's mother."

Hua Jing's expression was candid and natural.

"His...mother?..."

Before Song Huishan could decide whether to believe her or not, Hua Jing changed the subject.

But Song Huishan tried her utmost to explain things to herself. His mother?... Them?...

The car left the cemetery at three in the afternoon. Neither said a word the whole way. Hua Jing got out at the Exhibition Hall.

"Come eat at my place tonight," Song Huishan said, poking her head out the window.

"But I won't be home before dinner, so don't wait for me."

"You're busy tonight, too?"

Song Huishan felt depressed. Hua Jing's busy life often made her realize her own life's emptiness and aimlessness. Arriving home, she didn't feel like cooking; nothing tasted good when eaten alone. She rested on the sofa, overwhelmingly tired. Hanging directly across the room from the sofa was an enlarged black-and-white photo of him, its metallic frame shining coldly. Song Huishan suddenly felt cold, as if his unwavering gaze was cold also. The house faced north, and on sunny days the inside was invariably cooler than the outside. Better go take a walk, she thought.

The sky dimmed as night fell. The number of pedestrians dwindled as street lamps lit up one by one. The coloured lights illuminated pane after pane of storefront windows, making them even more eye-catching than in the daytime. Song Huishan strolled along, as if pushed by a gently flowing river. Her mood gradually lightened. Walking past a combination florist's and petshop, a department store, an ice cream shop and a boutique, she saw the newly remodelled cleaner's in front of her. With its new, dark brown display window, it looked quite resplendent. She had come just last week to drop off a soiled wool coat. Since it was to be ready in one week, she could now pick it up on her way.

Song Huishan approached the cleaner's and stopped. Just as she was about to step inside, her eyes involuntarily swept over the dark brown display window and caught sight of two reflected figures. Blurry yet discernible, they stood face to face, one slightly facing away. She couldn't see their faces clearly; she didn't want to know who they were, but she had plainly recognized them. It was Hua Jing and Engineer Yin.

"All this time.. All this time..."

In a panic, she hurriedly avoided them, crossed the street and fled, as if she herself had committed something shameful.

"All this time... All this time..."

Song Huishan walked faster and faster, like a horse that was being whipped. Her mind raged and seemed to turn back time. Memories of the past sharpened and intensified. Hua Jing had been so pretty then with her trim figure and delicate features, never saying much.

"All this time... All this time..."

Song Huishan didn't know how to clarify things to herself. All this time what? And now what? At the Huancheng bus stop, she jumped on to bus eleven. The vehicle started along a circular route: the starting point was the end, and the terminal was the beginning again.

"All this time... All this time..."

Song Huishan leaned against a window and looked out, a lost expression on her face. A thought flashed through her mind like a shooting star: Should she move? Change apartments so that they'd no longer be across the hall from each other? She had no idea how many stops they'd made, or whether they'd reached the end already and were now going in the other direction. She just sat there, not wanting to get off...

Translated by Joyce Soong

Under One Roof

GRANDMA had been dead over six months before they were finally allotted an apartment with two rooms and a small hallway. It was even situated on one of the fairly busy city streets. Distributed by the municipal education bureau, the flat was a reward to teachers who had made outstanding contributions, or to those who were nominated for the title "Special Teacher." This year Song Xiuzhen had once again won the title, and her husband Gong Pinfang had been seconded to the district education office, where he was in charge of compiling textbooks. Gong was good at his job and had published several pamphlets on problems associated with teaching materials. There was no doubt that the couple in all respects deserved to get the apartment.

The flat was ideally situated on the third floor. The rooms side by side, one bigger than the other, both faced south with balconies. The hallway was quite spacious, enough for a square table, a refrigerator and a washing machine. Only the bathroom was a bit small. They would have to get someone to tile the three walls and put in a small tub. And while they were at it, why not have the kitchen done too, with mosaic tiles? There was piped gas, which could be lit with one strike of a match, so quick and convenient. Just think of those four shining, white, clean, tiled walls! It was every housewife's dream. Song Xiuzhen did not exactly belong to the "every housewife" category, but she still had to cook three meals a day. However, she was a little different: she only had to cook for half a family. With Grandma gone, the couple and their two daughters seemed to have very naturally divided into two. Song looked after the younger girl, he took care of the elder, each managing his or her own business.

In fact, they had been living apart for several years, but to spare Grandma's feelings while she was alive, they had not broken up. Anyway, there really was no way for them to separate, since the five of them lived in one thirteen-square-metre room, so the most they could do was sleep in upper and lower bunks of a double-decker bed. There was no question of separating the cooking either, since three families shared a kitchen which contained three briquet stoves and three sinks. It was so cramped there was hardly room to turn around, let alone set up another stove. Crowded together like this, they saw a great deal of their neighbours and had to keep up some kind of a respectable front. And after all, they were both educated people, reluctant to bare their family wounds in public. The idea of breaking up distressed Song terribly, and she had refused to consider it. The trouble was, he would not change his mind either. She could do nothing yet remained unyielding and firmly refused to give in.

Now with a new flat they could divide things equally. When they got the keys from the housing office, they went together to inspect it.

"You have the smaller room with Elder Daughter, I'll have the larger one with the little one."

Song made the division equably. Their elder was a boarder in a vocational middle school and only came home at weekends. The younger was still in junior high. This meant they needed two desks in the larger room so they would not disturb each other.

"As you please." He had no reason to argue, because the small room, at twelve square metres, was not really that small, and quite ample for him when he was alone. When their elder came back, she could sleep on the sofa and would not take up any extra space. However, he did have one condition, "My fridge and your washing machine can go in the hall. As for that table, it's too old. Sell it to the junk man."

"What do we eat on, then?"

Song Xiuzhen could never bear to part with old furniture. They had been married twenty years, and everything they possessed, no matter how old or battered, was familiar and comfortable to her. Losing or selling anything made her unhappy. In those days, they had had to scrape and save for nearly one year to buy each piece. She recalled how both of them had gone without monthly bus tickets for one whole year in order to save up enough to buy a wardrobe. Every morning before light they each took a lunch box and walked twelve bus-stops to school to teach class. Each month they saved ten yuan, a hundred and twenty in one year. In those days, paying a hundred and twenty yuan for a wardrobe was a big event which created a sensation in their alley. All the neighbours came to have a look and to comment. The pride of ownership filled her heart. To be able to afford a few pieces of good furniture when one only earned some fifty yuan and had to support old people and children proved what a good housekeeper she was. She had never complained about her lot no matter how hard life was. Every day she watched her daughters growing bigger, going from primary to middle school. In another five or six years, they would graduate and become independent. Just a few more years to hold out...who would have thought he couldn't wait?

"Each cooks for himself. We'll eat in our own rooms."

He seemed to hate the square table. During the years of their separation, they had still been compelled to eat around it, especially at dinner time, which invariably was a proper meal with three dishes and a soup, vegetables and meat. For others, the evening meal after a busy day was a time for the family to chat, relax and be cosy. But for them there was only heavy silence as they ate. This table was like a slab of iron, embodiment of sullen coldness.

"I'll keep it and put it in the big room," she said quietly. She had long since got used to his indifference the moment he got home, and had gradually learnt to counter him with a calm, neutral manner which allowed them to keep up appearances. Sometimes, though, she could be very obstinate. She would not throw the old table away, she thought. It would come in handy for preparing her lessons and correcting home work. It didn't matter what she used as long as there was a place to spread out her books. No need to spend money on another desk either.

"The two bookcases..."

Of all their old furniture, those were the only things he was interested in. Bought three or four years back, they were made of dark wood, had glass doors and still looked quite new. There was a story behind them too. The money for them came from the prize she was given the first time she was elected to be "Special Teacher" by the district. She bought them three days after he withdrew his request for a divorce from the court. That day, she took the money out of the bank, borrowed a tricycle flatcar and went to pick up the two bookcases from the shop. She told him they were for the two girls, one each, but of course he knew they were for him. In the twenty years since he started work, he had taught and compiled conscientiously, never smoking or drinking, his only enjoyment and hobby a visit to the bookshops when he had some spare cash. There he would pick and choose, sifting and eliminating over and over before buying a few volumes. Over the years, the books had accumulated in cardboard boxes stuffed under the bed. During the damp "plum rain" season, others hurried to bring out their woollens to air, but he hauled out his books, spreading them around as if opening a secondhand shop, letting the damp ground under the bed dry out a bit. Every time he went through the whole rigmarole he would swear that the moment they got a new flat, he would buy a small bookcase. He never imagined that she would buy them for him with the first more substantial prize she won. But he was not in the least grateful to her. For six months the bookcases remained empty, because he refused to touch them.

"The bookcases can go in your small room."

Song Xiuzhen stood in the doorway of his quarters and in her mind's eye arranged the bed, sofa and bookcases, though she knew very well he would not do things her way. From the time they no longer lived as man and wife and he withdrew his divorce papers, they had nothing more to plan together, nor was it necessary to plan for each other. This awkward, strained situation had affected their two girls, who each clearly and willingly took sides. The older girl took his part (she had been brought up by his mother); the young one stood up for her "she was born in the cadre school and had lived in the dormitory with Song). How much longer was this situation going to last? She had no idea. However, thanks to her steadfastness, the family was still together, and things seemed to improve. After all, he had withdrawn the divorce suit; he had finally filled the bookcases with volumes from the boxes; he had signed the papers for the flat, so that they now shared new quarters...clutched in her palm were the two copper-plated doorkeys. The unease and disquiet which had tormented her for so long seemed to have calmed and to be gradually subsiding. A thread of hope even glimmered, as long as he did not give up the new flat, as long as he still needed the bookcases, as long as he did not file for divorce again, the hope shone more brightly now, and she said with warmth, "How about getting someone to fix the kitchen and bathroom? At least make a tub and put up some tiles?"

He remained indifferent, as if the kitchen, bathroom, tub and tile had nothing to do with him.

"I'll put up the money."

Her elder daughter had told her that he had used up all his savings on a double-door refrigerator. This had not been any advantage to her, just as he had never used her washing machine for his clothes, preferring to wash by hand or wait for the daughter to come back on Saturday to wash for him. In this way neither transgressed on the other. But after all, the kitchen and bathroom had to be shared.

"That can all be done some other time."

"When? It's easier before all the stuff is moved in."

"I'm moving next week."

His tone brooked no discussion. At last he was going to have a room of his own, and he was in a hurry.

"Well, let's move together then."

Song was annoyed but said nothing. Such mild displeasure was easy to control. All these years, she had endured so much unhappiness, and even put up with it rather well, she thought. Three years ago the court had sent her his request for a divorce just at the time the school was organizing a singing competition. Her thoughts and feelings in turmoil, all she had wanted to do was find a quiet place for a good cry. She had not believed he would really try to destroy their family. None of the reasons he gave were the real ones, just one complaint after another about how she neglected her home in favour of her work. Not one word about the real reason —— his fickleness, and with someone who had been her student too. It was unendurable and she made up her mind there and then that, no, never would she agree to a divorce, that she would fight with every reason she had. But he became colder and colder toward her, and sometimes they did not exchange a word for weeks on end. They were more distant than strangers. She was filled with despair yet had to put on a brave face and endure. After all, she still had many students to think of, and there was the competition and the singing to win. That day, the large school hall was lively and boisterous. Over twenty classes sang one after the other, and it was dark before the prizes were finally handed out. Her class came first once again. After everything was over and the students had left, she sat in the still classroom and stared vacantly ahead. When her younger daughter came to find her she complained of a headache and wanting to rest. Never would she tell the girl about the divorce request; she was prepared to bear it all alone until absolutely necessary.

"I've asked for a small truck from the education bureau." He was telling her in a roundabout way that he was only going to move his own stuff.

"The school's supplies department has agreed to borrow a big truck for me."

On certain minor things, Song was far less petty than he. Men, no matter how mature, could never quite rid themselves of childishness.

"We must ask some people to help us move."

He knew no one at the bureau.

"When the kids heard we were moving, many of the boys volunteered to help."

She carefully used the word "we," which felt strange and awkward to her from long disuse.

"It doesn't look good to get students to help."

How prim he sounded!

"It doesn't matter with mine."

At school Song Xiuzhen was more than able to deal with all sorts of problems. She just could not understand why in her private life she was such a failure.

"That's settled then: the move is for this Sunday."

"On Saturday I'll start packing."

This brief exchange on the house-moving was more than they had said to each other in years, it seemed. During that week, Song

went shopping as soon as she had spare time: curtains, bed covers,
sofa covers, all that she could afford to change she changed. Deep
in her heart, she pinned great hopes on this move. Years ago, it
was precisely because of insufficient housing when her sister had
come to help with the children that she had requested a transfer to
a middle school with dormitories. She had boarded with her
students and only returned home once a week or every fortnight.
She had thought that this would allow more room for Grandma,
and give her more time for her work. Who would have thought
that two years later the "crisis" would occur? She blamed the
housing and now pinned her hopes on the new flat.

2

On the day they moved, everyone worked hard, and there was
much coming and going. Even a family that was not well off had
enough belongings to make up two truckloads. Yet when these two
truckloads were divided up between the two rooms, the kitchen and
the bathroom, they seemed rather paltry. He took a single bed, an
old easy chair and the two bookcases; she had the big double bed,
the desk and a chest of five drawers. In her large, sixteen-square-
metre room these few things looked sparse no matter how she
arranged them. The dining table would just have to come in. Its
scratches covered with a tablecloth, no one would see how old it
was. In the hallway, as he had suggested, were the refrigerator and
washing machine. The fridge stood against the wall by his door,
while the washing machine just fitted the space between the
bathroom door and the hall.

The "movers" had to be fed, even if they were her students.
Song had prepared fully by buying a large packet of cold meats:
salted chicken, sausages, smoked fish. She also cooked two plates
of vegetables and a whole casserole of curried beef soup with

vermicelli and chicken-blood cubes. She was determined that there would be enough for a really good feed. This was their first move in twenty years of marriage, and not only was the flat much bigger, but they had everything they needed. It really was a happy occasion. Since it was Sunday, both daughters were home and could look after the guests. Song sent them to buy a crate of soft drinks and slipped a five-yuan note to them to pick up a bottle of good rice wine for him. One of his quirks was that he never touched beer, but had in the past drunk a bit of rice wine at festivals and the New Year. These last few years, his capacity for wine had increased quite a bit. On Sundays he would take an empty bottle to buy draught Jiafan wine from the grocer's and finish half of it at one meal. She couldn't intervene and so pretended to see nothing, but inside she said to herself, "What you sow you reap!" Of course, today was an exception. He had worked hard, and a bit of wine would warm the blood and relax the muscles. Everything had gone very well too: the mood had been harmonious, with everyone willing to be reasonable. Her students were a lively lot, full of jokes and laughter. He too had been in a good temper, making witty comments to the daughters and the boys and stimulating the young people to greater animation. Although she did not say very much, being too busy organizing and arranging, Song felt happy and at ease, as if a lump of ice in her heart had melted. This was probably why she felt she should buy him a bottle of wine.

"That's what she should do," said the elder girl.

"Dad never thinks of Mum." Her younger sister had a sharp tongue too.

"He's pretty unhappy himself."

"It's his own fault."

They argued as they did their shopping. In the past they had rarely spoken about their preferences, though each knew very well how the other felt.

"You know, Aunt Xiaomei had got married," said the elder with a sigh. She liked this Aunt Xiaomei.

"About time, too!" The other did not like her.

"You should not be ungrateful. Aunt Xiaomei was good to you. That time you got pneumonia, and Mum was living at school, she's the one who took you to hospital and stayed with you every day," said the elder girl in a reproving tone.

"Only because she wanted to impress Dad!" came the quick retort.

"You're just like Mum. You don't understand people."

"So you understand Mum?"

As they lugged the heavy crate back, the sisters bickered and chatted.

"Well, now that Aunt Xiaomei is married, Dad should stop thinking about her and be nicer to Mum," said the young one.

"You think people's feelings are that simple?" The elder spoke as if from personal knowledge.

"So what's so difficult about it all? At least they are still together and not divorced!" The younger sister was emphatic.

"What do you know?" The other spoke loftily. After all she was the elder.

"No less than you!" Her sister was determined to have the last word. After all she was the younger.

The sisters always quarrelled and made up. They returned home peeved with each other, but after setting up the table and spreading out the food and drink, they had made up again. The meal was very jolly, with much lively conversation. Song Xiuzhen spent most of it in the kitchen, leaving him and the two girls to look after the guests. Everyone ate heartily, the boys positively wolfing down their food. She decided to cook some more dishes. This was her first day in a kitchen with cooking gas, and she enjoyed being a "real" housewife. Anyway, it was years since they had had a proper meal with everyone so happy and relaxed. They rarely had guests, because neither he nor she cared to invite friends over and force the other to pretend hospitality, like acting in a play. Their closer colleagues, who had an idea what was going on, also avoided coming to visit. But today was their housewarming, and it seemed to bode well, Song cooked another two dishes of spicy pork and meat with peanuts and opened two tins of fish and the last packet of cold cuts. The small table groaned under the weight of stacked plates, and when everyone had finished, there was still a lot of food left over.

The boys departed. The daughters were worn out and went to bed each in her room. He disappeared into the bathroom to wash while she cleared up. Even after combining the leftovers, there were still four or five dishes. The weather was not very warm, and the food would keep for a while, but there in the hall was his copious refrigerator which was already emitting a purring sound. If the food was put in there, it would keep for several days. Song Xiuzhen purposely cleared the empty bowls slowly and left the four or five dishes on the table, so that when he came out of the bathroom and saw them, he would of his own accord say, "Put them in the fridge." After this happy meal, she had changed her mind and decided to let the table stay in the hall. The leftovers would last the whole family at least two days, he would not need to cook, and they could all sit around and have another couple of meals together. If after this he did not suggest they cook and eat separately, then... Carefully she wiped the oil-stains off the table with a rag, as if pinning her glimmer of secret hope on this table.

He came out of the bathroom in a set of new pyjamas, his hair still moist and warm. He glanced at the table, but perhaps because he did not have his glasses on made no sign and went into his room without saying a word.

Song's suddenly bated breath came out in a rush. She scooped up the dishes, took them into the kitchen and placed them on the cupboard by the window, hastily washed the sinkful of dishes and glasses and went into the big room. As she lay on the bed her whole body ached, but she could not fall asleep. The new room furnished with her old things was both stange and familiar, and she had difficulty adjusting. Maybe she was used to the crowded way they had lived before. Now there was more space, the top bunk was gone and so was he, and her whole heart felt emptied, like in a dream. It was impossible to sleep soundly. The bed stood against the wall which divided the two rooms. Just one wall apart, and yet she knew that now this thin partition really and truly separated them. Thoughts chased through her mind and fixed once more on the leftovers. The next day, after a poor night, she got up with bags under her eyes.

"Mum, all I have to do is heat the leftovers for lunch, right? I can do that. You needn't come home." The younger girl was already thinking of lunch even as she consumed her breakfast.

"I'm coming back to eat too. Don't lose the key," she cautioned. "If you get back first, put the cold rice on the gas."

The new flat was much nearer Song Xiuzhen's school than the old place, and she had time to come back to cook lunch for her daughter. Actually, the girl was no longer small and well able to manage lunch on her own, but Song felt guilty, because she had been unable to look after her daughters enough when she boarded at shcool. Now that things were easier, she wanted to make up for her past neglect. Anyway, she wanted to see how he behaved for the first lunch in their new quarters. Would he eat the leftovers? Would he eat at the table?

As soon as the bell for lunch recess rang, Song jumped on her bicycle and rushed home. Her daughter had the transistor radio on and had put the rice on to warm as directed. Song put down her bag and went to heat up all the leftovers, in the expectation that he would come back to eat with them. He usually did come back, because he worked a half-day in the office and a half-day at home writing teaching materials. With gas, things were so quick, and soon the four steaming dishes were set out on the table.

"I'm starving!" The daughter used her chopsticks to pick up a mouthful of hot food.

"Wait for your Dad."

"He said he would eat in the canteen and then come back. Save him cooking."

"When did he say that?"

"This morning, when we left together."

"Well, eat then." She ate silently, and the food tasted either too salty or too bland, not at all like last night.

"What are we having for dinner, Mum?"

"The same thing." Neither had a big appetite, and the leftovers would last them at least until the next day.

"Oh, no!" The daughter was tired of the food already. "Cook me some vegetables tonight!"

He came back from work with a number of big and small packages, which he opened and stocked into the fridge. Some of the food he washed and cut, and cooked himself two small dishes. By the time Song got back, he was already eating and drinking in his room, at a coffee table. She once more heated up the leftovers and cold rice and cooked a plate of greens for her daughter.

Mother and daughter ate silently and glumly at the table, as if fulfilling a task. The liveliness and fun of the previous night's dinner were finished and gone, just as all the hustle and bustle of moving was over. Thus the pattern of life for the next fortnight was set: he lunched in the canteen and ate by himself in his room behind a closed door; she came dashing back at midday to heat things up, only preparing a proper fresh meal in the evenings when there was enough time to shop and cook. The days passed peacefully. Patiently she endured and waited as before, steadfastly waiting for him to come to his senses and start to "thaw." Her daughter became more and more frustrated, and one day burst out, "Mum, take me away!"

"Where to?"

"To our old house. I prefer to have to light the coal stove every day."

"Nonsense!"

"Am I stupid, or are you? I know you can wait, but I have no hope."

"Why not?"

"Listen: Aunt Xiaomei got married last year. If Dad really wanted to patch things up with you, he would have done so long ago."

"How do you know?"

"Elder Sister told me."

Song Xiuzhen lapsed into silence. She had managed to sustain herself through these endless, suffocating days by the thought that some time or other Yin Xiaomei would get married, and once that happened, he would give up and slowly come back to her. After all he had a family and two daughters.

"Has she married recently?" She did not believe this "last year" business. He had been coming home right after work these days and seldom went out on Sundays. If the grapevine said she was married, it must be recently.

"If you don't believe me, ask Elder Sister. If you ask me, I don't think her marriage has anything to do with you and Dad. Dad withdrew his request a long time ago, didn't he?"

"How do you know he filed?"

"Elder Sister told me. Dad tells her everything, not like you," she said sulkily.

"Really, your father is the limit. What's the point of talking about this?" A resentful expression appeared on her face, and she felt a surge of anger. He still took this attitude, even with the other one married!

His door was always shut. He locked it when he went out and latched it from the inside when he went in. She had not stepped inside since they moved. The elder daughter told her he had bought two framed pictures for the wall, one of *mei* blossoms. How she hated that character "*mei*!" She had absolutely no desire to enter his room.

But after all, Yin Xiaomei was finally married. That night, Song Xiuzhen turned this piece of news over and over in her mind, and considered what this meant for him, for her and for this family.

3

Sunday again. After lunch Song Xiuzhen picked up her bag and prepared to go out, telling her daughter not to wait for her for dinner and that she could eat with her father and sister if she wished.

"Mum, where're you going that you'll be so long?"

"Home visits," she mumbled.

"Always the eager beaver! It's Sunday, and you're still visiting!" Her daughter was displeased again.

Without explaining, Song got on her bike and hurried off. She twisted and turned through many streets for about half an hour, then got off to examine a small slip of paper with an address. She was really far out, in the suburbs, twenty minutes away from Caojia Ferry, in an area of decrepit, run-down houses like a slum area. Yesterday she had got hold of Yin Xiaomei's address and since then had a strange feeling that even though the young woman

was newly married, her life left something to be desired. Which
after all was quite normal. She knew very well that Yin Xiaomei
had waited for him several years, and he had promised to get a
divorce to marry her. But for this plan to be carried out, the
consent of the three of them was needed.

Song pushed her bicycle and walked a stretch. On the handlebars
hung her bag, bulging with a new jersey she planned to give Yin
Xiaomei with congratulations on her marriage. And yet, she had
hated the younger woman bitterly, had gone to see her in the
laboratory where she worked and criticized her in front of her
colleagues. The next day Yin Xiaomei had sent her a letter
accepting the blame and giving assurances, "... Teacher Song, I
really must apologize to you. From now on I will not see Teacher
Gong any more. I swear not to come between you again." Song
had believed her and shown him the letter. His face had blanched
in anger, and he had snatched the letter from her and torn it to
shreds. For a while he had been in a very bad mood, ready to
explode for the slightest reason. Even his mother had had to be
careful what she said. But not two months later, she had noticed
that he often said he was busy with meetings and did not come
back for dinner. Once he had gone out of town on a business trip.
The day he was due back, she had sent their younger daughter to
the station to meet him, but the girl had come back without him
and told her sulkily, "I saw Aunt Xiaomei at the station." After
this she had moved to the office for a period, blaming herself for
believing those "assurances." When the initial shock had passed
and she had calmed down, she had returned home and prepared to
dig in her heels for the long haul. "Let's see who will outlast
who!" She had pulled herself together and thrown herself whole-
heartedly into her teaching and had been nominated a "Special
Teacher!" He had filed for divorce, but before she had got around
to engaging a lawyer, he had withdrawn the request because at that

moment the education bureau asked to second him, and the divorce would have been untimely. Things had dragged on. During those years, she had not been able to stand the thought of that Yin Xiaomei. But now, hearing that she had got married, a sense of pity stirred; she had had a hard time too. Song Xiuzhen felt an urge to see her; after all, she had been her student. Past quarrels were over, everything was finished; she wished to sit down and talk things over calmly. Maybe Yin Xiaomei could even work on him a bit.

When she found the place, the neighbours said no one was home. The couple had probably gone shopping. Song felt torn, wanting to leave and to wait a while. One of the neighbours noticed her hesitation and kindly asked her in to sit down. "Xiaomei is on duty today. Her husband will not be far away."

"What does her husband do?" Song asked, and hastened to introduce herself, "I'm Xiaomei's old teacher."

"He's a technician in a factory. He may be lame, but he can do anything: build a house, making furniture —— a really capable chap!" The neighbour was expansive. "With him, Xiaomei will be all right!"

A cripple! Song was stunned but did her best to conceal it. Why would she marry a cripple? Did he know? Yin Xiaomei was not beautiful, but she was tall and fair. In class she had not been anything special, had said little but had had lots of character and been very independent, refusing to get close to any teacher. After graduating from university, she had gone to work in the biology institute. One day, she had suddenly turned up at their home for a visit. The absent years had given her grace and poise. She had explained simply, "Each teacher has his or her place in my heart, and I never forget." That year Grandma had not been well, and Song had been working and unable to come back every day. Yin Xiaomei had often kindly offered to help Grandma. That's how it had started.

Song Xiuzhen did not wait any longer but took her leave and hastily left this district of jerry-built houses. As she climbed on her bicycle, her legs felt weak, and she could hardly pedal, as if the bicycle chain was rusty.

When she got back, the two girls were watching TV in his room. It was a small twelve-inch, black-and-white set that often broke down. Song was saving up for a colour set. Each time she managed to save enough the price went up.

"Visit over?" Her younger daughter came running out at the sound of the door opening. "Come and watch TV with us. It's Shirley Temple. She really is cute."

"You people watch." She wasn't in the mood; neither did she wish to go into his room.

"Dad's out."

"Where's he gone?" She didn't want to ask but did anyway.

"He said he was going to buy bookcases."

"But he has two already! How can he fit any more in?"

"Dad says those bookcases you bought should go in our big room," said the younger daughter. "Just what we need. Our room's very empty."

Song Xiuzhen sat down on a chair in the hall, resting her arms listlessly on the small table, still thinking, "Why has she married a cripple? Why?"

At dusk, he arrived back with two bookcases in a hired truck. The two girls helped him carry them up and move the two old cases into the big room, like lost property restored to its owner.

Song did not help. She was busy cooking in the kitchen with the door shut. She cooked four dishes and made a big bowl of dried shrimp and seaweed soup. Her daughter burst in complaining of hunger.

"Take everything out." Song reached for the chopsticks and

hesitated. How many pairs? He had not had time to cook, and there was the other girl.

"Hurry, Mum; the chopsticks!" Her daughter could hardly wait.

Song grabbed a handful, certainly more than four pairs. If they wished...

"What do you need so many for?" The daughter took a pair and started tucking in.

His small room was quiet. Were they still sorting books inside? She sat down but couldn't bring herself to eat.

"Why don't you eat, Mum?"

"What about them?" she mumbled.

"Dad said it's too late to cook, so they've gone out to eat. Dad got some commission money today, so he's treating," her daughter said with her mouth full.

Still she sat without moving, a stuffed-up feeling in her chest that choked her breathing. "Didn't your Dad invite you?"

"Of course, but if I go, what about you?" was the knowing reply.

Song Xiuzhen felt the tears rush to her eyes. She sprang up and went into the room and stared blankly at the two empty bookcases.

"Come and eat, Mum. Those two bookcases are nothing to look at. You should see Dad's; newest model, really beautiful." Her daughter followed her in.

She really wished to see the new-model bookcases, but as was his custom, he had locked the door when he went out. At her daughter's urging, she sat down and ate a few mouthfuls. After the meal, when they had wiped the table clean, she said to her daughter, "Come, let's put the table in our room."

"What's wrong with it here in the hall?"

"Your father thinks it's too old and shabby." As she ran her hand around the edge, she thought the time when it had been a place for family meals was really over.

They pushed the table into a far corner with a tablecloth on, and suddenly, with the bookcases and table, the rather empty-looking room of yesterday filled out and became homey.

But the hallway was emptier, with only his fridge and her washing-machine...

Shanghai, November 7, 1987

Translated by Shi Xiaojin